DEI

This book is dedicated to supportive wife Sandie, who had to share our crazy life with these disparate characters for many months and who contributed so much to the story. Also, to our wonderful children, Ben, Georgie, Rosie and Elliot and their unstoppable zest for life and adventure. Life is too short and the world too big to stand still. And finally, to my much-loved, much-missed brother, Toby, who gave so much love and happiness to everyone around him with his light and laughter.

I would also like to add special mention to the late, lamented Anthony Bourdain, who inspired me so deeply. Without his unique spin on life and appetite for travel, shaped by an identifiable blend of incurable insecurity and feigned arrogance, I would never have embarked on our blog, catsacrossamerica.net. The world lost his incisive but flawed genius far too soon.

Finally, it would be totally remiss of me not to extend my heartfelt gratitude to my good friends David Wade, Sara Hayward, Mark Matrazzo and Chantal Reed. Only with their help was I able to transfer this story from somewhere in a dusty corner of my head on to the printed page.

Copyright © Desmond Nichols 2021

All rights reserved.
This is a work of fiction. Any similarity to actual persons, living or dead, or actual events, is purely coincidental. Certain longstanding institutions, businesses agencies and public offices are mentioned, but the characters are wholly imaginary

ABOUT THE AUTHOR

Des Nichols was brought up in Rugby, England, before attending Mill Hill School in London. After a spell at Guildford College of Law, he surprised his family by taking the natural progression into greyhound racing. He spent seven enjoyable and successful years running various tracks, including Brighton and Romford, interrupted only by a 12-month break in 1976 for an adventure around the world. In 1979, he joined his good friend, Peter Anslow, in organising the Daily Mail Ski Show at Earls Court, London, before, in 1983, he was brought into the Daily Mail as Promotions Manager. In a newspaper career spanning almost 25 years, he was appointed Deputy Managing Director before becoming Group Marketing and Promotions Director on all Associated Newspapers' titles, the Daily Mail, The Mail on Sunday, The Evening Standard, Metro and dailymail.co.uk.

After retiring from this role in 2007, he moved to Naples, Florida, becoming a US citizen. In 2017, he and Sandie, with their four cats ensconced in their RV, embarked on a two-and-a-half-year tour of America, writing his popular travel blog, *catsacrossamerica.net*. as they criss-crossed the USA from coast-to-coast.

He has a son, Ben, and a stepson, Elliot, who live in England, and two daughters, Georgina and Rosanna, who have both emigrated to Australia. Today, he and Sandie while away their days in Spain - with their cats and an overworked keyboard.

LYING IN LOVE

By Des Nichols

'Once you have ruined your reputation, you can live freely'

CHAPTER ONE
THE DUKE OF WELLINGTON

TUESDAY, JULY 9

George Granby sat alone at the bar, his hands cradling his pint glass as if it was a prized pot of gold, his glazed eyes fixed in a frozen stare on the still surface of his companion beer. The chatter of the few drinkers at the other end of the bar muted in his head.

The Duke of Wellington was a typical historic London pub, a proud temple to the Victorian splendour that defines England's 19th century magnificence. It was a piece of pure theatre, with a beamed ceiling, leaded windows, rich red curtains and a glorious, imposing bar as its shrine and altar. The vast serving counter was of the finest mahogany, protected by a rich veneer of varnish that positively glistened under the soft lights. Above it, a legion of tilted glass mugs swung expectantly by their handles, each waiting to be taken down, filled and unleashed onto its next partner.

It was now 4.30 in the afternoon, a time when millions of Londoners were still at work, incarcerated in their offices, every man and woman focussed on their own corporate crisis of the day.

Ask anyone who knew him and they would all describe George as a tall, handsome man of the old school, with something patriarchal and venerable about him. Although only in his early fifties, he deported himself as a man much older, with the air of someone who had the worries of the world on his shoulders. His well-groomed dark brown hair carried the same side parting that his mother had carved when he was a young boy. With his height, elegant bearing and impeccable manners, you could have assumed that he had come down from a proud lineage of military officers, the sort that kept India in pukka order during the regimented control of the British Raj. His strong features gave him an almost stern appearance, belying his kindly nature, and with it came an authority that commanded respect and an attentive ear. He was a man of values and excellent manners, who acted out his whole life with a dignity similar to that which Hollywood gave Cary Grant in the 1930 movies. He was first to make sure everyone had a drink, to see the ladies seated at the table and, countless times a day, to hold doors open, even for total strangers, repeating his 'after you' deferentially at every opportunity. Women were treated like treasured objects, pieces of fine porcelain, proffered every courtesy with just a glint of respectful flirtatiousness in his attractive smile. George was the very essence of chivalry. All the vulgar modern-day familiarities and discourtesies were anathema to him. In his opinion, they represented the total collapse of civilisation as he knew it. He elected to remain locked in his own bygone era, a time when people behaved decently and the young called you 'Sir'. If he was honest, he was aware that these halcyon days had decayed and disappeared decades ago, but he continued to fight his one-man resistance against the disintegration of good old British politeness. His basic creed, instilled in him since his birth some 53 years ago, was based on duty and commitment. 'Noblesse oblige' veritably pulsed through his veins.

For George today, however, things were very different. He had the look of a man drowning in his own personal quagmire of desolation. For today was the day he had been cast aside, 'let go' as they euphemistically say, by his dynamic advertising agency after twenty-three years of commitment and dedication, twenty-three long years of sycophantically massaging the egos of boastful executives. He had served his colleagues well, looking after countless self-important marketing directors as they pompously confused the extent of their ability with the size of their expense accounts, while he all the time responded, without question, to every instruction from his corporate hierarchy. In truth, he had been always irritated by these cocky young swordsmen, who flashed in and out of his life in their expensive suits, but he never once showed them a scintilla of disdain, knowing that it was only a matter of time before they would move on, with an equally irritating successor replacing them as the scenario repeated itself once more.

He had known what was coming. Indeed, he had seen it first, long before even his lords and masters had come round to it. His time had been nigh for a while. They had got to him in the end. Like for so many of his generation, modern life was moving on at such a pace that it was leaving him behind in its wake. The internet, jargon, buzz words, brutal ambition and money, money, money had taken over the asylum and pushed out all semblance of the loyalty, predictability, security and sheer laddish fun that had defined his working career for so long. His world of commitment, civility and team-playing was now populated by self-obsessed thirty-somethings, who were so deluded by their success that they could not see that the fragility of their positions, while, in reality, they were as replaceable as the technology they depended on.

George was one of the good guys, a friend to trust, a colleague to rely on, and above all else a thoroughly good bloke to have a drink with. But it appeared that those qualities no longer held any sway at Forsyte Manners, a behemoth of an agency that had created a revered position for itself in the otherwise ephemeral advertising world. To George, it had been, in recent years, a complete mystery how something as abstract as an agency was able to maintain its lofty reputation with such a turnover of badly dressed, conceited hedonists running the show. In urbane George's view, these 'creative genii' looked more like scruffy gardeners than thrusting young bucks, something that he could not abide.

Sadly, it had gone unrecognised that one important contributor to the success of these high-flying companies could actually have been the assiduous efforts of the humble and unheralded Georges of this world. They were the 'account executives', who tended to their client's every need and whim, while the trendy creatives in their black shirts and the aloof, top-floor directors in their expensive suits seemed reluctant to engage with their clients, preferring to engage with one another. This brace of superior beings seemed to survive and prosper by permanently shoring up each other's importance, often dismissing the Georges as 'bag-carriers', mere shuttle diplomats whose role, in their eyes, was simply to cajole clients, arrange Wimbledon tickets and buy endless celebrity-chef lunches in the finest gourmet restaurants in town.

George sat on his stool churning his predicament over in his head, pensively grasping his dimpled beer mug tighter, before tenderly gripping the handle and raising the precious chalice to his mouth. The other drinkers had by now left and a cast of just two remained. George and the barman, Gerry. The popular steward of the Wellington bar had an imposing stature, standing well over six feet tall. His dark hair was frozen into place with gel and his dress sense was always smart, fashionable and relaxed. He was definitely aware of his irresistible good looks and made no effort to hide a vainglorious streak when he knew he had a captive audience.

"Everything OK, George?", said Gerry, as he wiped a wine glass with a flowing white cloth. George, having by now sunk half his comforting pint, could only just manage a polite, sardonic smile back but quickly and instinctively he reminded himself that not to reply was just plain rude, something that was not his style.

"Been better, Gerard", he replied morosely.
In his typical style, having learned on first meeting that the affable server's real name was Gerard, 'but everyone calls me Gerry", George insisted on giving him his full, classier moniker.

"Left the company today, old boy. All a bit of nuisance really", he replied with his characteristic understatement. George didn't do anger or hot-headedness. His English sang-froid maintained his permanent level of calm countenance.

"Shit", gasped Gerry "That's bloody awful". The sympathetic barman came over, his glass-cleaning continuing as he leaned down in genuine concern towards his head-bowed customer, who he liked a lot.

"What happened?".

"Usual thing. Re-structuring. Another bloody re-structuring. That place has been 'restructured' every damn year. This time I was the one thrown in the skip".

"Sorry mate. That's terrible. After all those years. And it isn't the best time is it, what with the divorce and all that".

"No. Timing could be better," lamented modest George.

"So, what now?"

"God knows. After finding myself a bit homeless, now I am just a bit unemployed."

"Where are you living now?".

"Well, Kate has the house, so I have rented a place around the corner. Nothing permanent. Just a one-bedroomed flat at the moment, but it'll do until everything gets sorted out. I got it to be near the office. Well, that didn't work out too well, did it."

Gerry didn't pull his words.

"And how is madam? Is she still being a complete bitch?".

Gerry had never met George's wife but, in support of his friend, hated everything about her and he was always keen to put in the bad word. He could not even call her by her name. But, curiously, George did not really feel anything like that degree of venom towards Kate, but he appreciated Gerry's well-intended support, even if it was far too harsh and unjust. He knew Gerry meant well.

George had no time to answer the question for, at that exact moment, he felt a friendly, boisterous pat on his hunched back. Gerry raised himself up behind the bar, his serious face breaking into a welcoming smile for his new customer.

"Hi, Georgie. How's tricks?" came the cheery voice.

It was Chris, or Christopher as George called him for all the same reasons that he called Gerry, Gerard. He had, for once, got out of work early. Chris was always the funster of any party with his impish demeanour being his biggest attraction to the ladies. Although he was quite handsome, he cared little about his appearance, his fair hair in a state of permanent dishevelment. No-one could ever call Chris a snappy dresser. His inexpensive shoes went unpolished and his Marks and Spencer trousers unpressed. He was, however, extremely likeable, and, as far as everyone knew, had never made an enemy in his life.

"What's up, mate? You look like your bloody world has collapsed".

Gerry shot a glance at Chris and puckered his eyebrows in an attempt to throw a silent sign that screamed 'shhh', forewarning him that they were in the middle of a crisis, but Chris was never quick on the uptake. He then reached up to get Chris his glass and proceeded to pump out his favourite pint.

Somewhat reluctantly, George outlined the latest dilemma to crash into his shattered world. Chris listened attentively. When the woeful tale of the day had been told, Gerry returned George's glass to him, freshly filled to the brim, with a sympathetic "get that down you, mate".

Chris always looked on the bright side and immediately, in his customary clumsy way, wanted to find something encouraging to say. With Chris, bulls and china shops came to mind. He was a simple soul, a good man, but not great at expressing a convincing deep level of concern.

"Sorry about that mate. They are all bloody idiots. I hope they're giving you a shedload of 'FYM'?". It was typical of Chris to go for the money first.

George was bewildered by this indelicate expression.

Chris explained. "F*** You Money? You know. A bloody big pay-off. Your 'F*** You Money'. Hang out for as much as possible. It's your two fingers back. You deserve a ton of cash after all you have done for them".

"F*** Off Money. I like that, Christopher. Your usual delicate vernacular, as see," George replied. "Oh, yes, there must be what I would rather call a redundancy package. I am not sure how much though. I have been there a long time so it should be significant. Haven't had time to give it any thought. But I am going in to see the Managing Director tomorrow morning to sign papers, you know, so that I don't run off and tell the papers about what the bastards really get up to. I expect we'll go through the payoff in the meeting." Hearing George swear was strange. It was as if the Pope had just called his faithful cardinals a useless bunch of shits.

The mood slipped again as the two huddled closely together, George having swivelled his barstool round towards Chris, who stood supportively, hanging on to his pal's every word. Their friendship, anchored in the bar of the Wellington, had become as deep as it was sincere. The genuine camaraderie between drinking mates can be an extraordinary bond and not always obvious. Usually, it manifests itself in uncontrolled laughter mixed with unbounded merry banter. Not today. This was the time when this special relationship showed another side and offered a rarely called-on masculine support system for a friend who felt the need to share a moment of true anxiety.

The two pals did indeed understand one another, even though, personality-wise, they were complete opposites. Chris was, by nature, a barrel of laughs, the sort who always lifted the spirits of everyone around him whenever he approached the bar. He was a Peter Pan, quite the best person to have around for that early evening drink. However, right now, the two friends were drawing on a far more serious bond, the same that had in recent weeks seen them join forces, shoulder to shoulder, like fellow King and Country soldiers defending Rorke's Drift against another relentless Zulu onslaught. For both had recently received divorce papers and the spears coming their way were from the merciless hands of their wive's lawyers.

There can be few experiences on this planet that are more disabling or disruptive than an unwanted divorce. Whilst in neither case was it unexpected, to both men the recent receipt of formal papers, outlining in legal jargon that proceedings were being initiated, had come as a punch-in-the-stomach, a bolt from the blue. Chris, however, had the greater resilience.

He was thirty-five, going on eighteen, with an infectious love of life that showed in his open, genial face. With his effusive personality, he welcomed everyone into his frivolous world with a hug and an unconditional acceptance. Although his dress sense was no smarter than his intellect, the urbane George thoroughly loved his company. In spite of their obvious differences, there was a seamless, complementary connection that had formed into a strong bond. Chris was one of those people who always skipped through life, with the uplifting help of the wings on his heels. He was never one to allow bad things to clip them. If his beloved Chelsea football team lost, he would inevitably get the drinks in and quickly look forward to the next game, bouncing on with the same childlike, unassailable enthusiasm he had shown before the kick-off. The word defeat was not in his dictionary. He enjoyed life to the full. Tomorrow was always another day. The thing that made this so easy for him was that he saw life very simply. He liked being happy more than being sad. So, he just did it. To him life was better that way. Perhaps George loved the fact that his friend was everything that he was not.

Chris was an engaging and energetic young buck, his uncombed hair and cheeky smile giving him a rakish appeal. Girls invariably fell for his humour and energy. He had never been long without a girlfriend but, right now, he was having to contend with a disgruntled Angela, his wife of eight years, on whom his magic had definitely worn off.

It surprised no-one that he had never had a serious career path. By anyone's standards, he had taken an unconventional route to his thirties, at no point ever looking for that steady job that his parents had wanted for him. He knew he was a disappointment to them but brushed it aside, concluding that they did not understand him. In his jaunty march through life, he had had any number of incarnations. He started out trying to be an actor but, frankly, he wasn't very good, something he always knew full well in his heart, although that had never stopped him. A complete inability to remember his lines had not helped. He had tried once, half-heartedly, to get what his parents would call a 'proper' job, but days spent glued to a computer in a boring office were not for Chris. It was far too dull for him. It lasted one whole week. He even had a go at being an Elvis Presley impersonator, not realising that his shock of Scandinavian hair, his incapacity to wiggle his pelvis in any direction and, crucially, his discordant singing that sounded nothing remotely like The King were never going to help him further his ambitions, which crashed and burned after just one rather embarrassing Friday night in a Croydon pub. But he brushed this aside in his own inimitable manner and moved on. Somehow, through one of his many friends, he had found himself getting a job in a sales promotion agency in central London. This suited his mercurial personality far better and, by chance, had brought him into the same career arena as George. It was all 'marketing', whatever that was. They had first met at this very spot in this very bar a year earlier and found they could chat away effortlessly for hours on end about all the things they had in common and many that they had not. Agency life has always been fed on gossip, scandal and schadenfreude and Chris loved tittle-tattling. This camaraderie quickly became a nightly routine, providing an hour of light-hearted distraction before each man took his soulless commute home to their somewhat depressing domestic lives.

Somehow, Chris's carefree approach to life had prevented him from seeing the divorce juggernaut that was careering at speed towards him, while George, in typical George style, had the antennae to see the early signs of impending marital collapse, even though he chose to ignore them for a long time. Chris' style was to carry on regardless and ignore the whole issue. He had totally failed to notice as significant Angela's indifference to him when he got home, the absence of any conversation when they slumped into their respective chairs to half-watch TV, the lack of any shared excitement when the word 'holiday' arose, the reheated solo dinners every evening - Chris was totally oblivious to it all.

As for Angela, she was just coping. She had made the decision that this all had to end. She had spoken with her parents, who were not surprised, and her Dad had even offered to pay for her lawyers. It saddened her to be the instigator of the end, but she knew Chris would never do anything. It had been up to her to make the move. If it was up to Chris, they would probably have been locked in limbo forever.

The two friends at the Wellington had, by coincidence, received their first divorce papers on exactly the same day. They had arrived as a massive wake-up call, announcing that life as they knew it was about to be turned upside down. And, whilst you might think they would both react very differently, in fact, at the moment of impact, they had mirrored each other's devastation. It was actually a bigger shock to Chris, who had not seen things as being that bad. George was just gutted that it had come to this, but it was no real surprise. For while he still held a candle for Kate, he had known in his heart that the situation could not go on forever. With both men, on opening those ominous envelopes, their jaws had dropped and they were stunned into silence. That night, when they met up in the Wellington, they were both lost for words as the enormity of what was about to happen sank in.

Angela, like George's wife Kate, had already been to several meetings at the solicitors, surreptitiously visiting their offices while Chris was at work. Each time, she met with a bitterly liberated, feisty lady, who was as plain as a Rich Tea biscuit and could not conceal her dislike for men. On each occasion, the fake-friendship between the two grew as the aggrieved wife enjoyed the sycophantic support of the skilful lawyer's charm-offensive, buddying up to her new client and ladling out sympathy by the spoonful, while stirring in lashings of vitriol over her client's unjust plight. The lawyer was very experienced at this.

The slender Angela was a bright, studious young woman. She was attractive, pretty even, although she made no attempt whatsoever to enhance her natural good looks with stylish dressing or alluring make-up. Lamentably, her choice in clothes was as drab as her ash brown hair, which had once been cut into a fashionable bob, but which now hung listlessly, almost touching her shoulders. It looked for all the world as if she had just stopped caring.

She worked in a small, well-organised book shop and was a bookworm herself, liking nothing better than going to bed early with a romantic novel and a cup of tea. She also had a voracious appetite for learning and consumed herself in reading hefty tomes on many esoteric subjects, with a special interest in Fine Art and classical opera.

Her marriage with the permanently affable Chris had been, almost from day one, a patent mismatch, his superficiality meeting her seriousness head on. She had slowly, and sadly, fallen out of love with that boyish boisterousness which had first attracted her to him. She now accepted that it had been fundamentally her mistake. Initially, he had been such a refreshing contrast to the dull academic types she had dated, a breath of invigorating fresh air. She had been captivated with him. When they did eventually get married, she was 31, he was 27. There had been a noticeable lack of enthusiasm for the match from her parents and they made no secret of their doubts. Unfortunately, it turned out that their doubts were soon fully justified as their much-loved daughter started to come round and pour out her heart to them, admitting that she was getting more and more unhappy in the marriage. It was not the age difference that created problems for her, it was their disparate personalities that really caused the fissure. Serious

Angela had always had a greater maturity, while Chris was stuck in a state of permanent irresponsible childhood. She knew that none of this was his fault, so she was careful never to criticise or chastise him in front of her parents but she could not help herself bemoaning her unhappiness in the relationship. To both their credits, they had learned to co-exist. Arguments were rare and they maintained a degree of politeness that enabled them to continue to live under the same south London roof. It was routine that dominated their lives. Chris went off to work on the same train each weekday, while Angela caught the bus to her bookshop. At weekends, Chris watched football and Angela read. Chris listened to his rock music, while Angela preferred opera. The marriage had stagnated and Angela, the sensible one, was the first to see that ending their union was best for both of them, the only solution.

Meanwhile, Kate Granby, George's wife, was a very, very different kettle of fish, as different as you could possibly get. She had been born Catalina Elena Mendoza in Granada, coming to England with her parents when she was eight but never losing her powerful Spanish accent. She was the polar opposite of the intellectual Angela. Although school lessons in English had been hard for her, she had entranced everyone with her explosive personality. Friends swarmed around her like bees.

After leaving school, where she had danced and sung her way through each term, she could not wait to get away from home and found a job as an au pair with a Mr and Mrs Cohen in north London. That was never going to suit her, but she stuck with it for a year, before applying to be an air stewardess with British Airways. With her Spanish, she was accepted immediately and soon put on long-haul flights to South America and Florida.

It was on a stopover in Miami that she first met George. It was a meeting that was to change George's life. Catalina Elena had a penchant for English men. No, a bit more than a 'penchant'. She did not do 'penchant'. It was better described as a red-hot, incendiary passion. She went weak when she met any handsome archetypal British man, with his posh, public school voice, foppish hair, irrespective of whether he was wearing either a smart Armani suit or a rugby shirt.

Kate was a ravishing head-turner, with her brazen walk and the swish of her long jet-black hair that got attention wherever she went. Her piercing dark eyes had a Latin fire within them, oozing sex appeal. To complement her undoubtable attractiveness, she paid enormous attention to her immaculate style in clothes, which never failed to complete this pulchritudinous vision. She had arrived that day with the cabin crew at a luxury five-star hotel on Miami Beach. They had all changed and dashed down to the bar. Kate had characteristically offered to get the first round and went to order the drinks, four Pina Coladas. George happened to be at the same hotel for some international marketing conference but, as usual, he preferred his seat at the bar to the uncomfortable chair in the conference hall. It was around 5.30pm and he was enjoying the company of his Manhattan, which he had insisted was made with his preferred Scotch whisky, not Bourbon.

As she grappled with a clutch of four drinks, she muttered an 'excuse me' as she eased her willowy way backwards from the bar, brushing the man sitting next to where she was standing. It was the debonair George. "No problem, my dear. You seem to be in need of some assistance. May I give you a hand to carry them?"

"You're English".

"Just a tad. Where are you from?" George responded poshly, picking up on her soft accent.

"I live in London, although I come from Spain originally," she replied, in an affected accent, clearly articulating every syllable in 'originally'. George had found this very attractive. He then took two drinks off her and followed her to her colleagues, who were sitting in the lounge.

"Thank you, darling. You are very kind". She started an introduction to her colleagues. "This is… sorry, I didn't get your name."

"George. George Granby". The seated crew mumbled a casual 'Hi'.

"I'm Catalina. Call me Kate, darling" instructed the forceful statuesque beauty.

It must be remembered that this was over fifteen years ago, when George was in his magnificent prime. He was in his late thirties, dashing, well-bred, cultivated and most imposing with his strong, upright stance. The best of British.

"Thank you, George. We have just arrived. It is a pleasure to meet you. I hope to see you around."

He smiled and returned to the bar, affording this exotic creature an occasional glance as he sipped his scotch and soda.

The next day, George found himself having a light breakfast of an omelette, some melon and a refreshing glass of Florida orange juice. He was sitting on his own at a small table in the breakfast room when he suddenly caught his breath as Kate swanned in. He was struck dumb by this long-legged vision of loveliness, coming straight from the pool, with her tumbling hair still half-wet and wearing a one-piece costume clearly visible under a billowing gossamer wrap.

"Hello George. May I join you? I am feeling a bit peckish. How is the omelette?" That Spanish accent was driving him insane. George half-rose as she sat herself down at his table. Right then, it was as if all his prayers had been answered at ten in the morning. If anyone else had been that forward or presumptuous, it would have horrified him. Not Kate though. She could do no wrong, everything was in perfect order, so bewitched was he by this Latina siren. A waiter came over and she addressed him authoritatively. "I'll have the same as my friend". She looked directly at George. "Is that just a plain omelette?". George was frozen to the spot, with a forkful of egg approaching his open mouth. He could only nod nervously. "I'll have exactly the same as my friend, but with cheese in my omelette" she ordered. He had never seen anything like this whirlwind, such poise, such confidence, and he went into a mild state of shock.

George was in heaven picking and prodding at his omelette. He soon relaxed and began chatting to her like an old friend, although at times he felt himself falling under her bewitching spell as he looked deep into those dark enticing eyes. Any awkwardness passed quickly. George and Kate in no time had hit it off as if this was meant to be.

Plates cleared away, Kate sipped her orange and asked, "George, what are you doing now?"

"Absolutely nothing" he replied, knowing that he had no intention of returning to the mind-numbing presentations that he had flown over to see.

"That is excellent. We shall go for a walk around Miami Beach, yes? I love it here. The art deco buildings are the best in the world."

George liked that style of architecture too and was extremely interested in having a look around. However, to be completely honest, that was not why he so readily agreed. It had more to do with the irresistible Señorita sitting before him.

After they finished their juices, Kate quietly addressed her breakfast companion. "Oh, George. I have to slip into something more decent of we are going out. Would you mind coming up with me while I change?" George positively blushed a bright red British blush but could not bring himself to say no.

"Y-yes. Of c-course" was the best stutter he could manage.

They went up to the sixth floor in the elevator, George closely behind Kate as she walked the length of the corridor, got her key card out of her small purse and opened her room door. She stepped back, letting him enter first before following him in and closing the door with a click, leaning back firmly against it with her scantily clad body. The spider had caught the fly.

What happened next, George still dreamed about. Things like this only happened in movies. Without any sort of warning, she morphed into this rabid animal. She started murmuring under her breath in heavy, guttural Spanish. Grabbing his shirt, she ripped it open, all the time kissing him passionately. George was stunned into inaction. She threw him onto the bed like a rag doll, whipped off her wrap, and leaped on him. She was on fire, an unstoppable force meeting a very British, barely moveable object. The Charlottes and Cassandras in George's life had never behaved like this. He was totally unprepared and utterly inexperienced in this sort of thing while she took complete control. Missionary George just went with it. She pulled him up, pushed him against the wall, moaning and kissing him with a vengeance, while wrapping her long lithe legs all around him with every move. George, by now, was loving it. All his English reserve had been squeezed out of him. He offered no resistance as he was shoved back on the bed and his remaining clothes were torn off.

The next twenty minutes were what gave her the nickname, the title that George called her in his head, but only in his naughtiest dreams. Kama Sutra Kate. She sat on him, jumped on him, flipped him over, tickled him, bit him, squeezed him, scratched him. There was no end to her ingenuity. When it all eventually came to an end, George and Kate sank back exhausted and passed out, jet lag kicking in. By the time they awoke, it was 3pm. Kate shrieked.

"Oh, look at the time, I have to go, darling. My bus leaves at 4". She was referring to the crew shuttle bus that would take her to the airport for the 7.45pm flight back to London. George had been unaware that she had to leave so soon. She immediately threw herself into showering, dressing, fixing her haystack hair and putting on her make-up in the bathroom. On hearing the shower, George, unnoticed, put his ripped clothes back on to say a polite good-bye, but not before courageously entering the bathroom and asking through the shower curtain for her phone number.

She poked her head around the curtain to tell him and gave him one last lingering kiss before disappearing back under the shower, shouting "See you in London, George". Our matinée idol was on cloud nine, stunned by not just the sexual Olympics he had just competed in, but also the fact that they both felt so perfectly comfortable with each other. For once, he did not even feel any need to apologise for anything, as he invariably apologised to women for everything out of old-fashioned civility, whatever the occasion.

He headed back to his own room in his tattered clothes, careful to avoid any prying eyes, and continued his nap, all the time questioning his short-term memory. 'Did that really just happen?", he asked himself. They never did get to see the art deco buildings.

That then was how it had all started. He had summoned up the courage to ring her a few days later. To his surprise and delight, she was miraculously exactly the same tempestuous Kate in London as the one he had met in Miami and they picked up where they had left off. They married the following year, amazing all George's friends, who thought 'lucky old George' as he walked proudly down the aisle with the biggest grin of conquest in his face.

But, after a while, it seemed inevitable that that level of intense passion had to cool, although it did last for a couple of good, energy sapping years. Sadly now, however, they found themselves where they were - in the grasping hands of voracious divorce lawyers.

George chose to freeze-frame Kate in his mind as that girl he had met in Miami, a vibrant temptress who fancied him like crazy. He had found her so sexy, exciting, passionate and totally irresistible, everything he had not experienced with the spoiled, upper-class English princesses that he been involved with previously. To have married his Spanish flame was the zenith of his whole existence.

At first, she had very much enjoyed everything about her new married life, adapting easily to the highest traditions of English homelife. She even looked forward to the corporate functions and together the pair were always superb hosts, convivial and engaging. She was perfectly cast for the role, flamboyantly fussing over guests, whether in their box at the Royal Albert Hall, at Ascot in June or Wimbledon in July. But, for Kate, it took only a couple of years of champagne boring company people attached to their dull wives and husbands for the novelty to wear off and for an irascibility to creep in. George began to get on her nerves just by being George and the unsuitability of the match to begin to show at the raw edges. Their characters, which had at first complemented one other, turned from Love Story to Taming of the Shrew in a matter of months. Shouting was an inherent talent to Kate, who could launch into a full vocal assault in a flick of her untamed confusion of hair. For her, arguing at the top of her voice was a national sport.

George was hopeless at holding his ground, something he thought later might have been the one thing that had lost him respect with his combative partner. Perhaps, he would mull, if only he had given her the same back, the rows might have ended more quickly in a passionate Latino crescendo like they had in Miami. Perhaps. But that just was not George. He always played the role of the correct English gentleman, standing up and taking his punishment like a man. He had tried unleashing unconditional apologies, even when he felt he had done nothing wrong, but after a few 'you are always apologising, they mean nothing' from Kate, he concluded that this tactic of capitulation did not work either.

It came to a full bust-up one summer night, with crockery being smashed and regrettable things said, concluding with Kate telling him to get out. He resisted the temptation to walk out into the unknown and had slept that night on the couch. On his journey to the office the next morning, he came to the heart-rendering realisation that this madness had inevitably to end. He still was not sure if he did the right thing in agreeing to leave the marital home, ending up in his drab little flat. It had happened in a haze, but as ever he puckered up his stiff upper lip, kept calm and carried on, in true stoic style. Of one thing there was no doubt. He still loved Kate. It was hard not to love Kate. He understood things from her viewpoint. He was not, he accepted in self-effacement, the most exciting man in the world and perhaps she deserved better.

Unsurprisingly, there was a painful sting to that Iberian tail and he came to discover that her leonine temperament that had been so protective of him in the early days could turn in the blink of her Andalusian eye into the fiery aggression of a tigress. One glare from her enraged face could kill a man at twenty paces. Kate always had the potential to be a fearsome opponent. In full flight, she looked like an enflamed Carmen, her raven mane shaking voluminously down over her shoulders. But Gentleman George could always forgive her. Any explosive outburst came, he accepted, with the package. He always appreciated that she had been a loyal, dutiful and faithful wife, qualities that meant everything to him. He liked making her happy and was pleased she enjoyed the trappings that he provided, a nice home, expensive cars and Caribbean holidays. Having married late in life and deciding together that children were definitely not on the agenda, it had been George and Kate against the world. He enjoyed his work in those days, while she loved playing the wealthy housewife, always finding plenty of time for shopping, having manicures and lunching with friends. Importantly, trust was never an issue. And he still trusted her with his life. But now it was over.

On their third pint at the Wellington, the two pals were gaining solace from one another, indulging in a moment of close comfort, as warm as their beer, and they sank deeper into their conversation.

One feature of this male-bonding friendship was that no-one was ever allowed to be down for long. George realised that that was enough, that they had too long on their problems. With a swashbuckling conversational volte face, he changed the subject in a trice.

"How's the job hunting coming along, Christopher? Heard anything yet?". George's tone jerked from doom and gloom to enthusiastic encouragement.

"Not yet" said Chris "But I had a good second interview with a lovely lady, Jill Spender, who is Head of Promotions at the Post. She seemed to like me. Yes, I think it went well".

Chris had heard that the newly launched Daily Post newspaper was advertising for a promotions man. They needed a whizz kid to come up with wacky ideas to boost their ailing circulation. The paper had been published for less than a year and clearly their multi-millionaire boss, Eddie Walker, had not seen his sales hit the circulation heights he had wanted, and expected, in spite of his bullish launch and endless TV appearances. He had confidently told the world about how he was going to shake up the whole newspaper market with his dynamic new paper. It sat mid-market, between the top-selling Sun and the rock-solid Daily Mail, which completely dominated the middle ground. For some reason, Walker thought he had spotted a gap in the market between the two, only to learn that people's reading habits were hard to change and that he was actually trying to squeeze into an overlap. He had once said on TV "I am also trying to reach the people who currently don't buy a paper at all and persuade them to buy one". This naivety had had his competitors in stitches. Chris was nonetheless incredibly excited about the idea of getting on board this new venture, especially about being able to tell his friends that he was now a big man in the newspaper business.

"I hope to hear any day now. Fingers crossed".

"You'll get it. You'll be brilliant", George reassured, with a broad smile. "They'd be mad not to have the famous Christopher Adams' genius on board. Anyway, good luck, old chap." On that positive note, George, having paid the bill for both men, rose and turned towards the door. "Drinks on me tonight. Got to go". This abrupt exit was perfectly normal.

"Thanks mate," Chris prepared to follow him out, "and keep your pecker up, George. See you tomorrow".

As George left, he was thinking about what Chris had said and mumbled "F*** You Money, eh. Hadn't really thought about that" and his step lightened as he strode off towards his lonely flat.

David Nugent sat at home in his little cottage feeling sorry for himself. It was that early evening time that he never knew what to do with. He was sitting in his solitary comfy chair in the little lounge reflecting on what a great weekend he had had with the children. Suddenly his face dropped when that drama at the house flashed into his mind. He had been simply picking up the children, but Moira never missed an opportunity. Why did everything that involved Moira always end up with confrontation and arguments? Why could she not be nice for once? Why did she always involve the children in every conflagration? His head was shaking in dismay as he replayed the confrontation.

David was an interesting man. He was in his mid-forties, Oxford educated, witty, much travelled, wealthy, clearly very bright, a successful City boy. He had stylish good looks, was of average height and had always had a charm that women loved. There was a cool sophistication about him. Nowadays, he mostly dressed casually but elegantly, albeit with an old-school predictability. He was brought up on rugby, cricket, golf and tennis, not football, something that positioned him 'above the cut' in British society. Such was his ignorance of the country's most popular game, traditionally the tribal sport of the working man, that, on one occasion at university, when asked by a colleague if he knew the result of the Liverpool/Chelsea game (which had ended goalless), he famously informed him that it had ended 'love all'. As a young man, after leaving his Alma

Mater with his degree in economics, he had set about trying to quench his insatiable zest for seeing the world by exploring the corners of the planet at every opportunity. He had always been a free spirit. The thought of marriage had never entered his head. His dream was of being stateless, a refugee from the Sixties, free from all responsibilities other than finding the next place to lay his head, before moving on over the next horizon the next day. He had a particularly warm glow whenever he recalled one of his first adventures, flying to San Francisco on a smoky 707 with the inspirational Grace, his original true sweetheart, listening to Scott McKenzie and bathing in Californian sunshine, with flowers in their hair. However, the gritty reality of working life was his inevitable destiny. Relentless hours in the office, entrapped within the daily commute, put paid to any ideas he may have had of being a maverick explorer. He had married Moira in a rush, swept away by her desire to become Mrs Nugent, and surrendered himself into middle-class village life. In no time, he had welcomed the arrival of Robbie and Jessica, and they changed his life immeasurably. With Jess' first cry, he became a new man, an altruist, an exuberant Dad and he loved every minute of it. Looking back, this was the seminal moment, he thought to himself. At that point, his life had then taken some irreversible turns. Firstly, he had become a father, something he had never truly considered. To his surprise, his new family totally fulfilled him more than he could ever have thought possible. Secondly, at that same time, his career in the City went meteoric. Money poured in, bringing him as a reward a magnificent Georgian house, which some might have called a mansion, a shiny new Range Rover that exuded youthful success and an accompanying lifestyle that competed with the rich and famous. He had even bought a couple of racehorses to complete the inventory of prosperity and, what is more, they actually won races. He had it all, everything he wanted or could have ever wished for. But what always meant the most to him, what he held most dear, were those two little children, who would run up to him when he got home and hug his neck so tightly that he felt his head might fall off. Now, sitting in his small cottage, he was finding this new, imposed isolation that his broken marriage had forced onto him thoroughly depressing, mostly because his cherished father's role had been snatched away from him so dramatically and so unjustly. As he sat in solitude, he felt no anger, no regret, just a deep sadness.

He had given up his job a few months before, walking out on the rapacious City world of vaulting ambition and self-obsessed greed. By that time, he had squirreled away a considerable nest egg, wisely recognising early on that he would, one day, be looking for his exit strategy. He had been able to take it all for what it was and for what he could get out of it, but only for so long. 'Ephemeral, Profitable, Forgettable' was how he once described his egregious life in the rat race. Although he had latterly congratulated himself on breaking free, having tucked away enough money for a lifetime, his masterplan was, in the end, anything but what he had anticipated. He had never foreseen that Hurricane Moira would have very determined plans of her own to suck it all up in her devastating maelstrom.

She had prepared herself well when she had called him in to the dining room that day. As she had presented him with her fait accompli, it had been immediately obvious that all resistance was useless. The die was cast. It had been less of a discussion, more of a case of a simple surrender to her terms, which she had laid out methodically, like a terrorist presenting demands for the release of a hostage. Negotiation had been out of the question. He never stood a chance.

"Sit down. I want you to listen, don't speak", she had barked out unequivocally in the opening gambit. "This has gone on long enough. It's time we should separate." More followed hot on its heels. Next came the detailed pronouncement. "You can find somewhere to live, and I shall keep the children here". She really had thought this through. She had then charged on. "They will stay at the same school. You will pay the fees. You will move out as soon as possible".

Moira was ahead of the game. She already had her lawyer in tow and had been well-briefed. Her choice of litigant prize-fighter was Hedgwick and Havisham, an exotically and expensively named firm of solicitors, who sat at the top of the modern, self-interested legal hierarchy. Their whole raison d'être was to extrude as much money as possible from the richest clients available. Their modus operandi was heartache, shattered families, broken children, and financial ruin - these were their stock in trade. They were seasoned and toned at getting their way through the ungentle art of mental brutality, invariably clubbing their client's victims into submission. Their sole objective? Maximum profit for themselves. The longer they could drag out the suffering, the greater their reward. Wives of Russian oligarchs and Middle Eastern potentates were their prime targets for recruitment as clients. And now their attentions were being focussed on him and this middle-class family from the heart of the leafy South of England.

As their latest victim, David had recently been pummelled by Moira's legal bullies, who sent him forensic threats by email every Friday evening at 5pm, timed to ruin his weekend. Everything from non-molestation orders to threats to confiscate his passport flooded in, all designed to intimidate and weaken. Their strategy was to wear their prey down until they lost the will to live. And it often worked. However, David had eventually become hardened to their shenanigans, although never to the hurt being caused by his enforced absence from his own children.

Sitting there in contemplation, he could not help casting his mind back to the carefree happiness they had all once shared, playing on the large lawn of his beautiful garden, jet-skiing in the Mediterranean, getting dressed up for the pantomime at Christmas. Looking back, he had had everything he had ever wanted. Now, it had all been savagely snatched away. His thoughts then drifted to the latest debacle.

He fell into a downcast trance as he flashed back to the previous Saturday. He was more in a daze than a sleep as he remembered the moment that he had pulled up in his aging Range Rover opposite his old house. It had been a stunningly sunny day, the kind that is uniquely June in England. He had arrived, full of excitement, to collect his two children, his son Robbie, aged 7, and daughter Jess, aged 9. This was his weekend to be a father, his decreed time to spend prized, fun-filled hours with the two people that he loved most in the whole wide world. A girl had walked by the car. He recognised her as the daughter of a neighbour. He had then rolled down the passenger window to say a friendly hello.

"What are you doing here?" she had snapped back coldly.

He remembered being slightly thrown. He never expected that sort of brusqueness and would certainly never have employed it himself. In a humble effort to restore common courtesy and possibly claim sympathy at the same time, he had imparted calmly, "Hi. Good to see you. I am just picking up the children from my old house".

"It might be old, but it isn't YOUR house. It is Moira's", snapped the belligerent girl before turning on her heels and shuffling through her gate. He was numbed. Welcome back to the village, he had thought. His heartfelt feeling was one of humiliation, which he had redressed with his usual dismissive sarcasm. 'Stupid cow,' he had thought to himself as he got out of his car and crossed the road.

He had not been put off by this. Not in the slightest. Today was the day he had looked forward to for two weeks and no-one was going to spoil it. He had exciting plans and he was bubbling. He was about to take the children to Legoland and had the tickets in his pocket. There was nothing he liked more than spoiling them and sharing in their silliness. He could not wait to hear their shrieks of exhilaration on the rides as they clung on for dear life. Seeing them happy meant everything to him. And, of course, he would be quick to buy whatever overpriced toys they wanted. He knew that the good parenting books would denounce him for indulging them, but, hell, he wanted them to have everything they could ever dream of in his few special hours with them.

He had phoned the house the evening before at 8pm. He was permitted, indeed had been instructed, to make two telephone calls a week, on Tuesday and Friday nights, to talk to the children. This was what had been 'agreed', agreed meaning what was ordered to by Moira's lawyers. Although it sickened him that his life with the children was governed by arbitrary rules, there could be no resistance. Jess had answered the phone. He had been unable to contain himself and blurted out his proposition.

"Hi Jess. Here's an idea. How about Legoland tomorrow?". He had then heard her say to her brother in an energized, stifled stage whisper "Legoland!". Robbie had let out a boyish shriek in the background. "Could you ask Mummy if it's OK if I collect you at 11 rather than the usual 12? It's a bit of a drive and I want as long as possible there".

"Hang on, Daddy". It then had gone quiet for a good minute. No hint of a conversation between daughter and mother could be heard. The longer the silence had lasted, the more he had been filled with dread. He knew his collection time was officially noon. Rules are rules. They must be obeyed. This was the diktat. He knew he was on the back foot. But, to his absolute delight, the simple reply came back. "That's fine", Jess had said, although it had been noticeable that her words had not been uttered in a burst of joy, but in a matter-of-fact tone that conveyed the grudging agreement of 'the other side'.

He had been a very happy Dad as he rang the bell at 11am on that sunny day. But no-one answered. He rang again. He paused. Then he rang a third time, this time for longer, imbuing into the ring a degree of his irritation. Still nothing. Stunned, he stepped back and looked at the windows. There was no sign of life.

He slumped back into his car, his crest well and truly fallen, and sat pensively for a good 10 minutes. He had decided not to get het up, instead he thought he would use the time positively to call in on his friends, Roy and Margaret Harrison, an affable, devoted couple who lived in the house next door, and so he invited himself in for a cup of tea and a bit of a moan.

It must have been a good half hour later that he left. He liked his old neighbours and had not seen them for months, so it had been good to catch up. They had had some good times together, especially at Christmas, when Roy traditionally invited what seemed to be the whole village into his living room for wine and mince pies. As he left, he had spotted that Roy had a stone bench against the wall between the two houses and he could not resist climbing up to peer over into the garden. His first thought was how neglected his brightly coloured borders were looking, having been once a kaleidoscopic forest of tall delphiniums, highly scented stocks and splendid irises. But he quickly refocussed. He looked at the back of the house. The conservatory doors were wide open. All of a sudden, out of nowhere, a furry flash of black leaped up the wall. It was Billy, his faithful old labrador, now re-identified as the 'family dog'. He and Billy had always been totally devoted to each other in their own special relationship. Every time that he got home from the station, come rain or shine, his faithful dog would lie in wait for his car to arrive through the gates at 8.20pm, before jumping onto his master, shaking, wagging and licking, the moment he opened his car door. Even on those wet winter evenings, David had never been angry when his drenched, muddy-pawed companion bound onto the lap of his most expensive suit. The adoration in his dog's kind eyes after all that waiting in the rain made chastisement impossible. As Billy had squealed and squealed at this long-awaited and unexpected reunion, he had stretched over lovingly, just managing to put his outstretched hand on the dog's head. The bond was still not broken. This was a bitter-sweet moment neither was ever to forget. Unexpectedly, he had felt a tear well up in his eye, indecipherable to him as to whether it was of joy or sadness. The children must be at home, he had concluded, presumably ready to go. He had had no choice but to go back to his car, to play the game and sit it out. At exactly midday, the front door swung inward. Moira, unseen, squeezed herself awkwardly behind it. This was her kind of theatre. A disembodied, charmless voice spoke loudly and severely.

"The agreement is 12. Read it. You'll be getting a letter from my solicitor on Monday".

He had tried to ignore this embarrassing scene, immune to her threats, and had held the hands of the two subdued children as they crossed the road and climbed quietly into the car. Robbie got into the front without argument. The children had already agreed that he would have it there and Jess would have it on the way back.

In spite of the delayed departure, the mood in the car had quickly picked up as the resilient three headed off for their day out. He recollected how pleased he had been to see the village disappearing into the distance in his rear-view mirror, leaving behind all thoughts of the unpleasant encounter that had just taken place.

He had learned in recent months how to throw the switch whenever he was reunited with Robbie and Jess, in order to generate an instant 'let's have fun' atmosphere. Robbie turned on the radio and tuned it to their favourite music station. David loved hearing the children singing their hearts out in the car. It gave him a thrill that they knew every word to their latest favourite songs, many of which he was hearing for the first time. It made him think back fondly to when he was their age and how he would sing along to 'She Loves You' and 'Please Please Me' in the back of his Mum and Dad's Morris Minor, as if he was a real Beatle. At the same time, he had not been able to stop his mind dwelling on the unnecessary and damaging fatuity that he had been remorselessly subjected to in the past twelve months. It had been all so unnecessary. He had never forgotten that morning they were going to board Eurostar for a long family weekend at Disneyland Paris. "Jessie and I aren't coming. You can take Robbie", Moira had suddenly announced as they got up at dawn. It cut him to the quick, but, as ever, he knew resistance was futile, so father and son just nonchalantly headed off for the station and had a great weekend as if everything was normal. But it was not normal and he knew it. It was just another day in Moira's world. And he never forgot.

David suddenly snapped out of his dream, or nightmare, finding himself back in the real world of his cottage. His despondent scowl was then wiped off his face to be replaced with a grin of glowing satisfaction as he relived the wonderful afternoon that they had spent eventually together, free of all the nonsense they were being put through, sharing some hours of good old family fun. He shook his head again, brushing his retrospection aside as he got out of his chair. "Mustn't let it get me down", he said to himself. "Time for another cup of tea". As every Englishman knows, a cup of tea is the solution to any adversity, the restorative of normality.

Chris got off his train at the usual time, 7.31. He popped a mint into his mouth as he walked from the station through the suburban avenues towards his home. For some reason, he was repeatedly playing Roxy Music's Avalon in his head and was striding out purposely in time. He was not quite whistling, but sort of inaudibly breathing the tune. This was his default good mood. However, as he walked, his mood changed and he became overwhelmed by an indescribable hidden fear. George's disheartening ill-fortunes had haunted him all the way home and tonight he could not shrug off an underlying feeling of unease. He began to walk more slowly as his mind drifted back to that awful night some weeks ago when Angela first grasped the nettle and brought up the thorny subject of divorce. The papers followed shortly afterwards. He remembered it all clearly.

Number 67 was anything but imposing, just a modest, reasonably sized, pebble-dashed semi with barely enough room for their Ford Escort to be parked on the paving slabs out front. The car had meant that any kind of front garden was impossible but, even though he was not a great horticulturist, he had planted a line of gladioli bulbs along the wall and they now added a splash of summer colour that made him proud of his green fingers every time he came home. He turned the key, walked in, picked up some uninteresting letters from the shelf on the wall, only to place them straight back again.

"Hi" he called out as he closed the door.

An indifferent "Hi" bounced back from the lounge.

Angela was sitting back in her chair, with a glass of sauvignon blanc by her side, a book opened on her lap and some unwatched game show on TV. The volume was low, so no adjustment had to be made for Chris' arrival.

"Had a good day?" said Angela, who had yet to look up to greet her husband.

"Very good thank you. And you?", replied Chris, indifferently.

"Fine thanks. There's a steak and kidney pie in the oven. I've eaten", she added, still looking down towards her book.

Chris had by now taken off his jacket and headed into the kitchen, returning to sit in his chair with a tray and his glass of wine. The next twenty minutes saw no conversation whatsoever between the two. Although it looked like Angela's novel continued to win out over the TV, her expression was vacant, as if even the book was not holding her attention. Even Chris, a stranger to intuition, could not escape a strange feeling that something else was brewing in her mind. He made no enquiry and ate his dinner, breaking the silence only to shout out an answer to one of the quiz questions and to congratulate himself with a clipped "yes" when he got it right.

After the overcooked pie has been devoured, he took out his tray, washed up his plate, knife and fork and returned to his chair. A half hour then passed while some police drama played out in the background as the night ticked away. All the while, a deafening silence reigned in the Adams' household. His mind went back to the day he had received the divorce papers and he had been sitting in this very chair. He knew that something serious was coming when Angela got up and turned off the TV.

"Can we talk?" she had announced. Chris had immediately took this as a rhetorical question and had steeled himself for whatever was coming next. His worst fears were confirmed with her next words.

"I don't want to fight, but we need to talk."

"Fire away" said Chris, leaning forward into a receptive pose, conscious that whatever was coming might not end well.

A feeling of foreboding smothered his usual flippancy and brought a furrow to his brow. It was as if he was in a play, that this was not really happening to him. No, it was actually more like he was watching the play in the stalls rather than being an actor on the stage itself. Chris and Angela had, of course, discussed the state of their marriage on a number of occasions, but this felt different. The worst night was on the day he had received the divorce papers and had hit the roof. That time, the thespian streak running through him burst forth and he found himself embroiled in a kitchen-sink drama. His performance that night could have been best described as exaggerated, as if in a bad melodrama. In keeping with his habit of over-acting, he then lost it and yelled, mostly at Angela but also breaking off into the ether of the middle distance, demanding to know what was going on. 'Why?' he howled in a hurt tone. 'Is there someone else?', 'How long has this been going on?' 'Why didn't you mention it before rushing to the lawyers.' 'What now?', plus a few more obvious theatrical questions which served to portray him as the victim. However, he quickly became conscious that, with his raised voice, he was now turning into the unfamiliar role of aggressor. He found himself in the role of the protagonist, a marital pugilist, facing an opponent on whom he was trying to land punches. But his punches had little chance of landing and certainly no chance of hurting. They went right over Angela's head. Her impenetrable defence was her detachment. He never shouted at her again after that. They both saw the futility of it, especially Chris. It was not their style. Since then, they had established a rational, more resigned platform of co-existence and had learnt to resolved issues in a decent, restrained way.

That was two months ago. Chris had managed conveniently to kick the whole matter of divorce into the long grass by simply ignoring it. And even though there was no denying the sound of silence that had hung like a pall over the home since then, the subject had not been brought up again. And on the plus side, there had been hardly one cross word between the two.

"Chris", said the controlled Angela, almost sympathetically. She had been practising these words for days and gulped before she embarked on her proclamation. "Chris... I think we have to call it a day. We have to face the truth. We can't go on pretending like this forever. We are just existing. It's time to accept we would be happier apart and I guess we just need to restart our lives. Both of us. I don't want a fight in court, but I do think we have to face facts". She paused before speaking more slowly. "I guess, if I am totally honest, I have just fallen out of love with you and I can't go on pretending any longer".

It was the words about 'fallen out of love' that hit Chris the hardest. He always wanted everyone to love him and could never understand why anyone would not do so because he loved everyone himself.

For the first time that night, they looked each other directly in the eye. And neither could speak. They shared a silent stare for almost a minute, before Chris said "I know. I know. You're not wrong. I have been wishing the whole thing away, hoping that it would just disappear".

This capitulation to the honesty of the situation immediately brought them closer together and defused the situation. They flashed a smile at one another, a sad, fatalistic smile. Chris got up and moved behind Angela, gently squeezing her shoulders with his hands. She put her hand on his in an almost motherly way, turning her face up towards him.

"I am so sorry Chris. You know I wouldn't hurt you for the world, but I think we have to get divorced".

"I know, Angela. I know. It's just a bit of a shock really". That was probably the truest thing he had ever said.

WEDNESDAY, JULY 10

By 6pm the next evening, George and Chris had assumed their usual places at the end of the bar of the Wellington, George perched on his stool, as was his wont, and Chris standing alongside. There were often several others who joined them in the after-work drink. Over the months, they had attracted a gaggle of friendly co-conspirators that might or might not drop into the Wellington at the allotted time, most of whom they had met either on their commute or at the office. But, recently, however, it had been left to the two stalwarts alone. Only George and Chris maintained the same ritualistic dependability. It would be impossible to imagine a night when these die-hards were not stationed at their usual posts, pints in hand, laughter effusing into the air just as the clouds of cigarette smoke had used to in the good old days. These two were the lynchpins of this unofficial 'club', George being the quiet, sensible captain and Chris the life-and-soul-of-the-party entertainment manager. So tonight, as no-one joined them, they were à deux, something each man was perfectly content with.

Chris always had a joke. Name any subject and he would launch into a gag. He was an engaging storyteller who could hold everyone's attention, especially by being able to do almost every accent on the planet, from Austrian to Australian, Birmingham to Belfast or Chinese to Chilean. For him, the longer the joke went on, the better, as he could employ his dubious acting skills to hold his audience. It was no surprise, therefore, that political correctness was notably absent from his extensive repertoire. 'Woke', he was not. But he never meant any harm. Jokes about stereotypes were bread and butter to him. Religion, of course, was the jam on top. Vicars, priests and particularly nuns were more than fair game. Being so good at accents, he loved to use them at every opportunity, meaning that Paddy was more often than not a feature, as was Ahmed, or 'this frog' or 'this kraut'. His defence was always one of innocence. 'People were meant to laugh at one another's differences, weren't they? It doesn't mean I don't like them. Quite the opposite. After all, foreigners are quite like us, really', he would say if challenged. For him, humour was what made the world go round and, vitally, he knew inside that he had not got a shred of prejudice or malice in him. He loved everyone. But, when around Chris, everyone had to be prepared that they could be the next potential target of his quick barbs. He felt he was funniest when catching his unwitting victims out. On this particular night, Chris had one of those lined up and threw it at George in the form of a casual question.

"By the way, something came up today you may be able to help me with, George. You're a bright guy. Do you happen to know what DNA stands for?", Chris asked, enquiringly.

"Ah. I do actually, Christopher. It's deoxyribonucleic acid", George said confidently, with a smile of satisfaction.

"Wrong, mate", said Chris, smugly. "It's the National Dyslexic Association".

George paused before generously rolling back, almost falling off his stool like an upturned cockroach, his laughter resounding around the pub, matched only in volume by that of the joke-teller himself. Gerry, listening intently from behind the bar, struggled to work it out but eventually collapsed in uncontrollable laughter at the trap George had fallen into.

In all this ribaldry, they had failed to notice the smart, well-dressed man who had come up to the bar next to them and who, after catching Gerry's attention, had quietly ordered a pint of best. Gerry passed the drink over with a smile and the man stood consciously alone as he took his first sip. He hadn't intentionally listened to the others' conversation, but such was the outburst of effusive laughter that he got caught up in the infectiousness of it. He chuckled accommodatingly as he glanced over to the merry pair, careful not to be considered as invading their privacy. The laughter eventually died down. For some reason, Chris then abruptly changed the subject and asked George how things were at home. This was an unfortunate downer and things crashed from a high to a low. George solemnly explained that he was due in Court next Wednesday, how he had had to expose to the enemy all his worldly goods and how he felt having his finances forensically examined by Kate's lawyers. He added with sadness that this was particularly painful for him as he knew it was the lawyers, not Kate, who were pushing so hard. A dark cloud had returned over the two men, a far cry from the air of hilarity that they had been sharing a minute before. It went quiet, giving each man a chance to pick up his glass and sink some more of his supportive beer. Then Chris returned to the whole depressing matter of his impending divorce and what he should do next. Chris always heeded George's advice.

A voice interrupted them. "Forgive me, gentlemen", came an authoritative voice next to them. The dignified, middle-aged, fair-haired man, with blue eyes and a strong rugby player's chin, was standing next to them at the bar. The two turned to see the new arrival addressing them both. George did not appreciate the impudent intrusion and flashed an old-fashioned look to transmit his disapproval. The interloper took a chance and carried on. He addressed them mimicking the articulate tone of a fine Shakespearean actor at the Globe in bygone times.

"Dear friends, I could not help but overhear your tragic plight. You appear totally discombobulated. Worry not. A kindred spirit is here. Help is at hand, for I too am experiencing marital machinations and am an expert in the ancient and mystical art of the disappearance of ex-wives, a virtuoso prestidigitator in making these nemeses vanish for good and it seems my services may be required. One visit to my humble barber's shop at 186 Fleet Street and..." (he pretended to pull a handle by his side), "Puff. Gone. All over. Dematerialised in an instant. Dispatched forever" He paused briefly. "Meat pies are, of course, my speciality. The name is Todd, by the way. But you can call me Sweeney. My card".

The man extended his arm and proffered his business card between his two forefingers. He stood proud and erect, resolutely fixed in his Laurence Olivier character, poised and expressionless, awaiting a response and hoping he had not just made a complete and utter arse of himself. He stood there uneasily. Why he had suddenly launched into this ridiculous charade was a complete mystery, even to himself. He knew it was completely out of character but, for some reason, could just not stop himself. Perhaps, he thought, that his hours of solitude had made him socially insecure. His bizarre perfomance, he knew, had been a bit of a gamble. To his enormous relief, after a heavy pause, his audience rose to the bait. This was, after all, a perfect Chris moment. Pure theatre, straight out of The Demon Barber of Fleet Street, staged in the gothic setting of a classic Victorian London pub. All that was missing was a flickering gaslight, a few raucous ladies of the night with heaving skirts and bad teeth and a chorus of cane-carrying men in black frock coats and top hats. Chris would have doubtlessly loved to have seen the Phantom of the Opera emerging from behind the thick dark red velvet curtain that hung over the door to the private room. Gentleman George took the card from the outstretched hand and examined it. Although he was not as naturally funny as Chris, he was always eager to have a go, joining in even though he often confused the themes. He read the name on the card.

"Dr David Nugent, I presume"., George remarked, switching characters. Where Stanley and Livingstone came into it, Chris did not understand, but he laughed anyway. Inexplicably confusing his filmography, George then switched to a James Bond villain's voice.

"Vee 'ave been expecting you, Mr Nugent". Chris and David laughed supportively.

Immediately, with that, David was embraced into the elite fold. His gamble had paid off, having passed the initial 'be funny' test with flying colours. His entrance had been a triumph. Chris then seized his moment to steal the stage, thoroughly enjoying the spontaneous dialogue.

"Mr Todd. Dear boy. You don't happen to have any promotional deals on at the moment, do you? You see, we both have an 'issue' that needs a trip to your barbers for a quick cut. Two for the price of one, perhaps? Or perhaps 20 per cent off now and the rest chopped off later?".

"Are you still working for Henry VIII?" butted in George, picking up on the head chopping line, still trying to do his best to be funny.

David drew himself up. "No, he fired me for letting that Anne Of Cleves get away. God, she was ugly. I tied her to the stake, but she was so ugly the fire wouldn't light".

As often happens when you are on a roll with a pint in your hand, the jocularity can all too easily spiral into complete nonsense, but they all laughed anyway, even if they didn't know what they were laughing at. An immediate bond had been formed, a bond that none of them, at that moment in time, could have possibly imagined would shortly to lead them together into a new chapter of life beyond their wildest imagination.

"I'm George, George Granby" said the seated member of their cast, "and this is my minder Christopher Adams".

"When I'm not here, I am his absent-minder", Chris jested.

"David. David Nugent."

They exchanged the traditional handshakes and, as is custom, each man then eagerly competed to get in the next round of drinks. David won.

An hour passed quickly. 'Divorce bore' tales of woe were rolled out in turn, with David chipping in with his own saga of purgatory. Each wallowed in his own individual morass of ridiculousness and injustice. David explained how he had just visited his solicitor that afternoon and that it was by pure chance that he had wandered into this particular watering-hole.

It was all cut short only when George took a glance at his watch, stood up and announced his abruptly, 'Got to go'. Chris always saw this nightly urgency as rather sad, thinking that his friend was heading out with absolutely nothing to rush home for. However, his departure was the cue for them all to finish their drinks and for Chris to head for the station. The leader of the pack had left.

"See you tomorrow", said George as he moved towards the door. He then added, "Hope to see you again soon, David. Very good to meet you. We're here every night. Apparently." He smiled and walked out into the mid-summer late sunshine.

George was the lynchpin, the cornerstone of the group. Whoever turned up, he was always central to everything yet probably the one that spoke the least, the enigmatic elder sitting on his usual stool, content to enjoy the conversation around him. He was the pivotal figure, the catalyst around which the whole social ritual revolved. Without George, there would be no nightly gathering of the clan. Once he departed, the leading man had left the stage and the show wound down. So, without George, Chris and David chatted slightly awkwardly for a while and it was not long before David said his goodnight and set off towards the station.

As David left, Chris said a generous goodbye to his new mate and turned back to the bar, head down, his half-empty pint in hand. He too was resigned to drinking up and catching his train. But as he placed his near empty glass onto the beer mat on the bar, he looked up, expecting to see Gerry in front of him. However, to his complete amazement, the handsome barman had somehow miraculously mutated into the most delectable creature of the female variety, with silky dark hair, absorbing blue eyes and a seraphic smile. She stood confidently before him, looked down at his glass and, in a disarming Celtic tone, said "Would you care for another one?".

Chris would normally have tried to impress with his humour and repertoire of accents with a predictable "Aye, Lassie" but he was stunned into paralysis by this sensation that faced him. He was usually quite good at chatting up the girls, his casual coolness tended to impress, but when faced with such a superlative beauty as this he knew he was out of his depth and he was completely thrown. He was unable even to look her in the eyes, let alone talk to her. Luckily, it was she who addressed him.

"Are you a regular here?", she said, as she pulled his pint, assuming he wanted one.

Chris's mouth quivered at the edges as he tried to get some words out. Any words. He was at heart so very British. Not in the traditional way, like George, but, when it came to meeting really, really pretty girls, all his confidence drained away as his face filled up with a tell-tale blush. What came out was spontaneous gibberish, some obscure utterance spluttering out, his brain having totally disengaged. He was a bag of nerves. To his immediate embarrassment, he just began blurting.

"I live in South London actually. I come up by train every day. I work in Holborn but am about to get another job and am looking for a flat and come here every night". He was then struck by what a complete idiot he had sounded, garbling at this lovely girl his staccato life story.

"Really", she said in a controlled tone, making him feel even more stupid. "I'm Bonnie. Bonnie Carter, by the way".

"Chris. Chris Adams".

"Nice to meet you, Chris".

Bonnie Carter was an eye-catching 27-year-old, a stunner by anyone's standards. She was adorably cute, with a kind, girl-next-door face. Her eyes were as blue as robins' eggs and her dark straight hair positively luminesced under the lights of the bar, while it was hard not to stare at those cherubic lips as she spoke in that seductively soft Edinburgh accent.

Chris's heart skipped a beat and, as hard as he tried not to say something daft, the best he could come back with was unbelievably disappointing.

"Nice to meet you too". 'Idiot' he thought to himself in self-disparagement.

He had expected Bonnie to walk away at this point, not just because there were other customers who needed her attention, but particularly because of his abject failure to make any kind of good first impression. It came as a wonderful surprise, therefore, when she continued to be anchored to the spot, facing him, letting Gerry do the honours with the waiting customers.

"There are some lovely areas around here once you get away from the offices and all the walking-dead commuters" she said. He was worried about this sleight as he was, after all, one of her 'walking-dead' himself. It was as if she had a sense of superiority about living right there, in the heart of it all. He quickly saw an opportunity to relate with her.

"Yes. You are so lucky. I have always wanted to live in this part of town". This was, of course, a complete lie, but he felt his confidence ebbing back as he started to share a common link with the bewitching Bonnie.

"Are you looking for somewhere at the moment?", Bonnie queried.

"Yes. Absolutely. Definitely." he said, with his conversation with Angela the night before spinning in his head.

"Where have you looked?"

Chris tried not to appear taken aback as he felt he was now actually doing rather well. In fact, he started to get quite nonchalant. "To be honest, I have only just started looking in estate agents' windows and on a couple of websites. Funnily enough, I am going to get serious about it next week - so if you hear of anywhere?".

"I shall keep my ears open. It's my first night tonight, but you hear a lot of stuff working in pubs and who knows, someone might just be moving out of somewhere nice".

They continued to chat away, the conversation getting easier and flowing more naturally with every sentence. That was until Bonnie interjected with... "You won't miss your train, will you?". Chris wasn't sure if this was a statement or a question. He realised he had lost all track of time and peered down at his watch. He had indeed just missed his train. But he acted calmly, trying to show no reaction, desperate to maintain an air of casual self-assurance.

"No, it's fine," he said, faking composure. "No hurry. Twenty minutes yet. I have time for another pint". He had already decided to catch the next train and be late home for once. After all, he thought, why would Angela be bothered.

She then said one word that made his heart leap, his pulse pound and his inner delight erupt. She looked back him, right into his eyes. "Good", she said slowly and softly.

That is all she said, in the most beautifully gentle voice he had ever heard. That was it. One little four-letter word. No word could have excited him more. With that single word, his world shook. She accompanied it with a coy, knowing smile and the lingering look they shared held an intensity that said another thousand words.

This glorious moment was broken by Gerry calling Bonnie over to help with the influx of customers. She had forgotten where she was for a second, on her first night's work, and she was quickly jolted back to the job in hand. Chris remained transfixed, standing alone in his own starry universe as Bonnie served an irritatingly large round for a group of lively office staff, who had just cavorted in. He was unable to take his eyes off her. Eventually she returned to that same spot, straight in front of him, the spot where he had first seen her, when time had stood still. She repeated that bewitching smile, as if to pick up where they have left off.

"Now, where were we?", she said enticingly.

The two chatted eagerly, but intermittently, as Bonnie broke away to pull pints for thirsty customers. But nothing could hide the immediate spark between them and they both knew it.

After a while, Chris spoke reluctantly. "Well, I guess I have to go. Can't stay here all night? Hope to see you again", he quavered.

"I'll be here. Monday to Friday nights from seven. Possibly see you soon then" she replied, adopting the same cool tone.

"Yes, soon", he stuttered nervously, knowing full well he was there every night.

Chris then left, turning in the doorway to raise a palm of farewell. Her eyes followed him and she raised her hand from the bar to give him a small, encouraging wave back.

Anyone sitting opposite Chris on the train that night might easily have confused him with a deranged simpleton. He gazed emptily at the window but saw nothing as the train sped through the suburban stations. His mind was elsewhere. He was in a daydream. Arriving at his station, he got out like an automaton, walking in a haze along the well-worn route to his home. He found himself whistling out loud.

As he turned into his avenue, he recognised in himself a completely different man from that who had left the house at 7.30 that morning. Gone was the downbeat, depressed homecoming Chris, replaced by the vital, bouncy one of old. He remembered for the first time in an age what it was like to feel alive inside. He knew though that he had to suppress his elation in preparation of what lay behind the door of number 67. Angela would be sitting in her chair, obligatory glass of wine to hand, TV on. "Act normally", he commanded himself as he took a large breath in and consciously brought his demeanour back down to Earth. He turned the key and walked in, ignoring the same pile of letters he had ignored the day before.

"Hi", said Angela from the other room.

"Hi", replied Chris

"You're late tonight".

"Yes, stopped in for a quick drink with the lads after work. Sorry about that". He didn't know why he had apologised. He had done it only to keep in character.

"That's OK. Your food is in the oven. Fish fingers. Sorry, I was a bit busy today". She had probably rushed off to the solicitors, he thought, after their big chat last night.

He was already planning his evening. He wanted to escape this tired routine and be on his own. The thing about arriving home late, he thought, was that he could now legitimately go to bed sooner than usual. He still shared a bed with Angela. In spite of the everything, he had never been dispatched to the spare room as usually seems to happen in these situations. Fortunately, Angela was not a drama queen and had been remarkably civilised throughout the whole thing. However, tonight, he wished that he had been given his marching orders. Tonight, after months of sleeping, back-to-back, motionless, every night, his total solitude would have been a blessing, alone with his thoughts, recalling that magical encounter in the Duke of Wellington.

"So, anything interesting happened today?", Angela asked, as he fed another fish finger into his mouth. For some reason, he was not particularly hungry.

"Nothing really. Just a long day", mumbled Chris, while trying to extract some taste out of the bland dinner. There followed a two-minute silence.

"Angela", he said, about to embark on a speech. He started talking to his wife unsurely, before gaining strength. "Er...I have been thinking about what you said last night". It was unexpectedly his turn to hold the floor. "I think you're right. I have been selfish. What you say is absolutely true. I think it IS time I moved out. It is only fair that you can now get on with your life". He waited for a reaction, which did not come. He hesitated before speaking. "So...if it's OK, I might start looking for somewhere next week".

Angela's attention immediately left the TV and her eyes focussed on him, like a heron focusses on a fish. She wondered where that had just come from.

"That's quick" she said curtly. Her female antennae were twitching and her suspicions had been immediately aroused, although it was impossible to discern whether she was surprised or hurt that he should be acting so readily to what were, after all, her wishes.

"No point in wasting time", he said accommodatingly, trying to move forward. Needless to say, this strong unaccustomed style of assuredness in her otherwise predictable Chris had already fired up her feminine intuition. He really was a lousy actor and an even worse liar.

"Is everything OK?", she probed, her caring tone disguising her deep curiosity.

"Yes. Absolutely. I have been thinking all day about what you said… and I agree. Let's talk about it tomorrow. Now, if it's OK, I think I'll get an early night. Heavy day tomorrow" he said.

With his Parthian shot, he took his tray out to the kitchen. He poked his head back into the lounge and reassured the bemused Angela.

"Don't worry. Everything's good". Angela's intuitive senses were working overtime.

THURSDAY JULY 11

The sun burst through the curtains in the bedroom of David's thatched cottage. He woke up, as was typical these days, without the help of his alarm. Since quitting his job, he knew he could start every day in his own time. Well, that was the theory but, in reality, he still always jump-started himself into life at 6.15am, the time that his faithful alarm had used to shake him into action for his dash to the City. He went down to the tiny kitchen and put the kettle on.

He looked out of the front window as he waited for the water to boil and was lifted by the sight of the busy collection of beautiful sparrows and blue tits vying for their turn to gorge themselves on his four bird feeders that hung off the conveniently long branch of a small tree. These were his favourite companions now, he often thought. The human race had let him down again and again and he felt less of a need to make any new friends, preferring his own company, that of his lovely children and, of course, of his little songbirds. In any event, he had never in his life had many true 'friends'. He looked with a kind of envy on people he knew who had close buddies, but he had never found that depth of relationship with anyone himself. Yes, he used to be invited to parties at university, but only, it seemed, after everyone around him had been asked first.

During his marriage, he had had a steady stream of dull, forgettable couples, mostly parents from his children's school, arriving for dinner at weekends, always at Moira's request. She would call them her friends. That is not how he saw it. He would nevertheless do his best to enliven the evening and play the jolly, genial host, not with the support of his wife but that of a copious intake of a half-decent French white wine. He found the whole concept of drinking in moderation on these occasions totally bizarre. 'If you don't want alcohol to do its work, why bother at all?', he used to think. To him, at that time, to stop drinking before its effects were felt seemed a complete waste of time and money. He would regularly hose down a bottle or two, while splashing it as liberally into his guests' glasses, hoping the evening would get better. In fact, his effusive hospitality only served to annoy Moira, who preferred to maintain a restrained, middle England sobriety. This, of course, failed to entertain David in any way at all and after the first hour of talking about teachers, holidays and 'do you know what she said the other day?', he was always, without fail, thoroughly disinterested. His energy and enthusiasm levels read like a downward graph, starting with his over-animated greeting for their guests and descending rapidly to his sitting back, slumped in his chair at the head of the table, enduring the asinine drivel that flowed backwards and forwards across the table in front of him.

All that was over now. Those tedious evenings had disappeared along with his marriage. And he felt no sadness but a genuine relief about losing both. The atmosphere for him and his children had been toxic. Although he had his insecurities, he knew inside that he was basically a good person and, in his rare moments of introspection, he found a lot to like about himself. While living in the state of holy matrimony, he had found himself having to build up his own confidence to cover any deep-rooted self-doubt that had been instilled into him. His natural self-assuredness and this new insecurity battled it out in his head occasionally but, through his strength of character, his inner faith in his own ability always won out. He recalled that he used to leave his office after a particularly bad day muttering to himself 'I am the best at what I do. I am the best'. Anyone hearing this weird mantra would think it was arrogance, but it was far from that. It was his way of keeping himself up there and winning.

Now he was right down there. Admittedly, he had managed to secrete away a considerable fortune over the past few years, but his prestige as a high-flyer had, well, flown. Although he in no way saw himself as a loser, he was aware that others might perceive him as such, especially his former work mates. No job, broken marriage, rented cottage, a five-year-old car parked outside, that is what they would see. How the mighty fall, they may think. But they would have badly misread the situation. While he had had his marital and career setbacks, he had always looked at life holistically and managed to absorb the good and repel the bad. The enthusiasm and purpose of the small birds in the garden were an inspiration to him. He was lifted each morning by the sight of his little friends, busily and chirpily starting their day. They were enviably free and, on seeing their hopefulness, he became able to put behind him the pointlessness of his miserable former existence and his unfathomably bad marriage. He smiled to himself as he began to appreciate his own new-found freedom after years of being trapped in his daily ritual commute, crammed into an overcrowded railway carriage, his body being jolted at every set of points, followed by the crushing walk to the Underground, shoulder to shoulder amidst a herd of other ensnared humans as they squeezed themselves into packed Tube trains. Yes, he was now a free man. He may have lost his reputation, he thought, but at least he could now live freely.

A nervous goldcrest suddenly landed on the branch outside his window. It was as if David had had an electric shock put through him. Could it be? He knew his birds well, having spent hours poring over the Observer's Book of Birds as a child. And he still had it by his side. He certainly thought he knew exactly what a goldcrest looked like, even though had never seen one in real life. He referred to the little book which confirmed his identification. This was his first ever sighting. No-one would understand his thrill. People might laugh for my excitement, he thought to himself. But he felt such an elation at this special moment, such a feeling of privilege. He had once read somewhere that this little chap, with that tell-tale stripe on his head, used to be called "the king of birds" in folklore. Sadly, the little monarch did not stay long. Nevertheless, he had had his impact. As David made his tea, he smiled to himself. 'Perhaps it's a sign', he pondered.

He sat down and put the news on TV. He had once been a news junkie, wanting to know everything that was going on in the world. Recently, however, he had concluded that the problem was that to be truly happy in life you have to know everything, or nothing at all - and that we all seemed to know half everything and permanently seek to find out about the other half. He had complimented himself at the time on this observation, crediting himself with the wisdom of a philosopher, and concluded that, as total knowledge eluded him, an existence of splendid isolation, living in a news vacuum, would be the best way to exist. Unfortunately, life could never be like that, as Moira and her lawyers reminded him every week. So, he sat down, another tea in hand, the TV turned low, and stared back out of the window.

"Something has to change", he said to himself in full voice. He had put his philosopher's hat back on, emptying his mind to achieve true clarity. Then, out of nowhere, he had an eureka moment.

"That's it. I am moving to London. Total re-invention is what's called for". This was typical David. He had this peculiar trait of presenting himself with a conclusion and then matching his thought process to justify it afterwards. Decision first, accommodating logic after.

"Yes, that's it. I am moving to London. A new start." Then he thought of Jess and Robbie. He had elected to stay in this area so that he could be close to them but, as he looked at it all through the lens of this new perspective, he rationalised that it was stupid to live in this isolation on a cycle of twelve nights alone and two nights with the children. Would his move away be seen by them as a betrayal, a desertion? His thoughts quickly eked out vindication for his new renaissance. 'They can come to London on my weekends. They would love it', he determined, positively. The opportunities opened up in his mind - the theatres, the museums, the aquarium, the zoo.

"Yes. That's it." He repeated, as he took himself excitedly upstairs, put on a smart jacket and headed to the car.

Next thing, he was on the train to London. His dusty road to Damascus took the form of train tracks to the big city. It was only when he reached Victoria Station that he stopped to think about what he was doing. The commuter mayhem had passed. He had rarely ever seen it out of rush hour. It looked empty. Only a few people stood on the forecourt under the gigantic Departures board. He strolled leisurely across the open space in the direction of the Underground before stopping himself. "No. It's a taxi for me from now on". He vowed at that moment never to go down into the oppressive labyrinth of Tube tunnels ever again.

It was, by now, 11am and he jumped into a waiting black cab. For some reason, in the absence of any other inspiration, he gave the instruction "The Duke of Wellington, please. Just off Fleet Street." The cabbie gave him a respectful 'right you are, sir' and pulled out into the busy London traffic.

As David looked out of the window, he saw the world differently, like a tourist. Heading off towards the Mall, he had time to study the gilded Victoria memorial, the stunning flower beds, the natural beauty of St. James's Park, and, above all else, the Royal Standard flying high above Buckingham Palace. The Queen was at home and all was well with the world. With Great Britain, anyway. He peered out like an excited child as he drove down the flag-lined Mall. It must be the Italian president's turn to come to town, he thought, as the road was bedecked in green, red and white flags fluttering from the masts. He had beaten this path often, moving across town for meetings and lunches. But this was different. For the first time, he felt relaxed as he negotiated the notoriously slow-changing traffic lights under Admiralty Arch, which had irritated him so much in his business days, but which now, in his new positive mode, did not annoy him at all. They merely gave him longer to absorb the grandeur of the edifice around him, something he had never fully observed.

But the best was yet to come. As he drove through, a classic scene opened up before him like a revelation, an icon that was all that was great about his homeland. For there stood Admiral Horatio Nelson, justly proud and aloof at the top of his column in all his glory, commanding over all that he surveyed, guarded protectively by Sir Edwin Landseer's Lions of Trafalgar, masterpieces of their art.

David's sense of patriotism, sublime pride in his country and new-found inner strength almost burst his body and he beamed as he passed the National Gallery and turned into the Strand. As he sat back, he passed the little alley on the right that led down to the Savoy Hotel, quirkily the only road where you have to drive on the wrong side by law, and he afforded himself a wry smile. He had lunched in the Grill Room often, mostly with clients but occasionally with his old boss, Cameron McKenzie. He remembered the formidable Mr McKenzie commenting over their boeuf en croute, with a julienne of vegetables and a rich au jus gravy, on how far they had both come in their careers, taking this sumptuous meal to be a marker of that success. David recalled the slightly awkward silence that followed his honest, but courageous, response. "Yes, but the best thing is, I don't need any of this. It's wonderful, but I don't need it". He could not help himself. He meant it. His free spirit could never be confined. It was an involuntary exclamation of his inner self breaking out, the one that had taken him to the Taj Mahal, Ayers Rock and Machu Picchu and so many other wondrous places that had to be seen. He had never lost sight of what he really was - never the corporate beast, for that was just his alter ego.

He came back to reality as he passed more opulent architecture of imperial years gone by. Today, for once, he looked up, not straight ahead, appreciating the buildings not just at eye-level but also all the fine masonry above, right up to the roof. He then came to the magnificent Royal Courts of Justice, London's High Court, the Pantheon of English law, standing nobly before him and he felt pity for the stony-faced barristers and their clients as they followed one another in and out of the palace-like entrance. His journey from the station, a trip he had done a hundred times, was suddenly a revelation.

When David was dropped off outside the pub, he knew it was far too early to have a beer and a pastie. In truth, he suddenly realised that he was not quite sure why he was there at all. It may have been simply that Chris had dropped into conversation that the Wellington did an excellent Cornish pastie at lunchtimes and he knew his name was on one of them. But he felt this was somehow his calling. Perhaps it was something more, maybe it was fate, he thought. So, he just started walking.

Fleet Street is synonymous with newspapers. Not long ago, this had been the home and relentless battleground of the biggest national papers, a Press cauldron. The Mail, the Express, the Guardian, the Telegraph and that interloper, the Sun, all had their fortresses here. Now only a few remnants of the great old days of publishing remained. Until a few years before, Fleet Street was the mecca. Nightly, the giant hot metal presses would pound sleeplessly below ground, deep beneath the grand buildings, giving warmth to any homeless men who could secure a survivable but uncomfortable bed on one of the large grilles on the pavement above. Inside these cathedrals to the Great British newspaper industry, the hectic, smoke-filled editorial floors had resounded all day and long into the night with the deafening clatter of old typewriters and the cussing of frustrated journalists. The demands of modern times, however, had caused the newspapers to disperse from their traditional hub. The macho editorial floors were now large, soulless smoke-free executive lounges, desks lined up regimentally, each under the silent control of the omni-present computer. The shouting and screaming of hysterical hacks had long gone, replaced by a hushed mumbling from a huddled gaggle of disgruntled old scribes, the only legacy of a lost era.

David strode on down this historic thoroughfare past the old newspaper buildings until there, before him, appeared the dominant dome of St Paul's in the distance. It drew him on magnetically, as a holy shrine would beckon a dedicated disciple.

Then, suddenly, his pilgrimage was interrupted. His attention was drawn to a large estate agent's window on his right. He saw this as another auspicious sign and stopped to look. One side had 'offices to let' and on the other were photos of several swish apartments in imposing new upscale blocks. 'I could see himself in one of these', he thought. He took himself through the door. A well-presented young man rose from his desk and approached him.

"May I help you?", the young salesman asked. He was somewhat boyish in looks and had patently had an expensive education, speaking as he did in an almost plummy voice.

"Thank you. I am looking for an apartment in the area," David said with the authority of the successful City entrepreneur he had once been.

"Please. Do come in and sit down. Now let's see what we can do for you."

David smiled back excitedly and thoroughly enjoyed the respectful attention he was getting from this polished young man.

"Yes, let's see what's out there, shall we", he said in his best voice.

George had been awakened by his brain-shattering alarm at the usual time. It seemed totally unjust that, on his first day without a job, the first day of the rest of his life, the earth-shattering bell still shook him into consciousness at first light. He had a meeting at 9.30am with Clive Urquhart, the Managing Director at Forsyte Manners, and, although he was dreading it, he knew that it was something that had to be got through. His morning ritual was as it always was, the obligatory cup of coffee, two slices of toast, butter, never margarine, and his favourite Dundee marmalade made with Seville oranges. George was a true Brit through and through, and proud of it. His soul lay in a bygone, gentler age and he thought to himself how his life might actually be better hereon now that he had been forced out of the uncivilised daily existence of corporate chaos.

As he was leaving his second floor flat, he saw his brief case sitting by the armchair in the small lounge. It sat there, waiting to be picked up as usual. "No, not today", he said to the bag. "Absolutely not. Those days are over. From now on, you can stay at home".

He was cringing at the idea of going into the office. For a start, he had a particular dislike for that security barrier at the entrance, another machine to which he had to pay obedient homage and that was monitoring his movements like a Big Brother. What happened to the friendly doorman with his "Morning, Mr Granby?", he would ask himself. Word travels fast in the company village and he knew that everyone would be glancing sideways at him as he walked up and put his little ID card into the mouth of that damn barrier. To his relief, it opened. He had not been 'cancelled'. Not yet anyway, he thought. This time, instead of gliding up the huge central escalator to the executive floors, he had to head ignominiously to the reception desk on the right. Unfortunately, the pair of uniformed security men were occupied with other people, so George shrunk in the humiliation of having to stand back, while the world and his secretary walked confidently past. He was trying to look anonymous, unsuccessfully attempting to hide in full view. Eventually it was his turn. George spoke softly, almost sotto voce, fearful that one of his former colleagues might witness his embarrassment.

"Mr Granby to see Mr Urquart for a 9.30".

He hoped he would be sent straight up as he had timed his entrance at exactly 9.25 and was not happy when, having put down the phone, the receptionist said to him, "Mr Urquhart will see you shortly. Please take a seat".

He settled himself into the highly visible, low-back chairs that were placed around a circular coffee table in the foyer, joining the other visitors who had just arrived, their Starbucks in front of them and their briefcases by their side. He sat uncomfortably on his seat of shame. They all ignored each other. George felt naked without his case or coffee cup. He managed a smile when he thought about these grey men's briefcases, probably permanently stuffed like his had been with the same useless mix of irrelevant papers and forgotten knick-knacks that had travelled with him for years. Bizarrely, the contents of most cases never change, yet they cover thousands of travel miles every year, their owners clutching them like lifebelts. Commuters, he thought, have to have the security blanket of these little portfolios, unless, that is, they are under 26, when their backs are invariably saddled with overpacked rucksacks, which knock everyone senseless as they get on and off the trains. Today, he was no longer a commuter or a corporate lackey. Today, he was a free man. Just one more scene to play.

He sat awkwardly as all the suited and booted execs marched past. He was hoping not to be spotted and it felt like being a freshly killed wildebeest being savaged by a pride of lions on the African savannah, while the rest of the herd returned to unthreatened grazing as the carcass of their friend was devoured by the predators. His thoughts were interrupted.

"You can go up now", a voice commanded. "Do you know the way?".

"Oh yes", he replied sarcastically. "I think I can remember".

He took the familiar lift to the top floor, feeling an instant anonymity as a crush of young people squashed him against the back wall. Mr Urquart's office looked out over the Thames, a view reserved exclusively for the Chairman, the Board Room and the few top men who were at the helm of Forsyte Manners. George did, of course, know the Managing Director well enough. Their paths crossed fairly regularly at meetings and in the executive washroom, but, more often, they had been together on umpteen social events when the cigar-smoking Clive, as he insisted on being called when off the premises, had held court and George had deferentially listened and laughed at all the right moments of his well-worn stories about himself. More often than not, these occasions had included wives and partners, something Kate loved, all dressed up and desperate to make an impression. The more she loved them and settled into her acceptance amongst the illuminati of the company, the more he grew anxiously uncomfortable, especially when she started to get too over-excited by the expensive champagne and began to compete with Clive in being the centre of attention.

George knocked gently and entered the anteroom. Sharon, Mr Urquhart's PA, greeted him warmly, springing up cheerily and offering him coffee. She clearly knew the dark circumstances of the meeting but used her years of service to pretend that everything was perfectly normal.

"Clive will see you in a minute". 'Clive' he thought. Normally it would be Mr Urquart. Today, however, he was ready for all the false camaraderie and the chummy arm around the shoulder.

The two sat silent, George with his hot drink in hand, Sharon going back to her typing, until the door to the Urquhart office suddenly flew open and a boisterous Mr Urquhart burst out, saying loud farewells to an important-looking businessman. "Give Sharon a buzz and we'll do lunch next week" he said to his guest gushingly. 'Life goes on', George thought, 'for some.'

In a rapid shift of tone, insincerely warm and slightly patronising, Mr Urquhart ushered him into the plush office with a "Come in, George". Without any ado, Mr Urquart started his spiel, clearly wanting to get it all over with as quickly as possible so that he could get on with the business of the day.

"Sorry about all this, George. Bloody shame. We have always got along so well, you and I, and you have been a tremendous asset to the Company...". 'Blah, blah blah" thought George, barely listening.

They then chatted briefly about the good old days and how things had changed and that, well, we all have our day and that everything has to come to an end. George just sat unmoved and watched him do his bit, observing his old boss acting out his role on autopilot, having this done a hundred times before.

A ream of papers was then produced. "Look old chap. This is a bit of a nuisance. It's got to be done, I'm afraid. I need you to take this stuff to your solicitor and let him check it out and then you sign it. It's just the usual stuff, non-disclosure and all that."

He put the handful of A4 pages into a large white envelope, stood up and handed it over.

"Oh. Nearly forgot. Just one more thing. I should really do this after you have signed everything, but we have both worked long enough together, haven't we."

He reached into the top right-hand drawer of his large oak desk.

"I think this will soften the blow a bit, old boy. Here. This is for you". He held a cheque out over his desk towards George, who leaned forward and took it without looking at it. "Now, George, dear fellow, I am sure you'll understand. I have to get on. If you have any questions, don't be afraid to come back to me. Just give Sharon a ring. Thanks for everything. Good luck old boy. Oh, and love to Kate." And that was it. All over.

As George turned half-way round to head for the door, he could not resist a nifty glance at the cheque. He was gobsmacked. There it was in the little box on the cheque, as clear as day, £345,000. Chris' words immediately exploded in his head.

"Bloody hell. What type of money did Chris call it? Oh, yes. F*** You Money!". With a rare profanity, George's thoughts spilled out into barely audible words, as he saw this huge number. Mr Urquhart thought he caught something George had uttered.

"I beg your pardon, George...?".

"Er, oh nothing, Clive", George muttered, "Thank you". He walked through the door, still staring at the cheque. 'F*** You', he said to himself once more in a hushed voice as he stepped into Sharon's office.

"Sorry, George?".

"Oh, nothing, Sharon. Thanks for everything. Hope to see you again one day".

He and his money then left the building.

Chris went into the office as usual. He liked the girls he worked with and they liked him. There had always been a bit of flirting going on and he loved every minute of it. He had a special fancy for the sexy Mia, a petite blonde at the desk opposite. He could never help his eyes following her delectable rear end as it swayed around the office - like two little boys fighting in a sack, he would joke. She knew exactly the effect she had on him and played him like a fiddle. The department comprised of seven girls and just two men, him and the uninspiring Colin. He had absolutely nothing in common with

Colin and he was perfectly happy about that. As Colin was no threat, it gave him exclusive rights over the pool of female talent. In Chris' eyes, his colleague was a humourless nerd, which therefore allowed him to be the unchallenged cheeky boy of the team. For some reason, today, Colin was late in, an exceedingly rare event. One of the girls sidled up to Chris.

"Now listen, Chris. Honestly. I want you to be serious for once and listen". Marianne was a popular, slightly stern brunette who worked hard and was a friend to everyone. Chris lent an attentive ear. "Look. Colin is on the Atkins diet, has been for two weeks, and you haven't noticed. When he comes in, can you please be nice to him for once and say something about how slim he looks. He had a thing about his belly and he's terribly pleased about the weight he has lost. I think it's 10lbs or more".

"Of course, Marianne. Why would I possibly say anything nasty? You know me better than that. Don't you?", he said with a twinkle in his eye. Marianne flashed a cynical glare back.

The girls then chatted about all that they had been up to the night before. If a new date had taken place, the whole gang was always eager to find out how it went. In no time, however, their boss, James Flynn, came out of his side door and did his start-the-day pep talk, not noticing that Colin was missing.

"Morning all. Jackie, did you finish that copy for the Robertson's leaflet? Can I see it? Now, please". That was the extent of his motivational speech. They always hit the ground running.

"Of course, James" she said as she flurried with him back into his office.

At that point, Colin walked in. He was flustered as he was never, ever late, throwing off his jacket and placing it behind his chair as he sat down, perspiration bubbling on his brow.

"Morning Colin" said the girls, almost in unison.

"Sorry. Train broke down at Clapham Junction. Had to change", Colin said apologetically.

"No problem, Colin. Don't worry about it", said Marianne. There was a pause before the silence was broken. Marianne stared at Chris in an obvious prompt. The girls all looked at Chris nervously to see what would come out of his mouth.

"Morning, Tubs", quipped Chris dismissively, without even looking up from to his work. All the girls scowled angrily at Chris, who obliviously carried on proof-reading some copy he was working on. It was at that point that Chris' mobile rang. He reached down into his pocket and put it to his ear.

"Is that Chris?", said a polite young lady.

"Yes. This is he" he responded grandly, still chuckling inside from his 'Tubs' line.

"Chris, this is Anne from Personnel at the Daily Post. I have some very good news for you. We are delighted to be able to offer you the post of Assistant Promotions Manager under Jill Spender. This probably isn't a good time. Could you ring me back at your convenience later and we can go through it all?".

Chris wanted to shriek with delight but just about managed to contain his elation. "That is excellent news. Thank you so much. If it is OK, I'll call you later on this afternoon", he replied properly. Chris had tried to be economical and unemotional with his words in order not to arouse any attention from his colleagues around him. In spite of that, he could not help letting out a minuscule, subdued squeal.

"Good news, Chris?" asked Mia. Nothing went unnoticed in an office with seven girls.

"Yes, very, thanks". His self-congratulatory grin could not be disguised, although he did his damnedest to conceal his excitement.

"Yes," he said again as he looked up at Mia. "Everything is good. Very, very good".

David had to give up any thoughts of lunch as he and Tristram, his newly adopted estate agent, had been charging around all over the area, jumping into Tristram's small BMW to get from one flat to another. David had briefed the young man that he wanted his own place, with a spare room for the children, furnished or unfurnished and he had a budget of £4,000 a month. He thought that it would be easy. There must be plenty of good choices out there for that, he had thought. He certainly considered it enough money for him on top of the extortionate school fees he had to pay each month. Even though he had managed to put a princely sum away after his glory days in the

City, he was only too aware that the current Mrs Nugent would soon be doing her damnedest to carve off at least half of it with her legal butchers. He was fairly confident that he had enough to set him up in his new life, but he was also aware that he had no real income and that his finances were totally at the mercy of her lawyers.

He set out with glorious optimism in his search for a new London home. In no time, however, disappointment loomed large. At the first place, he had to step over a barely conscious Rastafarian and bisect his cloud of ganja smoke to get to the front door. The flat then turned out to be minuscule, with bedrooms the size of the cupboards. This would never work, he thought. Next, they went around the corner to another option, an older ground floor flat in a mansion-style house. Heartened for a second by the grandiose frontage of the building, he thought 'this is much more my style' before entering the large baronial hallway. His hopes rose. Unfortunately, on walking into the flat, he was hit full on by a pungent 'old lady' aroma that made his eyes water. The pine furniture and net curtains added to the scene of an old people's home.

"Next" said David, after less than 30 seconds.

He could not hide the depression that he felt as they set off to inspect more candidates. He was, in truth, prepared to give up the whole idea completely after the first four. Tristram saw his mood and tried to boost his spirits, encouraging him to keep going.

"Prices have gone up a lot in the last few years," he explained.

"Are we talking about property or the ganja that goes with it?", David enquired wryly.

"Both, I guess", said Tristram. "But, yes, I can see that none of these ones are anywhere near right for you. Can you go a bit higher? That will open up a few more options"

"I could. I suppose find another 500, or even 1000 at a push. You should know that I am in the middle of a divorce and it is difficult to know what I will come out of it with. So I have to be sensible".

They then went to three more expensive ones, with the same reaction. In spite of his dream of a new incarnation, he knew he was not going to give up his cottage and his birds for any of these. They headed back to the office. David was, by now, totally despondent. Tristram liked David, remained calm and tried to be positive.

"Here's an idea. One thing you could do is try to find someone in a bigger place with a spare room looking to share. That would get a much larger living area".

"But I need two bedrooms. Don't forget the children", David pointed out.

"Mm. Forgot that. Yes, that might be tricky".

David started his goodbyes. Tristram, recognising his failure, politely said he was sorry he could not help him and wished him well.

"Look, I'll just have to think about it all", David said. "Thanks though for your time today. You've been great." They shook hands and David headed to the door. As he went to pull the handle, Tristram jumped up out of his seat excitedly.

"Mr Nugent. Wait. Wait. Hold on a minute. I've just had a thought. How about this? How about YOU getting the bigger place, much bigger, and YOU get the flatmates? Then YOU could rent a far better place to YOUR liking and YOU could pick people that you want to share with? That way you can get what you like, and who you like, and have the bedroom for the children - two if you prefer." After a short pause, he added "You could rent a whole house, or a large apartment".

David spun around towards him and his face lit up. He had always got things quickly and he saw in a flash the answer to all his problems. The goldcrest had landed, he thought to himself.

"Brilliant", he said. "That's brilliant. What have you got? Come on, let's see something much bigger then". A flow of enthusiasm flooded back into him.

Tristram enthused. "Let me get some things together and you can take them home and look at them at your leisure" He slid the top drawer of a large filing cabinet open and pulled out one glossy brochure after another and popped a bundle into a folder.

"There you go. Have a look at these".

"You are a genius, Tristram. I'll get back to you", David shouted back as he exited the office.

David's flat hunt had been a rollercoaster of emotion. He had woken up in his bed in his quaint little cottage prepared for yet another solitary day, before getting his flash of inspiration and zipping up to London. His exhilaration had sunk deep into a mire of despondency when checking out flats on the market, only to be uplifted by Tristram's revelation. This epiphany on the road to St Paul's gave David his bounce back as he now had a new plan to work on.

"Yes", he pondered to himself as he strode back down Fleet Street, "That's it. I'll get a huge, swanky place and find some decent, fun flatmates. Perhaps some racing people. My type of people". When it came to the actual house or flat, he already, in his mind's eye, had big ideas. He was used to thinking big. "Robbie and Jess can come up and they'll absolutely love it. This is going to be brilliant".

It was later than he thought. The hands on the clock outside the old Daily Telegraph building showed it was almost 5.30pm and his pace quickened as he marched towards the Duke of Wellington.

George and Chris were already getting towards the end of their first pint. David sensed they were having a serious tête-à-tête as he approached the bar and was careful to give them a respectful distance. Gerry, being the pro he was, remembered his choice of beer from the night before and immediately pulled his glass of draught bitter, without a word. It took, however, George just a second to spot him.

"Good evening, young David. Good to see you back so soon in this humble hostelry".

"Hello, George. Hi, Chris."

He was so excited that he skipped the usual social chit-chat and dived clumsily straight in. He could not stop himself.

"I've been flat-hunting and thought I'd pop in for a quick pint".

He had put it this way subconsciously to protect himself in case he did not receive the same genial welcome he had had the night before. He need not have worried. George and Chris dropped their conversation like a stone and reverted to their welcoming, upbeat banter.

"Did you find anything?" asked George. "I was really disappointed by what I found out there when I was looking a few months ago. Some bloody horrible places. And completely overpriced".

"No, you're right. There's nothing. It was a complete waste of a day. Some of the places were revolting and they were asking a fortune. I wouldn't have put my dog in them. It's a joke"

"I know. You may have to try further out, you know, Hackney or Brixton or somewhere like that." George said as an experienced authority on the subject.

"To be honest, George, I'd stay where I am in the country rather than get stuck there. No, I want somewhere in the heart of the city or not at all".

Chris piped up. "Don't know if I told you. I'm going to be looking myself next week. I have told my beloved that I'm moving out and I fancy being round here too. Not sure how my liver will enjoy it, being near the Wellington. But it'll just have to toughen up and get used to it. So let me know if you come across anything small that you think might suit me...".

David cut in, reacting like a lizard's tongue catching a bug.

"Are you serious? Are you looking for somewhere?".

"Well, yes. So, if you see anything you think I might like, let me know, would you?".

"Of course. You know I said it had been a complete waste of a day, well, one brilliant idea did crop up". David proceeded to tell the boys about his day, briefly describing the depressing old places that he had been shown and how he got the impression that there is nothing worthwhile out there in his budget. He then prepared to launch into his new master plan. He now had the total attention of both Chris and George. This was the time for his denouement.

"OK. Here goes. I have a plan. Let's start at the beginning. This guy Tristram from the estate agency has just dragged me all over the place, flat after horrible flat, and there is nothing, nothing out there. George, you mentioned that you have searched yourself and it is depressing, isn't it? But..." he dropped in a dramatic pause, "BINGO, our Tristram came up with the answer".

"Go on", said George, in a sceptical tone.

"The idea is this. It's simple." David saw the genuine, expectant look gripping his friends' faces as they glued their attention on him.

"If there are no decent small places and they are all so overpriced… what about flat sharing?"

Chris chipped in, stopping him in his flow, disappointed that this was the 'big idea'.

"Is that it? Nothing new about that. Thought about it. But, you know, being the last in, getting the worst room, going in with people who already know each other really well…"

David immediately interrupted. "No. No. No. Chris. You're right. Bear with me, there's more. How about this? What if…", he paused a second, "what if I rent a great big place that I like, or possibly a house if I can find one round here, and then I pick who lives there with me?". He gave them a knowing glare. His companions froze for a second. David grinned boastfully as if he had just cracked the Enigma Code. Then Chris' expression broke into a huge euphoria. The penny had just dropped. George was still digesting it all. His spark still had to fire up.

"That is a bloody fantastic idea", said Chris, recognising straight away that this could be the answer to his prayers. "So, you get a nice big place you like and get other people to join it. It's funny how long it takes to discover the bleeding obvious. That's great, David. How about me being your first flatmate?".

David looked quizzical as the enormity of what he had just heard struck him. "Seriously, Chris?"

"Too bloody right", replied Chris. "This is a fabulous idea. I need somewhere quickly too. When do I move in?"

Chris continued to race ahead in his usual over-excited way. George was still deliberating the idea in his head. Chris, half joking, went on.

"You in as well, George? It'd be better than that grotty little flat you're in now". George seemed slightly offended, straightened himself on his stool and raised an eyebrow at Chris' blunt description of his accommodation, something he had never had the honesty to utter before. Nevertheless, George did get his point and leaned back again, pensively considering what had just been proposed in a measured George-like way.

Meanwhile, the two younger men enthused together uncontrollably. The full blast of a new optimism had hit them. David chimed in.

"George, I've got a load of nice brochures here. If we pool our money, we could get somewhere amazing. What about one of those flash City apartments, with a view over the Thames?". David was now in full steam.

In his head, Chris had already made up his mind, packed his belongings and moved in. David was already imagining the lounge and the incredible view. George was slowly coming around to the whole concept.

David cheerily ordered another round of drinks as they talked animatedly for twenty minutes about their new glitzy world, with even George admitting that 'it is not the worst idea I have ever heard'. That, for George, was like a full-blown approval, one small step short of 'I'm in'.

The conversation ended with the more rational George saying his 'Got to go' but adding "let's have a board meeting here tomorrow and give it some serious thought. Are you OK with that David?"

"Can we make it Monday? I have promised to go to dinner with some friends in Tunbridge Wells tomorrow night."

"Monday is better for me too, if that's OK with everyone," added Chris. "I might have to miss tomorrow altogether, as I have to have a drink with the girls in the office, to tell them that I am leaving and all that. They'll be heartbroken".

"Tell you what", said David. "I'll check out some more places online tomorrow and over the weekend and print any good ones off".

To David's and Chris' surprise, the calm, unexcitable George chipped in. "I'll check some out as well".

David and Chris looked at each other. They both had the same thought. George was on board and they watched him raise himself off his stool, to take on the self-appointed role of chairman of the board.

"OK, gentlemen. Here, Monday, 5 o'clock", said George. As he had started to leave, David had another bright thought and he stopped George in his tracks.

"Hang on a second, George. Just one more thing." He then addressed both men. "Look, I have got a horse running at Sandown on Saturday. Bit of fun. I hope you don't mind my asking. I was going on my own. You don't fancy joining me for a day at the races, do you? It should be fun".

Both men were quick in their decision. They consulted their mental diaries and predictably saw a completely blank page.

"Yes. Love to, David. That'd be great. Thank you." said Chris.

Spurred on by Chris' acceptance, George said, "Good idea, David. Thank you. That would be wonderful".

"That's brilliant." David then explained how he would leave some owners' badges in their names on the gate and that they should meet him at 1.30pm in the Owners Bar by the paddock.

Chris repeated back "Sandown. Owners Bar, 1.30. Tickets on gate... It's a date". With that, George left.

"Fancy another quick one for the road, David", asked Chris.

"Just a quick one. Thanks", accepted David.

"Listen. David", Chris said hesitantly.

"What is it, my friend?"

"Thanks for asking us to the races. That is so kind of you". He became hesitant. "Hey, by the way, apropos of nothing, have you seen the new barmaid Bonnie yet? No, of course you haven't. Well, this girl only started last night behind the bar and she is absolutely drop-dead gorgeous. She starts in a minute, at 7, and, well, we had a bit of a chat last night..."

"You dark horse Chris. I hadn't seen you as a big Casanova."

"No, seriously. I really like her. And I just thought, would you mind if I asked her to join us at the races on Saturday? She doesn't work weekends. I don't know if she'll come, but you wouldn't mind, would you? She's really nice". Chris was totally smitten.

"Of course not. I'll put an extra badge on. No problem".

"Thanks David. You're a pal. She probably won't come anyway, but you never know".

They hadn't been watching the clock. It was after 6.50 and Chris suddenly saw Bonnie lift up the flap in the bar and swish though, taking off her light coat and getting ready to start work. She appeared not to have noticed him.

Chris nudged David with his elbow. "That's her".

"Wow. She's lovely. See what you mean. Use your charms, mate. Use your charms. Good luck. I'll leave you to it now. Go to it, Romeo". David picked up his pint and drained what was left in three gulps, giving Chris a knowing man-to-man wink as he left him at the bar. He took one more glance back as he stepped out onto the pavement, only to see that Chris and the delectable Bonnie were already huddled across the bar in close conversation. Lucky old Chris, he thought, as he headed back to the station.

CHAPTER TWO
A DAY AT THE RACES

SATURDAY, JULY 13

The gathering in the Owners Bar went perfectly to script. David had arrived early to meet up with his trainer, Charlie Walsh. They had not seen one another much recently. David used to drive up to his Warwickshire yard regularly to see Golden Oak on the gallops and to join Charlie and a huddle of other owners in the local pub, the King's Head, for Sunday lunch. It was one of his favourite things to do. This was a National Hunt yard, meaning that nearly all the horses were 'jumpers'. Their battlefields were mostly over the fences on the lesser known tracks like Stratford, Uttoxeter and Market Rasen. If you were a lucky owner with a good enough horse, very lucky, there might be an appearance on the big stage at Cheltenham, Newbury or Ascot. These were special days, every owner's dream. The few occasions that David had had a runner at one of these had been his very best of times, wrapped up on chilly winter days, Whisky Mac in hand, immersed in endless horse talk in the crowded bar and hopefully welcoming home a winner. These country folk were about as far a cry away from the insincerity of those slick City bankers as he could possibly get. They were the salt of the earth. And the farmers who owned many of the horses, and some of the yards, fascinated him. He loved talking to them. Most were deceptively well-heeled, owning the view from the window of their old country houses all the way across the rolling fields, each acre dotted with specks of black and white Friesian cows, into the distant horizon. But there was no ostentation, no flaunting their wealth as the cock-a-hoop City boys do in London. For most, transport was a beaten-up, 10-year-old Land Rover, which was as faithful and dependable as their obligatory brace of labradors.

David loved going to the small local tracks with a runner. It was how he started out as an owner. On these race days, it was routine for him to disappear discreetly out of the office, jump into a waiting car with a complicit driver, who would then speed him up the M1 motorway to the racecourse. He would stay just long enough to see his horse run and be back in the office by 5pm, making a lot of noise on his return to convince everyone that he had been somewhere in the building the whole time. If his PA, the loyal Annie, had a call for him in his absence, she would have a selection of three well-rehearsed replies. "Sorry. He's at a meeting", or "Sorry. He's on a course", or "Sorry. He's with his accountant", meaning, of course, his turf accountant. Annie had convinced herself that she was not really lying, just being a shade duplicitous with the truth, as all were factually correct in their own way

    David and Charlie had always got on famously well, in spite of their obvious lifestyle differences. Charlie, with his broad Yorkshire accent, always enjoyed David's company. David had been one of his very first owners and had supported him throughout the early days and as a result a lifelong bond of trust and loyalty had been formed. Charlie had started out as a journeyman jump jockey, often travelling hundreds of miles for one unsuccessful ride on a 25-1 shot. Although he had broken countless bones in falls, he had also had his moments of glory when winning a couple of big races. His name, though, had never been up there on the list of champions. That all changed ten years ago when, now as a trainer, he'd seen a complete change of status. Success had started to come rolling in. In no time, he found his true metier and he was winning races galore, including the most prestigious races at the Cheltenham Festival, the highlight of jump racing's calendar. With his congenial charm and infectious, relentless enthusiasm, he quickly caught the eye of the country's major owners, those whose unlimited wealth could enable them to buy the best horses at the best sales. To Charlie's credit, this never affected his loyalty to his original, smaller owners, of which David was one. In no time, he had the most powerful string in the land and, three years ago, won the coveted title of champion trainer. What is more, such was his grit and professionalism, that no-one had been able to wrestle that title away from him since and he was still going from strength to strength.

Today though, was a summer Flat meeting. That meant that there were no jumps to be negotiated and the races were much shorter. The horses on the flat are younger, and more expensive, with much wealthier connections. Sheiks, lords and multi-millionaires vied to splash money on the finest bloodstock and pit their charges against one another on the hallowed turf of Ascot, Goodwood and York. No Land Rovers for them. Chauffeurs would steer their purring Bentleys into the reserved car parks, stepping out briskly to open the rear doors for their illustrious masters. No, this was a completely different game and Charlie was certainly not amongst his natural ilk. A few of the elite were already congregated in the Owners Bar. Charlie rarely had a runner on the flat and he was never relaxed amongst this snobby group. For a start, he would kowtow to no-one and most of these people enjoyed a bit of sycophancy.

He walked in, bedecked in his trademark thick tweed suit and the faithful old 'titfer' that he wore year-round, and went straight over to David, who in contrast was dressed in his own predictable outfit of blue blazer and fawn flannels, looking as if he would be just at home at Lord's cricket ground or Henley Regatta.

His horse, Golden Oak, was an enigma, bringing his owner the sort of luck you pray for. It all started with a phone call to Charlie a year ago, before the word divorce had come into David's vocabulary. He had had a good year in the City and felt like splashing out on another turf adventure.

"Charlie, can you find me a nice young horse? No hurry. Nothing exposed. It doesn't need to be instant action". David had learned all the racing jargon. "I fancy getting an unraced youngster, a two-year-old possibly, and have some fun bringing him along. It might be taking a bit of a chance, but hell, let's have a punt. Ideally, when you look at the breeding, I'd like something a bit nippy that might make up into a two-miler". His dream was one day to win the Queen Mother Chase, the speed merchants' two-mile championship showdown at the Cheltenham Festival.

To say, 'can you find me a horse? - no hurry' to Charlie is exactly the same as saying 'I want a horse and I want it now'. In literally minutes, a message bounced back on the phone: "How about this one? Really nice horse" with a link to a page in a sales catalogue and a picture of a handsome beast. The one Charlie sent was a stunning, un-named flashy chestnut with a white blaze and four white socks. He reminded David of Nijinsky, not the dancer, but the fabulous 1970 Triple Crown winner. David always told the tale of how, at 17, he had hitch-hiked to Newmarket to see his favourite horse of all time race on what turned out to be his final appearance, in the Champion Stakes. Although the equine superstar (he had won all three Classics that year, the 2,000 Guineas, the Derby and the St Leger) anticlimactically ended up as runner-up, it had not mattered to David. Nijinsky was his star. Just seeing him in action had been the highlight of his racing life. Seeing this image of his all-time favourite, David could not say no to buying this magnificent young horse.

Well, as things worked out, Golden Oak, the name he chose, turned out to be a bit special, 'a flying machine' as Charlie called him. In no time, the trainer considered him so good that he ventured to have a go on the flat as a three-year-old. His faith was rewarded, winning his first two races over 5 and 6 furlongs at Chepstow and Bath. However, today was a big step up in class.

David's love affair with the turf had started very young, at school, where he would sneak down to the local bookmaker and have one shilling each-way bets on a daily basis. His very first live experience of racing had been when he was about nine. His father had taken him to Warwick for an evening meeting. His Dad had placed his first ever bet for him and it promptly won at 20-1, bringing him a staggering £4 pay-out, more money than he had ever had before. That was it. With that win, he was hooked. His love of racing had then grown as he moved on in life, until he got to the point where he could actually afford his own racehorse. Over the years, he had owned quite a few and he had enjoyed a good number of winners, admittedly mostly at small tracks, but each one was special to him and he remembered every indelible victory with a glow of pride. He loved nothing more than talking to Charlie about those early days, reliving the great moments. He was doing just this when

Charlie cut in, put his hand on David's arm and leaned his head towards David's ear.

"Had a call from that wife of yours the other day", he interjected in his broad Yorkshire accent.

David started and pulled back in surprise. "What was that about?", he asked inquisitively.

"She wanted to know the value of your 'orses." He said, before adding, "You're in trouble there, pal".

"What did you say?", asked David anxiously.

"Oi told 'er to fork off." Charlie said in his Northern brogue. "None of her damn business. It's David what owns the 'orses, not you, oi said. Never could stand 'er".

This summed up the 'boys' club' bonding that meant so much. In this case, Charlie had given both barrels to Moira and David could have hugged his friend for it, there and then.

Just then, George arrived. Charlie and George immediately hit it off. It may have been simply that Charlie saw the urbane George as a potential new owner, but they conversed freely, with George asking all the obvious questions as a new boy to racing and the trainer patiently, but engagingly, giving him the answers. David was very happy indeed. This was the time he loved most, away from all the hassle, on the racecourse with both friends and a runner, the sun shining down and a lively glass of Veuve Cliquot in his hand.

Next to arrive was Chris. David was thrilled to see that he had brought a lovely young filly to trot out with him. Bonnie had obviously fallen for Chris' charms and both positively fizzed with the spritely bounce of a new romance. Both David and George lit up when the delectable barmaid was introduced and clustered round her. The Wellington mob, playing 'away' and out of their familiar Victorian hostelry environment, immediately effervesced in their own shared excitement, laughter rising like the bubbles in their champagne.

Charlie quietly disappeared and moved off unnoticed to talk to others in the room.

David tried to explain everything that was about to happen, in layman's terms, to his greenhorn colleagues. There was not enough time to cover all and sundry about racing, but he gave it a go. Chris, obvious as ever, wanted to know just two things.

"What's the name of your horse again? What price is he?".

"It's Golden Oak, he's in the second and he was 8-1 in the paper this morning". This was a decent price, Chris thought.

"Chances?" said an uncharacteristically monosyllabic Chris.

"Well, you should have a few bob each-way. Don't go crazy though. Although Charlie did say he is showing all the right signs at home, so we are hopeful".

Bonnie stood close to Chris and looked up to him with a smile.

"Can you put a fiver on Golden Oak for me?", she asked him genteelly. He smiled back. "Of course. I am going to have a bit of a punt myself".

The parade ring outside the bar was empty, the runners for the first race having left to go onto the track. In fact, they were already being loaded into the starting stalls. Time flies at the races. No-one worried that they had missed the chance of a bet, as they were concentrating on Golden Oak and what might be in the next half hour. In fact, they were so absorbed in Golden Oak that they did not even watch first race on the TV monitors. Suddenly, David announced, "There he is". Golden Oak was the first horse of the second race to enter the parade ring.

"David, he's GORGEOUS! I love chestnuts" exclaimed Bonnie.

"Thanks, Bonnie. He is rather handsome, isn't he", said the proud owner.

Chris suddenly thought, for some reason that only he understood, that it would a good time to introduce some of his own humour into proceedings. He never could stop himself.

"If I got a horse, I wouldn't get a chestnut. I'd get a bay". The other three turned to see what on earth he was going on about, knowing full well that Chris knew next to nothing about horses. "And I'd call him Docker".

David had not yet come to grips with Chris' childlike humour and naïvely indulged him.

"Why is that?" he asked, in genuine interest, unaware he was falling straight into Chris' trap.

"Because then I could ride him around all day singing 'I'm sitting on Docker the Bay".

"Oh, for Pete's sake, Christopher. That's awful. Don't you ever stop?" snapped George, partly to protect David from any embarrassment. Chris felt an extra buzz of pleasure for catching a racing man out with his puerile joke. Bonnie did let out a subdued, supportive chuckle while David quickly got things back on track.

"Come on. You are all going to join me in the parade ring. Let's go".

They were surprised and thrilled in equal measure. Schmoozing with the owners and trainers in the parade ring was one of those things that they had seen other people do on television, at the Grand National and the Derby, for example. They never dreamed that they would get their chance to have this exclusive, privileged experience in racing's inner sanctum. They walked down the steps from the Owners Bar towards a narrow gap in the parade ring rail. David drew their attention to the horses being led round by their lads and lasses.

"Now, mind how you go. Be very careful to time going in between the passing horses. You mustn't spook them. Wait for a decent gap and then walk through quietly",

Chris had never been this close to a thoroughbred racehorse in his life. They were much larger close up than he had ever imagined. To him, they could have been huge fire-breathing dragons. David, George and Bonnie glided through elegantly when a suitable space between the runners appeared. Timorous Chris hesitated and got left behind. The others, now inside, turned round and saw him standing outside the ring, waiting for his moment. When a healthy gap did appear, they beckoned out "Come on, Chris". He started to move, then dithered nervously, and missed his chance. It took three attempts before he skipped through.

Charlie saw David, surrounded by his phalanx of friends, and headed towards him. The two talked, while the others listened in total silence. To them, most of the chatter was gobbledegook, unintelligible racing jargon. Nevertheless, they were loving their moment in the holy-of-holies at Sandown Park.

Golden Oak's jockey, Johnny Murphy, approached, deferentially touching the peak of his cap, whip under his arm. Chris thought he looked old and tiny, even for a jockey. 'Still, at five foot nothing, I guess what else is he going to do in life?', he mischievously ruminated.

It all moved quickly. The horse was pulled over, the rug thrown off, the trainer adjusted the girth, the jockey gripped the saddle and offered his right heel to the trainer, who flicked the rider onto the horse's back. Off went Golden Oak with his jockey, in the bright red and white colours, making two circuits of the ring before turning out towards the course.

"Now we have work to do. Follow me", said David, marching forth like a kindergarten teacher leading a crocodile of obedient children. They walked through the stands, negotiating a path through the bustling crowd, out to the front, which overlooked the glorious vista of the course. Sandown is a natural amphitheatre, with a panoramic view over the glowing green turf of the circular track. There was a sharp intake of breath.

"Absolutely stunning", came a rare superlative from George, who was not easily impressed at the best of times but was overcome with the magnificence of the course.

"Let's get down to the bookmakers", chipped in the over-excited Chris and they all set off cheerily as the anticipation mounted.

"Bloody small these jockeys, aren't they," Chris added as they walked. "They seem even smaller close up. I suppose that, at five foot nothing, being a jockey is the only job they could ever do, really", Chris said to the others.

"Yes", David replied. "They do have to be small to do the weights. Brave though. Mind you, they aren't stupid. Johnny Murphy is one of the brightest. He had wanted to be a brain surgeon as a boy".

Chris looked amazed. "Wow. Really. That is amazing. What happened?".

"He wasn't tall enough… so he became a gynaecologist."

George roared. "Bravo, David. Got you back, Chris".

"Hey, I do the jokes round here", Chris said to David jokingly as he put his arm around his shoulder.

They trooped down to the row of bookmakers, each of whom was standing on a stool against his illuminated board, which displayed the names of runners and their odds. Bonnie gave Chris her £5 without a word. Golden Oak was indeed 8-1. Then, as they took in what was happening, it flashed to 9-1 in front of their very eyes.

"That suits me", said Chris, seeing his cue to go in to place his bet. He bore down on a rotund bookmaker, smoking a large cigar. George watched this and then presented himself before the bookie to the right of him. David, at the same time, went to the one on the left, a skinnier, pale faced man in a cloth cap. Chris put £60 on, George £50 and we shall never know how much David wagered. True racing folk think it is vulgar to talk about these things.

"Am I on?" said Bonnie.

"You are very much on", Chris assured her.

"Come on, Golden Oak!", she cheered as they moved into the packed viewing area reserved for owners. Charlie Walsh joined them and the five stood edgily awaiting the start. Around them, dozens of binoculars were being raised towards the stalls. In no time, the commentator burst forth.

"They're under starter's orders. THEY'RE OFF".

Bonnie could not help herself. She yelled "Come on, Golden Oak" time after time, at the top her high-pitched voice, causing a few pompously stiff-necked punters to dip their binoculars to glare at her in disapproval. She was completely oblivious to this and kept up her vocal support unabated as the horses galloped past the stand. They crossed the line with Golden Oak only in mid-division, but it did not matter. There was still a whole circuit to go.

The field seem to clump together down the back straight, causing Bonnie to tug Chris's sleeve.

"Where is he? How's he doing", Bonnie asked Chris.

"He's about sixth. Plenty of time", Chris advised as if he was a racing expert.

As they turned into the home straight, Golden Oak had managed to improve one place. David saw that his jockey was sitting very still, a good sign, while those in front of him, except for the rider of Honest Harry, were starting to scrub away at their charges and whips were being drawn. Three furlongs to go. The crowd suddenly erupted. Honest Harry smoothly struck the front down the straight and went three lengths clear, looking all over the winner. Bonnie had, by now, gone quiet. Chris got a feeling of inevitable doom. A furlong to go and Honest Harry was now flat out, his jockey riding for all his worth for the line. Then, Golden Oak's flashy white socks came smoothly out of the following group and, under the urging of his jockey's arms that were pumping away forcefully, started to get into full speed. In a few strides, he broke clear of the pack, setting chase on the leader. With one crack of the whip, the beautiful chestnut seemed to change gear. Bonnie started to jump up and down and shout again. But would he catch him before the line? With just fifty yards to go, Golden Oak came alongside Honest Harry and the two equine athletes ran eyeball to eyeball before Johnny Murphy cracked his whip once more and David's champion eased away. Golden Oak had won. His ecstatic fan club roared and whooped uncontrollably. Bonnie threw her arms around Chris's neck and gave him a strangulating hug. When they pulled their heads apart, they gave each other that telling look of love. In a spontaneous action, they kissed.

David and George, standing in front of them, had not even noticed this burgeoning romance, so elated were they as they celebrated this unforgettable moment. Chris then abruptly broke away from Bonnie, seemingly embarrassed. Then he got back to the celebrations. It would be easy to think that Chris had dismissed this first kiss as insignificant. Nothing was further from the truth. However, he could only ever think of one thing at a time and, right now, he was totally distracted by his winnings.

"Let's get our money", he exclaimed pragmatically.

Chris started down the steps, Bonnie clinging to him snugly, tilting her head into his shoulder. George, David and Charlie followed. The winning owner and trainer were stopped in their tracks as they received countless pats on the back from acquaintances and strangers alike. They were the men of the moment. It was David's latest fifteen minutes of fame. Charlie then moved off and David collected his group together once again, requesting his friends to turn around and come with him. To Chris' surprise and horror, they were herded off in the opposite direction to the bookies. Chris was confused. He wanted his winnings and he wanted them now. He was like a little boy who had dropped his toy and was being hauled away by his mother. However, he followed David compliantly back through the stand. They looked bemused as he took them on a walk around the parade ring but soon all became clear. There, before them, stood the magnificent, glowing frame of Golden Oak in the winner's enclosure. They walked in like conquering heroes. The heroic, blanketed horse, soaked in sweat, was being walked round in small circles to help him wind down as steam rose off his exhausted back. It was a spectacular sight.

The photographers burst into action. A beaming David held the bridle as the cameras clicked, with the proud look of a champion boxer raising his Lonsdale Belt. Charlie congratulated David. David congratulated Charlie. They both congratulated the wordless jockey, who immediately rushed into the weighing room with his saddle under his arm, his next ride beckoning. A crowd had gathered around the enclosure and the group were the focus of everyone's attention. Chris loved this vicarious triumph and would have signed autographs if he had been asked. After five minutes, a bowler-hatted steward invited David to come to the 'presentation of the trophy' and his friends stepped back to allow him his solo moment. On the podium, a racing dignitary handed him a glittering Waterford Crystal bowl, suitably inscribed. It was David's finest hour, made more special by having his new friends sharing it with him. He positively beamed, while his fan club applauded until their hands hurt. As David joined them again, Chris wasted no time in bringing up the subject of his winnings.

"Now let's get our money" he said, with a hint of impatience in his tone, and they walked apace back to the bookmakers. By now, most of the winnings had been paid out and the bookies had no-one waiting in line. Each of the winning gamblers, marching abreast like the Three Musketeers, approached the bookie with whom they had placed their bet. The line of three strode up as if choreographed and handed over their tickets in a synchronized motion. Chris handed over his ticket to his florid bookie, who still had a half-smoked, burned-out Cuban cigar hanging out of the right side of his mouth as he begrudgingly handed over £600 in fifties. Chris held it aloft in his right hand, like Neville Chamberlain arriving back from Germany waving Hitler's worthless declaration of 'Peace In Our Time'. He shook the bundle of notes boastfully towards Bonnie. At the same time, George was being dealt out ten crispy new fifty-pound notes, which he discreetly put into his inside pocket with typical decorum. The two men and Bonnie clucked excitedly, like hens at feeding time, not noticing that David was taking considerably longer to be paid out. His hollow-cheeked bookmaker repeatedly sunk his hand deep into the bottom of his satchel. When all the fifty-pound notes run out, the gaunt bookie had to resort to handing over twenties. The crochety layer gruffly counted out the rising numbers. We shall never know how much it all was, but the expression on his bookie's face showed that it hurt. David had had a good day, for this pay-out was in addition to the £10,000 prize money the horse had just earned for his win.

They regathered, now glowing with a bonanza of new wealth. Bonnie looked up at Chris to say a polite "how much did I win?".

"Well", said Chris "I put another fiver on for you, so you get 100 quid" He went to his roll of money, peeled off two fifties and handed them over. She took them, came close to him and kissed him on the cheek.

"Perhaps we are just lucky together", she smouldered.

By now, even George had noticed something was going on between these two. He had, up to that day, not met Bonnie, let alone seen this as a burgeoning romance. He had, of course, heard about her from chatterbox Chris. As they walked back towards the Owners Bar, she found a moment to introduce herself properly and explain about her new job at the Wellington and how Chris had asked her along to the races. He was immediately caught in her spell.

"I shall definitely stay after 7 from now on", George flattered her, with a smile. His attention then turned to her escort, and Bonnie turned away to talk to David about Golden Oak and what he fancied in the next race.

George took Chris aside. "Well, well, well, Christopher old chap. You scoundrel. You didn't waste any time. Bonnie is a gem", said George with typical generosity.

"She is bloody gorgeous. And I think she likes me too"

"Oh, she does. Even I can see that. Life just suddenly got a bit more complicated, didn't it, old boy".

"Do you think so? Oh, I see what you mean", replied Chris. George just gave a big knowing smile. Bonnie returned to Chris' side, while David got caught up in a heavy conversation with what looked like a racing journalist, who was scribbling notes down on a small pad of paper.

"David says to get on Rough Passage in the next. Can you put another fiver on for me? And I do mean just a fiver", Bonnie said to Chris.

"Of course. I'll do it now." And Chris went off to place the bet, leaving Bonnie with George once more.

"It is so nice to meet you all", said Bonnie, picking up their conversation. "Starting in a new pub is always a worrying time and you all have been so nice. Thanks for letting me come and join you today."

"Our greatest pleasure, Bonnie", said George. "You have brightened up our day no end. Gerrard is great behind the bar, but you are so much more … er, how shall I put it? Decorative, if you know what I mean." This was George's maladroit form of flirting. He hadn't 'chatted up' a girl for years, a term that seemed to fall way below George's station in life. He had an insecure awkwardness with the opposite sex nowadays, something very different from the old times when he had a reputation as a bit of a swordsman himself. However, Bonnie put him at ease.

"You are so kind, George. I am sorry you have so much on your mind, with everything going on. I can't help overhearing things in the pub. It will all get much better soon, I'm sure. You are a fabulous man and you deserve the best".

These words filled George with a sudden rush of self-confidence. He now felt very avuncular, protective even, towards this lovely young thing as she put her arm in his, all the time saying the loveliest things to him. He felt a million dollars.

"Come on. Let me get you another glass of fizz. Don't worry about Chris. He'll find us. He can smell a good drink from half a mile away", George insisted as he continued chatting to her on their stroll back to the bar, her arm still locked in his.

Needless to say, Rough Passage ended up down the field, as did their other subsequent bets. None of the band of flatmates had had any more winners after Golden Oak's scorching triumph and there was just one more race to come. Curiously, no-one was the remotely bothered about the losses as the boys still had fifty-pound notes bulging their pockets and the copious champagne had put them into a high-spirited mood.

"Last race", enthused Chris, loving whole racing thing. "Come on David, give us the winner. You're the expert".

"I'm no expert, I can assure you of that. Let me have a look".

He glanced into his race card and mumbled as he went through the runners.

"It is a really difficult race to read, but I've got it. Come on everyone. Let's fill our boots", said David.

"Which one?" cried an enthusiastic Bonnie.

"Number 11. Fresh Start. I never back horses on names, but this one jumped out at me. That's meant for us. Fresh Start".

While George thought this was both silly and unscientific, he went along with it and pulled a note off his roll of fifties. Bonnie reached into her handbag and gave Chris a ten-pound note with a confident instruction. "Put it on Fresh Start. On the nose". She was already learning the racing terminology.

As things would have it, their pick was the favourite at 3-1, so they were not taking undue risks in placing their confidence in the auspiciously named horse. The last race is generally nicknamed in racing the 'Getting Out Stakes', a name obvious to anyone who has not yet had a winner and is trying to get out of their financial deficit. For the happy party though, it was more of a 'Getting In Again Stakes' as they beat their well-worn path to their 'lucky' bookies. As Fresh Start went from 3-1 to 7-2, the three marched up in line one more time.

They came together on the steps of the stand and waited anxiously for the race to start, the last chance for them to boost their fortunes still further. This was special, not just because it was the final race on an unforgettable day, not just because they could win even more money, but also because the name of the horse they had backed was not lost on them.

"Come on Fresh Start. Do it for US!", hooted Chris.

"They're off", the commentator announced.

It was a short race, a sprint, and their fancy got off to a fast start, grabbing an early lead. David was worried at this early speed as being in front so early is normally not a good thing,

"Ask a hare!", he would joke. The responsibility of having his friends plunge money on his selection weighed heavily.

Fresh Start was still in the lead as they approached halfway down the home straight. After having a few losers, they all fully expected something to come flying up and pass him. To their unexpected delight, Fresh Start just drew further away. And further. It was hardly a great spectacle but that did not matter a jot to the Wellington mob. Heaven had arrived on horseback. The further he went ahead, the louder they cheered.

Fresh Start won by eight lengths. They screamed with joy and then locked themselves in a group hug, like a standing rugby scrum. Even George lost his sense of propriety and gave a few hops as the others jogged up and down in a celebratory embrace.

After being paid out and without stopping for a drink, the Golden Oak team proceeded to join the stream of people heading for the exit. By now, David, clutching his trophy, and George were big buddies, chatting away merrily like old friends, not just about the racing, but all manner of subjects from the stock market to England's recent cricket win over the Aussies. A few steps behind, Bonnie clung to a cheerful Chris, as he worked out how much he had won during the afternoon.

David had to drive back to Kent and asked the others if he could give them a lift to the local station. George accepted the offer gratefully, while Chris looked at Bonnie and then back at David.

"I think we might go for a quick drink somewhere", responded Chris, going up slightly up at the end of the sentence with the nuance of a question, not sure whether it was a statement to David or an invitation to Bonnie. Even though Bonnie had not been consulted on this plan, she smiled approvingly. Chris added, "Thanks, though, David, for an amazing day. Golden Oak is bloody incredible. He is fantastic. I'll never forget it".

It was Bonnie's turn. "Yes, thank you so much, David. It was a fabulous afternoon. You have been so generous. Thank you again. Especially for all that champagne, and the tips". She unhooked herself from Chris to give David a kiss on the cheek. She then said her goodbyes to George, giving him a light, familial peck before reconnecting with her new beau.

George then announced, "Don't forget, everyone. Five o'clock...". Chris and David broke in in unison, "Five o'clock, Monday. The Wellington. We know", they affirmed. A cacophony of "Bye. Have a good weekend. Safe journey. Thanks again. See you Monday" followed. Bonnie finally took the trouble to single out George once more to thank him for being so welcoming and kind to her. His returning smile showed that he appreciated her good manners greatly.

"Bye, Bonnie", said George, chirpily. "Bye, Christopher. Have fun, you young things".

The two older men then stepped into the flowing mass and headed toward the owners' car park. Chris put his arm around Bonnie's shoulders. He then put a question to her, something he had been waiting for the opportunity to ask.

"Fancy a Chinese? The Good Earth is just down the road. I've been there before. It's one of the best".

"What a great idea. I'm really quite hungry now. Too much booze and not enough food".

The Good Earth restaurant was well known for its 'fine Chinese cuisine' with a reputation for some of the best aromatic duck in or around London. Chris had been there for lunch once before. His boss had had a morning meeting with a client in Esher and had invited Chris along for company. It went well and they ended up in the upmarket eatery. He had loved the food and was now very pleased with himself that he could impress Bonnie by effortlessly sweeping her off to a good restaurant.

Today, it was, of course, packed with racegoers. By sheer good luck, they were taken to a nice table, laid for four in the corner at the back. Chris silently gave himself another pat on the back for getting the best table in the house. In his adopted debonair, assertive guise, he chose that, instead of sitting opposite each other, they should sit side by side, both looking out over the other diners. He politely pulled back one of the round back chairs and seated his guest, taking a leaf out of Gentleman George's etiquette book. He then settled himself down beside her.

They both took some time to take in their surroundings. The dining area had a touch of English class about it, unusual for a Chinese restaurant, with the sumptuous, traditional feel of somewhere like the Connaught Grill or La Gavroche. It was, nonetheless, unmistakably oriental, as diners were reminded by a large mural of an abundance of sino-carp adorning one wall. The whole scene, with the ladies in their best hats and the gentlemen in smart suits, had a touch of quintessential English style.

This, the couple both knew, was their first chance to get to know one another. The attraction was obvious. The ease of being in one another's company was clear. Now they could learn so much more.

"What are you drinking? Champagne? Pimms?", Chris asked.

"No. No. Please. I am completely champagned out", Bonnie replied.

"I guess I am too, to be honest. Fancy a cocktail or a gin and tonic or something like that?".

Chris was doing his best to impress Bonnie and he felt he was succeeding.

"Oh, no thanks. A nice glass of wine would be very great".

Chris lapsed into a sommelier guise.

"Red or white, madam?"

"White, please"

"Sauvignon Blanc? Chardonnay?". Play-actor Chris was now in the part, all he needed was a white cloth draped over his arm.

"If they have a Pinot Grigio that would be lovely".

"That's my favourite too. Might as well get a bottle" and he picked up the wine list, pretending to resemble a connoisseur as he perused it up and down. At that point, the real sommelier appeared. Chris addressed him in his most man-about-town tone.

"Which Pinot Grigio do you suggest?" He just resisted saying 'my good man' as he held up the wine list in front of the waiter. Chris followed his finger to the wine he recommended.

"This one, sir, is a very smart wine, pale in colour, delicate and intense in taste with a hint of cashew", said the man in the white jacket, incongruously in a Chinese accent.

Chris hardly noticed the name of the wine, preferring to check the price first. £29. Not too bad, he thought. He then pushed his luck.

"Not too flinty, is it?". He had no idea what he was talking about.

"Oh, no sir. Not at all". The aloof waiter looked confused while Bonnie looked on in amusement. She knew Chris well enough by now.

"Let's have a bottle of that then. Well-chilled, of course. Thank you", he said with his new-found authority of a wine buff. He coolly handed the wine list to the sommelier, who left with a slow, "Thank you, sir".

Next thing to be decided was the food and together they pored over the menu of exotic dishes in silence. Such delights as crispy duck, spicy chicken with lemongrass, sizzling lamb and wasabi fillets of beef lit up the pages.

"Shall we share a couple of dishes?", proposed Bonnie, a suggestion that seemed perfectly in keeping with the harmonious melding of souls that had been happening throughout the day.

"That's a great idea", responded Chris enthusiastically. "You choose one and I'll choose one. How about that? Shall we also have a couple of spring rolls and some lettuce wraps to start with?" Bonnie accommodatingly said that was 'perfect'.

She then quickly decided on her choice, the sweet and sour chicken. Chris thought that, with the speed of her selection, she must always pick this same dish when she went for a Chinese, like he always ordered the chicken tikka masala when he went for an Indian, never bothering to check out the menu properly. Chris decided not to get anything too spicy, although the Hunan Chilli Lamb with cumin and special preserved chili would have been his first choice. But it was all going so well, he didn't want to risk it. She might not do 'hot', and it would spoil the whole 'melding' thing if he failed to get it right first time. "Is the Tangerine Kaarage Chicken ok with you?".

"Sounds delicious'" she said.

They ordered and set about getting down to business. They knew that searching interviews were on the agenda. With Chris, at this nervy first-date moment, a cartoon that an old girlfriend at university had above her bed flashed into his mind. It was a very simple set of six sketches. In each of the frames, a couple were sitting romantically over a candlelit restaurant table in what looked like an Italian bistro, gazing lovingly into each other's eyes. Each of the first four drawings were almost identical and had the young man with an animated, enthusiastic expression on his face and a bubble coming out of his mouth saying 'I,I,I,I', then 'I,I,I,I', then 'I,I,I,I,' then 'I,I,I,I,'. In the next frame, the fifth, the girl chipped in with her timid bubble "Me…". The final frame had the young man leaning back, instantly bored, yawning, with his hand over his mouth. It was because of these images in his head that Chris adopted the strategy of not speaking too much about himself, instead being first to ask the questions and he then made an exaggerated point of being seen to listen attentively. It had to be all about her, not him, he decided.

"OK, Miss Bonnie. Tell me about yourself".

"Not much to tell really", she said humbly.

"I don't believe it. Come on. Tell me Bonnie's story. Where were you born? Where did you go to school? How many times have you been married?". She laughed and started gently, in her soft Scottish accent.

"OK. I shall try and be quick." She took a sip of Dutch courage from her wine glass that the waiter had just filled.

"Cheers. Here we go. I was born in Edinburgh. As a young girl, I moved around a bit with my family. Dad played rugby league, you know, professionally, so Mum and I had to follow him from club to club. We moved all over the north-east of England, Halifax, Leeds, Wigan, exciting places like that. Eventually, he quit and we moved to Swindon where he got a job at a sports centre. I liked my school but didn't really like the town. Then I got into drama school in London and did musical theatre. I had always been in plays at school and people said I was quite good, so I fell in love with the idea of going on the stage. Although I enjoyed doing drama, I then decided to take a gap year. So, I left and went to Australia. I shared a place in Sydney for a couple of months with two Aussie girls, then travelled around, Melbourne, Alice Springs and the Great Barrier Reef - it was fabulous - then I went over to Perth, which I absolutely adored. I had a temporary work permit, so I worked in bars mostly. That's where I learned my immaculate barmaid skills", she joked and then paused. "I'm not boring you, am I?".

The cartoon came back into his mind and he realised he must try even harder at showing his concentration.

"Not in the slightest. I love it. Keep going". Encouraged, she continued.

"Well, then I came back and got a job at American Express in Brighton. I knew a girlfriend down there and she had a spare room in a house that she shared with two others, so off to Brighton I went." Chris resisted interrupting. He was dying to butt in. He too had lived in Brighton for a while and knew it well. Tempted as he was, he did not want to stop her in full flow.

"I was there for around two years in all. Met this guy Jeff and we got a place together for a while. Jeff and I split up after about six months - he was never right for me and I don't know for the life of me what I ever saw in him. Then I went off travelling again, with the Brighton girl I had shared the house with. Went to India. Sarah, that's the girl, just wanted to hang out in Goa, so I took off and did the Taj Mahal, the Rajasthan palaces and Delhi on my own. Very brave I was. Then we hooked up again and went to Thailand. That was fun, especially Ko Samui". She started to speed up. "Came back, thought I'd give my acting a go. Moved into a flat in Kensington, nice place, sharing with two others. Been to four auditions - without success - and got jobs in pubs to pay the rent and then one day I walked into the Wellington... You know the rest. Phew. That's enough about me. Now your turn. I need another drink."

Chris was his clumsy old self. He could never help it. Someone had said once that he only opened his mouth to change feet. Instead of coming back with interesting questions about her exciting travels, her courage, her sense of adventure or her ventures into the theatre, he came back with "So this thing with Jeff. Was it serious?".

"Oh Chris, you boys. Getting jealous, are we?".

He suddenly felt a complete fool and did an abrupt about-turn with his interrogation.

"Did I tell you I lived in Brighton for a while too. Where did you live?", enquired Chris.

"In one of those little terraced houses in Poet's Corner, Coleridge Street. It was really sweet", answered Bonnie.

"I know round there well. I lived not far away, just off New Church Road, on one of those roads down to the seafront. I love Brighton, well Hove actually".

Bonnie laughed. "That's what they all call it, isn't it. Hove actually. Yes, I loved it down there too".

"We should go there." Chris immediately realised he was being way too fast and over-presumptuous for a first date and quickly changed the subject again.

"I worked at the Hove dog track for a while. Just a summer job on the ground staff, cutting grass and stuff, sweeping up old tickets after the meetings and putting the greyhounds into the traps on the race nights. It was really great. I loved it. But it all ended one night when I messed up. One of my jobs was to organise the trophy presentations to the winning owners after the race, like David today, but nowhere near as grand. With the big races, after the winner was announced, the dog would be led down the straight from the kennels and the owner would go up some steps and onto the track for the presentation of the trophy under the lights on the winning line. Part of my job was also to MC it all. It all went well until one night, when we had a top-grade race for the best lady-dogs around. A dog called Rosie Posie won, I'll never forget it. Before the dog or owner arrived on the scene, I picked up the mike to address the large crowd." Chris put on his posh announcer's voice.

"I remember all too well. 'Ladies and Gentlemen. What a fine race by the magnificent Rosie Posie, trained by Johnny Dixon and owned by Mrs Marjorie Mountjoy…'. She was a local councillor and very snobby. At that point I saw the dog being led down from the kennels, along the track. What I missed though, which everyone else was watching, was the very posh Mrs Mountjoy clambering up the steps onto the track at the same time. I was looking one way, at the dog, as everyone else in the crowd was looking at Mrs Councillor bloody Mountjoy stepping onto the track." Chris had a gulp of his wine as he shuddered at the thought of what was coming next.

"So, there I was. As I say, I'd just spotted the dog coming down the track while the crowd was glued to the formidable old bat climbing the stairs in front of them. I started speaking on the mike. 'What a fine race by the magnificent Rosie Posie, trained by Johnny Dixon and owned by Mrs Marjorie Mountjoy. And here comes the bitch now. Let's give her a big hand'. The whole place collapsed in convulsions of laughter, with the exception, of course, of the severe Mrs Mountjoy. I had absolutely no idea what they were laughing about. It was awful. She didn't find it funny either and gave me a look that could curdle milk".

Bonnie creased up in laughter, just as the crowd had.

"That is so funny. It must have been awful. I hate those moments. I remember I was auditioning for a play once and had to say 'I divorced William and everyone says I only married him for the money. But that isn't true. I am not as rich as people think I am'. It was a big line. Unfortunately, nerves got the better of me and it came out as 'But that isn't true. I am not as rich as thinkle peep I am'. I didn't get the part".

"Oh no. That's hilarious. I feel for you", sympathised Chris, unable to contain his laughter. By now, their starters had arrived and inevitably it came to Chris' turn to tell his life story. Bonnie sat back to listen.

"I was born at an early age and can't remember going to school, although I must have done. Actually, my Mum always told the story of how she spent days getting me mentally prepared to go to kindergarten for the first time. She said she went on and on, telling me what it would be like, how I had to behave, about the teachers and all that. When the day finally came, it wasn't too horrible and, when she picked me up, she asked how it had gone. I allegedly said 'Fine, Mummy. It wasn't as bad as you led me to believe' and I told her about what I had been up to. I don't remember any of this. Next morning, she came into my bedroom and woke me early with a 'come on, up you get'. "Why?", I had apparently said, "what's happened?'. 'You have to go to school' she instructed. She says I then just stared at her and said 'What...AGAIN?' - I apparently thought that school was just one day and that was it".

The evening passed in this convivial, humorous vein. Chris did explain that he too had had a go at acting, admitting that he never could remember his lines. The Elvis saga was omitted, probably wisely. He hurried through some of the boring jobs he had done, skipping any detail, described how he had got into sales promotions and then broke the happy news about his appointment at the Daily Post. Although he was unable to describe the job properly because he had yet to start it, he explained that he had had his slightly premature farewell drink with Colin and his girls the night before and still had just one more long week to go before launching himself into his new newspaper career. Bonnie generously shared his excitement.

Chris, over the main course, also touched on his impending divorce. He told her about Angela. He was helped by her Jeff situation. In a way, it made them all square. He even repeated some of the words that she had used on the subject, dropping in 'I don't know for the life of me how we had ever got together, let alone got married'. Naturally, Bonnie had a few questions, but Chris thought he had fended them off well enough, even in spite of his dubious skills as a verbal fencer.

He then went through the whole story of David and the flat. He could not contain his excitement, becoming more animated as he went through it all. He mentioned that even George had told them he might move in and that they were going to have a good chat about it on Monday.

"Oh, that was the Monday board meeting reference. Now I get it", Bonnie deduced.

When the time came for the bill, as Bonnie offered to pay her half, Chris pulled out his wad of money and said, "No, Bonnie. Neither of us is paying tonight. This is on Golden Oak".

It was still quite early when they walked out into the street, pausing on the pavement as they thought what to do next. They went into a clinch and each wanted to kiss the other, but it was a bit awkward, nothing like that spontaneous moment at the races. Neither took the initiative until they were wandering aimlessly, arm in arm, down the High Street. Chris suddenly stopped abruptly, looked at Bonnie, put both arms around her neck and softly pulled her into him.

"You are amazing, Bonnie. I can't tell what a day I've had. You are.... just incredible." Bonnie put her arms around his waist and squeezed him.

"You're not so bad yourself" she said quietly, before they enveloped one another in a long, lingering kiss. As they released themselves from the tightness of the embrace, Chris looked into her eyes and spoke softly. "Meeting you was just the best thing ever."

He had already decided he would see her safely back to her home in Kensington. His problem was that, in suggesting it, he did not want her to think he was pushing for an invitation to stay the night. All far too soon.

So, he said, "I have to get home, but I would like to take you back to London first and then I can jump on the train from Victoria".

"No, no, Chris. That really isn't necessary. I'll be fine."

"No way. I would like to see you home safely. And anyway, this way I get to spend more time with you on the train."

"Alright then. Thanks", she replied with an appreciative smile.

They chatted incessantly all the way back on the train, before jumping into a taxi at their destination. "Drayson Mews, please", Bonnie told the cabbie. "Then on to Victoria", added Chris, cleverly saving Bonnie from any embarrassment.

He got out of the taxi with her, throwing a 'won't be a moment' at the driver and, after a warm 'thank you and goodnight' between the pair, they kissed again before Bonnie reached into her bag for her key and put it in the lock. As she closed the large red door, she peered around and blew him a kiss and whispered, "See you on Monday". He blew her a kiss back and he got into the cab, with a smile that stretched from cheek to cheek.

On the train home, Chris could not stop thinking about the whole fantastic day, not so much about the racing, Golden Oak and his winnings, but of Bonnie and how completely and utterly gorgeous she was. He could not remember ever being happier. He beamed inanely, like the Cheshire Cat, as he sat back, just like he had after that first meeting in the Wellington on Thursday. He was totally smitten.

He assumed that Angela was fast asleep when he got in, so he took off his shoes and crept upstairs. After undressing in the bathroom, he snuck under the covers and lay alongside his motionless wife. He lay there, in his own world, staring up towards the ceiling, for what must have been an hour, thinking about what the future might bring until he drifted into sleep, with that same stupid grin gripping his face.

CHAPTER THREE
MOVING UP

MONDAY, JULY 15

George was sitting at home in his slippers, reading his Daily Telegraph and sipping on his morning cup of coffee, when the entry door buzzer rudely shattered his peace. He had hardly had a single visitor since moving into his flat and he could not imagine who would be wanting to see him at this time on a Monday morning. He got up and went over to the little monitor and pressed the button.

"Hello?", he said inquisitively. To his total shock and amazement, it was Kate. George's voice, having not spoken a word for the past 12 hours, spluttered into use.

"K-Kate. What a surprise. Er, how nice. Come on in. Come up in the lift to the third floor, turn right, I'm number 14". Downstairs, the lock clicked to admit her. Kate entered the wonderfully old-fashioned hall, with panelled walls and a richly tiled floor, and went over to the particularly quaint lift, with its concertina sliding gates, like the ones that she had seen in old films.

Meanwhile, George hurriedly looked in the mirror, tried to smooth down his hair and prepared to greet Kate. His nerves were tingling. The 'ding dong' of the flat bell sounded. He took a deep breath and opened the door, trying to appear calm.

Kate looked amazing. She had styled and tamed her wild, tumbling locks and had altogether a trimmer, more striking appearance. Her make-up was toned down, less obvious and far more sophisticated. She stood there, totally composed and more elegant than George had seen her for a long time.

"Come in, Kate. What a lovely surprise".

"I hope you don't mind, George darling. I was just passing and I thought I'd pop in". They both knew that was a lie, but George did not care. He was always a willing captive to that sexy voice.

"Please sit down. Would you like a cup of tea, sorry, coffee?". Kate, like David, always drank coffee at this time of day. Her continental habit had caused George to change his regular wake-up drink years ago, from his favourite Darjeeling leaf to the Columbian bean. She settled onto the settee, crossing her long legs gracefully. George sat on the edge of his chair next to her.

"This is a nice little place, George. You have made it very homely". Her comment seemed to lack sincerity. The room was spotlessly clean and tidy, spartan almost, with one sofa, one chair, and a coffee table. The only splash of indulgence was an old display cabinet containing some colourful family chinaware. A small dining table and two straight-backed chairs against the wall completed the set.

Kate could not help noticing the one photo on the mantelpiece, a picture of them together, taken after an unforgettably excellent lunch on the beach in the Seychelles, on one of their unforgettable holidays.

She continued, with her Spanish twang. "I hope you don't mind me dropping in like this. I have been thinking about everything all weekend. It is really getting to me, George, this divorce. I don't like it. It is doing my head crazy. That woman solicitor I've got keeps pushing me and pushing me to demand more. Now she wants me to try and get the house and everything in it. Dreadful woman. I have had enough of her. I hate her".

George felt an ease washing over his whole body. His very first thought had been that this sudden visit was because she was going to say something serious about her health or that someone had died. He never expected this.

"I hate it all too, Kate. I hate the way these pompous idiots take it out of our hands and treat us like chess pieces in their nasty little games. I said to my lawyer the other day that I wanted to speak with you personally and he went ballistic, saying I should never contact you except through them. Bloody awful people."

"So, George, darling. I have given it a great deal of thought and I want us to have a chat, here and now, and sort this out between us. No more paying stupid solicitors. George, I really don't want much. I don't need much. If we sold the house, I would be quite happy in a much smaller one or even a flat - a bit bigger than this one though. This is a bit pokey, isn't it, George. As for money, I am not a greedy person. You worked hard for your money and deserve to have the most of it. I know that. I arrived with almost nothing. I feel bad when the solicitor says more, more, more. I just want enough to live. I know I need to move on with my life now. I have to be an independent woman. It is my choice after all. And I might even get a little job."

Up to this point, George had allowed her to flow but, at that last proposal, he could not help himself interjecting. "A job? You, Kate? Steady on old girl. Things aren't that bad". His mood had by now significantly lightened.

"No. Seriously. I have been thinking. I always worked before. I liked being on the airlines. I thought I could do some translating from home. You taught me lots of business words. There must be companies around that need documents translated from English into Spanish and the other way round. And there are visas and things."

"That's a terrific idea, Kate. You'd be excellent. By the way, I don't know if you have heard. I lost my job last week"

"I heard. Sarah Cowley rang to say what had happened. She said Geoff was really upset about it. He is disgusted". Sarah was the wife of Geoffrey Cowley, who had been a close colleague of George's at Forsyte Manners. Kate had got on really well with Sarah at the many functions they all went to.

"Don't worry. I'll be fine. But it does change things a bit".

"My poor George. I am so sad I am putting you through all this. I am so sorry..."

George cut in. "Kate. Kate. Kate. It is OK. I know you weren't happy. It isn't your fault. It is both of us. These things happen."

He reached out and took her hand in his. She held on to it tightly. They talked for an hour. Nothing would ever douse that flame that had once burned so brightly. On Kate's instruction, George then reached for a pad and wrote down everything they agreed. They would sell the house and she would get half the money - Kate had asked for less, George insisted half. They agreed some income for her, but only for five years. That was her idea. He offered 25% of his pension fund, which she accepted. "I am still young and will have my own job soon", she reasoned. Everything was agreed amicably.

He then, as the last item, came clean about his pay-off. Above all else, George was always honest.

"Kate, there is one thing. I may be receiving some redundancy money, you know, compensation from the company. What shall we do about that?"

"Darling, that is yours. It has nothing to do with me. It is between you, your hard work and your stupid bosses. Keep it, only please get out of this grotty little place. This is not a home fit for my George." They chatted only a few minutes more before she stood up. He rose out of his chair with her.

"I am no good at this sort of thing. You are the businessman. You get something to my solicitor with all this laid out and I will sign it. No doubt she will go crazy, but I don't care. I can't wait to be rid of her. I hate her. I trust you absolutely George and my heart breaks that it is ending like this. At least, this way, we can be friends".

George was moved by her generous sincerity and took her in his arms. She responded warmly. Both recognised the poignancy, although neither commented, that this might be their last ever marital hug.

"Now listen, George. See if you can get us out of going to Court next Wednesday. Understand? Please get on to your solicitor straight away. We have sorted it all out together and that makes me happy. You see, we never needed those terrible lawyers anyway". She moved towards the door. "Goodbye, George. You will always be my handsome George, you know that".

With that she left. George showed her down back down to the front door, where they parted, but only after he had given her a kiss on the cheek. As he collapsed back into his chair, every emotion rushed through him. Happiness, relief, but most of all, an overwhelming sadness at what he had just lost.

But he had work to do and sprung up after a few minutes to seize the phone. His call to Max Bannister, his earnest solicitor, received the reaction he expected. George read out his scribbled agreement with Kate. Even though the highly conditioned lawyer absolutely loathed what he was hearing, he recognised that the deal was very much in his client's favour.

"And Kate's agreed to this? This is a hell of a good deal for you, George. But there are ways of doing this. You have to leave it to your legal advisers. My job is to get the best deal I can for my client. You two can't just go running off and playing lawyers. It is for the other side to make their demands and for us to refute them. That's how it works".

George absolutely hated that 'other side' expression that the lawyers used. It defined their inflexible, unhelpful, confrontational stance. He was resolute. He had regained all his old confidence. He was going to do it his way.

"Max, with the greatest respect, that is the way you say it works. Kindly do as I ask. I am grateful for your help, but it is my life and this is a decision I have made with Kate. I shall email you the detail. Let's get it signed, sealed and delivered". With that, he put the phone down.

George received an email just three hours later documenting the draft proposal exactly as he had laid it out. Max asked for George's final approval before telling him he would like him to come in immediately to sign it himself in order to exonerate his legal firm. He explained that they would then send it to Hedgwick and Havisham, as Petitioners, to send it back to the Max as Kate's proposal. This was all very unusual, Max had stressed. George thought how ridiculous the whole system was but, having studied the document carefully, his reply was brief. His return missive read:

Dear Max,
Thank you for your email of today's date. Approved. See you in fifteen minutes.
Yours sincerely, George.

George dashed to his solicitor. A formal young lady ushered him straight into the book-lined office. He greeted him with a handshake.

"Good afternoon, George. You're having quite a day. Now, you are sure you want to do this? Last chance, old boy."

"Absolutely. How does it work again?"

"Well, you sign it and then we send it over. I want you to sign because you have gone a bit native here, George. I don't want you holding me responsible if you live to regret it later. When they get it, they'll go apeshit and call Kate. Then there'll be a few uncomfortable hours of them telling her not to do it, informing her that this is not good practice, threatening to quit and general feminist breast-beating. Then, if Kate means it and stands firm, they, as Petitioners, will have to send the deal back to us as their offer and you will sign it. It shouldn't take much more than 24 hours if Kate holds firm, I reckon."

"Then, is that it? Just like that. It'll all be over?", asked George.

"When you then sign their offer, that will be it. All done."

"Bloody hell." The sense of relief that this whole debacle might soon be over ironically served to heighten his anxiety. "So, it could be all over this week? Finish?".

"The financials could be done, yes. No Court next week. There's still a bit more work to do on the legal side yet though."

"That is fantastic. Thank you, Max."

"It seems I did very little, George. Let me be honest. Bloody well done to you and Kate. If I ever get divorced, I will definitely hire you as my lawyer." Both men laughed and George got up to leave. Max continued. "I shall ring you as soon as I hear something. But if, as you say, Kate does her stuff, I should have some good news in a day or so. She will be under a lot of pressure not to sign though, you know that. Are you absolutely sure she will do it?"

"Absolutely, Max. You don't know Kate. I feel sorry for her solicitor. When she makes up her mind on something, nothing will make her change it."

George departed the austere building breathing the fresh air deeply, like a released convict leaving prison.

It was almost six o'clock. David and Chris were already on their first pint in the Wellington. They were gathered around George's stool, neither man daring to sit on the hallowed seat, when the beaming George came in.

"OK. Let's do it", said a chipper George. The others looked at one another in amazement. This sort of reckless spontaneity was not in character with Gentleman George.

"Sorry, George? Do what exactly?", said Chris.

"Let's get a house together. Or a flat. I don't care. But make it a big one. How about it, Christopher? Let's do it. What's stopping you?". Chris could not believe his eyes or his ears.

"Have you been drinking, George?", Chris asked with incredulity.

"No. But let me get a pint and then let's all go and sit over there, around that table". Things were getting surreal. George now wanted to forego his precious bar stool and move over by the window. The three went over and sat down. George, on fire, acted as chairman, something his friends had expected and were perfectly happy with.

"Gentlemen. So, what have we got? I had a quick look this afternoon and have printed off a couple of places. I am not sure they're right though. I'll be honest. I couldn't find much, but that shouldn't put us off. What have you found, David?".

David responded to the somewhat formal board room format and briefed them in his business manner on what he had been researching.

"I decided we should look at houses or flats within a five-mile radius of here, at least five bedrooms, plenty of space, furnished. Is that about right?" The two nodded. They then proceeded to go through a collection of estate agent details, starting with George's finds. They passed each one around in turn, the last man consulting the others on whether it was a 'definite maybe' or 'definite no' before placing it on their appropriate pile. This took quite a time and they had a short break halfway for David to get in another round. After a good half hour, George dispatched the 'no' bundle to the floor and placed the 'maybe' pile in the centre of the table. They then went through the whole experience again, this time with greater scrutiny. However, the enthusiasm waned as each prospectus seemed less interesting on its second review. As they examined them again, they noticed some had different facilities than others and, before long, each was rejected as being less than suitable for their demanding needs.

"Not sure we have it here" concluded George with a sigh. "Anyone got anything else?".

David reached into his briefcase. "Well, there is this one, but you might think it is far too expensive. Still, I really want you to see it. I don't know why on earth Tristram gave it to me. Just to make me envious, I guess. It is a bit special". He brought out a large, highly glossy brochure and opened the gatefold on the table. Their eyes almost popped out of their heads. No words were necessary. There, before them, were the most amazing shiny photos of this glitzy, ultra-modern, super-trendy apartment with a balcony overlooking the Thames. All three got up and moved to the same side of the table, like a group of architects studying plans.

"Bloody gorgeous" was all Chris could say. David played the role of the agent and read out the description. "The epitome of luxury. A truly stunning apartment, located on the sixth floor of this prestigious modern building, overlooking the River Thames. Entrance hall, expansive dual aspect reception room, well-appointed modern kitchen, five bedrooms, each one en suite, spacious balcony with spectacular city views, underfloor heating and air conditioning. Flat screen TVs throughout and high-quality Bose sound system. Fully furnished, in outstanding decorative condition. Luxury facilities, indoor pool, fully equipped gym, spa, sauna, 24 hours concierge, ample parking."

They collapsed back into their wooden chairs, each man dreaming of what might be. It took Chris to bring everything down to earth.

"One small thing. Just one tiny detail", Chris said. "No way can we afford it". They had looked at the price and it was almost double anything they had seen before.

"Well," David always introduced his big next idea with a 'well' or a 'brilliant'. "I have been thinking. Here's a suggestion. This place has five bedrooms…"

"Be we don't need five bedrooms, do we," Chris interrupted. They knew all about David's children and Chris understandingly added "Your two will be OK sharing one room, won't they?". David affirmed that that was fine and then continued.

"Hold on, Chris. Listen. What if, and I am only saying what if, we get one more flatmate? What if we were to advertise for someone to join us? We would get to interview them and choose someone we like. We'd all have to agree, of course. Now, that way we cut our costs down."

Individually, they looked back at the monthly rent and did some mental arithmetic. Chris went quiet. The chairman broke into a smile. "That's doable for me. And you, David?"

"I'm definitely in". David confirmed.

Chris reluctantly addressed the meeting. "Bit steep for me, I'm afraid, guys. I have my new job but, even with the pay rise, it is more than I had in mind and much more than I can afford".

"This is how I see it". David put himself back in charge. "This isn't forever, is it. We shall probably only do this for a year. It's highly likely that we shall all buy somewhere individually in due course. But right now, we are where we are. Look, we have all had a shitty time, so why not push the boat out and have some fun. We deserve it, don't we? We don't have to give everything to the ex-wives and their bloody lawyers".

"Too damn right", enthused George "and Chris, we won't do this without you. We would never leave you out of this. One for all, and all for one. That is how it is going to be". He threw a glance at David, who winked back. "David and I will work out something that you can afford. You may be sleeping on a coat hanger in a wardrobe, but you'll be there. It wouldn't be the same without you. And, anyway, who is going to make the tea and the Sunday breakfast? Come on Chris. You are in. We won't take no for an answer".

Chris hesitated before announcing in an uplifted voice "OK. If you can work something out that doesn't leave me begging on the streets, I'm definitely in, though you guys do have to understand that it is a hell of a push for me financially."

David gave him solace. "Of course. Don't worry. George and I will sort it out. Hey, just had another thought. Tristram should still be in the office. Let me call him now". David pulled out the agent's business card, picked up his phone and punched in the number. George and Chris listened keenly.

"Hello. Sorry to call so late. Is Tristram there?". After a short pause, he continued. "Tristram, hi. David Nugent. You know you mentioned flat sharing? My good friends here think it is a brilliant idea. We would like to look at that incredible apartment in Thames Tower. Any chance tomorrow?" Another pause. "OK, I look forward to hearing back from you, or someone".

The other two looked a bit disappointed that no date had been fixed there and then. David reported back. "Tristram says he isn't handling the property himself and that he has to call the man who is in charge then he will get him to ring me as soon as possible". They garbled over each other ardently, with half an expectant eye on David's phone, which was lying in front of him. In no time, it vibrated and rang. They all perked up attentively.

"Hello. Yes. That's right. It is still available, isn't it? Great. When can we see it? You are out of town tomorrow? Wednesday then? That would be perfect". George and Chris leaned forward expectantly nodding their approval. "3.30 Wednesday? Let me check". He took the phone away from his ear and saw the other two nodding even more enthusiastically. "Yes, that's brilliant. OK. We shall see you at the entrance at 3.30 on Wednesday. What is your name again? Hugo. Thanks, Hugo. See you on Wednesday." They clinched their fists and let out a victorious 'YES' as they raised their glasses in celebration.

"Cheers. My round", announced the energised George. He felt good about himself, loving this re-invigorated George as much as the others were bemused by it. They returned to the bar, where he reclaimed his stool. No-one had dared to park themselves on it in his absence. Gerry came over.

"You all look like you have won the lottery. What's up?".

"Same again, Gerard. Have you got a rubbish bin? Do me a favour, old boy", and George handed him the large bundle of estate agent papers. All except that of the chosen apartment.

The new flatmates told Gerry about their plan, each chipping in to add to the story, first telling him of how the idea had come about and then showing him the fabulous pictures of the luxury pad. 'What's more, it's got a pool, a gym and a sauna", Chris threw in. Even the supercool Gerry was impressed, to the point that he said those magic words, albeit slightly grudgingly, "Drink those and the next one's on me".

As they got towards the bottom of their glasses, they were delighted to see Bonnie walk in. She joined them as they buzzed like excited children.

"So, don't tell me. I can see it from your faces. You've found somewhere?", she asked.

A jubilant Chris seized her and lifted her off her feet. "We might be moving into an amazing, film star apartment... with a pool, a gym and a sauna". Gerry watched on, suddenly expressionless.

"That's fabulous. Well, go on. Let me see it", Bonnie said, sharing their excitement. Chris lifted the brochure off the counter and handed it to her.

"Bloody hell, Chris. This is unbelievable. It's ridiculous. I love it. And how can you guys afford it?"

"We are working on that", Chris explained, "but basically, yes, David and George are the money guys and they say we can do it. We shall have to get a fourth flatmate though. We are seeing it on Wednesday at 3.30. I'll just tell them at work I have a dental appointment. They won't believe me, but I've only a few days to go so it is hardly worth them sacking me." Bonnie hugged him, sharing his moment.

"Come on Bonnie. There's work to do," called Gerry, peevishly.

"Sorry, Gerry. Right there," and she took up her duties on the other side of the bar.

They drank on for another twenty minutes and then George exclaimed 'Got to go' and the night broke up. David headed out at the same time. Chris hung back to chat with Bonnie for a while. It was obvious that Gerry was not in the best of moods and that he was irritated by Chris monopolising her time when she should be working. In his unabated enthusiasm, Chris all too hastily threw in a suggestion to Bonnie, even though they had not yet even been on a proper date. He was so over-excited that, as he was about to leave, he rashly brought up the idea of a weekend in their old stomping-ground, Brighton, for a second time. She visibly blushed and, in her embarrassment, sidestepped the proposal by saying she would have to think about it. "Let's talk about it another time'" she said. Chris knew from her tone that he had rushed things and apologised profusely, before saying his fond farewells. He knew he was annoying Gerry by keeping Bonnie from her work and that she was being put in a difficult position. As he left, the last thing he heard was Gerry scolding Bonnie. "Come on, Bonnie. Customers are waiting".

WEDNESDAY, JULY 17

Chris went into work and straightaway knocked on James Flynn's door. His boss had not been best pleased with him handing in his notice and enquired brusquely what he wanted.

"Sorry, James. I've had this awful toothache recently and I have managed to get an emergency appointment with my dentist this afternoon. Is it OK if I leave at lunchtime?".

"That's fine", he said curtly, not even looking up. Chris didn't care. That was one of the reasons he was leaving anyway. He was always telling everyone the man was a moron.

Soon after midday, just as he was starting to get worried that he had heard nothing, George's phone rang in his flat. It was Max. He had just received their papers, good old Kate had won the day and did he want to come round right now to sign himself?

"I'll be right there", he rejoiced. Hurriedly he put on his smartest jacket and his best tie before preening himself in front of the living room mirror, taking a second to observe that he was actually still quite dashing and dapper. The man in the mirror gazing back at him suddenly looked ten years younger and he flicked his hair in self-admiration, as he had used to do in his carefree days. Gentleman George felt pretty damn good about himself. His self-esteem had returned as he smiled back at himself.

"It's over. That's it. Stuff the job. Stuff Forsyte Manners. Stuff them all. They can keep their boring lives and I am bloody lucky to have got shot of them", he said out loud, talking to his appreciative reflection. He put on his mock flirtatious face. "Who will be the lucky woman tonight, Mr Granby?", he added. George was like butterfly emerging from his corporate chrysalis. His sparkle had come back. He straightened his tie and jauntily set off to the lawyers.

George and Max greeted one another like a winning team. George went up to the desk, perused the document with a cursory glance and dashed his signature onto it.

"I'll do the rest," said Max. "Now you have a free day as a free man, well, almost. If I were you, I would get yourself a damn good dinner at the Connaught tonight with some gorgeous woman. You are almost single again, after all". George laughed and scurried out, fully aware that he had another big engagement to keep.

David and Chris were already at Thames Tower as George stepped out of his taxi. They were standing in the shadow of a highly impressive modern building, bristling with the resonance of a five-star Dubai hotel. The three men were immaculately groomed, as if they were going to church. Although George, in his City suit, was bursting to impart his good news about his divorce settlement, there was no time as the debonair Hugo Carghill arrived on cue, immediately ushering them through the sumptuous foyer and into the plush lift, which barely made a hum as it smoothly elevated them to the sixth floor. Hugo let his clients exit first and then passed quickly between them to get to the door. "Here we are, gentlemen", he announced formally.

The door was pushed open. They entered in complete silence and their eyes widened as their feet sank into a deep pile carpet. They passed through the expansive mirrored hallway, onto a polished white oak floor as they stepped into a cavernous reception room. Marble walls and shiny chrome sparkled throughout. The space and the interior design left them aghast, with the contemporary designer furniture positively gleaming in its minimalist, but opulent, open plan setting. An impressive fireplace, with a modern stone façade and a faux flame-effect fire, was the centrepiece on the left. To the right, the room was flanked by a kitchen that screamed 'expensive', wrapped around a smart central island and with a swanky breakfast area by the window, plus, of course, only the most prestigious brand names on every appliance.

They headed for the outside patio, overlooking Old Father Thames. They slid the door effortlessly aside to emerge onto the large balcony, with its burnished stainless-steel railing and deluxe furniture, including a teak table for eight under a giant awning that protruded out of the wall.

Hugo exuberantly shared the panoramic view down the river, to the left Blackfriars Bridge, to the right London Bridge, while, in front of them, the dome of the indomitable St Paul's Cathedral loomed out of the metropolis. They stood mesmerized, before he guided them back in, leading them to the bedrooms. The apartment was positioned in one corner of the high-rise building and three bedrooms were to the left of the living area and two to the right, accessed by a short corridor by the front door. Each was superbly appointed. Almost with prescience, the three on the left had large double beds while, of the two on the right, one was a double and the other had two twin beds, the perfect arrangement for David and the children. Each had a flatscreen TV on the wall and electric blinds. The attached bathrooms, while not large, were well up to the standard of any high-class hotel. Finally, they were shown the small utility room that was subtly hidden away. Hugo continued his spiel in real estate speak.

"This is such an up-and-coming area. Your timing is perfect. Rents are so much more reasonable around here than in Mayfair and Chelsea. You are paying almost half the price. The South Bank is becoming exceptionally popular, a superb location with excellent places to eat. The OXO Tower Restaurant and Brasserie, my favourite, is a short stroll away. The National Theatre is just down the road, as is the London Aquarium and the London Eye. Now, if you have had a good look around, I will show you the indoor pool". He was making it sound like a bargain.

"Hold on Hugo", Chris said, "Can we have just a bit longer to take it all in? We haven't really seen the kitchen properly".

"Naturally", came the polite reply. Chris needed to have more time to absorb this palace of wonders. They returned to the living area and slumped into the soft sofas and chairs, then got up to rub their hands over the granite surfaces in the kitchen and open the doors of the massive fridge. They could not believe what they were seeing.

Eventually, Hugo led them out and took them on a tour of all the other stunning facilities. His spellbound clients followed him slowly and in silence, like a short line of Dominican friars. Once back at the front entrance, Hugo wrapped up his performance, noticeably tending to direct his gravitas towards David, whom he clearly saw as both the money and the sense in the group. They arranged to speak the next day and he then left on foot. The others remained in a stunned stillness. David broke it with a shout.

"Taxi". A passing black cab swung in. "The Duke of Wellington, please".

Few words were exchanged on the way to the pub. The three passengers were shell-shocked. It was only when they had re-immersed themselves in their natural surroundings of the pub that the blood started to flow back through their veins. The ever-present Gerry greeted them.

"Here they come. You're early tonight, gents. The usual I presume?". Without a reply, he went about filling the glasses. George took to his stool and, although he knew they were itching to talk about the flat, sorry, apartment, he had to get his news out of the way first.

"Gentleman. Before we go any further, I have something to report. Kate and I settled today. It is all over. Well almost. We have both signed and... I need a bloody drink, Gerard. Hurry up!", he shouted over the bar, jokingly.

"That's brilliant', said David. "How the hell did that happen so quickly?'.

George told the story of how Kate had come round and about the palaver that he had been through that morning.

David was delighted for him. "So, no Court, I guess. You lucky bastard, George. I've got my big showdown next week. That's going to be fun."

George looked sympathetic, although he did not want to get dragged into any more divorce talk.

"No chance of your wife being reasonable?", asked George.

"Not a snowball's chance in hell", David replied. But there was something much more exciting to discuss. So, George did one of his conversational about-turns.

"Now let's get back to the main item on the agenda, gentlemen. What do we all think of the apartment, then?"

Chris summed it all up in typical Chris style.

"Wow! Bloody hell. That was amazing," he hollered.

"You liked it then, Chris?", questioned David.

"It's the dog's bollocks". George frowned in disapproval at his language.

"Is that a real estate term?", asked David. "How about you, George?".

"I don't think I have ever seen anything like it."

"Shall we go for it, then?", said David inviting the others' support.

George pondered for a minute and his more rational side invaded his impetuosity.

"Hold your horses a minute, David. Let's not get too carried away. It is so bloody expensive. We would be insane to spend that sort of money, wouldn't we? And we don't really need something like that, do we?". David sensed his friend's jitters and thought he needed one more persuasive shove.

"We may not need such a fabulous place, George, but that shouldn't stop us. We deserve it. I told you, it's only for one year. See it as one full year of divorce therapy and recovery. On the practical side, we will get someone with a bit of money to pay a quarter share and we'll sort out the rest. It won't make too big a hole in your redundancy money, even if Kate does get half."

"She doesn't", said George with a triumphant smile. With David bringing that up, it had also dawned on him again, that, through her reasonableness, he had doubled what he might have had out of his redundancy pay-off if she and her lawyers had demanded half. Suddenly, the money mattered less. George went on.

"OK. I'm up for it, for a year anyway, but we do need to sort out the finances. Christopher, I need a talk with David to crunch some numbers". Chris took the hint and, together with his pint, slid down to the other end of the bar to talk to Gerry.

George called the barman back. "Gerard, do you have some paper, please?".

He brought them an A4 pad, tearing off the used front page. George and David took out their identical Mont Blanc ballpoint pens and started working on the sums. At the other end of the bar, Gerry went back to talk to Chris. There were no other customers apart from a couple sitting in the window and an old man in the corner, unhurriedly drinking his Guinness while studying his Evening Standard.

"So, Chris. What's happening with you and Bonnie?", Gerry asked.

"Oh, nothing." He paused. "Yet, that is. I really like her. We had a great day out on Saturday, by the way. Has she said anything to you about me?'.

"No. Nothing" said Gerry, unemotionally.

"Oh" continued a disappointed Chris. "Anyway, we shall see what happens. Don't say a word, but I am going to ask her out on Saturday, lunch in Covent Garden perhaps, and maybe a spin on the London Eye."

Gerry wished him a somewhat hollow good luck and then curtly changed the subject to the Chelsea-Arsenal game at the weekend. At both ends of the bar, the two pairs of men were locked in thoughtful conversation.

Soon, more customers started to come in and Gerry had to spring into action. As Chris remained on his own, he snuck stealthily along the bar, trying hard not to disturb his friends, who were in deep discussion. He picked up the brochure and began to study it thoroughly, bursting at the idea that he might soon be living there. Suddenly, he heard what sounded like a Sergeant Major's holler directed at Private Chris.

"Christopher. Here. Now", bellowed George. It involuntarily made him think of his Mum. The only time he had ever heard the shout of his full name was as a child, when he knew he was in trouble. The words 'Christopher. Here. Now' still made him quake. Fortunately, this was a less fearsome calling than his mother's. It was his 'call back', as Bonnie would say in her acting circles. Hearing the summons, he picked up his beer and went over. George addressed him, sounding uncharacteristically severe.

"Christopher. David and I have been thinking about your situation and we have come up with what we think is a solution. We fully recognise that we are not all equal partners going into this venture and that you have a slightly lower place than us in the hierarchy".

Chris did not like the way this was going. He looked at David to see if it was a joke, only to receive a deadpan glare. He was genuinely nervous about what was to come next. David took over, more slowly, but equally sternly.

"Chris. We know you are a young man, eager and ambitious. You are learning in life that only hard work will get you on". Chris did not appreciate being lectured but listened on expectantly. David continued pompously, in his lofty tone. "We have been looking at your 'problem' and may have found a way to accommodate you into our new luxury living. You will understand, I am sure, that George and I, in our new elevated status as wealthy, successful, retired single men, shall need staff. It is a big apartment and it will need looking after. So George has come up with a compromise. He proposes that we find a place for you with us, at a reasonable rent, on the understanding that you will be expected to vacuum everyone's room once a week, do the laundry twice a week and cook breakfast, eggs, bacon, sausages, mushrooms, fried bread, et cetera, every Sunday. To be honest, I thought this was a little bit too tough. So, I suggest we leave out the fried bread. No, seriously, in the end, after much discussion, we have agreed that the vacuuming and laundry twice a week could be taken out of the arrangement. So here, young Christopher is the deal". Chris braced himself. Still in character, David paused and proclaimed with a smirk, "The Board has decided that you can pay just 10% but get us a bloody good breakfast every Sunday, with or without fried bread, and that's the deal…how does that sound?"

The two older men then broke into laughter. Chris, after taking a moment to grasp what had just happened, joined in.

"That was superb, David", applauded George. "We should go on stage as a double act".

Chris retaliated. "You bastard, George. Both of you, you totally bloody got me."

"A taste of your own medicine, I say. We thought we would mess with your head a bit. Seriously though, Christopher, this is what we have decided". George set out the detail of the arrangement. "David has generously offered to pay 40%, because he has the children every other weekend and, more importantly, because he can afford it. He gets two rooms". The two older men smiled at one another. "I pay 25%, my quarter, as agreed, the new guy pays 25% and you, you spoilt boy, get to pay what's left, 10%. It had better be a damn good breakfast, though. Definitely no black pudding and only with the best British bangers. We agreed on that as well."

"That is amazing. Are you sure? Thank you both so much, guys," Chris gushed. "I really appreciate this. You have made a young chef very happy. My round, I think…"

"Make mine a large one", joked David, handing him his empty pint glass. Chris turned to the bar to order.

"Thanks, David. I cannot thank you enough", he said as he waited to be served.

"No, Chris, it's our pleasure. I reckon I have had quite enough stress this past year from the purgatory that Moira has put me and the children through. As I said, this is my curative therapy. The kids deserve a nice place as well. They'll love it. And, hell, as George says, I guess I can afford it. Even if things don't go my way on Monday, those years in the City mean she won't ever be able to leave me exactly skint. Or let's look at it another way. Golden Oak has just paid for the first month or two".

"Good old Golden Oak", Chris cheered, before turning to George again, giving him a friendly punch on the arm. "I didn't know you had it in you, acting like that, you rogue. You got me completely. I was seriously thinking 'a bit of cleaning, a bit of washing, this isn't going to be too bad'. I would have gone for it. You could have had your little maid, doing your cleaning and ironing your shirts. I probably would have even worn a foxy little miniskirt if you'd asked. Anyway, nice one George. I don't know what has happened to you, but I like the new George."

"Christopher, dear boy, this is the old George come back to life again. George Granby is back. Oh, and by the way, I like my eggs lightly poached. David likes his scrambled. And don't burn the bacon".

"You'll get what you're bloody given", replied the restored Chris.

Before long, George and David left the pub together, stopping on the pavement outside.

"We're going for it then?" asked David.

"Yes. I think we are all agreed. Do you want to take it to the next stage or shall I?", George enquired.

"If it is OK with you, let me do it. I'll phone Hugo in the morning and get the ball rolling. If they want a deposit, don't worry, I'll take care of that. I suppose it might be easier if I put the whole thing in my name as it might raise fewer questions. Are you happy with that?".

George did not hesitate. "I can't think why I wouldn't be. I am very happy. I suppose we should bounce it off Chris though, although he won't mind, I'm sure, not with the deal he is getting. He is a very lucky young man."

"Indeed. Mind you, he is just such fun to have around. We need Chris. I'm looking forward to my bacon and eggs every Sunday".

At that, the men went their different ways, George on foot back to his flat and David by taxi to the station. Both men felt that this was the start of something very significant, a farewell to their traumatic recent past and a welcome to a bright new dawn.

"What a day", said George aloud as he walked. "What a bloody amazing day".

Chris held back until 7pm, so that he could at least see Bonnie, even though he didn't want to miss his train and be late home. She had anticipated that he would be waiting there and arrived early, allowing them to sit at a table for a few minutes and have a quick chat. She walked in, looking as stunning as ever. He went headlong into the new flat arrangements and then on to something else that was at the front of his mind. He spoke out in his usual impetuous style. There was never any subtlety with Chris.

"Can we talk about the weekend, Bonnie?".

Bonnie looked down, embarrassed, before she replied,

"Look Chris, this is all a bit quick. I hope you understand if I say no".

Chris had forgotten about the earlier Brighton conversation and was about to ask her out for the day in London. However, she had misconstrued the question and he took her answer as meaning that she did not want to go out with him. He looked devastated and checked himself.

"Oh, gosh, wow, that's a blow. I thought we were getting on well. Was it something I did or said?".

"Not at all, Chris, but a weekend in Brighton? It's just too soon."

"Oh, shit, Bonnie. I forgot about all that. No, I didn't mean that. No. What I meant was, will you have lunch with me in Covent Garden and go for a stroll in the park or something?". A look of reprieve came over Bonnie's face.

"You are such an idiot, Chris. Of course, I'd love to go out with you on Saturday. I am even free on Sunday, if you have not had enough of me by then."

"That's fantastic, Bonnie". As he held both her hands across the table, he looked up to see Gerry glaring at them. Chris ignored him.

"What shall we do? Is there anything special you would like to do?"

"No, lunch sounds great", Bonnie reassured him.

"Have you ever been on the London Eye. Do you fancy a spin on that? And maybe the Aquarium after?", Chris offered.

"That would be incredible. No, I haven't been to either."

"It's a date then?". Chris squeezed her hand.

"It's a date", she confirmed, with a smile.

Chris did not stay much longer. He hated to leave her, but he knew he had to keep Angela calm and on his side. He wanted the next few days to be as 'normal' as possible, just in case she put some kind of spoke in the wheel. While Chris may have thought he was a master of cunning, he had, in fact, always been totally devoid of any second sense and had not noticed that she had already picked up on his odd demeanour, and, although she did not suspect anything specific, that she just knew something was up. She could read him as easily as one of her books.

Once home, the usual routine dropped into place, the polite greeting, the meal in the oven, the long silences between the two of them. Tonight, he used the times of quietness to contemplate about what he was going to say to Angela about the weekend. He had committed himself to Bonnie and now he had to find an acceptable story for Angela. It came down to two strategies. Should he lie, saying he was going to see an old friend? Or should he come clean and just say he has a date? He spent the whole of the nine o'clock news mulling over the two options, convincing himself one minute that 'Plan A' was best option, then switching to the honest 'Plan B' the next. Poor Chris. He was no sort of tactician. If he had ever had an affair, he might as well have worn a T-shirt with 'I am having an affair' printed on it. Even though he could not recognise it, he was hopelessly out of his depth, pitching his inept guile against the all-seeing wisdom of Angela. Even thinking he could outsmart his wily, intuitive wife with a web of deceit was naïve beyond naïve. Plan A would always have been a transparent non-starter. She would have smelled it a mile away. Anyone with half a brain could see that it would have to be 'Plan B', but we are talking about Chris. He trundled on with his thoughts, still juggling with what to say. In the end, it was all academic. For while he was deep in thought, wrestling with his complex conundrum, Angela spoke up.

"Are you seeing someone by any chance?", she asked calmly.

Chris was totally and utterly flummoxed. The blood drained from his face and his heart started beating like a drum. 'This woman must be bloody psychic', he thought.

"N-no. Why d-do you a-ask?", bumbled an unnerved and unconvincing Chris.

"Come on, Chris. I know you're lying. Look at you. You're a gibbering wreck. It's OK. I don't mind."

Chris was reduced to an amorphous mass. His spine had collapsed, his arms had fallen limp, his brain had completely clouded over. Angela looked straight at him.

"Do you think I'm stupid?".

Chris dared not answer, let alone look her in the eyes, having realised that some women seem to have the ability to pick these things up by some sort of sorcerous osmosis.

"Well, to be honest", he countered weakly, "and I was just about to tell you. There is someone I have met that I quite like."

Angela looked pleased with her powers of deduction. "That's fine, Chris. I hope you will be very happy. It had to happen to one of us first. But it does change things, you can see that. I think it makes it all the more imperative that you move out. I don't think you can live here like this and be out bonking someone else every other night."

Chris' relief was palpable. He poured out his plan in a galloping garble. "I have got somewhere in mind. I am going to share a place with George, that guy I know in the pub. You haven't met him, you'd like him, and there's this other guy we know. We are going to share".

"Well, Chris. You are quite the sly old dog. I see you've got it all planned. And when is all this happening?"

'I'm not sure", Chris said falteringly. "Probably in a few weeks. I was hoping to stay here at least until it comes available".

"Chris. This is our real test and I am not going to fail you. Of course you can stay. But I think the spare room might be more appropriate from now on. You are not jumping into my bed after rolling in the hay with someone else, that's for sure."

"It's not like that. But absolutely, yes. I completely get that. And you're not mad?"

The ever-logical Angela looked at him. "Chris, you are a great guy. But it is I who fell out of love with you. I know you could have gone on like this forever. That is not what I want. If you have met someone, have found somewhere to live and are happy, how can I complain? No, Chris, it's all for the best".

Chris, by now, had the blood back pulsating through his veins and his head had cleared. He went over to give Angela a hug. She froze.

"No, Chris. No need for that. Let's talk about it tomorrow night. Try and get home early. We could go to the Italian and sort everything out. Oh, and Chris, don't ever try and lie to me. It only makes you look stupid and I don't want to fall out with you."

"Thanks, Angela. When did I last tell you that you really are an incredible person? You'll be alright, won't you?".

She gave him a supremely confident smile, that of the strong woman that she was. She almost laughed at the question. When had Chris ever looked after her? But she would never want to humiliate him.

"Chris. Don't worry about me. I shall be fine", she replied simply.

"I'll go up and get the spare room ready then," stuttered Chris.

"Don't be silly. Not now. I'll get it ready tomorrow after work. Go to bed, Chris. I'll come up later. I need some time to myself."

"Of course, Angela. And thank you. You have been amazing. You are such a special girl."

Chris went upstairs and stretched out on his side of the bed. The relief from his tension made him relaxed once more. He tried to replay all that had happened that day but, in the shake of a lamb's tail, he fell asleep.

THURSDAY, JULY 18

David was up bright but later than as usual and sat patiently in the lounge with his morning tea. He was waiting until it was 9.30, the time that Hugo Carghill had said he arrived in the office. In the meantime, he allowed his birds to entertain him. A pair of impudent pied woodpeckers, who, David thought, had a vastly unfair advantage with their dexterity, pushed the little chaffinches and blue tits out of the way to hog the feeders, clinging on until they were satiated. The smaller birds had just reclaimed the food source when the time came to call the number on Hugo's card. It took a frustrating while to be answered. Eventually, a voice spoke.

"Hugo Carghill", the agent opened curtly.

"Hugo. David Nugent. Good morning. I hope you don't mind my ringing this early. I am calling about the apartment at Thames Tower. Not to beat about the bush, I would like to take it for a minimum of twelve months".

Hugo's tone immediately softened as the men discussed all the details, the price, the deposit, the utility charges, what was included and what was not. David asked if there could be any movement on the monthly rent and Hugo said he would talk to the owners, although he could not hang out much hope. Then he unsubtly dropped in a mention that other people were interested in the apartment, something that deadened any plans David had of taking a tough stance.

"Please see what you can do. Let me stress though, it is not a deal breaker". He realised that, by saying the last bit, he completely undermined any negotiating power he may have had. He baulked for a second when Hugo enquired who the occupants would be and concluded it would be best to play it down at this stage. He had pre-empted the question.

"The lease will be in my name solely if that's what you mean". He hoped that would suffice for now. "So, have I got it?". David then thought he would play Hugo at his own game. "I am looking at other places and would like to be reassured that you agree to my leasing it."

"Yes, basically, that is all fine. We shall have to do some background checks, I am sure you understand, and then you pay the deposit and it's yours. I assure you, Mr Nugent, we shall not let it to anyone else in the meantime. You can be at peace on that".

After a few minutes, they wound up the call. David sank back deep into his favourite chair and gazed out of the window at his little friends. The nimble finches and tits were in a fluttering frenzy, having totally reclaimed the feeders.

"You're going to have to learn to toughen up, little fellas. Life may not always be this easy. I am going to miss you guys", he sighed, "and I guess you are going to miss me".

He waited a while, glowing in the thrill of shortly sealing the deal on Thames Tower and thinking of the changes that were to come. His cottage amongst the trees deep in the lush woodland would be greatly missed. He had been happy there. This had been his sanctuary and as he looked around him in his modest home, he fully appreciated that more is not always better. The high-style life in the City, his large old family manor house and its glorious garden, all those ridiculously pampered holidays in five-star hotels, the new-car feel of a top of the range company car, they all amounted to nought if you were not happy, he thought. But now was his time. He just had to get through Monday. He was ready for the bruising in Court. He was after all a very wealthy man by most standards. But money in the bank did not matter as much to him as his rediscovered freedom. Yes, it seemed inevitable that he would lose half of his substantial savings in the legal mêlée, as Moira and her savage lawyers were hellbent in grabbing as much as they could with their opportunistic hands. Nevertheless, his half would still let him live in some comfort. He knew Monday was to be Moira's big day. She had always wanted her day in Court and that day had arrived. He laughed an ironic laugh as he thought how she must be wetting herself in excitement at hauling him over the coals. His hopes lay with the Sophie, his young, accomplished, and classy solicitor. All bets were on her.

He picked up his phone to ring George. As he told him the good news about the apartment, his new flatmate went into raptures at the prospect of their post-divorce life that they had so enterprisingly redefined.

George was over the moon. "Who would of thought that Sweeney Todd would walk into the Wellington and, within a few days, would turn our lives upside down. Thanks David. This is all down to you".

David shrugged off the compliment and went on to explain that he would not be coming to London for a couple of days and mentioned his trip to Court on Monday.

"You were spared this torture. You would have been battling it out with Kate by now, wouldn't you? Outstanding, you are so bloody lucky. I wish they were all like Kate", he said, with genuine regret in his voice.

"Yes, she is special. I can never be angry with her. She may be an explosive ball of Spanish fire, but she has the biggest heart of anyone I know. Damn pity I couldn't be enough for her though. To be honest, a Latin enchantress like Kate probably needs someone a tad more exciting than a middle-aged Granby to keep her flame alight," George said in self-deprecation.

"Never mind, old boy, you know what I always say, the best is yet to come", David said supportively. "You may soon meet some young, attractive, bright young thing who likes the same funny little things you like, including the odd pint in the Wellington. By the way, talking about bright young things, will you tell Chris the news? You'll be seeing him in the pub tonight, I assume?".

"No. Not tonight. He wants to get home early. I think he and Angela are having a heart to heart and they are going for a chinwag tonight. It's a rare pub-free night in for me. I'll have to take up crochet or something."

"Not where we are going, you won't. There'll be no time for that. Anyway, dangerous sports like knitting are banned in Thames Tower. I'll ring Chris then. He'll be over the moon."

He was about to ring off when George suddenly cried out,

"David, I almost forgot. I meant to say, it's not too early start thinking of the advert for our new flatmate, is it? No harm in getting it ready for the moment we move in."

David concurred. "Great idea. Do you want to have a go? I know you'd be the best at this, being from the advertising field".

"Will do. No problem. Something along the lines of: 'Room available, only apply if you are female, drop dead gorgeous, frustrated and rich. No divorcees'. How does that sound?".

"Bang on, George. Actually, I am starting to worry about you. I didn't know the old George, but it looks like we are all in for a roller-coaster ride. Go for it. But please let me see it first. I'm not sure you're joking".

"Good luck on Monday", encouraged George.

"Thanks. I'll try and ring you afterwards and give you the run down. You may have to lend me a shirt as I probably won't have one on my back by then."

Chris left work early, skipped the pub and headed home. Tonight was their 'big night'. Angela had booked a table for 7.00pm at the small, cosy Italian restaurant around the corner, somewhere she loved. As he arrived home just after 6.30, in the doorway stood Angela, looking a million dollars. He had not seen her like that forever. Her naturally curly hair had been straightened into a chic bob. Her face that was usually make-up free was adorned with coral lipstick, blusher, mascara, eyeliner, the works. She was wearing a stylish, knee-length, V-neck dress with a beige suede jacket draped over her shoulders.

"Welcome home", she said as she stood seductively in front of him.

"You look terrific, Angela. Absolutely amazing".

"Well, I am going on a date".

"With me, I hope. I had better smarten myself up then". He started to go upstairs. From below, Angela shouted up.

"I have put some clothes out for you. I don't want you wearing those stupid red trousers". Chris had no idea she felt this way about his favourite chinos.

"Thank you. But I thought you liked them. I think they're cool", Chris shouted back.

"They're ridiculous, that's what they are". Angela had withheld her feelings for months and now felt openly empowered. His liaison behind her back had put her in the driver's seat.

"I'll get you a glass of wine. I've started already. I'm on my second".

Chris then noticed that someone had left the light on in the spare room. Peeking through the half open door, in the light of a small bedside lamp, he saw that the bed was made up, with some fawn trousers and other clothes laying on it. This was it. He had finally been banished from the marital bed. No more back-to-back nocturnal, sterile co-existence. But far from being disconsolate at this landmark moment, he just shaved and got dressed for his night out. Chris mused how funny it was that, in all these recent years, she had made no effort at all. Now that they were breaking up and she finds out he is seeing someone else, abracadabra, this transformation. He had never had a very good understanding of women. He reasoned that it all had nothing to do with him, that she had just fallen out of love. It certainly was not any of his fault. But, in truth, it had everything to do with him. Chris, as ever, never quite got it.

A quarter of an hour later, he emerged, clean shaved and hair combed. He was wearing the smart denim-blue shirt she had given him for Christmas, the light brown chinos she had bought him for his birthday in February and had a white sweater over his shoulders, another birthday gift. She had certainly tried hard to smarten him up over the years, with little success.

They walked round to the restaurant, chatting like they had not done for ages. She told him things he never knew about her job in the bookshop and he listened attentively to every word. It was as if they were going out in those early days once again. When they entered Antonio's Trattoria, the eponymous owner greeted them.

"Signorina Angela. How are you? It has been too long. We have missed you". He then turned to Chris. "And welcome, sir. I have your table ready".

They were seated at a small table around the cliché raffia chianti bottle, draped in multi-coloured wax with a red candle protruding from the top. Just like the cartoon, he thought. They went through the menu. She selected the seafood risotto, which she always loved, while he went for chicken parmesan.

The wine was ordered and brought to the table. This was not yet the signal for battle to commence, so they continued their small talk, with Chris enquiring more about the bookshop and even asking about some of her friends, the one's whose names he could recall. But, of course, there was to be no battle. Thanks to Angela's mature sense of reason, the evening, under her tutelage and direction, was destined to be a lesson in civility and restraint. It was not long before the food arrived and Angelo himself came over, armed with a statuesque pepper grinder. Formalities over, Angela opened her questioning of Chris.

"When is your new place ready?", she asked her husband.

"Oh. A few weeks, no more".

"What's it like?", Angela enquired.

Chris proceeded to downplay every aspect of it. "Not bad", he said and by the time he had finished you would have thought it was a very ordinary pad in a very average part of London.

They eased gently into what they were both going to do. Chris told her more about his new job that he was starting on Monday and she explained to him, in the vaguest terms, what her plans were. It was not long before she brought out her big gun.

"Chris. About the house. I have given it a lot of thought. I would like to remain there". Chris went rigid, a roll of spaghetti dangling off his fork, in suspension halfway on its way to his mouth. Was this all about to go belly up? he thought to himself.

"Don't look so worried. I have a proposal to put to you. This is my suggestion. We have a fair sized mortgage, right? I'll put it all in my name and Dad will pay you your half share in the equity we have in the house. I've been talking to Dad and he is going to lend me some money to pay you. He said very kindly that he had saved a bit for a rainy day and that eventually it was all going to come to me anyway. So, I can borrow from him, give it to you and pay him back over time. As much as I can afford each month he said. It is so kind of him, don't you think?".

He paused and spoke to himself in his head. 'Kind of him, indeed. Her Dad never liked me and obviously cannot wait to see the back of me'.

Chris was not known for his business acumen. After considering the idea for a minute, all he could think of was a big cheque coming his way. He could not find a single argument against it.

"That sounds like good to me. I should be out within a month and, as the new place is furnished, I don't want anything in the house. I'll just take my clothes and be gone".

"Oh, Chris, you don't have to go dramatic about it. Don't you think it's the best solution? Honestly? You can even have the car".

"No, what would I do with it? You keep it here and if you ever sell it or trade it in you can bung me a few quid. I can't that it's likely, but if I do need to borrow it for the weekend, would that be OK?".

"Of course", appeased Angela. "Anytime".

They then agreed that he could stay until his apartment came available, that under no circumstances would there be any fighting between them, legal or otherwise, and that they would keep in touch. Angela suggested that they should meet up for an occasional lunch or dinner just to see how each other is getting along and, above all else, to stay friends. Chris readily consented, agreeing that a civilised get-together now and again so that they can talk face to face through this transition period was good idea. This was his way of keeping things harmonious.

The free-flowing conversation continued genially for an hour. It was like the old days. He thought of all that time in recent months they had sat in front of the TV in silence and here they were chatting away like best friends. Funny old thing, divorce, Chris pondered. He did not have the wherewithal to realise that not all break-ups were like this, far from it. In truth, he had Angela to thank for the triumph of reason over confrontation, but he was unlikely ever to see it that objectively.

They went home happy, got into their separate beds and each looked to the future, both dreaming of what was to be.

MONDAY, JUNE 24

"Only bloody Moira would pick the first day of Wimbledon to get me into Court", said David to himself. Outside racing, this fortnight was the highlight of his sporting calendar. He loved his tennis and, although he had not hit a ball for quite a while, it had always been his favourite game to play since his early schooldays. Today, however, he was heading to his own personal 'Match of the Day' on his very own Centre Court, the Divorce Court in central London. His solicitor, Sophie Cavendish was waiting in the lobby of the large modern building and they sat together as she ran through the procedure with her client. The hearing was mostly for the Judge to settle the contentious distribution of who gets what, to adjudicate on the other side's demands and to achieve what David and the fractious Moira had been patently unable to do between themselves, to agree on the division of their marital assets in a fair and equitable way.

David rated Sophie highly. She was only 32 and yet had a highly impressive blend of young intellect and mature authority about her, while still managing to maintain her femininity throughout. Professionally, she was excellent at her job. And in David's eye, she had it all and he had always had the ability to spot talent. To be truthful, he was also particularly drawn to the manner in which she deported herself, with a rare grace and elegance, her shining, silken fair hair crowning her extremely shapely figure. Beautiful and smart, the perfect combination in David's book. She always dressed immaculately, complementing her enticing good looks with style and panache. She was David's kind of woman. Right now, however, it was not her comely allure that was all-important to him. It was her legal expertise that he was relying on.

"Moira is asking for a lot", she counselled him. "She will play the victim, blame you for everything and want you to pay handsomely. We can expect some serious ranting from their side. But this will not be decided on a punitive basis. For the Judge, her throwing out accusations won't mean a thing, because there is no causal element in divorce these days. Who did what will be of no interest to the Judge. It is irrelevant. It is just the financials that are on the table, not behavioural issues. We shall not be discussing the custody of children or anything like that today. Just the money side of things. We have to push back hard on what they are asking. Leave it to me. Don't say a word. I think we are quite lucky having Justice Roberts, though. She is very fair in my opinion. She..."

"She?", interrupted David. "She's not another bloody man-hater, is she? The legal world seems packed with them."

"No, she's fine. I have been before her several times and I think she is, if anything, slightly down on rampaging, avaricious, 'poor me' women who play the blame game. And she certainly has one of those before her today".

Without further ado, the usher asked them to come through. The courtroom was not large, classroom size, with a similar cold feel. Its soullessness was mostly due to the lack of daylight and the characterless fluorescent lighting. The Judge's chair before them was empty. In the front row to the right, he saw steely-eyed Moira and her grim-faced solicitor, Hilary Hicks, a singularly unattractive figure, the sort of sexless woman David could not stand, the polar opposite of his elegant champion, Sophie. Ms Hicks, as she likes to be called, had short angry hair, pointed features and she wafted an air of superiority about her, as if she had a permanent smell under her nose.

The Judge then emerged. Those before her stood up respectfully, waited for her to be settled, then retook their own seats.

"Here we go," David whispered to Sophie.

Justice Roberts, on first sight, looked like one of the very smart, middle class, middle aged, straightforward businesswomen that used to cross his path in the City. He was familiar with women like her. 'She looks OK to me', thought David, obeying his lawyer's instruction to keep quiet.

"Good morning. Mr and Mrs Nugent. Ms Cavendish. Ms Hicks. Let me say at the outset, I am sorry that we are here together today," said the Judge, in a kindly, conciliatory manner. "It is always my hope that litigants can resolve these matters between themselves and that my services are not called upon. However, it appears you have not been able to achieve any sort of agreement between you, which is unfortunate. We are here today solely to sort out how we divide the marital assets. I have read the Petitioner's claims and I must make it clear at the start of these proceedings that I do find them excessive. I think today there must be some tempering of expectations on the Petitioner's side." She looked directly down at Ms Hicks.

Sophie, unnoticed, gave David the most subtle hint of a smile. It could not have started better.

"Now, Ms Hicks, would you like to proceed in justifying some of these items".

Moira's lawyer then went through a litany of the hardships her client had suffered, how she had tirelessly brought up two children, how she had given up a successful career to do so, while the Judge stared down at her papers, completely unmoved.

"Yes, Ms Hicks, that is all very well, but may we please stick to the business in hand." The Judge showed impatience with her predictable sob story. She continued dispassionately. "May we start with the claim for maintenance."

"Certainly, your Honour. Mrs Nugent has been a devoted housewife for many years and we think that a claim of £50,000 per annum is perfectly reasonable for a homemaker and mother who has committed herself selflessly to her role."

Sophie interjected. "Your Honour. May I respectfully point out that Mr Nugent has recently lost his job and is currently unemployed. His circumstances are far different from what they were".

Ms Hicks countered. "I understand that to be true, your Honour, but I am sure he did it deliberately and that he will find another well-paid post as soon as this is over".

The Judge responded directly. "Are you? That is a most disparaging accusation, Ms Hicks. Can you then tell be how you can be quite so certain?".

"Well, I cannot be absolutely certain, of course, but it would seem in keeping with Mr Nugent's character."

Justice Roberts paused a second, giving the lawyer a disapproving look.

"Personal accusations of that nature have no place in my Court, Ms Hicks".

At that point, Sophie jumped to her feet. "Your Honour. If I may. I think I should make it clear to the Court that Mrs Nugent, before her marriage, had been a qualified hairdresser, a good one by all accounts, and had her own thriving salon up to the time she had her first child".

The Judge looked at Moira's feisty lawyer.

"Is that the case, Ms Hicks?"

"Yes, your Honour. However, that was a considerable time ago".

"Nevertheless, Mrs Nugent is still relatively young and presumably it would not take long for her to rediscover her old skills. Would you not agree?"

Ms Hicks could not reply at first, but then said, "She is not that young, your Honour. It would be hard for her to get back into the work force now". The judge gave no reaction and continued.

"Next item is the matter of Form E, each party's income and assets, including savings and investments. I am aware that pensions are a contentious area and we shall come to that in a minute. The usual procedure is 50/50 but, in the light of Mr Nugent coming into the marriage with over 95% of these assets and taking into account the length of the marriage, I consider that a 60/40 division in the favour of the respondent would be more equitable. Times have changed, Ms Hicks."

Ms Hicks objected. "Mrs Nugent has run the home for many years, your Honour. Her dedication to family cannot be denied and must be taken into account. Mrs Nugent has sacrificed her career and elected not to work, preferring to be a selfless stay-at-home mother rather than to continue her hair styling business".

Justice Roberts seemed to ponder the issue. All the time, the grim frown on Moira's face indicated the fury that was brewing up inside her. She had never envisaged it going this way. David had rarely seen her with such suppressed anger. In the normal run of things, the ticking bomb inside her would have exploded by now.

"She was indeed in a privileged position. But let's move on. The pension fund. Ms Hicks, your client wants 80% of Mr

Nugent's fund. I fail to see how this could be considered in any way reasonable".

Moira's lawyer set off at her most bullish. "Mr Nugent has amassed a considerable pension fund, while my client has none as the homemaker. She has reasonably assumed that future support from her husband would be assured while she reared their two children. We believe division should be on the basis of Mrs Nugent receiving an equal pension annuity as Mr Nugent when each reaches retirement age, not the same fund, I stress, but the same annual pay-out. We have attached, therefore, a report from an actuary that projects that, for this to happen, Mrs Nugent, as a woman, needs a significantly larger pot to receive the same annuity as Mr Nugent on retirement and we have divided the current fund on the basis of what sum would be needed for Mrs Nugent to gain parity, assuming Mr Nugent continues to contribute into the fund at the same level during his working life. We have calculated the sum he would be expected to have accumulated at retirement and divided it into two amounts that would give each party the identical pension dividend. And my client's figure equates to 80% of his current pot, which we would like transferred forthwith".

"Ms Cavendish?", said the Judge, inviting her objections to their reasoning. Sophie rose confidently and addressed the Court.

"Your Honour, my client came into the marriage with a substantial pension pot already prudently secured, while the Petitioner had made the choice not to contribute into any fund, even though she was working full time and had been enjoying some considerable financial success. Ms Hicks also makes some very bold assumptions. The Petitioner's argument assumes that Mr Nugent will continue to pay into his fund at the same rate for, say, another 15 or so years, and then, they say, he could claim not half the fund but only an equal dividend, which incidentally means he will have a much smaller pot than that of Mrs Nugent. What if he decides not to convert it all into an annuity and takes some of it out in cash? He will have been short-changed. And yet, the Petitioner wants her share now, while Mr Nugent, they demand, has to work for his lesser share and no account is taken of possible unpredictable events or setbacks. They propose a disparate division of funds, which they demand to be settled today, based and calculated on this questionable future assumption of what they say the fund would look like when my client hits retirement age. The Petitioner seeks to establish her share solely on the assumption that 'Mr Nugent continues to contribute into the fund at the same level during his working life'. That is simply a wild conjecture. However, in truth, the facts are at the present time very different. The Respondent is currently not working and there is no sign of his being able to re-establish the same remunerative employment as he enjoyed before. City life is a young person's world. And to suggest that Mr Nugent left his last post deliberately is most disingenuous. Does that all seem fair to you, your Honour? We contest that it is anything but fair".

The Judge paused again, appearing to have sympathy with this argument and giving the frustrated Ms Hicks and her seething client another dubious glare.

"Let's move on to the family home. Now you are asking for your client to keep it until the children are 18, another 12 years, when it will be sold and the revenue shared equally, is that right?"

"Yes, your Honour", said the Moira's stony-faced lawyer.

Judge Roberts immediately challenged that idea. "Do you believe that the children would not be safe, happy and well-catered for in a smaller house?"

"But this is their home, the only house they have known", Ms Hicks pleaded.

"That's as maybe, but do your client and their two children really need a six-bedroomed home to survive and prosper? May I point out that it is not the house that makes a home but the love and support of the parents, both parents".

Again, Ms Hicks fell silent, before she repeated weakly, "But it is their family home."

"Let's move on. School fees. I understand the children go to the same private school, with total fees of £36,000 a year. Ms Hicks, you and your client wish Mr Nugent to pay these. This, I am afraid, is something on which I cannot rule. The choice of education, that is, in this case, where Mr and Mrs Nugent decide to send their children to school, is entirely a matter for the parents, exclusively their choice, especially when they happen to choose a fee-paying establishment over State education. I would recommend that the parties share the costs if they are both agreed that is the education they select. I cannot rule on this matter. Now, what's next. I see, Ms Cavendish that your client has three racehorses." David perked up as his adored Golden Oak became the next issue. He knew Moira would do anything to take away something he valued so highly and enjoyed so much.

"Yes, your Honour, two as yet unraced geldings and a three-year-old, Golden Oak, that is having his first season racing".

"Now, Ms Hicks. I see that you are asking for £60,000 as half the value of these horses. May I ask how you arrived at that figure?".

"Your Honour, the two unnamed, unraced horses cost £12,000 and £8,000 respectively. They were bought with family money at the sales so that is a matter of public record. The other one, Golden Oak is a very promising three-year-old and has won three races already, so we put a value of £100,000 on him".

"Ms Cavendish. Your thoughts", said the judge.

"I am afraid I cannot agree. Golden Oaks' value is a matter of conjecture and is unsubstantiated. The Petitioner has picked a figure out of the air, inflated in her favour. Any horse could get sick or go lame tomorrow, or worse. Unfortunately, for your argument, my client would have to sell him this afternoon in tip-top condition to determine his current value and we have no idea what he might fetch at an auction. He may fail the veterinary inspection. Or, if he went to auction, it might be a quiet day at the sales with low bidding. It is not black and white. We just cannot make these assumptions and pick numbers out of the air like this. We contend that the Petitioner's conjecture is wildly exaggerated."

The case went on in this vein for almost an hour. Moira was getting more and more flustered. She was not used to someone questioning her demands. Her philosophy had always been that whoever shouted the loudest won the argument. At one point, she lost control and stood up, yelling at Justice Roberts.

"You're on his side. This is all a joke. I've had enough of this. My children and I need more", Moira cried out, petulantly. She was immediately admonished by the Judge, who reminded her in a patronising tone to behave. Justice Roberts made it clear to her that she, as the sitting Judge, was on neither party's side. Moira ignored the reprimand with a huff and a puff, in her usual dismissive way. David was, by now, enjoying himself in his silence, knowing that Moira was doing a magnificent self-destruction job, without any help from him. As the session drew to an end, the unflappable Justice Roberts, after five minutes of contemplation and jotting things down on her pad, addressed the assembled litigants.

"I have listened to both sides and I am prepared to direct an Order after careful deliberation. However, it would be far preferable if the two parties could leave the courtroom for an hour to discuss between yourselves a settlement to which both sides can agree, taking into consideration my comments today. Are you both happy to do that? If no agreement can be reached, I shall be compelled to make those decisions for you". Both lawyers voiced their agreement. The Judge continued. "However, Ms Hicks and Mrs Nugent, I want to make it clear again that I find your claims generally far in excess of what is, in my opinion, fair and equitable. Divorce is not about hitting the jackpot or winning the lottery. I would like to see a much more realistic maintenance payment that takes into account Mrs Nugent's reasonable needs as well as Mr Nugent's current state of employment, or lack of it. I note also that Mrs Nugent clearly has the ability to return to work for a considerable number of years to come. To be a working mother is not an unusual status in this day and age and you are fortunate that, in your chosen profession, Mrs Nugent, you can return to the workforce without further training and make your work times flexible to accommodate the needs of the growing children. With this in mind, I would think a figure of more like £15,000 to £25,000 per annum should be appropriate, and that only until the children reach the age of 18. I shall leave child maintenance to you, but the guidelines recommend around £5,000 per child per annum."

Moira shouted out again. "My children need more than that to live on. This is an utter joke".

"Mrs Nugent. I shall not tell you again. This is a Court of Law and I shall not permit such disrespect. One more outburst and you will be asked to leave."

The Judge then added, "And, Mrs Nugent, they are not just YOUR children, you share them with the Respondent. Please, permit me to continue uninterrupted. Now, the pension fund. I am swayed by Ms Cavendish's logical and persuasive comments on the baseless assumptions being made in the Petitioner's case and find your argument, Ms Hicks, frankly absurd. There should indeed be a pension sharing arrangement, but you must take into consideration that Mr Nugent brought a considerable fund into the marriage, that Mrs Nugent chose not to contribute into a pension scheme prior to the marriage, even though she had a successful business, that the marriage not was unduly long and that Mrs Nugent has the capability in the future of earning her own income, thereby contributing to her own pension fund. In the light of all these circumstances, I would have thought a figure nearer 20% was appropriate. On the matter of the house, I have no doubt. I believe that it should be sold as soon as practicable, with the funds divided equally. Wherever possible, the law prefers a clean break. I have also given some thought to the horses and cannot agree at all with your assumed valuation of Golden Oak. How much did Golden Oak cost a year ago, Ms Cavendish?".

The lawyer consulted her client in a mumbled voice.

"£14,000, your honour".

"This is, I admit, a moot point. Nevertheless, I have listened carefully to Ms Cavendish's argument and feel that the only certified value is that of the purchase price, which was recorded fairly recently. The animal is still very young and anything can happen. We cannot determine here his success or failure. Racing is a notably risky game, without any guarantees, so I suggest a total figure of £34,000 for the three horses, meaning a reasonable settlement for the Petitioner would be £17,000 rather than 60,000".

"I shall leave the other assets, including cars and household contents, to you. I hope though that you can reach agreement and return to me in this Court within the hour. If no settlement can be reached, I shall have to direct my own Order".

With that, she got up, everyone rose and she left.

"You were brilliant", whispered David as he and Sophie moved outside. "What now?".

"We find a room, they find a room and then we lawyers shuttle backwards and forwards trying to get to a settlement along the lines of those that the Judge put forward. Well, actually, I, as Respondent solicitor, do the running. They are really on the back foot now because, if they don't play reasonably, they know pretty clearly what the judge will order."

Although David was beside himself with joy at the way this was all going, he was just able to hide his elation, trying to appear as professional as his cool, calm counsel. The usher showed them to a small room where they sat down and wrote down their idea of a deal, based mostly on Judge Robert's 'summing up', which was better than they would ever have dared to have come up with themselves. Then Sophie disappeared. David sat on his own, contemplating how well it was all going, especially with the horses. Sophie was gone a good fifteen minutes and came back with a curiously expressionless face.

"How did it go?", David nervously enquired.

"Predictably they want more than we are proposing. Maintenance £25,000, pension 35%, 50/50 on liquid assets, the house for 5 years then sold, we agree child maintenance and they have conceded the horses. I think she felt properly rebuked on that one. Oh, and they won't pay towards school fees. Your wife says she doesn't care if they have to go to the local state school. What do you think about that one, David?"

"The Judge made it clear she won't get involved and Moira is calling my bluff. But if it was my last penny, I would spend it on their education. Also, they are stable and happy there, and I would hate to have to move them with everything that is going on at their home".

"So?". Sophie looked for her instruction.

"Try once more but, if they won't budge, I'll take the school fees. I am paying now anyway. You can always use that as a bargaining tool. My children always come first, before any houses or horses."

"Got it. OK. I'll do my best."

"So, what do we do now?", enquired David.

"You trust me, that's what you do. I think they know they are on the back foot. Let's not rush. The clock is ticking. If they go back to Court without a deal, they could end up in an even worse position for not being cooperative. We have to be back in Court in about half an hour. Let's sit here and have a nice cup of tea for ten minutes while they sweat it out."

David liked her style. He poured two cups of tea from the vacuum flask. They talked generally for a few minutes. Sophie then took a couple of slow sips before eventually looking at her watch, bracing herself and saying, "Let's do this". She sprung up and out of the room. David was impressed. Another ten minutes went by. David paced the floor like an expectant father until, all of a sudden, the door flew open.

"OK. I think you are going to be happy. Well, you bloody well should be. Maintenance 17,500 a year until the children are 18. Pension 23% - don't ask me how we arrived at that silly number. Assets split 60/40 in your favour. House put on the market immediately and revenue from the sale shared equally. You keep the horses but have to buy her out for 16,000. And your child support stays at 5,000 each per annum until the children are 18. I have failed you on one thing though. They wouldn't budge on school fees. But you did say you were prepared to pay them. I had to give them one little victory. Sorry about that. Do we have a deal?".

"Of course. And don't worry, I am genuinely happy to pay the school fees. You, Ms Cavendish, are a genius. A bloody genius". David beamed.

"And one other thing you'll be pleased about".

"What's that?" said David.

"They are both really pissed off".

"Brilliant. That makes me very happy". His beamed smile broadened.

With that and a chuckle, they both went back into the courtroom and sat down. Moira and Ms Hicks had faces as long as his horses'. As David sat there, he imagined that the Judge might walk in and say dourly, "Have you reached a verdict of which you are all agreed?".

Suddenly, she entered. David knew he was going to enjoy the next few minutes and, while he wanted to stare at Moira's face, relishing her defeat, he resisted the temptation.

"Ms Hicks, do you have you an agreement with the other party?".

"Yes, your Honour".

"Ms Cavendish, are you in agreement on all the matters apposite to this case?"

"Yes, your Honour." Sophie too was quietly enjoying her opposite number's discomfort.

"Excellent. I congratulate you all. May I hear what has been agreed?".

Ms Hicks read through the whole package and the Judge appeared mildly pleased with it all and with her own day's work.

"Very good. You have all done well. I am pleased we have been able to conclude matters today," she announced. "All that remains is to wish you, Mr and Mrs Nugent, the very best of luck in the future. Thank you". With that, she stood up once more, as did the others, and she left.

Sophie leaned into David's ear. "Best we hold back here a second". He had learned to obey her orders. They sat and watched Moira start to take her exit, visibly devastated. Ms Hicks gruffly gathered up her papers with the same hangdog face. No words were spoken. Alone in the room at last, David and Sophie could talk in their normal voices. He put his arms round her and just said "you were brilliant, absolutely brilliant".

"Thank you, David. A team effort. Fancy a quick drink?" she asked.

"On one condition. I'm paying". They crossed the road to a small, dark pub and he ordered her a well-earned gin and tonic and a welcome pint of bitter for himself.

As she sipped their drinks and replayed the proceedings, he asked if there was anything else to worry about.

"Everything is good. No need to worry. We did really well today…"

"You did", cut in David.

"Well, in truth, Justice Roberts did. I shall speak to Hilary Hicks tomorrow morning. I am sure she won't be a happy girl, not after Moira has had a go at her".

"If she is a girl. That's a huge assumption".

Sophie continued in a more professional manner. "We should have the decree nisi very soon and it will only be a matter of a few more weeks until the decree absolute casts off your chains. You'll be a single man again".

"That is amazing. I cannot thank you enough, Sophie. You have been just brilliant".

"My pleasure. I am pleased it all worked out so well for you". She paused for a second or two.

"David", she added in a more tentative voice, "Now that you are a free man, I was wondering if you were doing anything a week on Saturday?".

This was totally unexpected and he immediately wondered what was coming next.

"No, I have the children this weekend, so I have no plans".

"Do you fancy going to the Women's Final Day on Centre Court at Wimbledon? One of my partners has invited me and a guest and it would be lovely if you could come with me, a nice way to celebrate on a different kind of court".

"Sophie, that would be fabulous. Are you serious? Of course, I'd love to come. You know how I love tennis".

"Me too. I try and play every week down at Roehampton. It's a 'yes' then?".

"Very much so. I could think of nothing better than seeing a final and taking in a few Pimms and strawberries. And spending a day with you, of course. You just can't leave courts alone for one second, can you".

She had heard that pun so many times, but still managed to produce a polite chuckle.

"How about we meet at Gatwick and then I drive you up there. Is that OK? This is my treat. It will have to be quite early, around ten at the latest, I think. It can take quite a while to get into the car parks and we are having lunch there. Ten it is then. But of course we shall speak before then. You have my mobile number. I'll keep you informed of how things progress on the legal front, but I think it is fairly routine from here on. Now, I am really sorry. I have to get back to the office. Congratulations again. We've had a good day".

"A brilliant day. All down to you, Sophie". With that, she smiled, turned on her expensive heels and left. David looked up at the Almighty in the heavens and said to himself, "I have no bloody idea what you are playing at up there. You give me years and years of hell and then, suddenly, you like me again. Keep it up, old son. We could start being really pally. Who knows, the way this is all going you might even see me in church soon". He could not stop himself clenching his fist and muttering under his breath, "Brilliant. Brilliant. Brilliant...". It was all over. It may have been a Pyrrhic victory, losing a significant slice of his hard-earned savings, but he knew it could have been so much worse and he could now move on with his life. That was the most important thing. He compared the euphoric feeling to that of a sad songbird, who, a century ago, might have been forlornly trapped in a small Victorian cage for the amusement of its captors, but who is suddenly set free again, spreading its wings to fly once more, to sing and feed with his flock in liberty and peace.

So, everything in the Thames Tower garden was rosy. George was ending his marriage amicably and with far more money than he had anticipated. He had never wanted a fight with his lovely Kate and, thanks to her sweet soul, a Court battle had been avoided. He, more than anyone, looked forward to moving out of that cramped, dreary flat and into the plush new home, which was much more in keeping with his style.

While David had taken a financial hit, it was not hugely painful and he was happy, having always put a far greater value on his re-discovered freedom. It could have been so much worse without the understanding of the Judge and the tough negotiating skills of the admirable and adorable Sophie, with whom he now, miraculously, had a Wimbledon date in just a few days' time. More crucially, however, he would be spending this coming weekend with the two people he loved the most, his children, Jess and Robbie.

Chris was amazed, confused even, at how things had worked out so well. Without any call on his dubious diplomatic skills, he had been unwittingly steered away from any legal stormy waters into a sea of calm by the ever-sensible, measured Angela.

Somehow, he had even outpunched his weight and persuaded the beautiful Bonnie to have some more dates with him.

And all three of them had this incredible, glitzy apartment to move into. Each man was transfixed by the prospect of those summer sunsets, sipping wine on the balcony, surrounded by panoramic views of the Thames as it rolled gently by. A new life was about to begin. Their vision was about to become their reality. But there was still one thing that needed to be done. They had to find their new flatmate. What could possibly go wrong?

CHAPTER FOUR
FINDING A MATE

TUESDAY, SEPTEMBER 3

Over two months had passed and the three companions were now officially installed in their luxurious new home. The move into the new apartment had been relatively trouble-free, although the lease had taken longer to sort out than they had hoped but David had always been in complete control. He had dealt with the deposit, signed all the paperwork and been handed the keys to Thames Tower without a hitch. As a result of his assumed responsibilities and, more relevantly, his greater payment, he had also been granted the privilege of being the first to choose which room, or rooms, were his. He had gallantly chosen what were arguably the two least appealing rooms, the two slightly smaller ones on the right, although there was not a great deal of difference between any of them. The other two flatmates had drawn lots for first pick on the others and George had won. Both then selected where they would be sleeping for the next year, leaving one room unoccupied, awaiting the arrival of the as yet unknown fourth member of the clan.

George, the marketing man, had been the ultimate professional in placing the advertisement for the new recruit. He had done his research and was confident that he had found the perfect internet site on which to place it in order to reach the sort of people they were targeting. However, after David had been asked to check the wording of the ad, a little editing was required and his censor's pen crossed out the typically George line about 'no uneducated or uninteresting people need apply'. There had been a number of responses already, though not as many as they had expected. They were not unhappy with these as they deduced that the high rent had deterred what George called the 'riff-raff'.

The three together had decided that the best way forward was to select just a handful of candidates for interviews and send the others a prepared rejection letter. They then got together at the Wellington one night and sat around the same table where they had gone through those estate agent details some weeks earlier. George had printed out all the applications and they checked through every single one, whittling them down to their top five. Unsurprisingly, no-one voted for the Vietnamese fish and chip shop owner from Hackney, the Halal butcher in the Edgware Road or the former brickie from Hartlepool who had just won the best part of a million pounds on the Lottery. In the end, the leading contenders emerged – a Scottish semi-pro golfer with a three handicap, a singer/musician who had toured throughout Europe, a grande dame who had once acted with the Royal Shakespeare Company, a newly divorced man from Preston who had only recently sold his engineering firm and a finance specialist with his own company in Mill Hill. George, the chief marketeer, spoke first.

"We need to get moving for two reasons. One, because they will find somewhere else if we don't act fast and, two, we need the money. We are all paying for an empty room right now and that's expensive. So, David, what do you think?".

David showed no hesitation. "I think you're right. We should get them in as soon as possible. It's logical that we should do it at the apartment, so that we can show them round. It's now Tuesday so why not go for Thursday night? If they're keen, they'll turn up. Chris, can you be home for 7pm?".

"As long as it isn't a Friday, I should be OK. That's the busy night, getting ready for Saturday's paper. It's not been a particularly busy week, so I am sure I can get away early for one night".

"OK", said David. "Let's do it on Thursday at 7. George, do you want to contact them or shall I?".

"I'll do it. I'll send them an email tonight. What do you think, should we offer them tea or should I get some beers in?", enquired George.

"That is a good point. We might as well discuss how we run the interviews now. I think no alcohol. I am not sure if they need anything at all, just some bottles of water, perhaps? Get some extra beers in anyway. We'll definitely need them ourselves after five interviews". They all agreed.

"Shouldn't we jot down some areas that we want to ask about, while we are all here?", Chris asked.

"Good idea." David responded. "Chris, could you get a pad from Gerry, please?".

They then proceeded to go through all their personal preferences, their absolute and often totally politically incorrect 'no-nos'. "No woke lefties", insisted Chris. David and George were more scientific, saying they had to probe each candidate's finances to make sure they could afford it, assess their employment status and find out their situation with any partners, wives, exes or children. There was a streak of snobbery in all of them and they were worried that the 'wrong sort of person' would be spending time lounging around the apartment. Chris was less rational and made it clear that his criteria were simple, no-one who was ugly, fat, or had bad teeth. 'Fat lasses take up too much space' was his reasoned argument. The others looked nervous as he then piped up again with another idea.

"I think we need a secret sign between us so that, if we don't like them, we can communicate it. There's no point in an interview dragging on for ages if we are all thinking 'no way' from the moment they walk in the door".

George considered this a sound idea and complied with his logic. "Actually, Christopher, that is a good point. We should do something subtle or say something cryptic to let the others know our feelings, good or bad".

"How about we scratch the top of our heads if we like them and our necks if we don't?", said Chris.

"They'll think we have bloody fleas or head lice in the apartment if we all start scratching away". David responded. "How about this. If we really don't like them, we mention something about, say, food. If we do like them, we drop into the conversation something about pets. Is that obtuse enough?".

George thought that David's suggestion was the better idea of the two, and, as no-one had a more creative one, they agreed and moved on.

"We should do it around the dining room table, at half hour intervals. Does that sound right?", George proposed.

"Perfect", approved David. "That's it then. Well done, everybody. Let's all be at the apartment by 6.30 on Thursday and I propose that George should be in the chair".

"No, David, that is definitely your job". David immodestly accepted the task.

THURSDAY, SEPTEMBER 5

The first interview was to be at 7pm and by 6.45 the three flatmates had prepared the expensive glass dining room table as if in a boardroom, with pads and pencils taken from Chris's office laid out before the interrogators and bottles of water at the centre. David would sit at the end, flanked by his two colleagues, while the interviewee would be placed at the other end, facing the 'Chairman'.

"What we need above all else is a bloody drink", Chris helpfully pointed out with ten minutes to go. He grabbed three beers from out of the fridge. "What's the sign we use again, you know, if we don't like them?".

David restated the rules. "If you don't like them, we say something about food. If you do, it's something about pets".

"Like pets, don't like food. Like pets, don't like food", Chris mumbled to himself.

At precisely 7pm, the concierge called up. David answered. "A Mr Johnson to see you, sir".

The instruction "Send him up" was given.

When the flat bell rang, they were all in position. It had the feeling of being on a stage, seconds before curtain-up. Chris and George sat motionless at the table while David got up and opened the door. Standing before him was a strong, six-footer, with red hair and wearing tartan trousers with an aubergine Polo shirt.

"Come in Mr Johnson, or can I call you Fergus?".

"Aye, that's ma name. Whit dad they cry ye?", he said in the broadest Scots accent David had ever heard.

"Oh, I see you are a Scottish person. From Scotland. That's nice. Everyone is welcome here." David almost bungled his attempt at politeness, in fact he very nearly made a right hash of it. "They call me David. Thank you for coming at such short notice. Come and meet the team and then let me show you round." As they passed the table on their tour, introductions were made. "This is George, and this is Chris."

They stood up and hands were shaken. The Scotsman had a strong golfer's grip.

"Guid evenin. A'm gled tae meet ye. How ye daein? Aye, t'is a bonny wee hoose, ye have".

"Excellent. You, too. How do you do", Chris replied, not having understood a word and thinking 'How I wish Bonnie was here to translate'.

Fergus took this greeting as a question that need to be answered. "A'm daein fine. Whit aboot yersself?".

"Yes, very nice to meet you too", a perplexed Chris replied.

Fergus then turned away for his tour with David, who, as briefly as possible, guided him round, showing the kitchen first.

Chris, meantime, leaned over to George and whispered "I can't understand a bloody thing he's saying. It sounds like he's gargling with razor blades".

David had learned the schmooze from Hugo, the estate agent, and he took on his guise. "As you can see, it is a wonderfully furnished apartment, very bright and airy, everything is brand new, with the added benefit of an amazing view. Come and have a look". He slid the glass door and they stepped outside. "Now let me show you your room". He was moving and talking as fast as he could. He then sat him down with the others and the questioning started. It was a singularly unrewarding experience, as they struggled unsuccessfully to decipher his Caledonian patois. They went over all the items they had put on the list but failed to understand any of his answers. With an agreed limited time of thirty minutes for each applicant, in this case twenty-nine too many Chris thought, they rattled through each point. Chris was thinking how he could bring up the subject of food.

A bemused Chris had only one question. "You, where from? Town you live?". He was beginning to talk to him like the British talk to Spanish waiters, in a slow, broken English with the words in no particular order and verbs completely dispensed with.

"A'm fae Glasgae", Fergus barked back with pride.

"Thought he was from sodding planet Mars", Chris murmured under his breath.

Finally, David asked Fergus if he had any questions.

"Aye. Whaurs's the wattrie?", Fergus spluttered. "Dinna fash. It's nae jobbies".

"Sorry, could you run that past me again?".

"Whaur's the wattrie? The cludgie? The lavvy?".

"Oh, the loo. I'll show you". David got up and pointed it out. In their absence, George and Chris talked to each other, covering their mouths with their hands.

"Can you understand him, George?", Chris enquired of the others.

George paused and then said simply "No, barely a damn word".

"Do you think they even understand each other up there north of the border? It's just a blabbering noise. He sounds like my first car when the clutch went. I think it's food time, don't you?", Chris added.

They all sat together once more. George unexpectedly opened up, speaking slowly, simply and clearly.

"Do you like curry? A good curry? That is food I like". He spat out the word 'food' deliberately for David's benefit.

"Aye, ay leek a bonny vindaloo on a Freeday."

Chris joined in. "I like food too. Yes, I certainly like food. Yummy". David got the message loud and clear. Fergus' time was up.

"Well, thank you, Fergus. Thanks for coming over. We have some more people to see but we shall come back to you tomorrow. If you like the apartment, that is?".

"Aye. Thank ye". He got up, shook all their hands to the point of crushing pain once again and went towards the door with David.

As he left, he turned and said to them all, "Thank ye agin. The bit is braw. Bye for noo. Guid nicht". David closed the door on the unintelligible Scot.

"What the bloody hell was that?", shouted Chris, putting his head in his hands.

"I shall take that as a 'no' from both of you. One down, or should I say one 'doon' and four to go", said David. "Who's next?".

Next, they were to be entertained by a certain Norman Cowper. They had liked the look of him on his application because he was a finance specialist, who added that he also liked sport. Even though he admitted to supporting Port Vale, no-one had held that against him.

The same process was repeated at 7.30. Mr Cowper was invited up and entered the apartment.

"Hello, I am Norman. My friends call me Norm", he announced, in an irritating, nerdy voice.

"Hello, Norman. Sorry - Norm. I am David". This time the handshake was as limp and flaccid as a wet fish. Not a good sign, he thought. "Come on through, Norm".

"Oh, very nice. Big isn't it. What's the square footage?".

"I am afraid I forget", replied David, accommodatingly.

"You really should know, you know. How can you work out the value if you don't know the cost per square foot?", Norm reprimanded David.

"I can always find out for you", he responded politely, "but as you are actually here and are seeing it for yourself, I am not sure numbers matter. What you see is what you get". Norm was already annoying David.

"What sort of heating do you have?".

Now David found himself choking up with irritation. "Heating? It's under the floor and warm air comes out of little vents. Sorry, I can't be any more technical. The wonders of science, eh? Let's move on, Norm". David felt he was the one under interrogation.

When they sat down, Norm was still asking questions. "Is the glass hurricane-proof? We are quite high up. There was one in October 1987, you know".

David continued to bite his tongue. "Do you know, Norm, as incredible as it sounds, I never asked".

"Oh dear. That was very remiss of you. On the sixth floor as well. You should always make sure you have the proper glass", reprimanded Norm.

"Well, it works for me," Chris interjected. He got up and went to the window. "It does everything I want from it. Look, I can see right through it. I always think that is quite a good test, don't you Norm?". He was ignored.

David invited questions. George went first.

"What do you do for work, Norm?".

"I am a financial adviser and I work from home. I see I shall have lots of space here for me to spread out my paperwork. Excellent. Let me tell you something that will amaze you. I didn't set out to be a financial adviser. No, honestly. It just happened. No, I started off as an accountant…"

"No need to apologise" interrupted Chris, with a slash of obvious sarcasm. Norm carried on regardless.

"I missed that. Sorry. Anyway, I found accountancy too much. You know, all that stress. But you know, I'll tell you a secret. Do you know what I really wanted to be… a lawyer."

Three cries rang out. The 'L' word made their blood spontaneously boil.

Chris: "Do you mind if I check the food?"

George: "Yes, see if the food is alright".

David: "What food do you like, Norm?".

Norm responded innocently. "Oh, very kind, but there really is no need to feed me. I had a big lunch. There is an excellent sandwich bar near me that sells…".

David cut him off. "Well, Norm, thank you for coming. I am afraid we have to restrict the time as we have other people to see".

"I understand", said Norm, who was already being ushered to the door by David.

"This is a nice carpet. A very deep pile. I expect it is made of wool mixed with a man-made fibre like nylon or polyester. Do you know what it is?".

David almost pushed him out of the door. "Goodbye, Norm. We'll call you".

He sighed and leaned back against the door to close it. "He's the bloody deep pile. What a joke".

"I don't think Stormin' Norman quite gets my vote", stated George.

"If there was a hurricane, I'd take him onto the balcony and tie him to a bloody kite", Chris cried out, with his usual powers of descriptive speech.

"Next please", snapped David. "Bring on the lovely Mrs Adair".

The fact that there was woman on the final roster had been controversial. Chris and David were initially completely against, but George said they had to have someone female in line with equal opportunities or something. His ingrained corporate indoctrination had a lot to do with his directive. However, David was surprisingly converted to the idea when he read the application and said that having a sexy actress around might be fun.

"This will be interesting", said an unconvinced Chris, looking at a print-out of her application. "She says here she's thirty-nine, an actress and dancer, former RSC, divorced. That's probably where her money came from. David, you were the one keen to see her, over to you".

George made his feelings felt. "I don't much care for having a woman in the place, but I'll give it a go if I have to".

After a short while, the apartment phone rang and the concierge sent her up. David went to greet her. He pulled back the door, not knowing what sexy siren might be on the other side. There, before him, stood a statuesque, over made-up, over-coiffured, over-the-top vamp, straight out of the Rocky Horror Picture Show. Her not recently dyed hair was stacked up like an eagle's nest above her overpainted face. She looked the wrong side of fifty-five and was dressed, if you can call it that, in a confection of colour, a tiered taffeta creation, carrying a fur, with its head still on, over her arm. She must have left the Pekinese at home, he thought. Her guppy lips and stretched eyes showed that the Botox had not been injected sparingly.

David tried to hide his shock. "Er, come in".

"Hello, dear boy. I am Fenella Adair." She said in a gruff, deep voice before swanning straight through grandly, hardly sparing him a glance. "I have come to see the apartment, darling. Who are you?". She stretched out her hand to invite his deference. He noticed she had long, cream opera gloves on, just the thing for a September evening in South London. His fingers took the end of her fingers and he wiggled them. She then spotted Chris and George.

"Who are these two? Hello, darlings. How lovely to meet you both. Are you gay? Most the men I meet these days seem to be gay, especially in the theatrical circles I move in. Are you in the theatre, darlings? I love all gay men. And they just adore me".

Before the two men had time to protest and to establish their hip-thrusting machismo, she was gone, sweeping David away in a blaze of gaudy colour. "Let me see my room and the bathrooms, darling. I hope there is a lot of cupboard space", she gushed as David looked back at his friends, pulling a face that screamed 'God help me'.

She came back from the room speaking at the top of her bellowing voice.

"No. No. David darling. It is all far too small. The wardrobe is not even big enough for my shoes let alone my furs and raiment of clothes. And the bathroom, darling. Please. Don't ask me to make myself beautiful in that rabbit hutch. No, I am sorry, darlings. This is not for Fenella Adair. I wish you well".

With that, she turned and sashayed out, leaving the door wide open as she strode down the hall to the lifts. David shut the door and sat down.

"You screwed that up, David", said Chris, sarcastically. "She was great. The best yet. I was about to ask her if she had any pets. A boa constrictor would be perfect. Can you imagine her dancing? She belongs in a bloody circus. 'Gay', eh. I'll give her 'gay'".

"Oh, do be quiet, Chris. Shall we just give up?", said an exasperated David.

George tried to lift spirits. "No, I am sure the next two will be bang on".

"I feel sorry for all that little furry animal that gave up its life only to hang off that woman's fat arm for eternity", Chris crowed. "I am having that beer. Want one?".

They all went into the kitchen and raided the fridge. Having downed them in a few gulps, they tossed the bottles in the bin and returned to the table.

"Who's next?", gasped David.

"Our man from Preston", blurted George. "Harry Wythenshawe".

"Brilliant. Is that his real name? How did we ever find these people? Were we pissed?", thundered an exhausted David as the phone rang once again.

This time a smart, middle-aged man with a ruddy, lived-in face came to the door. He appeared much more like the real deal, respectably attired in his tweed jacket, elegant tie and well-polished shoes. He was welcomed in.

"Hello, I am David. Do come in".

"Ey up, lad. I'm 'arry. 'arry Wythenshawe". His powerful North Country voice filled the room like a megaphone.

"Pleased to meet you...'arry", said David as he steered his guest on the usual course towards Chris and George, where the introductions were made. "Pleased to meet you, lads. Forgive me, I'm right paggered, me. Just got off the train from Manchester. It was tanking down when I left and I left me bloody umbrella at home. Had to wait yonks in line for a taxi at Euston. It's been a bloody nightmare. Now let's see me room".

David and his stiff upper lip carried on with British correctness, as always, conducting his full but fast tour before joining the others at the table with Mr Wythenshawe.

Harry spoke up firmly. "I like it. It's a belta, this place. Very posh, like. Very nice. Rent's a bit high though. I'm expecting you to knock it down a bit".

David took charge. "I am sorry, Harry. No can do. We cannot negotiate on that".

"I am a very wealthy man, y' know, but I don't waste me brass. I'm reet canny with me cash. Always 'ave bin". Harry started to lecture his audience. "I don't squander me lolly on luxuries like this normally. I don't go out for them fancy meals, neither. And I don't throw away me cash on beer and wine, neither. Nor should anybody else. Never touch the stuff". There was a collective gasp around the table.

"So, what food, or should I say 'grub', do you like, Harry?", asked Chris predicably, promptly declaring his hand.

"Nowt better than good plate of old roast beef and Yorkshire puddin'. Followed by rhubarb crumble and custard and then some Wenslydale cheese and biscuits. Bloody lovely".

"I like that sort of food too", chimed in George, once more stressing the word four-letter word beginning with 'f'.

They managed to get through the next ten minutes, pretending to be remotely interested in his engineering firm and his ex-wife Hilda, but his beer and wine line had killed off any slim chance he may have had.

"Well, we shall have to come back to you, Harry. The money thing might be a deal-breaker though. We shall let you know. Thanks for coming all this way. We appreciate it". David led him to the exit.

"Bye lads. Very nice here. Hope to see you soon. You work on the money, lad". His considerable frame disappeared down the corridor.

"Some bloody 'ope", muttered Chris in a mock Northern accent. "Can you imagine? Him, living here? It wasn't just that he doesn't drink, it's that he hates anyone who does. Imagine, divorced and sober, at the same time, all the time. Jeez, however does he get to sleep at night?".

They sat clustered around one end of the table in desperation.

"One more to go. Who have we got now, George?'.

"The musician".

Chris piped up again. "God help us. Bloody Johnny Rotten, I expect. Bet he hasn't got a girlfriend. You know what they call a musician without a girlfriend? Homeless", joked Chris, ineffectively.

"Let's be positive, Christopher. Perhaps he has a very nice, and wealthy, girlfriend", said George in a wisp of optimism.

The phone rang and after the usual procedure, David pulled the door back. George and Chris were peering anxiously to see if this one was any better. Another surprise stood there.

"Hi. I am Ricky Wilde. I've come about the room".

David invited him in. "Thanks for coming, Ricky".

Ricky was every inch rock 'n' roll. He was in his thirties with a striking, lived-in face, had tousled black hair down to his shoulders and was tall, six foot three at least. His open neck check shirt was worn trendily over a black T-shirt, with his straight leg 501s fitting him like a second skin right down to his elaborate Lucchese cowboy boots.

"My pleasure, mate. This looks a fabulous place. Been here long?".

"Just a few days. It was fully furnished so it was good to go. We love it here", said David. He then took the rock god over to meet the others. As they went to shake hands, Ricky apologised for the crash helmet he was carrying. "Sorry about this. I left my Harley in your car park. Hope that's OK?".

Chris' opinion had immediately changed. He was already starstruck. This guy was so cool.

David showed him round and Ricky enthused about everything. He loved his room, thought the view was amazing and said the whole place was just 'fab'. Then they all sat at the table.

"So, you're a musician, Richard. What sort of music do you play?", said a slightly out of his zone George.

"Well, I grew up on early Mayall and Fleetwood Mac, the Stones, Jeff Beck, early Rod Stewart - that sort of stuff".

This 'stuff' was music to George's ears. The first LPs he had ever bought were by Clapton, Peter Green and, of course, the enigmatic Jeff Beck. He was already a convert.

"Are you in a band?", Chris questioned.

"Sure am. They're called Street Fire".

Chris lent forward, suitably impressed. "Wow. I know them. You played the Brixton Academy a few weeks back".

"Yeah. That was a great gig. We had a couple of thousand people there, I reckon".

David thought he should join in. "Do you sing or play guitar? You're not a drummer, are you?".

"A drummer? Not bloody likely. I am the lead singer, lead guitarist and leader of the band. And I write the songs. I just don't get paid enough".

David asked the obvious question. "Does the music industry pay well, Ricky?".

"Not bad", Ricky replied. "I made shedload of money in Germany when we toured, mostly on merchandise, T-shirts, baseball caps and the like. They loved us. And we had a hit in Japan, which helped the coffers".

They all laughed to make him feel at ease and Chris spouted "I am just going to feed the pet goldfish. Can I get everyone a beer while I am out there feeding our pet".

"You'll have a beer, won't you, Richard?", asked a welcoming George.

"Love one". He totally accepted being called Richard. That's what his mother used to call him.

George went on. "While you are 'feeding the pet', Christopher, make sure you get Richard a beer won't you".

"Yes, give the pet goldfish a hug from me too", said David.

"What's this with the goldfish? You must love that fish", said Ricky.

David was so confident that they had found their man that he was perfectly relaxed about coming clean. He told Ricky about the 'food' and 'pet' signals.

"No 'food' for me then, Chris. Anyway, I don't eat goldfish", Ricky shouted to the kitchen.

"How did you get into music?", David continued, sensibly.

"I had my first band when I was at the LSE".

David came straight back. "The London School of Economics. That's where Mick Jagger went, wasn't it?".

"Yes, but I'm a better guitarist than him".

George had a question. "Where are you living now?".

"With my Aunt in Wandsworth. My Mum's sister. I only just got divorced. We had been married only a couple of years".

"Sorry about that", sympathised George. "We have all been through it in recent times. In fact, that's really how we all came together and got this place. It's a long story. We are living proof that there is life after divorce".

"Is there?", said a slightly morose Ricky. "I'm not so sure. But anyway, change subject. It's great to meet you guys. You've cheered me up no end. Living with your Auntie after all these years can be tough!".

Chris came back with the beers. He slapped his new best friend Ricky on the back and handed him a bottle.

"You're a great guy, Ricky. Have a beer".

Fifteen minutes later, it was all fixed. It was an easy decision. While Ricky had nipped to the bathroom, David had whispered two words to the others, 'All agreed?'. The hands went up, and it was done. When Ricky sat back down, David made his pronouncement.

"Ricky, are you happy to join us here? We'd love to have you in our little band".

"Guys, that would be fantastic. I cannot thank you enough. When can I move in?".

"Tonight?", exclaimed an excited Chris. "Your room is empty".

"I have to explain it to my Aunt first. But that won't take long. How about tomorrow, late afternoon? It's really quick but that'd be great. Can I talk money with you then, David?".

"Of course, Ricky. Welcome aboard".

They gave a chorus of welcome to their new flatmate. Chris was thinking, 'can't wait to tell them at work. Ricky Wilde of Street Fire. Living here. This is so cool.'

CHAPTER FIVE
A LITTLE MISS UNDERSTOOD

SATURDAY, SEPTEMBER 7

Bonnie and her two friends, Adya and Samantha, piled out of their taxi in Covent Garden in fits of laughter. As Chris had told her that he was having a lads' day at the football, followed by a few drinks after the game, Bonnie had got together with her two best friends for a girls' night out. Chris and Bonnie's relationship had gone from strength to strength since they first met and they spent all the time they could together but a day apart, with friends, was something they both knew they needed now and again. The three girls were on top form and, as ever when they were together, a good time was guaranteed to be had, whatever they were doing and wherever they went.

Sam was the sort of eye-catching, bubbly blonde that women want to go shopping with and men want to date. Fun went with her wherever she went. Not only was she everyone's friend, but she was also very beautiful. Her long flaxen hair had this alluring way of dancing behind her as she walked, helped by the occasional nonchalant flick from the supremely confident Sam. She and the dark, beguiling Adya made a stunning pair and to see heads turn as they skipped by was the norm. Adya was also extremely pretty, a gentle Indian girl with glossy black hair and kind, deep brown eyes. Her parents had come to England almost thirty years ago from Mumbai, then Bombay, facing up to all the challenges that come with starting life all over again in a strange new land. She had been brought up very much as the English young lady, well educated, respectful and beautifully mannered. She and Sam had been best friends for the past three years and were inseparable. Bonnie had come on to the scene earlier that year when she met Sam at an audition for Chicago. They had struck up a conversation during the long wait to perform and, afterwards, a glass of wine to commiserate one another after their rejection helped seal a special relationship.

"My agent, Jeff, rang me yesterday and said they are auditioning for girls in a new revival of West Side Story", Bonnie told Sam. "I am going to have a go. You should too, Sam. I'll send you the details when I get them".

"That'd be great. Blimey, I had better get to the gym, fast. The only exercise I have done recently was three weeks ago with that Lucien, the French sex-on-legs I met in Ibiza, and that was all horizontal", Sam confessed.

"What happened to him?", asked a curious Bonnie.

"He took his frogs legs and hopped back to Paris and I never heard from him again. Although he did leave me with some great memories and a sore back. I have only just recovered".

The girls giggled and stepped out into the square. Their nights out were always a major highlight and were eagerly anticipated, particularly by Bonnie, who needed to get out after five long nights working in the Wellington. They had all met up earlier at her flat, where they had promptly downed a bottle of wine to get in the mood. The plan was that they would go on a pub crawl in the West End before having an Italian meal, or even a Chinese in Chinatown. After that, if past experiences were anything to go by, whatever happened next, happened. More often than not, they ended up in a club surrounded by handsome male admirers, who would invariably line up to buy them their next drink.

On the way downtown in their black cab, Adya had been telling the other two, in her comical dry way, about her disastrous online date earlier in the week with a balding German chef, who spent the whole night talking about his favourite bratwurst and why he preferred a Teutonic sausage to the Anglo-Saxon variety. The obvious innuendos were flowing freely.

"Let's start off in Covent Garden". Adya then suddenly exclaimed, "That'd be great fun". The other two agreed that it was an excellent idea.

The famous tourist spot is one of the liveliest places in London, especially on a Saturday evening. The surrounding buildings still captured its fascinating past, while dozens of street performers claimed it as their stage. Its chequered history had started off when it was part of an abbey, Convent Garden. Henry VIII had snatched it off the Church after his tiff with the Pope, who had refused to set him free from Catherine of Aragon to marry the coquettish tease, Anne Boleyn. He had promptly given it to some Earl or other, to whom he had owed a big favour. The Earl then had commissioned Inigo Jones, King James I's favourite architect, to redesign the square in an Italian style, with grand houses and elegant arcades. Soon, a small fruit and vegetable market had emerged to add colour and chaos. At this point, all was going well. However, that was not to last. Before too long, it fell deeply into disrepute and became a notorious den of iniquity, with taverns and brothels galore. There was suddenly a far bigger interest in pimps and prostitutes than pears and potatoes apparently, so the greengrocers moved out and the red lights moved in. Things did change, though, when it had a renaissance as a flower market a hundred years ago. As London grew and the traffic got worse, the market moved to a more accessible home and the square underwent another re-invention into what it is today, a vibrant place to eat, drink and be entertained by all and sundry.

Together, the three of them, arms interlinked, looked like a triptych of modern sassy glamour as they bounced amongst all the energetic, supple street entertainers. A unicyclist whizzed past them, shouting 'Good evening ladies, hop on', a knife juggler perilously tossed his blades high into the air and a man tied up in heavy chains was twisting sinuously in his invariably successful attempt to wriggle free. Covent Garden, a once dignified square sitting in the shadow of the Royal Opera House, had become a mecca for weird and wonderful acts. Sword swallowers, acrobats, magicians and stilt-walkers vie for the appreciative donations of the amassed carousing audiences. Bonnie took a particular shine to the bare-chested hunk with long dreadlocks, who somehow managed to cram himself into small, clear perspex box. She commented to the amusement of her two friends that his lithe, sinewy, contortionist back-bending could have any number of interesting applications. They were on excellent form as they strolled round, occasionally dropping some loose change into the tip baskets, exploring the length and breadth of Covent Garden.

"Oh, this is the restaurant Chris took me to on our proper first date", Bonnie pointed out to her pals. "We had been to the Aquarium and then we came here. It was lovely". They stopped outside the bustling Italian bistro and peered searchingly through the window.

Bonnie went ashen. She spat out some barely audible words under her breath.

"Shit. The bastard". Her bemused friends immediately showed their concern.

"What is it? What's happened?" inquired an anxious Adya.

"It's Chris. He's in there, with another woman", Bonnie bayed.

Sure enough, Chris was sitting two tables back on the left, enwrapped in a deep conversation, facing the window. She could see him clearly, while his dinner partner had her back to her. The three girls stared through the glass, transfixed.

"I am going right in there and…", threatened Bonnie, her anger almost brewing over.

"No, stop", interrupted Adya, "you most certainly are not. Making a big scene in a restaurant isn't smart thinking. Come on. Calm down. I'm sure there is a reasonable explanation. Don't let him get to you".

"Get to me? Get to me? I'll bloody get to him."

But she did not need to. He had already spotted the three girls, peering obviously through the window at him. He rushed out and came up to Bonnie, brimming over with excuses as he tried to take her arms in his hands.

"Get off me." Bonnie shrugged him away, brusquely. "You said you were out with your football friends tonight. You lied to me. Here you are, buying dinner for some bloody woman or other".

"That's no woman, that's Angela. It's only Angela. We are just catching up".

"I don't bloody care if it's bloody Madonna. You lied to me".

"Listen to me. I am sorry, Bonnie. I wouldn't do anything to upset you, you know I wouldn't. But it's just Angela. Please. It is just that we meet up occasionally to have a sort of chat and to check if everything is OK. Nothing more than that".

"Oh, so you meet up 'occasionally', do you? So, this happens all the time, does it?".

"No. Since our divorce we said we would try to stay friends. You know, try to keep it all amicable".

"I'm sorry, Chris. You bloody lied to me. I can't have that. Get back to your 'amicable' dinner with your precious little ex". At that, she turned to her companions. "Come on girls, we don't need this. Let's go for a drink".

She stormed off with Adya and Sam, leaving an embarrassed Chris standing there in front of the watching diners, who were staring back through the window at this impromptu Covent Garden display.

"I'm telling you. That's it, Sam. I was lied to before in Brighton, by a guy I trusted. Never again. It's over. That's bloody it".

They walked away sharply, Bonnie in the middle, to a nearby wine bar and Bonnie marched straight up to get the drinks, her rage barely contained. Both Adya and Sam tried to console her, to calm her down, but Bonnie was clearly shaken to the core. Sam then attempted to inject some logic into the situation.

"Look, Bonnie, it was all really quite innocent. In fact, if I'm honest, I admire the way they were so civilised throughout their divorce. You told me all about it and it is a shame more couples can't behave like that. I really don't think he meant to hurt you. He does love you, you know". Bonnie would have none of it.

"Sam, it isn't about him seeing bloody Angela. I couldn't care less. It isn't even about him taking her to OUR restaurant. He bloody lied to me. If only he had told me the truth instead of sneaking off behind my back and telling me some bullshit story about his football mates. It's the lying I can't stand. I just can't forgive that".

Adya tried to be the soothing balm. "OK. Now let's all calm down. Let's have drink, take a deep breath and have a nice evening, we are the 'girls on tour' remember?".

Bonnie was still scowling but heard what Adya had said and realised she should not be the one to ruin their evening. She did as instructed. She sank her glass of wine, breathed in and forced a big smile.

"OK girls. Let's get this party started!".

SUNDAY, SEPTEMBER 8

George, David and Ricky were sitting around the high-top breakfast table, as they did every Sunday morning, even when David's children were staying over, while Chris, in his natty apron, was busy frying, poaching and scrambling. He had become quite the expert chef by now, adeptly throwing his spatula into the air as if he was a cocktail barman. George was reading his Telegraph, and the other two were sitting quietly looking at the sports pages in the tabloids, all perched up on the high stools. David scrutinised the racing sections, while Ricky scanned the football reports.

George spoke from behind his paper. "There's this economics so-called expert here who says in 20 years, we shall all be poorer, probably lose our houses but we will be happy. That's bloody great, isn't it. I am perfectly happy now thank you, but, in 20 years, according to this idiot, I'll be happy with no money and no bloody home. The man's a genius".

His audience of two showed no reaction, except for Ricky who added, "Coventry City lost again. That's three weeks running". David ignored everything, absorbed in the racing results.

Chris ceremoniously delivered the plates, stacked high with bacon, eggs, mushrooms, tomatoes, baked beans and the best British bangers to each of his flatmates and then joined them.

"Here we go. Three cholesterol specials". David put down his paper and looked at Chris.

"How are we this morning?", he asked.

"Bit pissed off actually. No, a lot pissed off. Bonnie phoned at midnight, went crazy and finished with me. Just like that".

He had deliberately left out the details of the whole furious twenty-minute rant that he had been subjected to, with an intoxicated Bonnie giving him the full works, telling him in no uncertain terms that she didn't want to see him ever again. Although he had tried pleading the same defence again and again, it fell on deaf ears. She would have none of it. He had lied, been summarily tried, found guilty as charged and duly punished.

He was, of course, shattered by what had happened, although, while he had fallen head over heels in love with her, he knew he could do nothing after she had turned from his lovely little poodle into a rabid attack rottweiler. He had never seen her like this and was stunned that she could change so quickly and so completely. But Chris never allowed his emotions to run that deep and he was already in superficial recovery mode.

"I am sure there must be more to the story". David said intuitively, raising his eyebrows, urging Chris to come clean.

"Well, I was having dinner with Angela in Covent Garden last night and...", Chris began.

"Stop! You were doing WHAT?". David stopped him in his tracks, yelling the final word.

"I was just having dinner with Angela, that's all, what's wrong with that? And, of all the people in the whole wide world to walk by, Bonnie pops up. I look up and there she is, gazing at me through the restaurant window with her two friends. What are the odds on that?".

"Oh, Chris. Don't tell me you were having a secret Saturday night tryst with your ex-wife and Bonnie caught you. Are you crazy?".

"Not you as well, David. It wasn't a secret. I just hadn't told her. It was completely innocent."

"Completely stupid, more like. You lied to her?", snapped back David. "You must have a death wish or something. Can't you see how mad that would make Bonnie. I suppose it didn't cross your mind to tell her what you were doing beforehand?".

"Er, no. I just said I was going out after the football for a drink with some mates".

"Oh, Chris, Chris, Chris. Won't you ever learn? Ex-wives and former girlfriends are strictly off-limits, mate. Unless, of course, you had told Bonnie first and she had said it was OK. But you lied".

"Don't know what all the fuss is about", Ricky cut in, unsympathetically. "Women can be ridiculous. So bloody unpredictable. You might be well out of it, mate".

Chris fought back. "Oh, shut up and eat your sausage, Ricky".

"Your goings-on are interrupting my Sunday breakfast, Chris", countered Ricky. "Just pass the ketchup".

At that, the talking stopped. There was starting to be a heavy atmosphere over the bacon and eggs, and no-one wanted it to turn into an argument. As soon as they had eaten, each man left the table, quietly moving into the lounge to continue reading the papers. Chris was left to load the dishwasher and clear up, all part of his agreed duties. All the time, he was still thinking about the injustice of his situation. Inside his head, he was having a little chat to himself. 'This is awful. I did nothing wrong. I can't understand why she got so steamed up. I'll never understand women. Never mind, I guess I'll just have to get on with it. It was all so stupid. She just wouldn't listen. Nothing I can do, I guess". Chris was being stoical. Inside, though, in spite of this bluster, it hurt him very deeply.

"Sorry, Christopher. I know how you feel about her". George volunteered warmly.

"I have nice gig on Tuesday", Ricky threw in, wanting to get off the subject. "Anyone want to come?"

Chris perked up. He viewed life so simply that it never took much to detract him from one train of thought to another. "Where is it?", he asked Ricky.

"Nice venue. The Blue Bell in Islington. It's big. It's a really cool place and they always get a great crowd. Loads of hot chicks, mate".

"Might do", replied Chris, hesitatingly, "but then again, it would probably mean I'd get into even more trouble, so best not. I would like to come and see you play soon though".

"No problem", said a laid-back Ricky. "Anytime".

Chris retired to his room.

It was an "Easy Like Sunday Morning' kind of day. Inactivity filled the hours, colour supplements were being flicked through, as more cups of tea and coffee were being consumed. Ricky sat reading more football reports, while George had moved from the financial pages to the features on the latest Middle East crisis. David was absorbed in an article about exploring the Amazon. At around 11.30, Chris came through to the lounge.

"Psst. David". Chris was being unusually coy. "Can you come here a minute?"

"What is it?", said David, looking up from his magazine.

"Just come here a minute. I want to show you something".

David got up and went with Chris back to his room. "Close the door behind you", Chris instructed secretively.

"I am intrigued. Go on, Chris, what's this hush-hush all about?".

"Well, I have just signed up on this dating site, Loveline 100".

David was surprised. "Bloody hell Chris, you don't waste any time. Are you serious? You've signed up for online dating already?"

"No, I was just looking to see if Angela was on it and look what I found. It's your Moira. She's on there. No doubt about it. It's her alright. I saw her that day I came down to your old house with you to drop off the children. She didn't see me. I stayed in the car if you remember, while I watched every second of your ten-round scrap outside the front door. She is impossible to forget. She terrified the bloody life out of me".

"Let me see. Let me see".

Chris sat himself down in front of his computer, while David peered over his shoulder. He tapped a key and Moira's face suddenly filled the screen, staring a scary stare back at them both, all dolled up and glamorous.

"Bugger me. That's her. That's her alright. She must have been photoshopped by someone good. What does it say?".

Chris read the words in her profile, paraphrasing some of it.

"Loves travel and adventure...with a zest for life...thirty-three...loves dancing, the opera, the theatre, a good film at home on the sofa...enjoys all Asian food and fine wine...great sense of humour, blah blah...wishes to meet gentleman who shares the same interests and is prepared to have fun."

"It's unreal. Where's the bit about liking a good argument and the occasional mass murder? And thirty-three? She should be done under the Trades Description Act", said David.

They both studied it again, David shaking his head in disbelief throughout. His emotions were mixed. He felt angry, amused, bitter and sick that she was meeting people off the internet while having Robbie and Jess around. He thought of strange men coming into the house and a rage started to well up inside him. But, as these reactions churned, he reminded himself that she was single now, that he was free of her and that she could do whatever she wanted.

"Oh, well. There's some poor sucker out there that she will get her fangs into, I expect. I wish he would talk to me first. He might be a nice guy, poor fellow. Anyway, I hope they enjoy spending my money". David's bitterness showed.

Chris had refrained from offering his invaluable worldly advice, simply adding, "She looks a lot fitter than I remember her". He never could say the right thing.

"Thanks, Chris. Thanks a lot"

David left, went back to his chair in the lounge and sat motionless, staring into space for a good ten minutes, thinking about what he had just seen, replaying the whole experience. His mind started to drift as Chris' words kept coming back into his head, 'fitter than I remember...'. That annoyed him, although he was not going to say anything. Or was he? Suddenly, he jumped up again and went quickly into Chris' room, closing the door behind him.

"Chris, Chris. Do you really think she looks 'fit'? Do you?".

Chris turned cautiously and started to back-peddle.

"Well not fit exactly, but not bad, if you know what I mean".

"Chris." David got serious. "I have been thinking. You know we are good mates and that I would do anything for you. In fact, you know how I helped you with the rent situation when we moved in? Make no mistake, I was pleased to do so, you know, as you have become one of my closest friends, someone I have come to admire and respect"

Most people might have got suspicious at this point, with all this gushing admiration. But not Chris. He simply agreed that they had a special friendship and that he would always be very grateful for all he had done for him. He should have wondered what was coming next and seen a 'you owe me one' coming round the corner. But, of course, it went right over his head.

"You know I love your company", continued David. "In fact, we must go racing again the next time Golden Oak runs"

"That was an amazing day, David. I shall never forget it".

"Well, Chris, dear friend. I've had this idea". David stopped his flow for a second, then went for it. "How about this? Why don't you date Moira?".

"What? Hold on a minute. What the hell are you saying?". The bombshell had been dropped.

"Why don't YOU date Moira?", David repeated.

"Now, David. Come on, mate. You're not serious. I haven't given up on Bonnie yet". Chris looked closely at David's face. "Oh my God, you are serious. David, what are you thinking?".

"Well, look. I'll come clean. There is method in my madness. I need some help with Moira and this has just given me a golden opportunity. I won't go into it all but you could do me the most enormous favour. The thing is that it is impossible for me to find out what she is up to these days and, most importantly, whether the children are OK in that house. She doesn't know you. It's all perfect. If you could take her out, just for a drink, and find out a bit more, it would help me so much. You know how much I love Robbie and Jess and you would be doing me the biggest favour", he repeated. Little did Chris know that David had a bigger plan afoot.

"No. No way, David. I'd do anything for you, but not that".

"Why not?", persisted David. "It will be for just a couple of hours. I'll brief you on what to ask and you can use your inimitable and considerable acting skills to bring the conversation round to the subject. You'll be brilliant".

"Not doing it, David. Sorry. I still want things to work out with Bonnie. This would be dynamite if she found out".

"Come on. She'll never know. It's not much to ask of a good mate, for someone who has had tried to help you along the way. I'd be really, really grateful".

"This is so unfair", thought Chris as he pondered his options. Say 'no' and he would be letting his mate down. Say 'yes' and he would be putting himself in the epicentre of a web of deception. On the plus side, he thought, it was a way of paying him back. After all, if it wasn't for David, he wouldn't have been able to live in this fabulous apartment. His resolve was weakening.

"What's she like, your Moira?", enquired Chris, buckling under the emotional duress.

"Well, she isn't unattractive. Actually, she is quite good looking. She has a lovely figure although she has put on a bit of weight recently, but she isn't what you'd call fat or anything. And she has very nice skin, just too much of it".

With that reassurance, Chris seemed to be coming round.

"Just one date? Only one?".

David's face lit up. He saw hope. "Just one. We just need to find out what is going on".

"WE?", cried Chris. "So, are you coming on the date with me?".

"Don't be daft, Chris. We are a team, you and I. I scratch your back and you scratch mine. It's what pals do".

Chris went very, very quiet. He had been outmanoeuvred. And he knew it.

"Let me think about it. I take it you'll be paying for the drinks?".

"Naturally", agreed David, scenting victory. "Lunch, if you want. You give it some thought and then say 'yes'. I'll be in the lounge".

"Just one date?", Chris asked again.

"Just one date", reassured his friend.

David, well used to negotiation tactics, left him to fester in his dilemma. He returned once more to his chair, this time in a much more relaxed and optimistic mood.

Chris was bamboozled. Moira's fixed gaze glowed in front of him on the screen. David had been extremely good to him, he considered, and perhaps one date with Moira might not be as bad as all that. He was a good actor, he told himself, so he could pull it off with no problem. And how could he say no?
He already knew in his heart that he had no choice other than to agree to help his pal. He made up his mind. He would do it.

He started bashing away at the keyboard again, realising that, to make this work, he would have to change his profile to fit in with hers. He had signed up earlier with the sole purpose of seeing if he could find Angela on the site and had planned to cancel his membership immediately after his search. His current description of his personal 'likes' would in no way win Moira over. He went straight back into his profile, firstly registering his name as 'Brian Jackson-Brown' and replacing his photo with a poor, slightly blurred one taken at a drunken party, one from which Bonnie could never identify him if it happened to come to her attention. He had suddenly thought of the horror if one of Bonnie's friends spotted him on the site and told her. That would put an end of any hopes that he had of getting her forgiveness. Also, if Moira mentioned his real name to Jess or Robbie, they would probably work out exactly what was going on. He then wisely checked her 'likes' again and changed his from football, beer and the blues to tennis, Chinese food, and musical theatre. Moira would go for that, he thought.

Happy with what he had done, Chris raised himself out of his chair and went over to David, who was biting his lip trying not to smile too triumphantly. Chris leaned into him and whispered into his ear.

"OK, I'll do it".

"Excellent", David responded, sotto voce, without a hint of surprise. Then, the two furtive co-conspirators returned to Chris' room, trying to appear as normal as possible. Chris sat down at the computer.

"Close the door", he ordered, hitting the keys. David smartly did as he was told.

"I knew you wouldn't let me down", said David. "Thanks, Chris. Now, it will have to be next weekend. I will have the children here, so she will be free. You can drive down. I can always rent you a car. If I may make a suggestion, you could have a pub lunch with her on Saturday or Sunday. The Manor in Stonebridge would be perfect. It's about six miles away and really nice. She loves their roasts. She'll have the chicken, she always does. Go Tiger. This is great. Oh, and thanks Chris, I really appreciate this".

"Hang on, David. Will you stop organising me, please. It's my date after all", Chris insisted, feeling protective of his new assignation. If he was going to do this bizarre thing, he wanted to do it his way.

David backed down, not wanting to rock the boat. "Sorry, mate. Only trying to help".

"I'll tell you how you can help. I have already redone my profile and changed my photo. Now I need you with me while I message her. I need your help, big time, if she comes back at me with something I don't know how to answer," appealed Chris.

"I don't know anything about this computer dating lark. But I'll help in any way I can". David went and got a chair from his room and sat down next to Chris.

"OK. This is how it works". Chris was in charge. "I send a message, then she looks at my profile and hopefully she writes back. So, here goes".

CHRIS: 'Hi. My name is Brian. Brian Jackson-Brown'.

David broke in. "Brian? Is that the best you can do?"

"Shut up, David. Let me do it. Brian Jackson-Brown is the name on my profile. I can hardly use my real name, now can I", Chris explained.

"I get it, you cunning fox. But 'Brian'. Honestly", said David.

Chris carried on, anything but honestly. The big lie was being unleashed. He picked up where he had left off.

CHRIS: 'Hi. My name is Brian. Brian Jackson-Brown. You will have to excuse me. I have just joined and have never done this before. I saw your profile and realised we have so much in common. I wondered if you would like to meet up for a coffee or a glass of wine some time. I look forward to hearing from you'.

"Is that OK, David?", Chris asked, seeking approval.

"You're the expert. Seems fine to me. What now?". Chris hit the 'send' button.

"That's it. We just have to wait for her to come back now".

David was chewing his nails before doing what every true Englishman does when he is anxious – reach for the kettle. He went out to the kitchen, with a 'Tea anyone?' to the others, took their grunts as an affirmative and made three cups of tea and a coffee for George. His nerves were jingling. He could not get back to Chris fast enough, arriving back to the control room armed with two teas. "Anything?".

"She has just come back. Wants to know more about me". He began typing again.

CHRIS: 'Brown hair. Blue eyes. Some people think I look a bit like a young Michael Douglas. I like a glass of wine and a good laugh'.

"Wait. Wait. Michael Douglas? Are you kidding me?", an incredulous David questioned. "You don't look anything like bloody Michael Douglas.

"Well, Moira reminds me of Catherine Zeta Jones, so naturally I thought she'd like to go out with someone who looks like a young Michael Douglas", replied Chris, in his own peculiar logic.

"We are getting a bit carried away, aren't we? No, on second thoughts, leave it. I think she liked Michael Douglas in that film he did with Demi Moore. She is going to get a hell of a disappointment though. Oh, and so are you. Catherine Zeta Jones indeed".

Chris hit 'send' and sat back. The reply was immediate.

MOIRA: 'How about this? How about we meet up on Sunday for a bite of lunch? Are you OK to come down to Kent. I'm not far from Sevenoaks.

CHRIS: 'Perfectly OK. I've heard The Manor in Stonebridge is nice. I can meet you there or I can pick you up'.

"Slow down, Chris, slow down", heeded David. "You are not meant to know where she lives yet. You need to be a lot more subtle or we'll blow it". There was an ominous delay before the reply came back.

MOIRA: 'How funny you should pick that place. It is very near me. What a co-incidence. How about I meet you at 12.30 in the car park of St Peter's Church, Wychwood. That's my village".

Chris knew that she would never want to give her home address to a stranger she was talking to online.

CHRIS: 'That is perfect. I shall be in a silver BMW. I really look forward to it'.

"Stop right there, Chris", David interjected. "You haven't got a silver BMW. You haven't even got a car. And I never said I would rent you a bloody silver BMW".

Chris was feeling more in control every second. It was his turn to make the demands.

"Well, who do we know with a new one? Let me think. Any ideas?"

David thought and then the penny dropped. "Not George. You don't mean George, do you?". George had just taken delivery of a brand new, very smart, silver 5 series BMW. Chris smiled mischievously.

"But what if he won't lend it to us. What then?", said David.

Chris came straight back. "He will, because you are going to persuade him to. Now shall we get back to the business in hand?".

David was speechless. Chris hit 'send' on the message. By now, he was enjoying himself. In no time, a reply message had been posted.

MOIRA: 'Are you still there? Let me tell you about myself'.

David felt a need to rescue his pal. "She might go on for hours. Say you're busy. You've got to go to see your old Mum or something". Chris acted on his advice.

CHRIS: 'Would love to but promised to see my mother at 1. Let's keep it for when we meet'.

MOIRA: 'Yes, let's. The Manor is great. So, it's Church, 12.30, next Sunday. I shall look for a silver BMW, with Michael Douglas in it'.

CHRIS: 'That's the one. See you next Sunday'.

MOIRA: 'Yes, I am looking forward to it. Have a good week'.

CHRIS: 'Thanks. You too'.

Chris ended the conversation, leaned back and beamed with pride, thoroughly pleased with his performance, completely forgetting that, just ten minutes ago, he had hated the whole concept.

"There you go. That's how to pull them. All done. I have a date". All of a sudden, his expression changed to one of utter terror. Reality had hit him like a brick as he realised what he had just done. "David. What about Bonnie? Shit. You must keep this between us, please. We had this massive bust-up last night. I am hoping she will come round when she has calmed down. I bloody well hope so. Please keep this quiet. Just promise me".

"I promise. Cross my heart and hope to die", said David.

He then left Chris on his computer and moved out on to the balcony to lie on the lounger, feeling very happy with himself. It was a lovely day and he was enjoying the sunshine and the magnificent view across the Thames. George and Ricky were still where he had left them, totally oblivious of the Machiavellian plot that had just being hatched under their very noses. Chris emerged from his lair, slid the glass door and sat himself down next to David. The latter simply rubbed his hands in self-congratulation, a smug smile on his face.

"You'll like The Manor, it's very nice with excellent food", he said. He then proceeded to give him some ideas on how to convince Moira that Brian was the man for her. "Get into the musicals, like Les Mis and Phantom. She's nuts on them. Chat about films. She loves Love Actually and things like that, her favourite is The Holiday, although she hated Jack Black. Rebecca is her best old film, I think. Talk about travel. She has always loved Italy and goes on about Venice, somewhere she has never been and really wants to go. And mention her nails, she is very proud of her nails. Spends a fortune on them. And play some Mozart in the car. Marriage of Figaro would be best. Tell you what, look up a piece called 'Sull'aria'. It's a 'duettino' or short duet about the Countess Almaviva arranging a tryst between Susanna and her husband, the Count. Fabulous stuff. One of my favourites".

Chris listened carefully as David proceeded to brief him even more thoroughly, giving him other snippets of detail that he should drop into the conversation to make himself look even more perfect. Chris took careful mental notes and then added cautiously, "Got it. I think. I bet she'll love me being a film and opera buff. By the way, maestro, I hope this place isn't too expensive. It would be such a shame if I accidently spent all your money on champagne and caviar", Chris taunted David, with unconvincing concern.

David reacted sharply. "Just don't go crazy with the drinks bill, OK?".

Chris fought back against all these instructions and made his own demand. "Seriously though, David, we must keep this between ourselves. I repeat that the last thing I want is for Bonnie to find out. I mean this. You mustn't say anything to anyone. No-one. Our secret. Otherwise, I promise to resort to dirty tactics, like shouting 'Champagne all round. The Bollinger's on me' across the dining room and bar in the Manor".

"You bloody won't. Of course, I promise not to say a word. Except that I shall have to mention it to George if we need his car. He is a good sport. He'll understand and he can keep a secret", said David in reassurance.

They both relaxed, in this bond of trust, thinking about what they had just accomplished. Chris broke the silence.

"What shall I wear? I want to look nice for the first date".

"Something sexy, Brian. Something Michael Douglas would wear?". Chris stared back and gave a sarcastic laugh.

MONDAY, SEPTEMBER 9

In spite of his upset with Bonnie, Chris walked into the office with a spring in his step. Everything had started well at the Daily Post. He had joined a small, energetic young team, led by the dynamic Jill Spender, a tough career woman in her forties, who had been hardened from working in newspapers for years and years. It was understandable that some of her softer, more feminine edges had been worn away long ago, having been subjected to that male-dominated environment for a decade. Women who managed to climb to the top in the newspaper business tended to be even more brutal than the men. They invariably overacted the bullying thuggish role that they had seen from the editors and managers to a tee, shouting and swearing to create this aura of complete power. She believed that authority went automatically with the job title and her style and behaviour had become more extreme as she progressed up the ladder, and whereas the older, wiser execs knew that authority is actually earned, not given, that underlings work better out of respect than out of fear. This was a lesson she had yet to learn. She threw her weight around, lost her temper easily and could be a nightmare after a good lunch. However, she had taken an immediate shine to Chris and he had responded well to this. The others around him, glued to their computers all day, had welcomed him into their fold and he was put in charge of contests and giveaways. Jill had taught him in her enthusiastic style, "What's the most important four-letter word beginning with F in newspapers?". She instructed him, "It's FREE. Get me lots of 'Free for Every Reader' giveaways". Spurred on, he called around everyone and every company he could think of. Before long, FREE was splashed all over the front pages. Free maps, free books, free drinks, free chocolates, free everything. He had already had some notable successes. One of his recent promotions was giving away 20,000 Lady Diana roses. This had seen a massive response and a visible spike in sales. The roses, which he called Lady Diana Tribute Roses were the same type that were on her coffin at her funeral. They were actually sent out as small sticks on a skinny root, with blossoms a year's growth away. Chris had seen this as a definite marketing opportunity. His cleverness in getting a horticultural company to let him have them in return for some promotional space for a cut-price spring bulbs offer had got noticed, even by the fearsome Editor downstairs.

"I am setting myself a challenge", he had said to Jill. "I have noticed that the circulation increases when we do a good free offer but when we then have a week of no decent promotions, we lose all those gains. I am going to come up with something good every single week so that new readers won't want to leave us. They will look at all the competitive papers' front pages spread out in the newsagent and say, 'why wouldn't I pick up the Post when I get a free gift every week'. That's my mission".

Jill loved his energy and enterprise. It was noticeable that she was calling him into her office to bounce ideas off him more and more frequently. She had mentioned to him too that the Editor had congratulated her on boosting sales.

He was sitting at his desk, thinking up his next promotion, when there was a bellow from her office.

"Chris, the Editor wants to see us". This shout would normally send a chill down the spine. If the Editor 'wanted to see you', it was nearly always for a 'rollicking' or worse. He immediately went into her office, where she told him exactly how he should conduct himself, not to say too much and to address as him 'sir'.

The Editor's office was down one floor, so they took the stairs. They then passed through two swing doors and stepped onto the hallowed editorial floor. There, filling the whole area, long desks were spread around with feverish journalists crouched over each in their uniform chairs, heads bowed over their computer keyboards, intensely typing away on their story of the day. This was Chris' first visit to the epicentre of the paper. His boss pointed out what was what.

"There, in the front, is what's called the back bench, where the main editors and night editors sit in the evening when they are getting the paper out. That is the nerve centre when things hot up. That's the news desk next to it, that's foreign there, that's features, sport is at the back...". At that point, a camp cry screamed out from the midst.

"Coo-ee. Chris, love. What are you doing here?". An effeminate young man sprang up from his desk near the back, looking straight, well not that straight, at Chris. It was his old colleague Ashley, whom Chris had known briefly at his former agency but who had left the company over a year ago. Ashley was now the Post's TV critic working on the showbiz desk. He was also a very proud 'Friend of Dorothy'.

All the tough old journos lifted their heads. There were only three people standing up on the whole floor, him, Jill and a gesticulating Ashley. All eyes watched them. Chris wanted the ground to swallow him up. He spontaneously reacted with an uncertain raising of his right wrist in what looked like an unmanly wave, compounding the first impression he had already made with the old hacks.

"Well. You seem to have made quite a start with the editorial team", Jill commented. Chris could have crumpled into a heap and died on the spot.

Before anyone got to see the Editor, there was the small matter of passing through his PA's office to be contended with. Clearance for entry had to be granted by the formidable Betty, the Editor's gatekeeper and effectively the most powerful woman in the building. She was his personal, long-standing, faithful watchdog. Wherever he went in 'Fleet Street', whatever paper he had been on or will move to in the future, Betty came as part of the package. Her appearance was deceptive. Her flame of bouffant red hair, her heavy mascara and her intimidating lip-liner made her look anything but fierce, but you underestimated her at your peril. She knew everything and everyone, from Prime Ministers to the doormen. Above all else, she was the Geiger counter of his moods and also knew where all the skeletons were buried.

"Hi Betty", said Jill assuredly. "Is the Editor free?".

"Yes, he is expecting you. You must be Chris Adams. How are you enjoying yourself here, Chris?", Betty asked affably.

"Oh, it is fantastic. Thank you. Jill has been amazing. I am loving it".

"Excellent". Betty picked up the phone. "Jill Spender and Chris Adams to see you." She then smiled at Jill. "Go on in, Jill".

Chris walked behind Jill into the office feeling as grown up as he had ever felt. This was no place for his flippancy. As they entered, a large, old-fashioned man rose from behind an equally large, old-fashioned bureau, a far cry from the modern, grey desks that his staff had to make do with outside. In fact, the room was a complete contrast to the functional, minimalistic environment of the journalists' floor. It was power-dressed in carved wood-panelling, giving out a proud resonance of a time when the industry ruled the world and this office was the throne room. It was a step back into the opulence of former times, to an age when newspaper editors were kings, heading up the most influential organs of information in the whole world. Two paintings hung confidently behind the Editor, one showing a scene of the raucous, pounding presses pumping out the next day's paper, operated by sweating 1930's workers. The other was a cheeky, cloth-capped newsboy holding up a paper, from a similar 'Read All About It' era. These portraits reminded everyone who sat timorously before the Editor of the one-time dominance of the Press in the days before that soulless interloper, the internet, upset the paper cart.

"Jill, good to see you. This must be young Chris. Sit down". Around them, they were encircled by simple leather chairs, pushed back against the walls of the room, used by the editorial department heads when the Editor had his two daily 'conferences'. These were high pressure meetings, every mid-morning and mid-afternoon, when the top journalists presented their proposals for what stories they were planning on that night's edition. Two more comfortable chairs, with arms, were placed directly in front of the desk. Jill and Chris took their place on these. If they were not slightly lower than the Editor's, they certainly felt so to Chris as he shrank opposite the imposing man.

"Chris, I want to say well done. That promotion with the Lady Di roses was a stroke of genius." Genius is one of the most overworked words in newspapers, like its opposite, the 'c' word, both being liberally thrown around in this office at every opportunity, in equal measure. Journalists were used to receiving a regular number of each. "I didn't even know there was a Lady Diana rose. You know, when she was alive, we called her 'the patron saint of circulation' - one good picture on the front page and sales would go up ten per cent. You've done it again. It seems you have a bright future here. Make sure you hang on to him, Jill. But we want more, Chris. You are only as good as your last success. Keep them coming".

Chris felt emboldened. Such an endorsement by his boss' boss was as good as it gets and he felt brave enough to launch into his new-found promotional strategy. He had to be careful not to sound off too much in front of Jill, he thought, or this could backfire. Nevertheless, he knew this was an opportunity not to be missed. He took it with both hands.

He presented, or garbled more like, his promotional theory to the big boss, with an occasional glance at Jill so as to include her. He launched into his mantra.

"I think, sorry, we think, we should redouble our efforts and make promotions a huge weapon in your armoury, sir. We are committed to bringing you the best offers and competitions so that, when the readers see all the papers laid out in the newsagent, they would think 'I would be mad not to pick up the Post with such great news coverage and fabulous giveaways'. So, we don't want stop-start promotions, but we have to have a relentless barrage, something good every week, salvo after salvo of irresistible deals".

As Chris heard himself talk, it was like an out-of-body experience and he could not believe where all this was coming from or how well he was doing. He had unwittingly equated the importance and effectiveness of promotions to that of editorial excellence in the circulation war. This came with risks, but any fears were quickly allayed.

The Editor indulged him and then offered his encouragement. "That is excellent. Well done. Just keep it all going, you two. Let's get the circulation moving. I know as much as anyone that news is news, every paper has it. It's the added value that will shift extra copies. We should all have a lunch some time. I'll get Betty to get a date". Being invited to lunch by the Editor is, in the newspaper world, the equivalent of a mere mortal being invited to dine at Buckingham Palace. After all, the great man usually ate at the Savoy Grill with top Government ministers and powerful leaders from the business world.

They talked congenially for a while longer, the Editor taking the floor to impart his wisdom, including a salutary bit of advice that Chris would never forget.

"Remember one thing, young Chris. This is a tough game and these are not your friends", he said concisely, cryptically and chillingly. He was saying, in newspaper terms, 'watch your back'.

After ten minutes, their time was up. He stopped sharply and pushed a button on a speaker box, "Betty, call conference". That was their cue to exit and they passed back through Betty's office with a glancing 'thank you very much'.

Having narrowly escaped another 'cooee' from Ashley, they climbed back upstairs to their offices. Chris was worried that Jill would give him a blast for being full of himself after only a few weeks in the job. She had, after all, been around forever. To his pleasant surprise, she was effervescent with delight and told him how pleased she was with how it had gone.

"That went well, Chris. He didn't even call you the 'c' word. He must like you". The golden boy gave a broad smile and went back to his desk in the main office. There was a team of just five people working there, all go-getters and hotshots in their own way. The Colins of the world would not have survived five minutes. Chris had initially been nervous about joining this energetic, professional team after his old job. In the end, this turned out to be right up his street. He was starting to thrive on deadline pressure, something he had never experienced at this level before. His once eagerly awaited early evening trips to the Wellington had been willingly sacrificed as he worked late most nights to get things finished for the edition, but with life in his new apartment, he did not miss those six o'clock pints with George, as he still had a beer with him most evenings at home anyway.

That night, it was unusually quiet down at the Wellington. George's stool was nowadays more often than not vacant and, although he did still pop in occasionally, things were not the same. George knew that the old ritual, which had been a cornerstone of his existence, was over. In truth, he missed it more than Chris. It was a Monday night and the whole pub was more empty than usual, just two men sitting at a table doing more talking than drinking. When Bonnie arrived at 7pm, she walked into an almost rarefied atmosphere. Gerry was holding the fort single-handed.

"Evening, Bonnie. Don't rush tonight. We have the place virtually to ourselves".

"Doesn't look like it'll need two of us. This is going to be a long night. Where is everybody?", asked Bonnie.

"Well, they're not here, that's for sure. Good to see you. How was your weekend?". He thought this was a perfectly innocuous question. He was wrong.

"Bloody awful".

Gerry looked at her with a concerned expression as she took off her coat. She then joined Gerry, who saw in her eyes that something was very wrong.

"What happened? Something to do with Chris?".

"You could say that. If you are talking about him going out with his ex-wife and not telling me, yes. You know what? I caught him, red bloody handed, on Saturday night, having a cosy little dinner for two, at our restaurant". Her anger then turned to sadness. "It's not bloody fair, Gerry. I thought I could trust him, him of all people".

He saw she was about to burst into tears and went to put his arm around her. She put hers around his waist and pulled herself into him, sobbing into his shoulder. Gerry, while being overtly sympathetic, was also in no small way enjoying the physical closeness of the lovely Bonnie. He had secretly fancied her for some time, but when he watched how happy she was with Chris he had never made a move. Having her in his arms, and with Chris possibly about to disappear off the scene, he thought that this might be his chance and was tempted to lead the conversation, eventually steering it towards him asking her out. But, right now, was not the time. He played the consoling best friend and listened to her every word as she told him about that night in Covent Garden.

As she spoke, he had to tackle a dilemma. Should he say what a complete bounder and cad Chris was, that he had never trusted him and that she should not waste her time with such a two-timer or should he bow to his conscience and try to comfort her and give her hope that everything will be alright? To his own personal amazement, his better, kinder, more human side won the day.

"Oh, come on, Bonnie. I'm sure it was all a big misunderstanding. You've got to realise that Chris and his ex-wife were married for quite a while and have been incredibly civil, or so Chris tells me, over the divorce. According to Chris, she has no problem with you at all and wants Chris to be happy. At least you don't have a demented, jealous ex rampaging all over the place. They still probably have a few things to sort out, the house, car and things like that. Unhooking yourself from a marriage can take a while, I imagine".

Bonnie looked up at him. "But he should have told me. And it's not just this once. They have been meeting like this before. He lied to me, Gerry. He lied".

"Look, Bonnie. Men are sometimes too stupid for their own good. You have to see through the action and think of the intent. I am certain he has no plans to get back with her and that he had absolutely no intention of upsetting you. Perhaps if he had told you, you would have gone ballistic anyway and that was what he was frightened of".

"Am I being unreasonable?". Bonnie asked humbly.

"Let me answer your question with a question. Do you love him? You love him, don't you. That's why this is hurting so much".

Bonnie stepped back, thought for a minute and said softly. "Yes, I think I do".

"Then Bonnie, don't ruin things over the bloody ex-wife. He adores you. He comes in here early some nights and just talks about you non-stop. If I were you, I'd make your point to him and then let it go. He is a really nice bloke and I don't believe there is a bad bone in his body. Chris isn't clever enough to play games". Bonnie and Gerry both laughed in agreement, breaking the intensity.

"What should I do?", Bonnie asked, meekly.

"That's up to you", said Gerry. "I think that if I were you, I'd do something as simple as saying 'sorry, I overreacted'".

"You may be right. Not yet, though. He can sweat it out for a few days first. He won't lie to me next time".

"Atta girl, Bonnie".

Gerry broke off to serve the two customers, who had just come in, but all the time his wicked side was ruing what he had just done. 'I must be mad or a bloody saint', he concluded. 'I am just far too nice'.

TUESDAY SEPTEMBER 10

Ricky was in the small, makeshift dressing room at the Bell. It doubled up as a storeroom with beer kegs standing around, tonight being conveniently used as stools or just somewhere to throw clothes. The singer was looking vainly at his reflection in the mirror and playing with his long hair. Nerves still got the better of him before every performance and tonight was no difference. Unfortunately, this anxiety nearly always manifested itself in a short temper. A Jekyll and Hyde metamorphosis seemed to occur when he was to take the stage, transforming him from the funny, genial Ricky into a rock monster.

His drummer, Mitch, sat back in a corner, the smoke off his joint permeating the air like a London smog. The other two bandmembers, Jake and Rupert, were calmly tuning their guitars, oblivious to everything around them.

"OK, guys, we are nearly on. Make this a blast", Ricky said motivationally, before letting rip. "Let's get it right tonight. You were complete crap last week. Go easy on that dope, Mitch. We need you to be shit hot tonight, not stoned like some old hippy. There's a big crowd out there and I want you on top form, OK?". This was typical of Ricky. One minute you were his best friend, the next you would be stung by his tongue lashing out like a gaucho's whip.

Ricky was the self-appointed leader of the band. The others usually fell obediently into line, probably as they didn't care quite as much as Ricky did. Flare-ups were routine. To say Ricky was difficult to work with was an understatement. They put up with it because, as the lead singer, the lead guitarist and the songwriter, Ricky's position was unchallengeable. He was the star of the show and they all knew it.

There was knock on the door.

"It's 8.30. You're on..." bellowed a Cockney voice.

"Let's go, guys. Let's burn this place down. C'mon".

The club manager grabbed the mike. "Ladies and gentlemen. Tuesday Night is Rock Night at the Blue Bell. Make some noise. Let's hear it for Street Fire!". They walked out to the frenzied cheers of the heaving, raucous audience. Ricky held back off-stage to let the others get settled and then made his own lordly entrance, with a strutting, godlike poise. The crowd erupted and Ricky soaked up the veneration. He had a presence, of that there could be no doubt. Tall, good-looking, long hair, T-shirt and jeans, he was every inch rock 'n' roll. The band smashed into their opening number. In the front, girls screamed hysterically, all with their sole focus on the enigmatic front man, who responded by intermittently taking his right hand off his guitar to reach out and touch their extended, suppliant fingers. They loved him. He loved their love. It was a rock love-in.

The gig was a blast. There was a short interval of about twenty minutes, just enough time for the audience to get a fresh drink and for Ricky to get off stage and lay into his fellow band members. This time it was bass guitarist Rupert's time for the tongue-lashing.

"Jesus. Where are you playing tonight? The Royal Opera House?" was one of his comments. "A gorilla with a broken wrist could play better than you'" was another. Rupert, as ever, soaked it up, without any reaction. It was just another Street Fire gig.

They came back on and played for almost another hour before leaving the stage. The roars for an encore filled the hall. After an appropriate break to let the frenzy to grow, they came back on and threw themselves into a powerful rendition of

'Satisfaction', a fitting finale. They then left the baying fans wanting more and returned to their modest dressing room.

"Wow, that was a blast!", cried out a panting Mitch, lighting up another joint.

"You were complete crap again, Mitch. You were way out if it tonight'" attacked Ricky.

"Give it a break, Ricky. You can be such an arsehole. That was a great gig. Have a beer and chill", said Rupert, treating him like a child who was having a tantrum.

Ricky listened and got the message, snatching the bottle of beer out of Rupert's hand. "OK. That was a fun night. Well done, guys. We killed it". Dr Jekyll was back in the room.

They were used to him. His personality was not so much split as cleft clean in two. The rock Ricky had always been a beast, right from the first band he had as a sixteen-year-old. Someone must have told him that this was how stars behaved. His reputation in the business for being 'difficult' was renowned, not helped by his dispensing with the services of fellow musicians and managers alike at a whim. To him, everyone was an idiot. In total contrast, however, the friend Ricky was generous, loyal and funny, albeit with a tolerable arrogance. In fact, this egotism could be attractive and, anyway, those who really knew him were well aware that it hid a huge streak of insecurity. Like so many, he built up his own self-confidence mostly to overshadow his own self-doubt.

After the one roadie, Alvin, who they all called Stardust, had organised the packing of the gear into their truck, Ricky turned to the boys and said simply, "Nice one, boys. We were shit hot tonight. Let's do that again at Brighton next week". All was forgiven. As always.

That same night, Bonnie was about to leave for work at the usual time. It took her a good twenty minutes to cross London to get to the Wellington but, with the traffic, she always gave it a bit longer. She was just finishing her make-up when the doorbell rang. She opened the door to a lovely little lady carrying a huge bouquet of flowers almost as big as herself.

"Are you Bonnie?" asked the woman. Bonnie nodded, struck dumb by the sight of the flowers. "These are for you", and she handed them over. "Somebody loves you."

She thanked her and took them inside, lay them down on the kitchen table, before opening the card.

It read 'Bonnie, one day without you is a pain I cannot take. I don't know how to be without you. I am so sorry for my stupidity. I never, ever meant to hurt you. I never meant to hurt us. Please forgive me. I love you. Chris XXX'.

The tears rolled down her face. She cried so much that she had to redo her make-up. But she now knew not one but two things - he loved her and she loved him.

She did eventually get to work, still with a tear trickling down her cheek as she sat in the bus. Some fellow passengers did look round at her, but she simply gave them a warm smile back to let them know that they were tears of happiness. Gerry noticed immediately that she was a bag of emotion.

"Well, Miss Bonnie. Feeling better? You look it".

"Oh, Gerry, he has just sent me the most beautiful bouquet and such a lovely message". Tears welled up again and she reached for a tissue.

"Say no more, girl. Go get him. Don't lose him if you feel like that." But that would have to wait. She still had a night's work ahead of her.

It was a busy night for the staff at the Wellington, the opposite of the night before. A large office birthday party raised the noise level and boosted the wine and beer turnover at the same time. On the good side, it certainly made the evening go faster and kept Bonnie's mind off her personal drama. Last orders were always at 10.45pm and they closed at 11 sharp. However, it was always near 11.30 by the time she could leave.

Outside, at that late hour, London was still buzzing. The pavements were still busy. Many people had been to the theatre and were either heading home or searching for a late-night bar. Bonnie stepped out into the throng and there, in front of her, was one sole person standing completely still, while everyone around him was bustling and shuffling to and fro.

"Hi, Bonnie". It was Chris.

She just threw herself at him, wrapping her arms around his neck and kissing him as hard as she could. The tears returned.

"You stupid, crazy bastard", she said.

"Thanks for your kind words. That's very nice, very romantic. I love you, too. Seriously, Bonnie. I am so sorry. You were right. I was an idiot. I should have told you. From now on, nothing but the truth. Always. Please forgive me".

"Oh, Chris, I do. Of course I do". She was about to say something like 'but don't do it again' but stopped herself. She knew when enough was enough and that they must both put it behind them. His mind then went back the day at the races and Good Earth.

"Fancy a Chinese? Shall we go into Chinatown and start again?".

"Let's do just that", and she grabbed his arm tightly. They took a taxi to Gerrard Street, the hub of Chinese restaurants, all of which were doing a roaring late-night trade, mostly filled with unsmiling Oriental folk who had just finished work.

"Can we have Dim Sum? I know it's late and they may not have it but it's my favourite.", Bonnie asked.

"You can have whatever you want", Chris replied and asked a local, using up all his Cantonese on two words 'Dim Sum?'. The man pointed down the street, on the other side, saying something unintelligible. They walked down, passing about four restaurants, all displaying scrawny, bronzed ducks, skewered by their necks, hanging in the window, until the came to one with a sign that read 'Dim Sum Special'.

They went in, found a table and were immediately presented with an invasion of trolleys, lining up like London buses. They picked out pancake rolls, coconut buns, deep-fried shrimp balls, beef short ribs, and potsticker dumplings by the plateful. They both had, thankfully, a healthy appetite, stoked by the emotional car crash they had been just gone through. After a shot of sake, they changed to Tsingtao beer. It was a reunion filled with love, warmth and laughter. When they were not wrestling a dumpling, they were holding hands across the table.

It was after 12.30 when they came out. They walked down Gerrard Street to the taxi rank at the end and they both climbed in a cab.

"Drayson Mews, please", Chris instructed the cabbie. Bonnie interrupted.

"No, Thames Tower, please". Chris managed his shock by taking her in his arms and kissing her. The driver looked in his rear-view mirror and smiled as he saw true love entwined.

They crept back into the riverside apartment, turning the key as silently as they could. An overexuberance of love, happiness and alcohol resulted in several suppressed fits of laughter. Even Chris raising his index finger to his lips and going 'shhh' was hilarious. It was very late and the others were in bed asleep. Even though they tried to be as quiet as mice, they could not hold back the deep vibrance of the love and joy they were sharing at this moment. The artificial light that rose from the London streets below gave a soft illumination throughout the apartment, helping the two sweethearts as they staggered into Chris' room and quietly closed the door. Bonnie kicked off her shoes, lay her jacket on a chair and threw herself on the bed, into a spreadeagle of sheer delight. Chris immediately followed her every action, taking off his shoes, laying his jacket over hers and jumping onto the bed beside her.

The kiss that followed was as passionate as it was long and, in no time, they had discarded their clothes and were both entwined, naked, on top of the bed. Her body collapsed eagerly into his and he consumed her in his doting arms, all the time kissing her tenderly. His embrace enveloped the softness of her skin as he cradled her and they melded seamlessly into one. He was absorbed into her adoring eyes, which closed only as she surrendered herself to his limitless love.

WEDNESDAY, SEPTEMBER 11

George and David were sitting at the breakfast table in the kitchen, accompanied by tea, coffee and some toast. It was a beautifully warm and sunny September day. However, the normality of their morning routine was about to be shattered. Walking across towards them appeared Bonnie, wearing one of Chris' white England football shirts and little, or nothing, else. The two men looked thunderstruck, their mouths falling open, their eyes popping out of their heads. Bonny had enough sex appeal even when she was pulling pints behind the bar, but to see her emerge like a Botticelli Venus, her ruffled hair tumbling unbrushed onto her shoulders, was too much for the boys, especially at 8.30am.

"May I make a cup of tea?", Bonnie asked as she came closer towards them.

David shot up to help her. "Of course, let me show you where the cups are".

George was not to be left out and sprung from his seat to offer further assistance, both men eager to help this apparition. "Let me show you where the tea bags and sugar are", he gushed.

She prepared two cups while the infatuated men buzzed about her like bees round a honeycomb, both barely able to string a coherent sentence together.

"This is an honour, Bonnie", bumbled David. "Can I take it from your attire that you and Chris are friends again?".

"You could say that", she said cheekily as she poured the hot water into the cups.

"That makes me very happy. Chris can be a such a blithering fool sometimes, but he is genuinely a great guy. Just too stupid for his own good on occasion and I have told him so".

Bonnie appreciated the support and vindication. "That's all over now. I don't think he would ever dare go behind my back again. He has learned his lesson. I don't know what he told you about it, but the truth is that I caught him out with his ex-wife and he hadn't told me. But the worst thing is he lied to me.
I cannot bear that. You don't blame me for being angry, do you? It wasn't pathetic jealousy, that's not me. It was the lying I objected to. But, as I say, that is behind us now. He bought me some amazing flowers and took me to dinner last night. He was really nice and very apologetic, which means, guys, I am back. Sorry about that!".

"We are delighted, Bonnie. I must tell you though that he was very upset about it all, you know", said George. "It is just so good that you two are together again. You make such a lovely couple".

Bonnie picked up the two cups and walked back into the bedroom, fully aware of the stares that followed her every step.

"Well, well, well. There's a surprise," commented David quietly as they gawked at her. "We had better start raising our own game, dear George. We can't let these youngsters have more fun than us".

"I think you're dead right. Bugger, I just thought", George's expression changed. "How the hell is he going to explain about the Moira thing?".

This was a thorny problem that Chris had already been sweating over. To admit that he was about to go on a date with David's ex-wife would be incendiary. To lie again, on the other hand, could be fatal and there was no way he could hide the deception from her, even if he had wanted to. No, he thought, she would have to be brought on board, and quickly.

Ten minutes later, the happy couple appeared together and went slowly onto the balcony. She still looked ravishing in her over-large football shirt, Chris less so in his T-shirt and jeans. As they passed, David just had time to ask if he was going into work today and Chris explained that he had rung in to say he would be late with another dental appointment. The couple then slid the glass door behind them unhurriedly.

Chris and Bonnie sat at the table with their hands clasped around their warm tea. Chris had had some time to consider how he was going to explain his mucky intrigue to the girl he loved. He had no choice. He could not lie, again. In the end, he just plunged in and told her about David's evil plan. The only part he changed was the bit about him finding Moira on the internet, saying it was David that had been surfing the web, not him. Her eyes were fixed on him, eking out any potential untruth as he hummed and hawed his way through the complex story. He eventually came to the last and the most dangerous detail, his 'date' with Moira at the weekend.

"Let me get this straight. You are going on a date with David's ex-wife and you want me to be happy about it?", Bonnie scowled.

"Not a date exactly, Bonnie. It is all just a game. I agreed to play along, and that's all it is, acting out a part, and I promise there is absolutely nothing to it. I just want to help out a mate. God, I wish I hadn't agreed now".

To his complete amazement, Bonnie said, "No, Chris. It's brilliant. Did you come up with all this yourself?".

Chris turned his temerity into a little puff of pride, taking ownership of the cunning plan. "Yes, well, I did actually, sort of. You don't mind?".

"Mind. Not at all. If you are helping David and his children, I think you are being very noble. It is actually hilarious, the whole thing. But you won't run off with her, will you?".

"Bonnie, no, no, no, I won't do anything. If you don't like the idea, I'll get out of it right now".

"You will not, Chris", she said firmly. "You boys have made a pact. There is one thing that I must insist on though, or else we have a problem".

"What Bonnie? Anything", Chris said in total fear of what was to come.

"I insist this, that you meet me tonight at 11.15 outside the Wellington, like last night, and whisk me back here. And I don't need flowers this time".

Chris smiled and reached out to take her hands in his.

"Bonnie, you are the most amazing girl I have ever met. And the sexiest. I love you so much".

It was lunchtime. David was sitting at a table for two at Daphne's, one of his favourite restaurants, where London's society came to relax and chat over excellent food and a crisp glass of Italian wine. While the upscale Etruscan eatery was understated on the outside, the inside epitomises 'la dolce vita' with unassuming elegance. It has class written all over it. David was waiting for his special guest, a lady of whom he had grown extremely fond over the past few months.

As his guest approached the table, he stood up and kissed her on the cheek.

"I hope I am not late".

"Not at all. It's lovely to see you. Now, what are you drinking? Will you have a glass of champagne with me?".

"I'd love to. Thank you".

Sophie Cavendish personified style. In or out of the office, she never failed to appear anything other than refined, fashionable and sophisticated. David had been swept away by her composure and intelligence, as well as her captivating beauty, from the moment she had battled for him in Court. After their day at Wimbledon, they had several lunches. Lunches then became dinners. As the relationship developed, they had decided it was best to keep their liaisons secret as they both felt it was too early to introduce Sophie into the lives of Jess and Robbie. They had been through so much already. David did not even tell his flatmates about the trysts. The covert dinners then inevitably became clandestine dates, two or three times a week. David had seized every opportunity to spend all the time he could with her and had become completely infatuated, as Sophie had with him. Yet, to see them together, sitting correctly at that table, you would not have known there was such a fire burning within them. It was a very British affair.

"How have you been?", David asked.

"It was only last Thursday that you came over so not a great deal has happened since then. I saw my parents for Sunday lunch. You remember it was my Mother's birthday. I am very close to my Mum but she has been poorly recently so it was nice to spend time with her. I also busied myself around my apartment and that's about it. Not very exciting I am afraid. I missed having my man around".

David smiled affectionately and the champagne arrived.

"Cheers, Sophie. It is just so lovely to see you. I missed you too. So, you haven't ruined anyone's life recently, have you?" David joked, referring to her professional capacity.

"A few perhaps", Sophie joked. "I have a client that has this ghastly husband who is having a fling with his secretary and we found out that he has now set her up in a little love-nest in Chelsea. I think my client is about to become the proud owner of a million-pound flat in The King's Road".

"You are brilliant, Sophie. Brutal, but brilliant. I am just glad you were on my side. I'd probably be eating at McDonalds now if you had been on Moira's team. So, how was your Mother's birthday. Did it all go well?".

"Yes, it was fine. She's been very poorly lately but I think she really enjoyed it. I'll tell you all about it, but let's sort the food out first, shall we? I'm starving".

They ordered their lunch, washed down with a delicious bottle of Tufo di Greco. Conversation always flowed easily between the two. She talked about the birthday and he chatted at length about Jess and Robbie with Sophie asking what his plans were for the weekend with them. Inevitably, she brought up about how she would love to meet them, not in a pushy way, more enthusiastically. Although David had often been tempted to introduce her, he had always thought better of it. As much as it galled him, he did not want them to feel any more division in their lives and, if Moira found out, he was well aware that she would do everything in her power to make his, the children's and Sophie's lives as uncomfortable as she could.

He thought, quite rightly, that it was far better that he and Sophie enjoy the time they had together below the radar. He was, however, waiting for the day when all that could change, the time when they could be free to bring their relationship into the open. He just could not see when that day would be. It was what they both wanted and deserved. However, his protection of the children came first and, in Sophie, he had someone who fully understood and respected his dilemma. After all, she dealt with marital bust-ups every day.

"I haven't been a great Dad, Sophie. Not really. Looking back, I was always at work and I should have arranged things better. I should have done so much more. In my defence, though, I wasn't really allowed to be a good Dad", he confessed. Sophie looked at him sympathetically.

"David. This is the real world. You were and are a wonderful father. I see all the time how you dote on your children. It's obvious that they adore you. I see it every day in family break-ups. In nearly all my cases, four parties are involved in the divorce process, the husband, the wife and their respective lawyers. If any one element is hellbent on a fight for a fight's sake, just for their day in Court, the system completely fails. Working hard, commuting, getting home after the children have been put to bed, that's not being a bad parent. It's providing, it's protecting, it's reality. Parenthood should at best be teamwork, two complementary contributors to the marriage, ideally working in harmony. The quality of the time you spend with the children is the important thing and it is Moira who has cast her shadow over everyone's happiness for a very long time. Don't let it get to you. Moira will always be one thing, whereas you can be anything."

David was lost in awe at her wise counsel. His admiration for Sophie knew no bounds and during their many secret nights together his feelings had grown into something far deeper. She had become his trusted lover and confidential companion, his soulmate, whose every compelling word of advice he accepted faithfully. Sophie had an incisive, intelligent way of seeing things so clearly that her sagacity never failed to enlighten him.

"I would like to ask you to consider one thing though", she continued. "While I totally agree with you that I should not meet the children just yet, I do think that keeping me away from them indefinitely serves no useful purpose other than to let Moira's control extend into the future. You are divorced now. It has been tough on the children and they have come through it in spite of the horrendous atmosphere and rows. You have always been there for them and they know that. To perpetuate this veil of denial will achieve nothing, other than to play into Moira's game-plan. You all have to move on, even Moira. Especially Moira. When Moira meets someone and feels like we do, do you think she would keep him out of the children's lives? Of course not. I am, of course, talking about real relationships, not casual flings. Please don't think I am interfering. It is just what I see every day. David, I would like to think that I can enjoy their company for Christmas this year, not the one after, and that we can together provide an environment that they deserve, loving, stable and fun. That's my professional opinion anyway". She finished with a touch on his hand. "I guess what I really want is for all of us to be family".

"Sophie. You never fail to amaze me". David wanted her to know the highest regard in which he held her. "Your clarity, your wisdom, you are incredible. I cannot disagree with a single thing you have said. In those few concise words, you have the ability to make me wake up and rethink everything. You are right, so right. We do need to move on, all of us, and not be held back by dancing to Moira's tune. Her vindictiveness and negativity have dragged us all down. I make a promise to you here and now that I shall make this happen, way before Christmas. In fact, I wish we could all go away together at half-term, but that is too soon".

"David, I know that that is too soon, for you, especially. Nevertheless, looking ahead, let's aim to have a good Christmas, together. If it takes longer, then so be it. It is not a rush. I am not going anywhere. I just think that you will be happier if you saw some light at the end of the tunnel and can finally shed the shackles of a failed marriage. And I wouldn't worry too much about the children. Take it slowly and you will be surprised how receptive and accepting they can be. I am sure they will like me".

"Sophie, for once, I am lost for words. I have nothing to add. They will adore you. You are astounding".

At that point, their food arrived. Sophie thought it was time to change the subject.

"David, I have a question for you. How would you fancy having a consultancy in a very successful financial investment firm? I have a lovely client who, like you, is going through a horrendous time. We were talking the other day about his business and he is looking for some experienced, energetic, handsome, engaging help to share his load and I naturally thought of you. I think he wants a good lunch pal too. What do you think? I know you'll like him".

"That sounds unbelievable. It would be perfect. I can't sit around the apartment like a pensioner all day".

"Great. His name is Greg Chapman, he's really nice and I think you two would hit it off. I shall get him to call you if you are up for it. I know you'll get along famously".

"Thanks, Sophie. That'd be amazing. Any more surprises? Are you going to carry me off into the sunset on some exotic beach?".

"I wish. Not yet. But I will. One day. That's my promise to you". She gave him a loving, kittenish smile.

David smiled back warmly, stretched out his hand and placed it on hers. She, in return, proceeded to turn her palm up and clutch his affectionately. She blew him a silent kiss.

CHAPTER SIX
HOT DATES, BEST SERVED COLD

SATURDAY, SEPTEMBER 14

It was David's big weekend. Not only was he having the children at the apartment but also Chris was going on his mission to date Moira. After an uneventful drive down to Wychwood, David parked up and went to the door at precisely 12 noon, expecting the usual confrontation. To his utter amazement, instead of the familiar delays or conflagration, it opened with a gentle ease.

"Hello, David, nice drive?" said Moira, with an uncharacteristic smile. "Come on children. Daddy's here. You mustn't keep him waiting". The children came out as happy as the birds of May and gave him an enormous hug. "Have a nice weekend, you guys. See you tomorrow. Don't forget choir practice, Jess, back by 3.45 latest". With that she closed the door, softly for a change. David was dumbstruck with this rare civility, until he remembered that she had a date with 'Brian' the next day. That explained everything, he thought.

They drove up to London, singing away merrily with the radio, arriving at the apartment at about 1.30pm. The children loved it there, immediately running in, bouncing around the furniture and rushing out onto the balcony. George tended to find something else to do when the children came and lost himself in the Wellington for a drink, while Ricky had skipped breakfast and was settled into a lazy Saturday with his acoustic guitar. David went to have a shave and freshen up, leaving the children on the sofa with Ricky. They had taken to Ricky, especially when he played his songs to them. They snuggled round him in complete admiration. 'My youngest superfans', he called them.

They adored him and he was terrific with them, letting them clamber all over him and join in as he sang. This was the 'nice guy' Ricky at play. He was working on his new song, a melancholic number with more than a touch of personal pain in the lyric. On the coffee table in front of him, he had a large pad on which he had scratched down the words. As he sang, he would stop occasionally, pick up the pen and change a line. He was working on the opening verse.

'The cheers were so loud on that opening night.
You looked down on the crowd like a Phoenix in flight.
'You went down a storm as you smashed your guitar.
Since the day you were born, you were always a star.

'So proud and so strong, my hero that day,
Why did it go wrong? You just threw it away.
Then came the day for our curtain to fall,
Can you honestly say that you gave it your all?

'My whole body's dyin'. I've no more to give.
There's something 'bout lying I just cannot forgive.
The truth's a good friend, my companion, my guide.
Right up to the end, I'll have truth by my side.

'That truth became trust but what did you do?
You turned it to dust. What has happened to you?
You've broken my heart. You've broken our home.
While you're lying in love, I'm lying alone'.

There was a moment of stillness and then the children started clapping. Ricky gave them a modest smile.

"That's what it's called, guys. 'Lying In Love'. What do you think?"

"We love it, Ricky. Will you play it for Daddy?", asked Jess.

"It's a bit sad. Are you going to make it into a record?", swooned Robbie.

"Do you think I should?", Ricky asked.

"I would buy it, even though it's a bit sad", Robbie repeated.

"Then I will record it next time I'm in the studio, just for my two most special superfans. You will have to come with your Dad and see the band play one night, won't you".

"Can we? Can we really?", the wide-eyed children asked with unconfined excitement.

"We'll see. I'll talk to your Dad about it.

The two children shifted closer to Ricky as he went into a slow rendition of the Beatles' 'If I Fell'. David came back in and Jess could not help herself. "Daddy, Ricky says we can go and see his band. Can we? Can we?".

"I don't see why not. Let me talk to Ricky about it."

"Daddy, you must hear his new song. It's amazing. Will you play it, Ricky".

"It's nowhere near finished. Just the first verse and the chorus? Is that OK?"

He played a cut down version once more, and when he got to the chorus, both Jess and Robbie joined in at the top of their voices. David applauded the trio loudly and told Ricky that he really loved the song.

"Ricky's going to record it, Daddy. For us", Jess said.

"Is that right, Ricky? That really is excellent".

"Well, if my superfans demand it, then it has to be done. We are in the studio next week and I have about six of my songs I'd like to lay down, plus some covers. I thought I'd do that classic Elmore James number 'Shake Your Money Maker', Curtis Mayfield's 'People Get Ready' and Bad Company's 'Feel Like Makin' Love'. I really love that track. George would know them, I'm certain. He's a dark horse that George. There's a little rocker inside him trying to burst out, I reckon. I am now thinking of putting this new song on the album and perhaps even make it the album title - 'Lying In Love'. What do you think?".

"I think it's brilliant", David enthused.

The children looked at the singer adoringly. "Do it Ricky. You have to record it", begged Jess.

"Alright. I definitely will", he said to the overjoyed children, as he put his guitar back in its case. "Just for you two".

David had tickets for the Lion King that night, so he suggested that the children should have a quiet afternoon, watch a film in their room if they liked, and then they would go out at around five to grab a pizza near the Lyceum Theatre. Even he knew that he spoiled them too much. That would never stop him though. Just to see the smiles on their faces and get that thank-you hug meant everything to him. They obediently disappeared to their room and David went off to his for a short nap. As he lay on his bed, he was thinking about the Machiavellian plan that was about to be unleashed. 'How on earth will Chris survive a date with Moira?', he asked himself.

SUNDAY, SEPTEMBER 15

By 9am, the first stage of the dating game had begun. After a late night with Jess and Robbie at the Lion King, David was up and about, albeit moving slowly. He had tucked them into their beds at almost midnight and they were understandably having a very late start to their morning.

Meanwhile, Chris, excused from breakfast duties, was well on his way, having already morphed himself into the charmingly compliant Brian Jackson-Brown. He had set off early in George's new BMW, far too early for his 12.30 tryst and, as a result, he had driven slowly, listened to the radio and thoroughly enjoyed the luxury of the leather seats with that new car smell, before stopping for breakfast at a roadside café. When he pulled into the church car park just after 12, it quickly became apparent that being there so soon was a far from good idea as it gave him much too much time to think about exactly what he was doing. As the witching-hour approached, he was a bag of nerves. His bravado had started to wane, replaced by doubt and uncertainty. All of a sudden, there was a tap on the window. He looked up. Moira looked older than her photo. When Chris had seen her with David a few weeks back, he had watched her from a distance and in full flight, or in full fight would be a better way of putting it. Having got into the car, she bizarrely put on a regal pose, grandly proffering her hand as if she was the Queen. Chris gave her fingers a duly deferential shake. "Hi, Moira, nice to meet you at last", said Chris, starting up the engine. His initial feeling was one of total disappointment, but it eased his nerves. "I hope you are hungry".

"I am and I am so pleased you have chosen The Manor. It's so weird that you knew. It's one of my favourites. They do a wonderful lunch there. By the way, I don't want to be a killjoy, but I do have to be back by 3.30 at the latest. I hope that doesn't spoil your plans".

In truth, Moira talked while he listened, bringing up their online profiles and saying how amazingly similar they were before getting back to the subject of lunch.

"I used to go there quite often before my ex-husband decided to walk out on me. He always put himself first. He never thought about anyone else." It took no deduction for Chris to realise that she was talking about David, while thinking to himself, 'bloody hell, straight out of the traps, she's off and running already'. Her vitriol continued at the same pace and in the same vein for a few minutes before David's instructions rushed into Chris's head. 'In case of emergency, put the opera on', he thought.

"Do you mind if I play music?", Chris interrupted as politely as he could. Moira just smiled, with a hint of dissatisfaction at having to stop her diatribe.

'Let's see if this works,' thought Chris, as he fiddled with his phone. He had set up the stereo on Bluetooth and pressed play. Miraculously, the exquisite Sull'aria from the Marriage of Figaro filled the car. Moira, stunned into a rare silence, put her head back to listen.

"Oh, Brian. I just adore Mozart. I love this".

Chris, in an effort to impress, attempted to regurgitate some of the educated facts that David had primed him to drop into the conversation, all about the vocal duettino in the opera, the Countess Almaviva, Susanna and the tryst. Unfortunately, his attention to detail failed him as usual.

"Yes, this is my favourite of all the great 'suet divos'", he said confidently, nearly getting it right. His mispronunciation went completely unnoticed by Moira who, in truth, knew no more about opera than he did. He was now on a roll and continued unchallenged, with the puffed-up authority of an opera buff. "Act Three, if I recall. Yes, that's it. I simply adore the way that Viv woman tells her friend Susan about 'twisting' with her husband. No wonder she started singing so loudly. Who can blame her? It is so clever". While Chris allowed himself a smug smile, Moira hid her bemusement and gave no reaction.

Silence reigned. It did not last. The full three minutes of this glorious aria had tamed his fiery passenger as David had said it would, but not for long. As it came to an end, she let rip again, spewing out more caustic comments about David and how he had been such an despicable husband. Chris noticed that, so far, there was no mention of Jess and Robbie.

He somehow managed to block her ramblings out as Voi Che Sapete came on in competition to his companion's cacophony. He wanted to hum along loudly to drown her out but managed to refrain. After a while, he made some feeble efforts to regain control of the conversation, failing dismally every time. He did, however, eventually get his opening when she asked, in full flow, "...have you been married, Brian?".

"Actually, I only recently got divorced. It was...". His contribution was short-lived. Moira cut in. She preferred to be heard than to listen.

"Yes, divorce is horrible, isn't it. I don't know why they always want to fight. Did yours fight?". She said 'yours' as if talking about her pet dog. She went off on a rant again. Chris let her carry on, shutting her out by absorbing himself in Mozart's masterpiece and following his satnav.

She was still going strong when they arrived at the pub although, mercifully, she actually stopped talking as he parked the car. They walked in without a word being exchanged between them and Chris, putting on his best 'after you' manners, guided his guest to a table with a 'reserved' sign on it, next to the old inglenook fireplace. The Manor was indeed much more than a normal pub and much classier, a splendid Jacobean country house, filled with opulent interiors and antique furniture. The atmosphere was eerily subdued as people toned down their natural noisy banter to reflect the grandeur of their environment.

"What would you like? A glass of wine?", Chris asked in his poshest voice. On receiving her order of dry white wine, he went to the bar and returned with his pint of real ale and a large, overpriced glass of Sancerre. If it had been down to him, he would have bought her the house white but, after all, David was picking up the tab. In his absence, she had started to think to herself that she too needed to quieten down her yapping a bit. She hadn't been on a date for quite some time and was definitely getting over-excited, she realised. Taking a long, deep breath, she re-opened the conversation, appearing much more relaxed. "So, Brian, tell me about yourself", she said with an insincere interest. Brian bridled his sigh of relief as he had a turn to talk. "Well. I live in London and I am working in newspaper marketing. I have only just started my new job at the Daily Post, but I love it", immediately kicking himself for mentioning the name of the paper. His hopes of dominating the conversation for a while were quickly dashed.

"Were you ever unfaithful, Brian?". Moira threw out this oddball question and glared scarily at him. "Did you have affairs?" she asked bluntly.

Chris was taken aback by the question, even though he quickly saw exactly where it was leading. "No. Not at all. Never. Why do you ask?". Chris readied himself for the answer.

"My husband had a string of affairs. He was cheating on me with this young girl in his office...".

This time, he interrupted. Did he just hear that right? He could not believe what she was saying about his friend. It seemed so out of character. He was so amazed that he nearly gave the game away.

"What? Davi....", he stopped abruptly, realising that she had not yet mentioned David by name.

"What was that?", screeched Moira.

Chris had to think quickly to get out of trouble. He was never any good at thinking quickly. What came out next was utter rubbish.

"Er. What Davi..s Cup tennis player is your favourite? You, er, like tennis, don't you? I think you said so on your profile. I do too". That was just pathetic, he thought. Needless to say, he need not have worried. Moira was not listening anyway and was off again, bleating on about her former husband, his many mistresses and how he had stashed money offshore. It may have been all made up in her head, but she had said it so often to anyone that would listen that she now clearly believed it. He thought the best policy would be to get some food as soon as possible, thinking that that might put an end to her ranting. He thrust a menu in front of her.

"I fancy the Sunday roast. There's beef, pork or chicken. I am definitely having some rare roast beef with roast potatoes, Yorkshire pudding and horseradish. There are other choices though. What would you like? You look like a chicken girl", Chris suggested.

"No. I think I'll have the pork".

"Not the chicken? But I thought you would be a chicken sort of girl. I had this intuition". Chris stopped himself sharply. He had once again acted on reflex, jumping in without thinking. He was trying just too hard and getting clumsy.

"Funny you should say that. You do know me well. I would normally have had the chicken. Today though I really fancy some crackling and apple sauce".

Chris went to the bar and ordered. No sooner had he sat back down than Moira unleashed another lashing of the same monologue. It went on until the food came out. And even then, it stopped only for a minute. Chris ate his roast beef in silence as his lunch date went on, without pausing to eat or breathe, about the litany of David's treachery and deceit. It was only when her plate was empty that she ran out of steam. He thought of his cartoon and that he should come in at that opportune moment with a "Me" question. He went back to his briefing notes.

"What theatre do you like? I used to act, you know. Personally, I love musicals. Les Mis, Phantom, Cats, Miss Saigon, stuff like that".

"That's incredible, Brian. Me too. Those are my favourites too".

"And films? What are your best films?", he asked when he could get a word in.

"Well, I don't like films that are unbelievable, like Game of Thrones or The Matrix, stuff like that".

"No. I don't like those either. My favourites are Love Actually and The Holiday".

"Brian, you are incredible. I'm the same. I can watch The Holiday again and again".

"I thought Jude Law was fabulous. I couldn't stand that Jack Black. So miscast", Chris tossed in nonchalantly. "Oh, and when it comes to the old films, I just love Rebecca and Gone with the Wind". Chris thought he was on a roll, albeit perhaps sticking to the script too literally. Moira fell for every bit of it, leaning over towards him, smiling adoringly and, more importantly, without reverting to a further character assassination of David.

"Oh, I so agree. Wasn't Jude Law great? If I had to choose my favourite films of all time, those two would be right up there. We really do like all the same things, Brian. Isn't it amazing?". Chris had one ace more up his sleeve. He did not worry in the slightest that the juxtaposition was odd. He went with it anyway. "And I have just noticed your beautiful nails. They are lovely. I do like girls with well-manicured hands".

At that, Moira positively grinned and proudly held out the back of her hands towards him, fingers outstretched, her false nails gleaming. "Oh, thank you for appreciating them. I like to look nicely turned out".

Chris thought he had better move on, having used up all his well-rehearsed ad lib lines. He was now flying solo. This was a dangerous time.

"Do you work, Moira?". He mistakenly thought this was an innocuous question.

"It depends what you mean by work. Do I have a paid job? No. But I am a 24/7 mother and that is a full-time job for anyone. I used to be a hairdresser , a very good one if truth be known, and I had my own salon. It was actually a very successful little business, but I had to give it up when I got married".

Chris lost interest and was not really concentrating. He was miles away thinking about what else he had on his briefing notes. He then remembered his mission - he still needed to find out if the children were alright and what they were up to.

"How are your children, Moira? Sorry, I meant to say, how many children do you have? I mean, do you have any children, Moira?", Chris' blunder appeared to go unnoticed.

"I have two. Robbie, aged 7, and Jessica, 9. They live with me".

"Really. Are they OK?", Chris said ineptly, caught up in his own duplicity.

"What do you mean?". Moira looked perplexed.

Chris panicked. "Oh, are they, er, healthy and everything. No colds or flu?".

Moira was confused and put his erratic questions down to first-date nerves. She was already thinking of the second date and did not want a little thing like partial insanity get in the way.

"No, they are fine. How caring of you to ask", she said, trying to put him at his ease. "They are with their father this weekend, so heaven knows what stories he is telling them about me. He has them every other weekend".

"I know...", Chris checked himself as he tripped up again, just stopping before giving the game away. With the speed of light and the verbal dexterity of an inebriated bull, he tried to continue seamlessly. "I know... not very much about children. I don't have any myself. I quite like them though". He squirmed uncomfortably at how awful that had just sounded while Moira continued to ignore his weirdness.

"They are lovely kids and we all get on well. It is better without their father around. We don't need him. They both go to a school nearby and get on really well together and have lots of friends. Robbie is a good rugby player, scrum half, and Jessie likes hockey, so I spend a lot of time watching them. They like singing too. Jessie is in the choir. She is really good. Not sure how much she enjoys though. I think she'd rather be in a girl band", she said with a chuckle.

Chris, apart from noticing that Moira always called her daughter Jessie, suddenly became aware that he was getting a lot of pap and not enough hard news to report back to David.

"What else do you do with them?". He probed, going in hard, thinking he was some kind of investigative journalist. Moira thought this was an odd question and gave a suitably vague answer.

"We do lots together. The thing is that, even though they get on brilliantly, it is hard to find things they both like. We like to go for long dog-walks and they used to like going to London. Now that my ex-husband has moved there, they do that with him".

"Oh, that's nice for them", said Chris, all too gladly supporting his friend.

"Not really. I think they find him and his mates boring to be honest. They don't talk about it much".

Chris almost flinched but carried on. "How about holidays?".

"No plans. Last year, we just stayed at home. We have a lovely garden and they love playing out there. David wants to take them to Disneyland Paris for half term. I think it is a really bad idea. He just wants to spoil them. I don't want him filling their heads with shit for a week and buying them everything. We can find somewhere nice to go if we need to, but I don't want them damn well going with him".

"But he is their father". That was the red rag. With a flash of her viperine eyes, Moira gave him the full, terrifying glare.

"Brian. With respect, you know nothing". Brian knew that if anyone used the words 'with respect', they mean the complete opposite. "The man is a cheat and a liar. If he had wanted the children, he should have kept it in his pants".

Chris rocked back at her bluntness and immediately felt that this could all go badly wrong at any moment if he did not immediately change the subject back to safer territory.

"Isn't Phantom of the Opera just incredible? Personally, I prefer it to Les Mis. That's too long. The first act seems to go on forever."

Moira played along. "I agree with you totally. Phantom is probably the best thing I've ever seen in the theatre. Andrew Lloyd Webber is a genius".

Chris changed the subject once again.

"Have you been to many places in Europe, like, er, Venice for example".

"It's funny you should say that. I have been to quite a few places in Europe, Paris, Amsterdam, Rome, Italy is my favourite. Sadly, I've never been to Venice. That's one place I'd love to go. I've heard it's fabulous". Chris could not respond, never having been there himself.

At that, she excused herself and went to the loo. He reflected on how it was all going. He shivered when he thought how close he had come to blowing his cover. But, in spite of some jittery moments, he convinced himself that he had actually done a pretty good job overall and that surely nothing could possibly go wrong now that he was on the home run. A couple of minutes went by.

"Brian", a voice called out gently across the pub." There was no reaction. "Brian", the voice became louder. Still no reaction. "BRIAN" came a shrill yell, "are you deaf?"

'Shit, that's me. I'm Brian', registered Chris. He turned to see Moira at the bar, frowning at him.

"What do you want to drink?", she asked snappily, now watched by a few fellow customers.

"Sorry. I was miles away. Just a half of Harveys bitter, please. I'm driving".

Chris' went into a glowing red flush as he thought how he had so nearly messed up yet again by daydreaming about how he hadn't messed up. He was not very good at this, he concluded, thinking that he would make a lousy spy.

They sat together for at least another half hour, chatting away, mostly about divorce, Thai food, and Netflix. At around three o'clock, Chris dropped into the conversation that he should be getting back as he had to drive to London and the traffic might be bad. Moira said she also had to get back to take Jessie to a final rehearsal of the Hallelujah Chorus practice at school before a concert on Tuesday night. She told him that David was dropping them off at 3.45, adding caustically, "He had better not be late". Chris paid the bill, carefully keeping the receipt for David and they left. As they walked towards the car, a slightly awkwardness came over them both. The thought of a second date loomed large.

On the drive back, Chris managed to bring the subject round to his job, although he didn't want to give much away. He deeply regretted saying he worked at the Daily Post for fear that she might try to contact him, as Brian Jackson-Brown, of course. He was about to say that they don't like personal phone calls at work as a deterrent but then he thought that nothing would ever deter this woman. He came up with a better idea. He blurted out that he would like to give her his mobile number. She put it in her phone. Chris had once again failed to think things through. Unfortunately for him, she took this as the signal that he wanted another date.

"I shall call you then", she gasped with an expectant smile as she got out of the car in the church car park. "It has been fabulous to meet you, Brian. We get on so well and share so many interests. I agree with you, we have to do this again soon. It's amazing. And I don't mind coming up to London one night if it is easier for you, with your work and all that."

She opened the car door and started to get out.

"I'll ring tomorrow. Thanks again, Brian. It's been great". She was dying to add that he looked absolutely nothing like Michael Douglas but managed to hold herself back. The door slammed. Chris was left alone, stupefied. He drove off slowly, in a daze, trying to puzzle out what had just happened. He had no answer. His mind spun like a whirlwind all the way home.

After being held up in the Sunday traffic, he eventually got back to the apartment. It was nearly six o'clock. David had taken the children back to Wychwood as arranged. In fact, he dropped them off just minutes after Moira had got there. He was now already back home, having dodged the jams by taking side routes that he knew.

Chris entered to be met by an interrogation squad. David was the first to confront of him, champing at the bit like one of his horses. He bombarded questions onto his tired secret agent, who had just returned from his mission in the field.

"How did it go? What did she say? Did you find anything out? Tell me everything".

George came next. "Forget all that, how's my car. Is it OK? Did you fill it up?".

"Hold on. First, I need a drink", said Chris, heading for the kitchen. The other two followed him. "But yes, George. Thanks a million for the car. It is beautiful. And it is fine. And I filled it up just down the road. Thanks again".

George looked hugely relieved. "That's good news. Let me get you that beer", he said, beating him to the fridge and reaching inside for two bottles. He prized off the tops and handed one to him, before taking a swill out of the other.

"David. We need a chat. Grab a beer and come out onto the balcony", Chris said.

David did as he was told and followed him to the patio table outside.

"What did you find out?", David pressed expectantly.

"Well, I'll tell you what I did find out. I found out that that mad woman can talk. And she definitely doesn't like you. Put it this way, I know everything about Moira, a lot about you and she knows next to nothing about me. She just can't listen and she really isn't a fan of yours", he repeated.

Chris then told him everything that had been discussed and what she had said about the children, omitting any mention of his close-call cock-ups. He then told him that she expected another date.

"Brilliant. That is excellent, because I have a plan."

"Oh, no, no, no, David. It's not going to happen. You promised, just one. I have done enough. That's it, no more."

"Look Chris. You don't know how much this means to me. You are being the greatest friend anyone could have. Probably the greatest human being on this planet. I love you like a brother". David then proceeded to put his arm around him. Chris had a total inability to resist flattery, however insincere it may be. He smiled at David and, having soaked up David's affection, started to show less resistance to 'the plan'.

"Alright, I'll hear you out. What do you have in mind? And why? Haven't I done enough?"

David had thought of nothing else all the way back to London in the car. He already had formed a master plan in his head but he had developed the blueprint further on his drive home. David realised he needed to give his friend one more persuasive push. The strategist laid out his proposal.

"Let me get you another beer first", said David. "This might take a while".

Armed with further refreshment, the two men leaned forward towards one another conspiratorially, like Guy Fawkes conversing with his chief plotter.

"Chris. I am going to be honest with you. You have seen what Moira is like. She hates me with a vengeance and will do anything to hurt me, including using the children. Now, I want to take them to Paris for half-term. They have a week off and I haven't been away with the two of them for almost two years. These 'every other weekend' visits are OK but we need what I call some 'lumpy time' together, without all that dashing around. We need time to relax and just be a family. I have missed that so much and I think they have too. It's not so much that Moira thinks this will turn them against her, it is that she thinks they may come to like me more. She has said such terrible things to them about me that she doesn't want them to see that I am actually not the monster she tells them I am". He took a large swill of his beer.

"I get that, pal", said Chris with genuine understanding. "I know how hard it has been for you. Really I do".

"So, I was sort of thinking, you know, what if you were to help me as my pal. How about it if you asked her to go away with you at half-term, to somewhere nice, just a few days, so that she actually wanted me to have the children...".

"Whoa, cowboy. Are you seriously saying that you want me to take Moira away for a holiday somewhere? Me and her? Is that what you're saying? No way. I'm absolutely not doing anything like that and ruin my chances with Bonnie. I just nearly bloody lost her and I'm not doing anything that would have that happen again. You know that", Chris asked incredulously.

"No, Chris. I get that. I understand. It's not like that, not at all.".

"I don't get it. You just said I should ask your ex-wife to go away with me at half-term for a few days somewhere. Yes, Bonnie will really love that idea, I don't think".

"No, Chris. That's not what I am saying. Well, it is... and it isn't", David obliquely replied.

"I still don't get it. You just said I should ask her to go away with me at half-term and then you say that is not what you are saying." Chris, easily confused at the best of times, was now completely befuddled. "What the hell are you saying?"

"I am saying, yes, ask her to go away, but then no ... don't go".

David could see that Chris was still trying his best to catch up and unravel the plot.

"Let me put it more clearly. One, I want to go away with the children and, two, I don't mind messing with her head after all she has done to me over the past couple of years, cancelling holidays, making me live in friends' spare rooms, threatening me with all those Court Orders. This is very important. Now focus, because you are about to become my saviour. What I am proposing is this. You ask her to go away, to Spain or Italy or anywhere nice and sunny, for, say, three days in the middle of the half-term. You could say you have a conference or meeting or something, staying in a five-star hotel, all expenses paid and that the company will let you take your 'partner' with you. She agrees and then when I ask her again about taking the children away, in an answer to all my prayers, she'll say yes, because it suits her, and whoosh, Jess, Robbie and I set off together to gay Paree. Bingo!"

"And I get stuck with Moira?", Chris complained.

"No, that is the brilliance of my plan. All you have to do is not go to the airport. You stand her up and Brian then disappears forever. I would love to be there to see that. She deserves it"

"Wow, that's really mean. So, basically, I ask her to come away with me and then I stand her up? Is that it? I need a second to unscramble all that. Give me ten minutes. Make me a tea or get a beer or something. I need to think"

"OK. I'll go and grab us another beer and you give me your answer when I get back", David said compliantly.

"Don't hurry", Chris told him.

Chris mulled over the whole scenario. By now, he was beginning to enjoy his sense of being the key player, the lead actor on his stage, and he took on a new commanding authority over the situation. He knew David needed him. He quickly realised that this was a strong moment for him, one that he was going to grab with both hands. He felt empowered. In truth, David felt he had dealt his emotional cards well and knew Chris had no real choice other than to play along. He also knew everything depended on his flatmate saying yes. There was no Plan B. He knew that Chris was now the master and so he shuffled subserviently off to the kitchen to get his beer. He returned five minutes later.

"OK, Chris, have you ruminated and come to conclusion?".

"Yes, I have finished my ruminations. Cows do that don't they? Isn't it something to do with methane and the ozone layer? But I digress. Yes, I have come to my conclusion". Chris announced pompously. He then lapsed into a pause, frustrating David.

"Well? A simple yes or no will do".

"Not so hasty, my friend. After much deliberation and careful consideration with due concern for the onerous responsibilities and elements of all...", replied Chris, in a lofty tone.

"Oh, just get on with it", said an impatient David.

Chris sat motionless for a good ten seconds, twiddling his thumbs. While his acting skills did not amount to much, he had learned some sense of dramatic timing. Then he spoke.

"Well. Not to put a finer point on it, weighing up the pros and cons, after much deliberation...I'll do it".

David could not hide his elation and grabbed him excitedly. "Chris, I love you. You are the best. Thanks so much..."

"Wait. Wait. Not so fast". Chris had adopted a man-in-charge manner about him. He lapsed into a Nazi Commandant voice. "However, you must understand. Zis is a verry dangerous mission. I have my conditions. There are three conditions. Conditions that must be met or there vill be consequences".

"You are enjoying yourself far too much. Go on then. What are your conditions?"

Chris reverted to his normal, but assertive, voice.

"Number One: I think leaving Moira at the airport is far too brutal. I know you have a brutal 'get your revenge in first' streak from your City days, but I'm not like that, David. Even though I know you want payback, I am not going to be the one to deliver the blow for you. I just cannot go along with something as cruel and unkind as having her unceremoniously dumped at the airport, with her bag packed and passport in her hand. No, that's not me. If I do it, I'll do it my way".

"What do you suggest?", asked David.

"I'll come back to you with the detail, but basically I'll go along with the bulk of the plan and when you guys are safely in the Channel Tunnel on Eurostar, then I would let her down - gently. No airport nonsense". David asked what was next.

"Number Two: This is an important one. You are not going to like this". Chris saw the look of trepidation on David's face and was enjoying his moment.

"Number Two is easy. From now on, you make your own sodding Sunday breakfast"

"Got it. Agreed. No problem. Next?", demanded David.

"Number Three is simple. It's just this. We all do it."

"What do you mean? We all do what?".

"I mean that we all have ex-wives. We all want to know things about them, like you do with Moira. Why should I be the only one doing this? If I do it, then you other three must do it too, have one date, just one, with another's ex. Nowadays, it's a pretty sure bet that they will all be on some dating site or other. I shall hunt them down and you can ensnare them in your evil trap. And I will pick who goes out with who".

"George and Ricky will never go for that. I am not sure I will either."

"Then, nor will I. Simple. All for one and one for all. Or I quit. And that's fine by me". Chris leaned back having delivered his mischievous terms. A seriousness had entered the negotiations.

David stood dumbfounded, a rare time that he was lost for words, except for a hushed 'shit' under his breath. Then he gave Chris a long hard look.

"Alright. I think we can get One and Two out of the way quickly. With Moira, I don't disagree. My plan was probably overly tough. No more than she deserves though. But you are right. As long as I get on that train, I'll be happy. You play it your way. With Number Two, the big breakfast threat, the boys may not like it, but it was my idea in the first place. I think it's high time we either take turns or just do our own thing. No big deal. One and Two are agreed, subject to George and Ricky going along with it, which I am sure they will. Now Three. On your crazy idea about dating each other's exes, even if somehow, and it is a massive 'if', I can persuade the others to go along with it, I completely reject the idea that you, Chris the bloody Joker, match us up. No, I wouldn't trust you a yard. Knowing you, I'd probably end up going out with Ricky or something. No way. If, by a miracle, I do get George and Ricky to agree, we shall pick names out of a hat. One date only. That's it. OK?".

"Alright, agreed", Chris could now be magnanimous in victory. "And I shall get the next beer. That's the sort of guy I am".

"You're a devious little shit, that's what you are. But we love you. What we need to do now is to sit around a table with the others and get them on board. One thought though, a small thing, if you pick out your own ex, like if you picked Angela, we shall have to draw the whole thing again. Actually, I'd like to pick

Ricky's Alex. She's a bit of a mystery. He doesn't talk much about her. I am really curious what a rocker's wife looks like. Or I might get your brainy Angela and find out all your little secrets. Or the man-eating Kate. That'd be interesting. You know something. The more I think about it, the more fun I think this could be."

"Exactly", said Chris. "Let's get everyone together tonight. I think we are all in. It might not be possible next week. You never know when Ricky's going to be in or out... and I am bound to get a call from the vampire-woman tomorrow so I have to know what to say".

"That's certain. Moira won't let you out of her grasp, I can tell you that. I'll call the troops together right now. Leave it to me".

David went into the lounge and announced that he wanted a house meeting and, having read the papers all day and with nothing particular on TV, George and Ricky readily agreed, especially as David had got their drinks ready. They all sat down at the dining table and David opened the meeting, curious faces gazing at him.

"Thanks, guys. You are probably wondering what could be so important. Well, something has come up that I, and Chris, need your help on. It is a bit of a long story, but I shall try and keep it short. Don't look worried Ricky. Everything is fine. This is just some personal stuff". David had their attention, took a swill of his beer, and went on.

"You may have noticed that Chris and I have been up to something".

"No", said Ricky with a slash of sarcasm, "I haven't noticed anything. Sneaking off to the bedroom together seems perfectly normal behaviour to me". George remained silent.

"Well. It is quite funny actually. A week ago, Chris found Moira on a dating site..."

"What were you doing on a dating site, you hussy?", Ricky sniped at Chris.

"Not what you think, Ricky. I was just looking to see if Angela was on it, that's all. I found her by the way", Chris replied.

"Ricky, Chris", continued David. "Can I just get through this and then you can have your chat later. Now, where was I? Oh, yes. Chris found Moira on this site and showed it to me. After a bit of a laugh, I then got thinking. I'm having trouble with Moira and the kids and I really wanted to know what she was thinking and what she was up to. So, suddenly, it dawned on me, what if Chris went out on a date with her?".

Ricky's face was classic. His eyes widened and his mouth dropped open, expelling a loud "What? No, he didn't".

George was sitting quietly. He already knew this part of the story, having had it explained to him when David asked if Chris could borrow his car.

"Wait, Ricky", said David, trying his hardest to keep going. "Anyway, Chris agreed and they went on this date, today, while I was out with the children. And it all went incredibly well apparently and, surprise, surprise..."

"They're engaged?", butted in Ricky.

"No, not yet, but Moira is holding a bit of a candle for young Chris and wants to see him again. Now I have a new plan. This is it". David took another sip of his beer. "Chris has kindly agreed to see her a few more times..."

This time, Chris cut in. "'A few more times?'. We never said 'a few more times'".

David kept his composure. "Hold on, Chris. OK. Just enough times, then, to get her to agree to taking a couple of days away with him."

Eyebrows were raised around the table. David could see Ricky and George's confusion. This was a lot to take in.

"No. Hear me out. I am not explaining this very well. Let me put it more simply. You see, I want to take Jess and Robbie away to Disneyland for half-term in October. That's only four weeks away. It shouldn't be a lot to ask. After all, they would love it. I have asked Moira several times, but she won't let it happen. A flat refusal. It's all a power game to her. I could take her back to Court but that would be horrible for everyone, especially the children and it would start the whole show all over again. So how about this. How about Chris getting her to agree to go away with him for a few days, then she will let me have the children, because it now suits her? The children and I could then whizz off to Disneyland in Paris. Once we are safely on the Eurostar train,

Chris then tells Moira that his trip has been cancelled and 'gently' lets her down...", he looked at Chris and repeated, "...gently".

"All very enthralling. What's this got to do with us though?", said Ricky. "Ah. I am coming to that." David grabbed his beer again. His nerves were getting to him. "I am only too aware of and grateful for how you have all been so understanding about me and the children. You've been great. Now I need one more big favour from each of you. Chris has already said he would help me as a good friend. He has said he is up for it. However, typical Chris, he wants to leverage a bit of a deal. He has asked three 'favours'".

"Here we go", said Ricky.

"He has agreed to play along if, first, he lets Moira down 'gently', which I have agreed to and I am sure you'll have no problem with that. I originally wanted him just to stand her up at the airport but, being a nice, cuddly old Chris, he said that that was too cruel, so we have agreed on the 'gentle' approach. Second, he thinks he has done his stint as breakfast cook and that we should either rotate the chefs or just do our own thing. He's been a great egg scrambler since we moved in, but it can't go on forever. Personally, I think it's time to release him from his Sunday morning chef duties. Do we have agreement on these two items?"

George showed his approval with a nod of the head.

Ricky, typically, had a word. "He overcooked the bloody eggs every time anyway. Let him go, I say".

"Thank you for that Ricky. So, we are agreed." David continued. "Now we have just one more and the final condition as proposed by Chris... and seconded by me. We have you two, Ricky and George, to convince. Chris?". David handed the floor to Chris, something the younger man was not expecting.

A sceptical Ricky muttered, "Here we go. Go, Chris baby".

"Well, look, I am doing this for my friend, our friend. I am not tackling the mighty, fire-breathing Moira for fun, but for little Jess and Robbie. If this is the only way they can get to Disney with their Dad, then I shall make the ultimate sacrifice. Like me, you all know what Brother David has been through and, comrades, I think we should rally round him in his time of need. However, it seems, at the moment, the only one doing the bloody rallying is me. That doesn't seem fair. What I am asking for then is this…". He took a deep breath. "To put it simply, if I do it … then we all do it".

"What do you mean?", bumbled George.

"What, we all date Moira? She must be a nympho", chipped in Ricky.

"No. What is not what I mean". Chris expanded. "Here goes. What I want is for you all to do the same as I am doing, have a date with one of the other exes. I say it is only fair if we all date another's ex. Just one date. If I do it, we should all do it. That's what mates do. And anyway, think about it. One date need only last a couple of hours or so and, in that time, we can all get the latest goss on what's happening with our exes and can find out what we need to know. We can, through our planted agent in the field, ask any questions we want. And it could be a riot because I think we can all be in on it, each one of us goes on a date and the two of us who have never met her can go along to watch. The ex-hubby can even go too if he keeps out of sight. If, say, it was in a restaurant, we can have our observation corps on a table nearby. It'll be hilarious. What do you think?".

For some reason, Chris and David looked straight at George, fearing that this is where the major resistance would come from.

David addressed him. "George? What do you think?". He braced himself for the worst. After a long fifteen seconds' deliberation, George uttered forth.

"I think…I think… it is a brilliant idea. Who came up with this? You, Chris? Simply brilliant. Where is the harm in it? The exes get a good meal and I get to find out if Kate is OK and what she is up to and I get to meet Chris' or Ricky's significant other. Genius. Just one thing though, how do we arrange the date? I can hardly just ring them up and say, hello this is George".

David took up the mantel once more. "Good point, George. Chris has found a possible answer. He is confident that he will find them all on some dating site or other and is prepared to search through them all. He says nearly all newly divorced women go on them just to see what's out there and he has already found Moira and Angela. If he doesn't find the other two, we shall have to think of another cunning scheme. Oh, and you don't have to use your real name. Chris didn't. Isn't that right, Brian?".

They laughed at Chris' expense. "Is that right, Brian?", joked George, who was by now getting in the spirit of it all.

"Give over, you lot", Chris countered. "By the way, we might get some really interesting mucky stories on our own flatmates. Any skeletons in your cupboard, Ricky?". Ricky had gone very quiet and dropped his head with a grunt.

"Ricky, what do you think?", David asked.

Ricky looked worried. All eyes focussed on him and he felt the pressure. He did not want to do it but, at the same time, he did not want to be the one to let the team down. Nonetheless, he looked as terrified as a cornered rabbit and was clearly extremely reluctant.

"Not really my thing, guys. I'm not sure about it at all. It's like wife-swapping without the sex. No, sorry guys, I am not keen at all."

Each of the three pleaded with him in turn.

Chris went first. "Come on, Ricky. Be a sport. I'm doing it to help David. It's only fair that we do this as a team".

David recognised that it was time for some emotional blackmail.

"Look, Ricky, you know I am really grateful to you for being brilliant with the children. They really love you, especially Jess. She's got a bit of a schoolgirl crush on you, I think. Let me tell you the truth, the full story. A couple of years back, I was about to take the whole family to Disneyland in Paris for half term. I had it all booked, Eurostar first class from Ashford, nice hotels, everything. The children had been looking forward to it for weeks. On the morning we were going, we got up very early and Moira suddenly announced, dramatically, that she wasn't coming and nor was Jess. It was horrible. The only way to avoid huge row was to comply. I went with just Robbie, leaving Jess behind, and, even though we had a great time, I couldn't help thinking of Jess. I hated the thought that she was being made to take sides at her age. It was awful and this is now my chance to make it up to her. I am pleading with you, Ricky, please help me make this happen. You have become a pal, a real pal. And this is about being a team. It is all about Jess and Robbie having a great time and I know how much you have come to love Jess. You know I would do the same for you if needed. Please help me and don't deny the children the chance for some happiness after what they have been through".

George put it more simply. "Wow, how could anyone say 'no' after that. Come on Richard, old boy. Just look at it as a bit of fun. It'll be a laugh. And as Christopher says, we can go along and watch each other's date if we want. That would be very amusing".

Ricky was cornered and knew he could not say no. They waited for his reaction. The whole scheme now depended on him saying 'yes'.

"Seeing you all in agreement, I guess I don't have a choice. It seems I have to go along with it. I just hope no-one regrets it, that it doesn't deliver too many surprises along the way. OK then, I'll do it.".

"That's fantastic, Richard. Thank you. A couple of hours chatting can't do any harm. I can't see what could possibly go wrong", George said. Ricky raised his eyebrows. David took the floor once more.

"Thank you so much Ricky. That means a lot to me. So, we are all agreed then. We shall put all our exes' names into a bag and whoever we pull out we have a date with. No going back. As Chris said, 'all for one and one for all'. Agreed?", pronounced Musketeer David. "Hands up all the ayes...". All four men raised their right arms, Ricky less enthusiastically. "That's it then, motion carried. Oh, one more thing. Not a word to the children. If Moira finds out we are up to something, it'll ruin the whole game". Ricky muttered something inaudible under his breath.

"Let's do the draw now," said an enthusiastic George. No-one could believe that the reserved Mr George Granby was suddenly the leading protagonist.

David stood up. "Right. This is how it will work. Chris is already dating Moira, so he can organise the draw. Chris, can you tear three pieces of paper off the pad in the kitchen, write either Kate, Alex and Angela on each one, screw them up into a ball and put them in that large mixing bowl."

Chris left to get it all ready, while the others jested about who they wanted and who they preferred not to pick. He came back and placed the bowl at the centre of the table. He then took over in his role as MC, something he had done with mixed success at the dog track all those years ago. He could not resist mimicking a game show host.

"Gentlemen. Welcome to 'PICK YOUR DATE', the new show where you could meet your dream girl who could change your life. First date, shagging optional. Now, contestants, here's what you have to do. There are three scrunched up pieces of paper in the bowl. Each has the name of a date on it. You will pick one out, all at the same time. Whoever's name is on the paper will be that person's one night stand, sorry, date". David whispered in his ear. Chris added "Oh yes, if you pick out your own ex, you have to remarry her - no, only joking - we just have to do the whole thing again from scratch. Is that right David?".

"Absolutely", supported David.

"And remember, there's no going back. Right. Get an image in your head where the bowl is, turn your head, no cheating, and, on the shout of 'Go!', you pick your piece of paper. OK. This is it. Ready. Steady... GO... PICK YOUR DATE!". Three heads turned away and three hands fumbled in the bowl, each grasping a scrunched slip of paper.

"All done. Now don't look yet", announced Chris. "Now. This is it. Contestant number one, George. Read out the name on your piece of paper".

He opened it slowly, as if opening a birthday present at a party.

"Angela" he shouted.

"Give it here, George". Chris took the paper and held it open theatrically so everyone could see. "George has picked Angela for his date", he announced. "Good luck with that, mate. You're going to need it. Now Ricky. Read out who have you got".

Ricky unravelled his piece of paper. "Kate" he said calmly and handed it to Chris.

"Thank you, Ricky. Lucky Ricky has picked Kate for his date. You'd better go out now and get some more Viagra, my friend". Ricky then went very quiet, almost subdued. George sensitively picked up on this and continued to worry about his reticence.

"Don't you like the idea of seeing my Kate, Richard? Honestly, mate, she is tremendously good fun. You'll love her".

"No, George. It isn't that at all. Please don't think that".

As they all knew by the process of elimination who David's date was, there was no need for the final denouement. Nevertheless, Chris wanted to go through it anyway.

Chris completed his duty. "David, tell us who you have picked. Surprise us". David made his announcement.

"Yes! I get to meet Alex, lucky girl". He was actually quite pleased as he was intrigued by the mysterious Alex.

"David has picked Alex for his date. Thank you, contestants, we hope you all have a cracking date. Thank you for playing Pick A Date and good night". He then added, "Hey, I even have a name for our little intrigue. We should call it Project EX".

They immediately entered into a vibrant cross table banter about who they had got and what questions they wanted answered by their former partners. Ricky, however, looked stunned and sat back quietly, not joining in.

"Are you really OK, Ricky? You've gone very quiet", a concerned David asked. Ricky seemed not to hear him, paused and then started to address the table, softly at first.

"Hold up. Listen. Everyone. I have something to tell you." Ricky looked petrified.

"Shush everyone, quieten down", said David. "Ricky has something he wants to say". Ricky paused before speaking, almost bashfully.

"Look guys. I have been meaning to tell you this for a while, but it just didn't seem to matter. This now seems a good time. Ok. I hope you're ready for this. So, this is it... I'll just tell it as it is. I'm gay".

There was a collective gasp. You could have cut the silence with a knife. No-one knew what to say next. Eventually, Chris, of course, found words.

"Well, bugger me, Ricky. Whoops. Sorry mate, not appropriate. What I mean to say is, yes, well, wow, that's a surprise, but who cares. I for one don't give a shit. I am sure none of us do. Bloody well done coming out like that. You are amongst your pals and we love you".

"Hear, hear", said George. "Richard, you are our friend and companion, and we couldn't care less. In fact, it is a good thing as it makes this apartment more socially representative. Bloody good for you".

All eyes turned on David, who had gone pale.

"David? Are you OK?", prompted George. "Say something". David looked up and spoke slowly, taking a slightly different tack.

"Yes, I am really proud of you mate. Truly. That takes courage. Well done. We have a lot of love and respect for you. One thing though. Does this mean, am I right, that Alex is not entirely and completely a woman of the female variety?".

The now liberated Ricky replied. "That's right David. Alex is a six-foot, black, athletic, gorgeous male dancer from the West Indies. Antigua actually. We met while I was playing on a cruise ship with another band. It is a long story. David, I'd perfectly understand if you wanted to back out".

"No. No. Not at all", David stuttered through his shock, somewhat hoisted by his own petard. He did not wish to appear in any way either prejudiced or, worse, a bad sport. All eyes were fixed on him. "I really admire your honesty, Ricky, and I am sorry if all this put you in a difficult situation. We are your very best friends. Of course, I'd love to meet Alex. And, anyway, I never kiss on my first dates. But I think we do need to talk it through, Ricky".

"You can't back out anyway." Chris chimed in, trying not to split his sides in laughter. "We all promised. I'll tell you something, David teaming up with Alex is one date I am definitely going to be there for. That's a promise".

"I assure you that I am not backing out. That wouldn't be cricket. All for one and all that. It just wasn't quite what I expected, that's all", said David.

"You'd better take your dancing shoes. Best no heels though, eh? Can you dance backwards?", teased Chris.

That lightened the atmosphere and the four musketeers relocated to the kitchen to grab a top-up on their drinks. Everyone wanted to show their liberalism and Ricky was lovingly embraced by each of them in turn, amidst a flow of effusive 'acceptance' speeches.

"Listen", announced Ricky, bringing the 'glad to be gay' chatter to a halt. "I have an idea. Street Fire are playing in

Brighton next Saturday. Why don't you guys support me and come to see the world's greatest rock band in action? It's at a club called the Concorde, a neat old Victorian hall in Madeira Drive, right on the seafront. I reckon there will be five or six hundred there and Brighton fans are great. How about it?".

Chris bounced in first. "Fantastic. Brighton! Bonnie and I will definitely be there. We'll try and embarrass you as much as possible in the front row".

Sensible George had a concern. "I'd love to come, Richard. It does seem a long way to go for one night, though".

Ricky had the answer. "Let's make it a weekend. Let's go down on Friday night, and then come back on Sunday. There are some great restaurants down there, George. Come on, guys. It'd be ace. And you don't have the children next weekend, do you, David? You're free". David perked up.

"I'm up for it. Let's do it. Great idea. George, it'll be fantastic. We have to support our friend Ricky, after all. You'll come, won't you?". George immediately capitulated and said it sounded a 'terrific' idea.

They set about making plans. Chris, who knew Brighton well, said he would book the hotel, saying that the Grand did some really good deals at this time of year. They decided to leave cars and Ricky's Harley behind and take the train. This was going to be a weekend to remember.

David sidled up to Ricky. He had something else on his mind and whispered in his ear. "We need to talk. Fancy a curry across the road tomorrow night?". Ricky readily agreed. Meanwhile, Chris' turned to George.

"I need you to help me navigate my way through dating sites to find Kate, if she is there. I have no idea what she looks like. Can you give me an hour one night after I get back from work?".

"That is no problem. I can't make it tomorrow. Or how about Tuesday?".

Chris told him that around 7.30 on Tuesday would be perfect. Now he needed to enlist Ricky's help.

"Boy, am I going to need you, mate", said Chris. "I am out of my comfort zone on men's dating sites and I know nothing about Alex. When are you free to sit down with me and do a search? Could you do Tuesday night?".

"Tuesday would be good", replied Ricky, "but I really don't think he will be on any of them. It just isn't his style. By the way, you will probably have to sign up to get in properly. You can always sign up as David though. After all, he is the one having the date. Are you OK with that?".

"That's fine, I think. George and I are on the hunt for Kate that night so I can tackle both her and Alex. What fun", he said sardonically. "If Project EX demands it, then I'll do it. Out of interest, what should I put on David's profile?". Chris then thought for a second. "How about: Likes - flower arranging, crochet, making quiches and the Pet Shop Boys. Dislikes - dirty nails, dust, Donald Trump and AC/DC – no, change that to Iron Maiden. I don't want to limit his choices".

"We're not all Mrs Doubtfires, you know. You are such a tosser", said Ricky with a laugh. Chris responded with a roguish smile.

CHAPTER SEVEN
PROJECT EX

MONDAY, SEPTEMBER 16

Chris hated Monday mornings. It was not that he disliked his job, far from it. It was the whole 'the weekend's over, playtime's over, now back to work routine' thing. Sunday had been extraordinary, to say the least, and he was tearing himself apart because he could not tell anyone just how weird it had been. He was drained from his Casanova exploits with Moira and was struggling to concentrate. He had taken his time getting up and was unusually late getting into the office, refusing to be any part of the early mindless commuter rush. It never mattered on a Monday anyway, he justified to himself, as things were always very quiet for the first two days of the week. However, he was jolted back to reality when he heard one of the girls cry out, just at the moment he sat down.

"Has anyone here heard of a 'Brian Jackson-Browne'?". Marianne called out. She looked around and then, holding the phone away from her ear, shot a piecing glance at Chris, inferring in her expression that perhaps he might know someone of that name. He shook his head, as if totally nonplussed. She returned to the phone. "Sorry, no-one here by that name". Chris took out his own phone and saw three missed calls.

He went into a mild panic and left the office to stand by the lifts. That was where people went to make private calls. This was about to go badly wrong, he feared. He had to act with lightning speed. He redialled the missed call.

"Hi, it's Chrrr... Brian. Sorry, I have a cold." He faked an unconvincing sneeze. "Apologies for missing your call. I was in a meeting with the Editor".

"It's me, Moira. I just wanted to thank you for lunch yesterday. I really enjoyed it". They then exchanged pleasantries for a few minutes before she said, "I meant to mention that I have to be in

London on Wednesday afternoon, by chance. Do you fancy meeting up for an early bite to eat in the evening?".

"That'd be great, but I don't finish work till 6.30".

"That'll be fine. I have a lot to do in town. So where shall we meet?". Chris was caught on the hop. He had not prepared for this.

"If you are near Knightsbridge, why don't we meet in the bar on the fifth floor of Harvey Nichols? Does that sound OK?", he stumbled.

"It sounds perfect. I shall be there around 7. Very excited about seeing you, Brian."

"Me too", said Chris through his teeth. "We can have a long catch-up then. Sorry to be brief but I have a lot on this morning. Editor stuff, you know".

They said their fond farewells and the conversation ended. A shroud of relief came over him. His heart was racing. 'I got away with that, I think. Perhaps I should have chatted longer though', he thought before returning to his desk.

That night, David and Ricky were sitting at their table in the twilight of the Jewel of Jaipur restaurant. It was a typical Indian, the same you see throughout the country. On the outside, the frontage was a large, uninspiring plate glass window and, above, two smaller, dirtier windows were draped with shabby net curtains, presumably hiding the living area upstairs. Once inside, apart from the well-worn red carpet, it was perfectly clean and acceptable, with white tablecloths, attentive waiters, the inevitable sitar muzak and surprisingly good food. The smell was also better than most, not at all musty but an aromatic blend of cumin, coriander and cardamon which wafted gently over the senses. David had ordered a chicken tikka masala, Ricky his beloved lamb rogan josh. They started their chat over the popadoms.

"So, tell me what happened, Ricky. The truth. The others may have not noticed, but I have seen how upset you have been since you arrived. Perhaps I can help in some way. Why not start at the beginning".

Ricky took a deep breath and a sip of wine, before adopting a rare serious tone.

"OK. I'll start at the beginning. I shall try and be brief. We first met when I was fronting the four-piece band that I had in those days, the ridiculously named Ricky Wilde and the Wilde Things. We were playing on a five-day 'Sixties/Seventies' fun cruise. You'll laugh but we were a Troggs tribute band who put on mophead wigs and we played three gigs with other groups from that era, some real, some lookalike bands, like us. The audience was mostly made up of middle-aged married women desperately reliving their youth. It shot my musical credibility to bits but it paid the bills. Alex was a dancer in the shows on board. We met backstage and it was a match made in heaven. Well, on the Bay of Biscay actually. After I got back, I then managed, through my manager, to get bookings onto a couple of more cruises where I could join Alex and, in no time, we decided to get married, partly to allow Alex to move to the UK. I guess it was a bit too much of a rush really. It took place on October 23rd, three years ago, while we were docked in Madeira. We were on a transatlantic crossing from Southampton to Port Canaveral in Florida when we pulled into Funchal. The wedding itself had actually been a bloody disappointing affair on a very average cruise ship but it was still special for us. After the briefest ceremony in the small chapel, where the Captain oversaw the blessing, it was straight back to work, without a honeymoon. We eventually got this nice flat in London together and, apart from me flaring up now and again, we got on really well. Anyway, it was all so bloody stupid, David. I was away on a gig in Birmingham and, well, not to put too fine a point on it, I got drunk and had a bit of a fling, a one-night stand with this guy in some grotty hotel. I was a damn idiot. Pissed and stupid. Anyway, Alex found out. It must have been one of the band or the roadie or someone, I'll never know, and he went berserk - rightly. Alex isn't the forgiving type and he just said that was it, told me to get out, just like that, and next thing we are in a bloody divorce Court. It all happened so quickly. I let him have everything. He has his own income anyway. So that was it. I moved in with my Aunt and the rest you know. I have been an absolute jerk and I have never regretted anything so much in my whole life".

"You still love him, don't you?", said David, understandingly.

"Between you and me? Like forever. He's amazing. You'll see what I mean when you meet him. I think you'll get it", mourned Ricky.

"What's he like? I need to know", David asked.

"He's a sweetheart. The kindest man you could wish to meet. You'll love him, not as much as me I hope, but he is great company, kind, caring and very talented. You know, big guy, big heart. He could have been a top ballet dancer. Sadly, he had a really tough upbringing in the West Indies being gay and all that. Although he lived in Antigua, his Dad was an old-fashioned Jamaican - totally intolerant. He had some horrendous Billy Elliott problems growing up. His Dad gave him a hard time. Alex is the sweetest man, but you don't confuse kindness with weakness with Alex. Inside, he is a real toughie, a survivor, mostly from being very hurt by his bullying father"

"Does he still love you?", enquired David.

"I just don't know, David. I just don't know. He simply flat refuses to talk to me, has done since this happened. He has completely shut me out. I don't know what he is thinking. We did have something so special though. I can't believe he has lost it all just because of one stupid night."

"Look, perhaps this is a perfect opportunity, Ricky. If we do find him online and I can get to see him, I can find out all about it, how he feels about you and what he is up to. Are you OK with that?". David suddenly fully realised that he could be the key to getting them back together again and that his task now had a very serious side to it.

"That would be amazing, David. I am short of a conversation with him. He is so stubborn. I think, because of all the hurt he has suffered in the past, he protects himself from pain by shutting it out. I just don't know what is going on in his head. Weirdly, as you say, this dating thing could be a stroke of luck. I doubt though that he will be on a dating site, it just isn't him. You never know, though. I am checking all the dating sites with Chris tomorrow night. Fingers crossed".

They continued to talk deeply all evening, finishing off two bottles of a surprisingly drinkable Château Neuf du Pape, followed a brandy or two. By the end, they both felt uplifted and hopeful that this whole exercise could actually turn out to be a blessing. A ray of optimism had appeared on Ricky's horizon.

At the same time that David and Ricky had arrived at the restaurant, over at the Wellington, Bonnie had just got to work and was preparing herself for another long, slow Monday night. All of a sudden, Chris rushed headlong into the empty pub and up to the bar.

"Chris, I wasn't expecting you in. Are you OK? Can I get you a pint?", offered Bonnie. Chris accepted the offer and, unusually, sat straight down on George's stool. "You look odd sat there. It doesn't seem right somehow. How is George, by the way?". She got no answer as he was breathing so heavily. She handed him his beer. Chris had to get his panting under control before he could tell Bonnie his news.

He had rung her the night before to reassure her about his Sunday lunch with Moira and she gave the impression of being completely comfortable with the whole scam, even though, in truth, she was understandably far from happy about his seeing another woman. She had pretended to be supportive because she liked David a great deal and understood that this was the only way for him to find some peace after the mayhem of his agonising divorce.

Chris puffed out his words. "Bonnie. Firstly, I love you. You know that. No, I really, really love you". Bonnie blushed as she saw Gerry glaring down the bar, listening to their every word.

"You have come in to tell me that? That's very nice, Chris, but I think I know".

"No. It's not that. Not just that. I mean it is that, but it is also something else", Chris garbled.

"I could have guessed as much. So, what is it? Have you won the Lottery or has Chelsea sacked another manager? What's going on?".

Chris went straight in. "Are you doing anything at the weekend?", he asked.

"Nothing special, why?", replied a curious Bonnie.

"Do you remember, when we first went out, I talked about a weekend in Brighton and you were understandably reticent because we hardly knew each other?", he gasped. "Well, we know each other quite a bit better now, don't we and…"

"Spit it out, Chris. What are you saying?".

"It's just that Ricky is playing with his band in Brighton on Saturday and I was wondering if you would like to go along with me. It'll be so much fun. We could go down after your shift on Friday, on the 11.32, and be come back on Sunday. It would be fantastic for us to go back to Brighton together and we have never seen Ricky play. I am so excited. You will come, won't you?".

"And you get your dirty weekend in Brighton after all. That's what this is about", she said naughtily. "I am only joking. I'd love to, Chris. It's a great idea. I haven't been out of London in ages. Just you and me. We need some time alone".

Chris was suddenly stymied and stopped in his tracks. "Ah, now Bonnie, there is just one little detail I missed out. David and George are coming too. And, of course, Ricky will be there", Chris quickly added "but they will do their own thing and we can do ours. Is that OK?".

"Of course, it is Chris. I love those guys. This is going to be fantastic. I can't wait. I'll see if Gerry can let me go a bit early. But you will make sure we have some time to ourselves, won't you?".

"I promise we will have most of the day and all of the night alone together. How's that? Bonnie, you are an angel. We can walk through the Lanes, go on the Pier, have lunch at Browns and you can take me to all your old haunts", enthused Chris.

"Not sure about my old haunts, to be honest. Many are best forgotten. It will be absolutely wonderful. I love Brighton and I think it is going to be nice weather this weekend".

"I love Brighton, too. We could go to the dogs". Bonnie flashed him a look. "Only joking. Thank you, Bonnie. Thank you for just being you. I love you so much. Now, there is one more thing I have to mention. I promised never to keep anything from you again, right? The thing is, please don't be cross. I have another date with Moira on Wednesday".

Bonnie was not amused. "You promised, Chris. One date, you said. Don't push your luck. You're not going to make this a regular thing. I am not putting up with this ridiculous charade if you are seeing her twice a week".

Chris knew he had overstepped the mark and explained that it was not his fault, that Moira had called him and that he could not think of anything worse but that it had to be done for David's sake.

"Then, bloody well hurry up, get her to agree to letting David have the children and get out of it. It could start to be too much, Chris. You have to get it over and done with".

He sat for a few minutes, pensively drinking his pint while she served other customers. Every time she came near him, he would throw out more words of reassurance. His glass empty, he told her once more how much he loved her, again, and how understanding she was being. Then, he did a perfect George. He stood up sharply and simply announced, "Got to go. Project EX is calling me".

Bonnie gave him an ethereal smile of affection. While he could be childlike, living in the moment, she loved that side of him, particularly his boyish zest for the next thing on his mercurial mind. He leaned over the bar, kissed her economically, aware the Gerry was watching and fled back to the apartment. He had a job to do and wanted to do some research into all the dating sites that might be relevant. He had already tracked down Moira and Angela, now he had just Kate and Alex to find, on very different types of sites. But it was all for the good of his Project EX and he was enjoying being pivotal to its success.

TUESDAY, SEPTEMBER 17

Chris got home from work at 6.30. George and Ricky were watching the news on the huge TV in the lounge. David was out. He had mentioned something about meeting his lawyer out of town and that he might have to stay in a hotel overnight.

"Hi, guys", Chris announced. "I'll give you a shout after I have grabbed some food. George, you are first up, if that is OK. I think you will be easier. We can see if Angela is at home and is up for a date, then we can try to find Kate on one of the sites.

Just another day in Chris' world. We can tackle Tricky Ricky later".

Chris had some major challenges to overcome if he was to arrange all three dates in one night, but, ever the positive thinker, failure never entered his head.

After he had reheated curry and rice in the microwave, Chris went to his room, the nexus of mission control. He logged on to the site where he had found both Angela and Moira. Angela's profile was pulled up and George was called in. Chris was at the helm, the Captain Kirk of Project EX.

He spoke to George with rare authority. "This is where we are. I hope you don't mind but I put up your photo and profile last night. I used your real name, as I saw no reason not to. I hope that's OK. A message was sent. Now let's see if she took the bait".

George, new to this computer dating and not understanding what Chris was saying, was transfixed on Angela's picture. "She is lovely, Christopher. Not like I imagined. She is really attractive".

"I'm not sure what to make of that, to be honest, George. I never said she wasn't attractive", Chris replied in his defence, focussing on the screen. "It was just that she didn't make much effort, not for me anyway. When she puts her face on and dresses up, she can look really lovely. I actually think you two will get on well". He started to tap away on the keyboard to see if she had replied to the message.

"Result. Well, that surprises me. She's come back and she is definitely interested. Let me see if she is online right now". He started typing.

GEORGE: 'Hi. George here. Thank you so much for coming back to me. Are you there at the moment?'

She replied with her typical courtesy.

ANGELA: 'Hi George. Lovely to hear from you. I have seen your profile and we do seem to have similar tastes. I am pleased you are a bookworm too! I work in a bookshop and you will always find my head buried in some novel or other. And, like you, I love art and really enjoy visiting the galleries in London'.

Chris imagined her sitting in front of the TV as she always did, with her laptop on her knees and a glass of wine at her side. She asked some more questions about his work, where he lived and what sort of books he liked reading. George dictated the answers to Chris. It went well.

ANGELA: 'I would love to meet up with you. Perhaps we could have a late lunch one day?'

George had a hint of excitement in his voice. "Christopher, tell her I'd love to take her to the National Gallery, if she would like that. There's a Vermeer Exhibition on next week and I'd love to see it. We could go one afternoon and have a bite of lunch in the Garden Café as well. Tell her I have to go away this weekend and see if she can get the afternoon off on Wednesday the 26th, otherwise it will have to be the following weekend and that seems a long way off".

Chris typed everything as he was told, stopping only to ask how to spell 'Vermeer'.

ANGELA: 'Midweek might be a bit difficult. I shall have to ask my boss. I shall try and get the whole day off though and I'll let you know. I am owed some holiday'.

GEORGE: 'That would be amazing. If you succeed, let's meet at 12 in the entrance of the National Gallery?'.

ANGELA: 'I am sure it will be fine. Let me confirm it with you tomorrow'.

They then said goodnight and agreed to get in touch in the morning.

"That was fantastic, George", Chris said, triumphantly. "It could not have gone better. You and Angela, eh? You know something? You two might actually get along. Man, the world is getting to be a very strange place. You going out with my ex-wife. Well done, mate. But enough of this. We now have to find Kate. Let's do it".

They stayed sitting together, entering some details to narrow the search as they studied the photos, face after face, flicking through the screen. Dozens of women of all shapes and sizes looked back at them but Kate was not amongst them. After twenty minutes, they gave up and tried another site, and then another. It was nine o'clock when they gave an exasperated sigh of failure. The whole of Project EX was on the verge of collapse.

"Those are the biggest and best sites for her age-group. I can't think for a minute she'd be on the younger bonking sites."

"You never know with Kate. It's hardly likely though", said a despondent George, before a light went on in his head. "Hang on, Christopher. I have had a thought. Let me make a quick call".

He took out his phone and pressed on a name. As it rang, he gave Chris a hopeful look.

"Juan, buenos noches. Soy yo George. Cómo estás? Necessito un favor, old boy". He then reverted to punctuated English. "Juan, you mentioned a dating website for Spanish in the UK. What was its name?". There was a pregnant pause. "Amantes UK. Excellent. Thanks so much. Got to rush, mate. Let's have that drink soon. Gracias, Juan. Te veo pronto. Adios por ahora".

Chris was impressed. "Who was that? You speak Spanish really well. I got the 'buenos noches' and 'adios'. What was the rest about?".

George explained the website to his friend. "There is this dating site that my good pal Juan used to talk about that is specifically for Spanish-speaking expats in this country. He fancies himself as a bit of a stud and uses it quite often, he tells me. He tried to get me to go on it. Not bloody likely. One mad Spanish woman is enough for my lifetime. Anyway, I just thought that Kate might go there. She would be using her Spanish name of course, Catalina Elena Mendoza".

"Wow, hot stuff, George, you naughty boy. Now, what was it again."

George spelled out the website address and her name, while Chris typed feverishly. Up it came, Amantes UK. "It is all in bloody Spanish. Here, you'd better do it".

George uneasily crouched down at the keyboard and took the helm. In no time, he had discarded his hesitance and was bashing away like an old hand.

Chris chimed in. "Oh, new to this, are we? I don't think so. I bet you are on here all the time".

"Not for me, old boy. Give me a nice British girl at my age. They don't move so fast, if you know what I mean", George uttered. Then he sprung upright. "Hey, stop, stop, there she is!".

Sure enough, Kate's face looked back at her ex-husband. "OK, let's have some fun. And that's what this is, just fun. Better get Ricky in".

Ricky came when called and saw Kate on the screen. "She's really hot, man. How on earth did you ever get to pull a chick like that?".

"Thank you very much, Richard. My being suave, sophisticated and very English with a decent hair cut had a lot to do with it. That's another story. Now let's sort out this date and get it over with".

The three of them worked together. They registered Ricky and filled in his profile, giving prominence to his rock fame as George knew she would find that exciting. They also added dancing and going to concerts as his hobbies. His favourite food was, naturally, paella. Fortunately, Kate was at her computer at the other end of the link and messages bounced backwards and forwards. They started in George's broken Spanish, deciding it would give Ricky an educated, polyglot status as well as giving the covert operation greater veracity at the same time. After some friendly exchanges en español, they moved to English. Ricky edged George out of his seat.

He came straight out and asked her for a date. Caterina Elena accepted. He never beat about the bush and 'fancy a date?' was the best he could muster. It mattered not. She could do Thursday next week. He suggested just a drink, or dinner at Lorenzo's, her choice. George was struck by how unromantic this was, like booking a car service.

Kate was warming up. She began to show her usual Latin passion and was soon edging towards being flirtatious. A message arrived. 'You know what I'd love to do. I'd love to go dancing. I haven't been dancing in years and years. Take me dancing, Ricky'. George felt not only left out but also guilty and embarrassed. He saw his own inadequacies.

"Not a much of a dancer then, Georgie?", Ricky jibed. He then typed his one word reply in a flash, 'Done'. They arranged to meet at 8pm on Thursday the next week and to then go dancing. She agreed, asking where they were going. 'My surprise', he sent back. That was it. Ricky had his date with Kate.

"Next Thursday's going to be a late night", Ricky mumbled, with a rascally smile. "She won't know what hit her".

George was dismissed. He went back to the lounge, confused by what he had just done. His lovely Kate was now at Ricky's mercy. He then remembered that the hirsute rock-god was, if fact, gay and went back to watching TV feeling more relaxed. Meanwhile Ricky was now faced with the task he had not been looking forward to, to try and track down Alex.

Before starting, he went and grabbed a couple of beers, while at the same time passing a few reassuring words to George. When he joined Chris at the computer, his friend pretended to be on one of the men-only sites.

"Not now, Ricky. I am just accepting a date with this hunky lorry driver from Romford. He's stunning", Chris thundered.

"You're such a prat", exclaimed Ricky as he grabbed him around the throat and jokingly threatened to strangle him.

In order to get into the site, they had to sign up, giving personal details, and Chris set about registering as David Nugent. He knew David's photo album lived in his wardrobe, so he went and got it out of his room. Back at the computer he set about posting a raunchy old picture of his friend in his Speedos, taken while he was on holiday in the south of France years ago. Ricky took one look at it and objected loudly.

"For Heaven's sake, Chris. Your idea of gay men is a good thirty years behind the times. Haven't you got one of him looking smart and business-like?". Chris immediately went and replaced it with one of David in a suit at the races.

The site they were on happened to have a specific show business and entertainments section. Ricky had a feeling that, if Alex was on it at all, he would stick to dancers, singers and actors. He was right. It took just ten minutes of scanning through and then, miraculously, he appeared like the genie out of the lamp, looking lean and magnificent. Ricky gulped.

"That's Alex. That's my man. Bloody handsome, isn't he".

"Not my type," said Chris. "I prefer blondes. Right, go to work, Ricky. I can't think of a better man to do this". He put in a contact request and they crossed their fingers.

"He'll be working in the theatre right now, no doubt. Let's see if he comes back tomorrow", commented Ricky.

"Let's really hope so. If not, Project EX becomes Project Why?". He was not sure he understood that either. He simply had to say it.

WEDNESDAY SEPTEMBER 18

Breakfast in the apartment was usually a drowsy, uneventful affair but today there was a buzz in the air. At around 9.30 David came in the front door and joined Ricky and George, in their morning ritual of toast and tea, or coffee in George's case. They could not disguise their self-satisfied grins as they told him that they had found them all and that George was fixed up with Angela, Ricky with Kate and he had almost his date with Alex. It was all systems go.

"So he's up for it?", asked an apprehensive David.

"We shall know for sure later. We have put in all your details and he will hopefully come back to us in the next few hours. Exciting isn't it. You'd better start thinking about where you are going to take him", teased Chris.

"Oh, please. Why on earth do I listen to you, guys. By the way, what name have you used?".

"David Nugent, of course", confirmed Ricky.

"You haven't put my real name up on a bloody gay dating site, have you? You bastards. Jesus, if anyone sees it, my reputation will be ruined". David was almost hyperventilating.

"What reputation? You lost that years ago. Anyway, that's a bit prejudiced that, David. You should be proud to be gay".

"But I am not bloody gay. For Pete's sake. Sorry Ricky. You'll have to change it".

"Too late" said Ricky. "It's gone. You have requested a call back from Alex as David Nugent. I can't do anything about it now. Don't worry mate. If people come on to you, you can always turn them down. Just tell them you already have a boyfriend".

"Brilliant. This is awful". David cupped his head in hands.

Chris, having at first found it funny, now felt sorry for David. "As soon as we fix up your date, I shall take it down. I promise".

"Well, I hope your Alex is up early, Ricky. Let's check the computer now, Chris. I want that taken down a.s.a.p. I want my name off the damn thing". David and Chris marched into the bedroom and went onto the site. To their excitement, there was indeed a response from Alex.

"Ricky, come here. He's on".

"Let me see him", insisted David, straining over Chris' right shoulder. "Mmm. Not bad".

Ricky then burst in, pushed Chris out of the chair and started conversing with Alex. He typed furiously.

"Not too much, Ricky. We don't want him to get suspicious", David insisted.

Ricky typed some more and, after a few minutes, sat back and sighed.

"That's sweet and sour, that really is. My Alex has just accepted a date with another man because he loves all the things I like. It's like that bloody Piña Colada song all over again. Anyway, thank God it's only you, David, and not some hunky beefcake".

"Just a minute. That hurts. Alex might find me very attractive", protested David.

"David", yelled Chris. "You are not gay, mate. Keep reminding yourself. 'I am not gay'. You are taking this far too seriously"

"Sorry. I forgot for a minute. You are right. I mustn't get jealous", David jested roguishly. "But what if…".

Ricky pointed his finger at him. "You'd better not even think about it".

"So, what have you arranged for 'us', Ricky? When and where is our date?".

"Alex can't go out at night because he is working in the West End. He has suggested you meet him by the Gate Café in St James's Park at 1pm. As we are away in Brighton this weekend, you suggested next Tuesday to me, so Tuesday it is. Is that OK? He didn't say what he wanted to do. I guess a lunch in the park is as good an idea as anything".

"Just try and keep out of the bushes", piped up Chris.

Ricky just glared back.

Moira arrived at Victoria Station soon after 6.30pm. The whole story about having to be in London for the afternoon had been only a poorly disguised ruse to fix up a second date. She headed straight for the taxi rank and told the cabbie to take her to Harvey Nix.

Chris had been waiting for twenty minutes, mildly irritated as he did not want to be there in the first place. Nevertheless, he knew the deal, what he had to do and why he was doing it. And, in any event, he was seeing Bonnie in a few hours' time. Suddenly, Moira came swinging in, saw him immediately and gave him a familiar, affectionate smile.

"Hi, Brian. This is lovely. I hope I haven't kept you".

He looked startled. Thank heavens she had called him Brian, he thought, as he was so distracted by recent events that he had not yet slipped into his alter ego.

"Hi, Moira. This is a lovely surprise. What are you drinking?".

A waiter came over, she ordered a glass of wine and they got down to talking. She asked him how his cold was. He asked her how Jess' concert had gone and then let her run loose on all that she had been up to. After half an hour later, in an effort to hurry things along, he announced that he had thought it best that they should head off to eat, suggesting a restaurant called Boisdale, which just happened to be very near Victoria Station.

"That way we can have longer together", he explained.

"No hurry. There's a train at 11.25", she countered.

Chris' heart skipped a beat. He had to think fast. He had promised to meet Bonnie at closing time. However, he could not think of anything better than 'I have a big meeting at 9 in the morning, with the Editor'. He then added, "I'd love to have a late one with you but, midweek, I can't do late nights".

"Oh, never mind. Next time. Oh, Brian, I meant to ask you. I rang your office and nobody had heard of you."

Chris had to get a good response, and quickly. "Oh, you probably got through to the marketing department. That is a completely different team. I work in a sort of special projects capacity, for the Editor. All very hush hush, you understand. Best that you always use my mobile number".

Moira appeared to be impressed and told him she completely understood. They finished their drinks and took a taxi to

Boisdale restaurant in Ecclestone Street, just down the road from the station's side entrance. Chris had the exit strategy well arranged.

You can spot Boisdale from a distance, not because it is big but because it is very red. There's a lot of red at Boisdale. The bright red frontage welcomes you into a red interior. This apparently has something to do with its Scottish heritage, which also shows itself in the menu, with a selection of good Hebridean fare such as haggis and Arbroath smokies.

Their table was in the far corner and they settled down after ordering some more wine. Moira seemed altogether a lot calmer than on Sunday and she had not mentioned her ex-husband once.

Time passed, slowly for Chris, and they both tucked into their steak and thrice cooked chips. As they finished, Chris asked her what train she was planning to take. She had now had a couple more glasses of wine and was definitely loosening up.

"What time would you like it to be?", she smirked with an undisguised hint of wantonness. While the thought of anything carnal terrified him, he had to remind himself that his job was to steer the dalliance towards a liaison abroad with the minimum of distraction. He took this as the moment to nudge the exchange nearer to his objective and gave no answer to the question.

"You said you had been to Rome. Did you like it? I think Italy is wonderful, don't you?". Chris was using all his questionable skills to navigate the conversation in his desired direction.

"I loved it. The Italians have a great lifestyle. I think I could live in Italy, especially with all those gorgeous, dark Italian men".

"Don't I remember you that you mentioned you'd like to go Venice?", Chris asked.

"Oh, yes. I'd give anything to go to Venice".

'Jackpot' thought Chris, affording himself a barely perceptible congratulatory smile. He could not believe she had got there so quickly. David's words had flashed through his mind. He did not have the savvy to be creative. He tended to think in straight lines. Venice had been put into his head and Venice it would be. He remembered David's suggestion of a conference. She had just played right into his hands, he thought. Chris was an Aries and as such could not help himself rushing forward without engaging his brain. As Chris had once said about himself, 'I may not be the best, but I'm the quickest'.

"That's amazing. By complete and utter coincidence, we have a small, top secret strategy meeting in Venice soon and they want me to go, just three days, next month sometime. It's a sort of mini-conference with other top European newspaper executives. No-one knows about it here. Just me, the Editor and a couple of key people", embellished Chris.

"You are so lucky, Brian. I'd jump at the chance. Venice is one city that I would die to see. I have seen the photos and it looks incredible."

This was going unbelievably well, thought Chris. If he could get her to say that she would go, if asked, he could probably get away with just one more date before Project EX delivers its coup de grace. That would make Bonnie very happy. It would be so much easier letting her down after just three dates, before things got tricky. However, there was a snag. He immediately realised that David had not told him what week it was that he wanted to go to Disneyland. He was just about to blurt out 'when is the children's half term?', but just stopped himself in time. Nevertheless, he did take it to the next stage.

"If I do go, I think it is with wives and partners, you know". He often said 'you know' when he was lying. "I don't want to sound forward or anything. I am very aware that these are early days and that we must take things slowly, but if I do have a free ticket and you want to come, would you like to? I'll be busy at lot of the time but you can wander around Venice at your leisure. I'd be very happy if you could. It doesn't mean we have to, you know...".

Moira spared his blushes. "No, don't worry about that. We are both grown-ups and we can always have twin beds". Moira sounded like she was already packing her suitcase. "But, Brian, are you serious? If you go, I could come along with you, as your friend?".

"Absolutely. I should know tomorrow. I can ask my boss, you know, the Editor, and I am sure he'll make it happen".

"When is it?", asked Moira.

Chris was tongue-tied. He put on a thoughtful expression before speaking.

"Oh, damn. It is next month, not sure when, it's so top secret that even I don't know."

An intrigued Moira helped guide him. "If it was between October 12th and 19th, I can always get David to have the children. That would be fantastic". Chris choked on his drink and let out a muffled yelp. She was doing all his work for him. He also noted that she had called her evil ex-husband by name. She had to be mellowing, he thought.

"Funny. Those dates do sound familiar", he said.

Moira talked some more about Venice. She knew a great deal about it and was telling him enthusiastically what she had always wanted to see, St Mark's Square, the Doge's Palace, the Bridge of Sighs. Faced with all her genuine enthusiasm, he felt a guilty twinge, as he began to feel like a complete cad in kidding her along. Chris was, after all, a big softy underneath. However, typically Chris, he didn't suffer his guilt trip for long.

"I shall call you the moment I find out, hopefully tomorrow", promised Chris. At that, he suggested he should get the bill and see her to her train. It was now almost 10 o'clock and she had mentioned there was a train at 10.15. It was only a short walk and she was so elated about her planned trip that she almost skipped her way to the station. As they reached the barrier to her platform, she turned to kiss him. He froze and then tried not show his shock.

"Brian, you are wonderful. I am so excited. Let's hope you find out tomorrow. Thank you for the most wonderful night. You're the best".

She kissed him once more, turned and walk away down the platform. Chris controlled his eagerness to rush off and did his obligatory railway farewell, standing there waving as she waved back. He stood anchored to the spot for what seemed ages, wishing she would move a bit faster. She was heading towards the front of the train and so a lot a waving went on, so much so that his arm was aching by the time she climbed on board. There was, curiously, in spite of everything, something about Moira he admired. Chris always managed to see the best in everyone. She was definitely a go-getter, he pondered, and she probably got whatever she wanted, most of the time. Checking his watch, he saw it was 10.20 and rushed to get a taxi across town to the Wellington.

The rear cabin of a London black cab has always been a serene sanctuary in the heart of the teeming metropolis. Outside, the thronging pavements, packed with the heaving masses, create a hectic backdrop while the calm cocoon of the taxi is a place to reflect, to plan or, if you choose, to reveal some home truths to the cabbie through his little window, like a guilty parishioner would tell all to his Father Confessor. Just as women seem to be able to talk to their hairdressers about almost anything, men can do the same with their cab driver, as he sits behind the wheel, an anonymous back of the head with whom you can discuss your innermost secrets. For that reason, these London stalwarts are also the font of all gossip and scandal. Chris was dying to blurt out about this whole crazy adventure. However, he sat in silence. It was all getting so involved that he could hardly keep up with himself. He was contemplating what he had got himself into and how he and Bonnie were now getting on so well. His time with Moira weighed heavily on his conscience. The deeper he got into it and the more Moira seemed to be showing genuine excitement at the way things were going and the less comfortable he was becoming. He wanted to get this whole Project EX behind him, kill off Brian once and for all and concentrate on Bonnie. Fortunately, tonight had taken him to the brink of completing his task. There simply remained his confirmation of the trip to Venice, followed by Moira's request to David to have the children, and then his job was done, apart from the dreaded cancellation of the jaunt. Then, and only then, could he finally arrange the demise of the treacherous Brian Jackson-Brown. Perhaps he should put his obituary in the Times, he thought to himself. He could choose his own death. Mountaineering, parachuting, deep-sea diving, he thought. But the more he went through it all, the more he hated what was to come.

The taxi dropped him off at the Wellington and he went in, against the flow of merry drinkers coming out. Bonnie had already started wiping down of the tables as he approached her. She could see the disquiet in his face.

"Everything alright, Chris? Didn't it go well?".

Chris gave her a hug. "It actually went bloody well. She says she wants to go to Venice and I think we are almost done, thank heavens".

"Already? That was fast. You have had a successful night by the sounds of it". Bonnie proclaimed, generously.

"Yes, I guess so. Well, not really. I have had enough now. I just want to get the whole thing over with. What started out as fun is now horrible. I hate it. I just want to get back with you, without any of this".

Bonnie, seeing he needed consoling, went and had a word with Gerry before collecting her coat. She came out, took his arm and said, "Gerry said he'd finish up. Come on, let's get you home".

She had been bursting to tell him her own exciting news, that she had a big audition the next day. However, he had decided to keep it to herself as she fully expected to get the usual rejection. It was at the Theatre Royal for West Side Story after all, a bit out of her usual league. Nevertheless, she had been practising like mad, belting out the irritating 'I Feel Pretty' until it drove her insane and powerfully serenading the timeless 'Somewhere', a song she adored and hoped she would be called upon to sing.

However, this was not the moment to bring that up. It was rare to see Chris so downbeat and her role right now was to be with him and to support him. She recognised his vulnerabilities. While, at the same time, she was very conscious that comforting him for going out with another woman was extremely bizarre. Nevertheless, this was Chris, in whose life nothing was ever quite normal and she selflessly tucked him up into bed, brought him a cup of tea, slipped in beside him and gave him a cuddle. As she lay down beside him and they drifted off to sleep, she appropriately heard the distant strains of 'There's A Place For Us' echoing in her head.

CHAPTER EIGHT
WEST END STORY

THURSDAY SEPTEMBER 19

Bonnie got herself back to her flat early after her night with Chris. As she changed into her audition gear, the front doorbell rang. It was Samantha, whom she had told about the audition a couple of weeks before and who had decided to take her chance too. They were going together to give each other moral support. They both looked stunning in their leotards and tights, with sexy wrap-around skirts. Even more touches of glamour were added in front of the mirror as they delicately touched up their make-up with all the care of a fine artist applying his final brush strokes to a masterpiece.

The Theatre Royal, Drury Lane embodied all the magnificence, confidence and splendour of a time when Britain ruled the waves and Henry Irving ruled the stage. It was, and still is, without doubt, one of the finest theatres in the whole country. For a start, it boasts the largest stage on the oldest theatrical site in London and its history dates back to 1663 and Charles II. There is so much magic captured on this spot, even though this building is the fourth incarnation. The current version, built in 1812, still held within its walls eons of mystery and romance from the days of David Garrick and Ellen Terry. Legends abound. The only things missing are the flickering gas lights and the lords and ladies in their gilded boxes. Bonnie and Sam felt a glow of satisfaction as they walked agog through the vast, glorious auditorium towards the raked stage. They spared a moment to turn around and observe the balconies that climbed up toward the heavens, intimidated and exhilarated in equal measure. It was awe-inspiring. They were in their palace of palaces.

"One day all this will be ours", Sam said softly, squeezing Bonnie's arm.

The audition was for casting the girls in the chorus. A serious little man stood by the pit with a clipboard, taking their names and resumés before instructing them to take a seat on the left side of the auditorium. The two friends joined the gaggle of other hopefuls who had already arrived. Bonnie reflected with some satisfaction on how she had done her homework over the past couple of weeks, having practised singing along with the soundtrack scores of times, learning the words like a pro. 'I really hope they ask me to sing 'Somewhere'", she mused.

They waited anxiously, bathing in the glory of their celebrated surroundings. The drama started for real when a stern-faced group of five, three men and two women, descended from the rear and sat down four rows from the front. Bonnie and Sam knew that their fate now lay in their hands. The most senior looking man went onto the stage and addressed them.

"Here we go", Sam purred. "This is it".

"Good morning. Thank you all for coming. My name is Derek Jackson and I am the Director of our new production of West Side Story. The leads have already been cast but have to remain undisclosed at the present time. Now we need a chorus. We are embarking on THE most exciting stage production of this classic musical ever and want nothing short of the best. This is London, theatre's home, and we shall have the finest cast that anywhere has ever seen. Nothing short of that will suffice. Today, we want to see if you can show the excellence that is demanded for Leonard Bernstein's immortal score and Stephen Sondheim's superlative lyrics. We hope that some of you will show us that extraordinary talent we seek and join us on our exciting, ambitious journey. It will be a long day, a tough day, at the end of which we shall hopefully be casting up to ten of you into the chorus. There are forty-eight of you here now, and we have picked you out of hundreds. We shall be asking each of you to give us your own audition piece. Then, later, you will be put into groups to dance under the direction of our choreographer, Lynda Rossi and, after that, to sing a number from the show. There will be no call-backs. I intend to have the whole thing wrapped up by 6pm. So, again, thank you for coming. I shall leave you in the charge of my Assistant, Oliver Moss. Good luck to you all".

With that, he left the stage to a spontaneous ripple of applause and the Assistant Director took his place. Bonnie and Sam felt the blood drain from their legs and a jittery doubt creep into their heads.

"Please don't let me be first", prayed Bonnie under her breath.

"Hi there, everyone. This is how it works", announced the smart, slightly camp young man. "To start off, we want each of you to do your solo audition piece which must include a monologue followed by your song and dance. We have an excellent pianist, so please hand him your sheet music. That will take until lunchtime, when you will have a break for one hour. OK, let's go. We shall call you by name. Good luck, everyone".

All morning was taken up with individual virtuoso performances ranging from Shakespeare to Chicago. Third up was a nervous Sam, who managed a short reading before belting out a rousing version of 'All That Jazz'. Half an hour later, Bonnie, after a solid rendition of Ophelia's 'O what a noble mind is here o'erthrown' from Hamlet, shook the auditorium with the incongruous 'One' from Mervyn Hamlisch's A Chorus Line, with the unflinching support of a gold top hat that she had brought with her in her bag. She had done it dozens of times before, either at other auditions or at drunken parties, but this time her singing and her high kicks reached heights that she had never reached before. She felt she had done well. She sat back down afterwards to watch the others, even though, all the time, the appropriately titled "I Really Need This Job" from the same show resonated in her mind.

Lunch came round and the two friends nipped out to find something to eat. There was a small café nearby and each girl grabbed a sandwich and a smoothie, returning to their seats to enjoy a few minutes of calm. Before long, it was back to reality as Oliver Moss appeared on stage once more.

"Back to work, guys. I hope you haven't eaten too much because it's dance next. To loosen you up, our choreographer Lynda Rossi would like you all to file up and form four groups of twelve". Oliver Moss went back to sit next to his Director.

The girls obeyed the order in silence, filing up in an orderly line, with Ms Rossi bringing up the rear. She helped marshal them as they shuffled into four bevvies of troupers. Bonnie and Sam were, naturally, inseparable. Ms Rossi had chosen the jazzy 'Dance at the Gym' and the redoubtable hoofer proceeded to teach the nervous ensemble a complex routine, each group performing it in turn. Some girls inevitably completely lost their way. Bonnie was pleased with what she did. As was Sam. The stage lights were ablaze and, try as she may, Bonnie could not see the reaction of the adjudicators in their seats. She felt very alone, boosted though by Sam being at her side.

Once done, there was a pause while notes were made. Ms Rossi thanked them before she started to point out a number of individuals. Those identified then had to call out their names. The finger of fate pointed at Bonnie. "Bonnie Carter", she barked out, followed closely by an envious clap as others congratulated her. After a minute's euphoria, she watched more intently as the more noteworthy dancers were singled out. She crossed her fingers for Sam and desperately hoped that she would be selected. It took a while. "And finally...". Ms Rossi raised her arm slowly and her finger stretched directly at Sam, who gasped loudly before shouting out "Samantha Scott".

Ms Rossi concluded her task. "Thank you everyone. Don't be too despondent if you didn't get to call your name. There is still a long way to go". She then left the stage.

The girls' faces reflected their difference in fortunes. Bonnie and Sam both beamed. Others looked sourly dejected.

Next was the song from the show and a friendly, gaunt-faced man of about 30 sat down at the piano to put them through their vocal paces. The Assistant Director, Oliver Moss, then stepped out of the wings, stage left.

"OK. You have done really well so far. Well done. Now, the chorus song I have selected is the fabulous, wonderfully iconic 'America", which I want you to sing in unison, one group at a time. I want you to live this song. Let go of yourselves. Be there on the back streets of New York. Let rip. I am looking for my top ten. Good luck all".

This was the lighter moment they all needed after the complicated demands of the dancing. Bonnie had always found this anthem one of the easiest songs to sing. She and Sam's group were first up and they threw themselves into it, singing at the top of their voices, flicking their skirts and stamping their feet in an energy-sapping ad hoc routine. The two girls went into a world of their own and, boy, did they give it everything, as if singing their hearts out to the boys in their best Puerto Rican accent. They had to perform it twice, with direction coming in between the two performances. Once they had finished, they moved to the side of the stage, huffing and puffing exhaustedly, to watch the next group. After all four performances, a spontaneous ripple of appreciative applause broke out for the likeable pianist, echoing around the empty theatre. Everyone looked happy. For now.

"I hope we didn't go too bananas", Samantha said to Bonnie. "That was amazing. At least we shall go down fighting!".

After a lengthy, anxious pause, Oliver Moss appeared once more to repeat the process of choosing his protégés. Smiles dropped off the faces, replaced by expressions of nervous apprehension.

He walked over, armed with his index finger, which was loaded with a cache of hopes and ambitions. He started his selection. This time Sam came up first and she jumped into the air. "Samantha Scott", she announced wildly, turning to Bonnie for a congratulatory hug. Each girl that he pointed at after that shouted out her name with similar uncontrolled excitement. With just one place left, Bonnie's name had not been called and she felt resigned to her fate, that her chance had gone. She looked solemnly at the Assistant Director's arm and followed it as it made a slow, sweeping movement across the stage before it stopped and his finger flicked out to point directly at her. "Bonnie Carter" she cried out with unfettered relief and the two girls hugged one another and bounced up and down, before realising that out there, behind the lights, were the big fish who were taking things extremely seriously. They quickly regained control.

With that phase completed, the raw brutality of auditions reared its ugly head. At Oliver Moss' direction, half of the girls were summarily dismissed with a cursory 'thank you'. For the survivors, a more serious, more competitive tension overtook them as they prepared for the next session of the afternoon. After each new challenge, a few more were shown the exit and by four o'clock the forty-eight had been reduced to fifteen.

Bonnie and Sam had reached the final showdown. Auditions take no prisoners. It can be a cruel experience. This one was particularly merciless. This was big-time. The Director took to the stage and tried to calm their obvious nerves.

"You have done extremely well. I am very pleased. I think we could be taking all ten from amongst you today. Now I would like to look at you all for one final time. I want you to do 'America' again. This will be the last chance for you to show us why you are right for the show, so don't hold back. Good luck".

The girls knew this was their last shot. The adrenaline was pumping. After a few minutes of trying to calm their jitters, they settled down and concentrated as the pianist cued up the music. Then, the first few notes triggered their energy and they burst explosively into 'I like to be in America! OK by me in America' once more. Sam and Bonnie seized the moment. They whooped, they stomped, they danced their little white socks off. Once over, there was an eery silence followed by audible sighs of relief. Everyone had given it her all and now they were resigned to the outcome, good or bad. They waited edgily for a good fifteen minutes. Derek Jackson, the Director, slowly came back on stage, building the tension. Impressively, he knew the girls' names by now and started to read them out without ado.

"Melissa Wright, Jan Bendik, Caroline Clarke, Maria Rowland, Olivia Williams", he hesitated for a few seconds and continued in the same perfunctory tone. Bonnie and Sam gave each other an uncertain, apprehensive look. He continued. "I am sorry. You five haven't made it this time. Don't let it get to you. You all have great talent and ability. Keep going. Never give up. There is definitely a part for you out there. Thank you all for coming today". And that was it. For those five, the dejection was a hammer blow and they slunk off the stage, heads bowed. Meanwhile, the expressions on the ten other faces transformed from resignation to nervous elation. They were still in it, but would they all get through? Bonnie and Sam held one another's hand and squeezed tightly. The Director paused briefly before he turned to the remaining ten and his stern face broke into a broad grin. "Now what am I going to do with you lot? I tell you something. You had better cancel any plans you had after Christmas. The streets of New York are going to be your second home from now on. Congratulations. You are all part of the new West Side Story cast".

The girls just shrieked. Bonnie and Sam hugged each other and everyone around them, leaping up and down with tears in their eyes. The Director let them calm down before adding something no-one had ever expected.

"I want to thank you all. We have all your details and will be in touch very soon. If you have any reason you can't commit to a long run, please advise us now. In the meantime, well done. I am very happy and very proud of you all. But before you go, just one more thing. We are looking for an understudy for Maria. We think we may have found her here today. So, can I ask Bonnie Carter to stay behind please. Everyone else, thank you again, well done, you can leave now or, if you want, you can stay in the auditorium and watch. We'll contact your agents. See you again soon. Bonnie, can I have a word?".

Sam, showing no envy, embraced her again and whispered in her ear.

"Bonnie this is it. You'll get this. Trust me. You'll get this. You are so much better than everyone else. Now concentrate. Go for it, Bonnie. You're the best. I love you".

Bonnie then went over to the Director, in shock, lost for words and shaking. The stage was cleared, except for the girl of the moment. The pianist re-emerged.

"Right", came the Director's voice from behind the curtain of light. "Bonnie, let me say first that you have a rare talent. You have a great future in this business if you work hard and make the right choices. As I say, we need only one understudy and we would like to see if you are right for it. We have some mixed views on the panel, so I want you to sing 'Somewhere' for us. Give it all the emotion you can. Forget what has gone before. Don't over-sing it. At the same time, I want to see the audience in tears. Bring down the lights please. Good luck". He left the stage.

She was handed a microphone and the beam of the single spotlight isolated her from the darkness. She cut a lonely figure on such a vast stage. Closing her eyes for a second, she eased her nerves by transporting herself back to her bedroom, where she had sung this song in front of the mirror, again and again.

She opened them to see the pianist offering her the sheet music and lyrics. She brushed them away, took a breath and nodded that she was ready.

Bonnie sang like she had never sung before. Sam sat in the second row with floods of tears pouring down her cheeks. Those around her were also reaching for tissues. Bonnie performed like the star she was, with all eyes in the front seats rigidly captivated by her commanding dominance of the stage. After she sang the last note, the silence was deafening for a good five seconds. Every one of the girls had stayed on to see her and they then erupted into spontaneous applause and cheered enough to fill the majestic hall.

The house lights came back up, allowing her to see the Director surrounded by his team. They were on their feet, clapping their hands, smiling. She stood there, motionless, holding the microphone. Finally, his voice burst through. He turned to the other girls and then looked up at Bonnie. "Not a dry eye in the house. That's what I asked for and that's what you gave me, Bonnie. We are all agreed. You are exceptional and I am delighted to offer you the role as understudy to Maria and we are all thrilled to have found you. Well done. There's a lot of work to do but we are so excited you have joined us. By the way, you will probably be playing the lead in a lot of matinées. Who knows what that may lead to. Congratulations, Bonnie. We shall be sending all the details and financial terms to your agent. Thank you. That's it for today. Have a good night. You deserve it.".

With that, he sat down. Bonnie skipped off the stage straight into Sam's arms. But instead of uncontrolled exhilaration, Bonnie just said, "Fancy a pint at the Wellington, girlfriend?", in a modest, matter-of-fact way.

"Not sure it is grand enough for a diva, darling", replied Sam with a squeeze. "Bonnie, you were incredible". They both then shed some tears before gathering their things and heading for the pub.

It was now just after 6pm and in the taxi on the way there, Bonnie phoned Chris, trying to keep her voice as deceptively calm as possible. She told him in her theatrical serious tone that she had to see him and for him to come straight to the pub after work. She said that she would not take 'no' for an answer.

"You are messing with him, Bonnie", Sam said. "Won't he be terrified?".

"It's payback time for that night in Covent Garden. Let him suffer for an hour. It will do him good". Bonnie replied. She then phoned George and left a message about her good news, telling him that no-one should say anything to Chris.

The two girls, still in their audition kit, arrived at the pub and bounced up to Gerry arm-in-arm. Sam knew Gerry from her occasional nights in the bar, while Gerry always lit up when he saw Sam because she was 'so bloody, drop-dead gorgeous', as he put it.

"Now this a wonderful surprise, two for the price of one. You two look as sexy as hell. Hi, Sam, great to see you. You still look irresistibly edible", the vain Gerry joked.

"Hi, Gerry, I think you should be more respectful when you are talking to the friend of a West End star", Sam said aloofly.

Gerry looked baffled. "What's happened? Look at you two. You look like two cats who've got the cream. Something good has happened. Come on, what's going on?".

"Not much, except that we have only been at an audition for West Side Story all day and the Director said he wants us both, because we are fabulous, hugely talented and altogether amazing, that's all", Sam exclaimed immodestly.

"Bloody hell, guys, that is fantastic. Bloody well done".

"And it doesn't stop there", continued Sam. "What Bonnie hasn't told you yet is that she was hooked out from everyone and given the understudy role for Maria". She then burst into song with an over-excited Bonnie immediately joining in. Gerry sang the bits he knew.

'Curtain up! Light the lights!
You got nothing to hit but the heights!
You'll be swell. You'll be great.
I can tell. Just you wait.
That lucky star I'm talking about is you!
Honey, everything is coming up roses for me and for you'

"Drinks on the house", shouted Gerry, before he realised how loud he had said it. He looked across at the people at the other end of the bar. "Sorry, guys. Not everyone. Just these two gorgeous girls". He then went and poured them two large white wines and a half of bitter which he raised in the air. "To you two. Congratulations. This is just wonderful. The good news, I suppose, is that I get to be a friend of a real star. The really bad news is that I lose the prettiest, most adorable workmate in the world". He feigned sadness and then jumped back into his usual upbeat demeanour. "Now, Sam, what are you doing at the weekend?".

They drank and chatted for half an hour when a panting Chris came bursting in.

"What's up? What's happened?".

Sam went first, immediately relieving Chris of his worries, saying slowly, "Guess what. Your clever girlfriend just got hired to play Maria in West Side Story, that's all".

Bonnie was quick to correct her. "Not quite true, but I did get cast today in West Side Story as Maria's understudy. We went for an audition together, and Sam was incredible, and we both got picked for the chorus, which was amazing enough, but then they asked me to sing 'Somewhere' and they loved it. Next thing I knew, I was made the understudy to the bloody lead. It's just unbelievable".

Chris clenched his fists in excitement. "Oh my God, that's amazing. I thought something bad had happened. I had no idea. You bloody star. I knew you'd get your break. And you too, Sam. Both of you in the same show. I can't believe it. Come here, let me give Maria a kiss".

He took Bonnie in his arms and kissed her before giving Sam a hug too. Gerry pushed Chris' usual pint across the bar.

At that moment, George, David and Ricky came in together and the party started. The story of the day was replayed and they all celebrated lavishly, George from the security of his favourite stool. It was like the best of old times, but better. Gerry insisted that Bonnie have the night off and stay on that side of the bar. All the time, he flirted outrageously with Sam. By closing time, thanks to countless rounds of wine and beer, they were all vertically challenged and holding on to each other, as much for support as in affection.

Outside, Sam grabbed the first taxi to head home, only after receiving a confetti shower of farewell kisses and congratulations. The others decanted themselves into two taxis and the rest of the night was a blur, but Bonnie could not get a certain tune out of her mind. "Somehow, Someday, Somewhere", spun in her head, on a loop.

CHAPTER NINE
BRIGHTON ROCKS

FRIDAY, SEPTEMBER 20

When the gang woke up, none of them felt in great shape for a trip to Brighton. In turn, each hazily grabbed a tea or coffee and crashed into the nearest chair. Poor Chris had to go off to work.

"A bloody Friday as well. What a day to have the hangover from hell. Boy, were we hammered last night", he muttered as he kissed Bonnie goodbye at the door. Bonnie was ghosting around in a dressing gown that Chris had 'borrowed' from some hotel or other. David and George slouched deep into their seats, grunting occasionally, struggling to use joined-up sentences. Ricky appeared to have come out of the melee best. He was accustomed to boozy nights and his constitution coped much better as a result. In fact, he was almost perky. Bonnie left at around 11, casting out a hurried farewell across the room as she went through the door.

"See you later, guys. Chris and I will be down there by midnight. If you are still up, which I very much doubt looking at you, we shall see you in the bar. I expect you to be there Ricky. Real rockers don't have early nights".

The morning crawled by. George and David spent most of it in their rooms, either packing or laying down on their beds, or doing both at the same time. Ricky set off at midday to meet up with the rest of the band, before heading down to Brighton in their van. He had wanted to go down on his Harley Davidson but had decided it would be better if the boys stuck together, with Stardust in the driving seat.

Chris dragged himself through the day. Although his mind was not truly on the job in hand, he did his best to concentrate on behaving normally, something that was always a challenge. In the middle of the afternoon, a sudden thought hit him. He promptly headed off to the lifts. Pulling out his phone, he dialled Moira. She answered keenly. Chris spoke a curious, punctuated form of English.

"Moira, it's me. Can't talk long. Very busy. Lot on. Good news. Venice is on. Would you still like to come?"

"Yes, yes", howled Moira. "Definitely. What are the dates?".

Chris pulled out a scruffy piece of paper that David had given him.

"Monday, October 14th, flying back early on the Thursday. Are you OK with that?".

"Absolutely. No problem. It's perfect. By complete chance that is half-term week. The children are off school, but my ex-husband can have them. He'll be thrilled as he gets his way now", Moira said grudgingly.

She wanted to chat, but Chris cut her short, saying that the Editor was calling for him. He then mumbled something about how he hoped she would have a good time with the children this weekend and that they should speak again on Monday. As the call ended, two girls walked by and gave him a dubious look as he gave out a massive, victorious yell of 'Yes!'.

Meanwhile, George and David had each crushed everything into their overnight bag and put them by the front door. They left the apartment at 3.00pm to get the 3.32 from Victoria, arriving in Brighton an hour later. As they carried their cases to the taxi, they looked like two lost little boys going back to boarding school for the first day of term. By the time they got to the train, the Brighton buzz was starting to hit them. They sat in a first-class carriage and, the moment they had left the station, the tempting drinks trolley came down the corridor and David stopped it.

"Two beers please", he ordered.

"Please", begged George. "Not yet. I still have to find a piece of my brain. Are you sitting on it?".

"Come on, George. Hair of the dog and all that. We are off to Brighton and the fun starts right here, right now". He handed his friend a can and a plastic cup. "Get that down you".

As they flashed through Clapham Junction, they supped their beers in silence. By the time they got to East Croydon, having sunk their drinks, both were collapsed back, comatose, snoring heartily. The shake of the train had rocked them back into a deep, deep sleep. The next thing they knew was the shake of a guard's hand on their shoulders.

"We are here, gentlemen. Brighton. You're the last ones left on board. Unless you want to go back to London, I'd get off here. This isn't a hotel as far as I remember. Off you go". They sheepishly left the train, headed for the taxi rank out front and were driven off towards the seafront hotel.

Brighton is a colourful city on the south coast of England. It comprises of two conjoined old towns, Brighton and Hove. Fifty years ago, Hove was the posher, better behaved one of the two, where elderly, well-heeled widows would live or spend their summer weeks in staid temperance hotels on the seafront. Brighton itself was always its irritating neighbour, brash, noisy and vulgar, where people went to have a good time or to get up to no good on those infamous 'dirty weekends'. It was understandable, therefore, that the more mannerly, and snobby, residents of Hove, when they were asked 'Do you live in Brighton?' always recoiled and said the same thing. 'Hove, actually' was the invariable superior reply, in reference and deference to their far classier side of town.

One of the city's must-visits for George and David was the epic and spectacular Royal Pavilion, the ostentatious seaside palace built by John Nash in 1823 for George, Prince of Wales, the then Prince Regent, who later ascended the throne as George VI. His coastal holiday home was elaborately designed as a fanciful meld of Moorish and Indian extravagance, with onion domes and grandiose minarets. The humbler Queen Victoria, inheriting it as monarch in 1837, considered it far too frivolous, not at all fabulous. For her, it was too indulgent, too cramped and too close to her subjects. 'The people here are very indiscreet and troublesome', she had moaned before selling it to the city. Nothing much had changed.

The Grand Hotel was another of the many noble landmarks of Brighton. Chris had picked it out to be their home from home for the next two nights and had chosen well. It stood aloof, in all its Victorian splendour, on the seafront, with its bold white frontage, topped off with two Italian-style follies looking out in defiance over the English Channel. It was built exclusively for the upper classes of the nineteenth century and exudes a superior presence over all the other buildings around it. The opulent interiors continue the elegant theme. The marble pillars and an imposing staircase, which spirals up to the top floor, confirm the exclusive heritage of this magnificent hotel. Perhaps it is 'defiance' that should be the hotel's middle name, since it had to rise Phoenix-like from its own ashes following the IRA bomb that ripped it asunder on October 12th, 1984. It was here that a devastating device had been placed in the bathroom of Room 629 earlier that summer, timed to explode months later at 2.51am when Prime Minister Margaret Thatcher was staying in a neighbouring suite for her Party Conference. The Iron Lady, who was putting the finishing touches to her speech in the middle of that fateful night, survived the assassination attempt, but five others died. The perpetrator was eventually caught through a fingerprint that he had left on his hotel registration card.

Today, it showed no scars from that dreadful tragedy. George felt entirely at ease as he checked into these refined surroundings. David shared the sense that some old-fashioned sophistication was much more in keeping with his style, rather than the cold, functional accommodation of most modern hotels. They had each booked a single room. Ricky had originally suggested that they should share a room. It would be a riot, he had said. Initially, there was general agreement, that was until Chris reminded them that Brighton was the 'gay capital of England'. When that little gem of information was released upon them, they both decided that single rooms would be more appropriate.

On the way up in the lift, David suggested that they should take an early evening stroll into Kemp Town, the Bohemian, where a number of small bijou restaurants were hidden away in the old backstreets. George agreed but added, "Only after a short nap first".

Bonnie managed to get off work early and Chris, carrying two suitcases, met her at the pub at 10.30pm. She gave Gerry a coy kiss on the cheek, thanking him profusely for letting her go before closing and she dashed out of the pub with her weekend swain. Gerry had to have the last word, trying deliberately to embarrass the two lovebirds in front of the locals. "Have a great dirty weekend in Brighton, guys. Do everything I would do, given half the chance", he shouted loudly across the bar. 'Lucky bastard', he muttered to himself.

They got to the station five minutes before their train's departure time and scurried down the platform, each carrying a case. It looked like the scene from Some Like It Hot when Joe and Jerry rushed with their instruments to get on board their train. The excited couple managed to find two seats with no-one opposite them.

"I have to say something, Bonnie. I have an announcement to make". He broke off for a second and dramatically cleared his throat. "I want you to know…. that I bloody love you. Here, let's have a drink. Let's celebrate the West End's newest star". He pulled a half bottle of Veuve Clicquot Rosé champagne and two plastic wine glasses out of a bag, popped the cork and splashed it in.

"Cheers, Chris. Thank you for supporting me all this time. You have been wonderful. I love you too".

She spent most of the journey with her head on his shoulder, fizz in hand, watching the lights go by outside. The wearing after-effects of the night before were pushed aside by the sheer rapture of being with each other and going back to the town they both knew so well, together.

It was not long after midnight when they arrived at The Grand. As they approached the reception desk, Ricky bounded up.

"Welcome to my little seaside cottage, you two lovebirds. Georgie Boy and David have gone to bed, lightweights, so come and have a drink with the lads".

If Chris was honest, he had something else on his mind. He had upgraded his room earlier to one of supreme luxury. He wanted to surprise Bonnie and, once they were alone in the room, he planned to lock the door firmly and had absolutely no intention of leaving it until late the next morning.

"Just a quick one then, Ricky" said Chris, with a singular lack of enthusiasm.

Registration over, they went over to meet the band, their cases having been taken up to their room by a helpful bellboy. Sitting around a large round table, the boys introduced themselves as Mitch, Jake, Stardust and Rupert. While Ricky went to the bar to get the drinks, they discussed their favourite music and talked about the next night's gig. All the time they chatted, Bonnie gripped Chris' hand, continuously giving it a hard, knowing squeeze while flashing him an occasional 'let's go' look. Chris not only got the message, but completely agreed with it. He tried to chivvy things along.

"Sorry, boys. I have to go. Had a really tough day at work. But we shall see you tomorrow. Perhaps a drink after the show?".

Ricky explained that they would probably be going straight back to London, adding that they may just find time for a quick one in the Grand and that they should come backstage for a beer immediately after the show ends. The four tickets would be left on the door, in his name, he added. Chris gave him a knowing, suggestive wink, something that Bonnie fortunately missed. The couple then said their goodnights, bounced off to the lift and up to their room.

Chris opened the door in a dramatic sweep and a 'ta-ra!'. Bonnie went speechless as she walked into their sumptuous suite. It was a large, lavish room with Wedgwood blue walls and plush, velvet salon chairs, a voluptuous chaise longue and a bed the size of a small Caribbean island. Bonnie pulled back the long, luxurious curtains to reveal the sea, which shimmered under a bright moon. The breaking waves caught the lights from the coastal road in front of the hotel and sparkled in a graceful, rolling movement. Chris came up behind her. She turned to him and they kissed with a deep, meaningful passion. Her romantic beau then reverted to his more usual excited childlike countenance.

"Hey, come and see the bathroom. It's enormous". Bonnie followed him. "Just look at the bath. We could save water. It's the perfect size for two".

Bonnie said nothing. She just reached over and turned on the taps and poured the contents of a small bath salts bottle into the water. This was a signal that even Chris understood. He took her in his arms again.

"Need a bath, do we?", he cheekily added, "I thought it was called a dirty weekend".

While the bath ran, they returned to the bedroom and lay on the bed for a minute, gazing at the ceiling while holding hands, before Chris turned towards her and started to undress her. Before the last few clothes could be removed, she sprang up and ran to the bathroom. He was left, motionless.

"Come on in, big boy. The water's lovely", she called out while submerging her body below the bubbles. Chris joined her and they bent forward into a hot-blooded clench. They soaped one another slowly and invitingly. He softly rubbed her arms, her legs, her back, while she dropped her chin into her chest in pleasure. They indulged in the exhilaration of their foamy nakedness before Bonnie reached over for a towel, stepping elegantly out of the tub to dry herself with the soft, fluffy cloth. Then, taking a sumptuous white dressing gown down from the back of the door, she slipped it over her glistening body. The wet ends of her silken hair fell across her shoulders.

"Come up and see me sometime", she mouthed seductively, slipping the gown off one shoulder.

Chris grabbed her old towel, dried himself and then wrapped it around his waist. Bonnie was already under the sheet, her dressing gown discarded to a heap on the floor. He came over, casting the towel down, and slid in beside her. Their legs intertwined, plaited together in a weave of passion. Her tender touch as her hands soothed his body took him into a height of sublime bliss. They lay joined together in an ardent embrace. He looked into her beautiful eyes and, slowly and sensually, made love to her with a gentle, meaningful, unhurried intensity he had never felt before.

SATURDAY, SEPTEMBER 21

Breakfast at 9.30am on the Saturday had sounded a very good plan when George had proposed it two days earlier amidst an orgy of enthusiasm, but, now that the moment had arrived, for Chris and Bonnie it was more of a torture than delight. Chris, though, was a man of his word and was struggling into his clothes to go downstairs, as his girlfriend watched him from the warmth of the vast bed.

"You go down, Chris. Make my excuses. It has been an exhausting couple of days. They'll understand", directed Bonnie.

"Can I bring you something back? Toast and tea perhaps?" She accepted his offer with a smile and turned over to get some more sleep.

When Chris arrived downstairs, David and George were already attacking their English breakfast with gusto, while planning how they were going to spend the day. A refreshed George greeted his friend.

"Good morning, Christopher. Sleep well? Welcome to sunny Brighton. Had a good journey? What are you up to today? We thought we'd wander through the Lanes, if you and Bonnie would like to join us, and then have a gander at the Pavilion. The Music Room is incredible. Old King George, no relation, loved his music and he used it as his private concert hall. It is unbelievably extravagant. Good job Ricky isn't playing there. It wasn't built for his bloody speakers that go to eleven. They'd smash the chandeliers to pieces. After that, we'll probably go for a good lunch at English's. It's the best seafood in town. How about you two? Fancy coming along?".

Chris listened politely and explained that they were doing their own thing as they hadn't had much time together, suggesting that they might go for walk along the seafront to the pier and get some cockles there, adding "we don't have your budget. I expect our seafood lunch will be a whelk on a cocktail stick".

He wasted little time chatting. He wanted to get back to Bonnie. He sank David's glass of orange juice, grabbed some of their toast, spread it with a smattering of butter and marmalade, grabbed a cup of tea from the next table, filled it from the large teapot, added some milk and sugar and promptly fled.

"Got to rush. Sorry about this. A lot to do. See you later, guys. Have a great day. What time are we meeting up tonight?".

David proposed that they should be back at the hotel by five to prepare for their big night out, and then they could all meet up at six in the bar, adding the suggestion that they could grab a pizza before the show. George, usually a debonair dresser, was more interested in what everyone was wearing, to be told that jeans and T-shirts were essential, the only outfit for this sort of thing.

"I've got my flannels and a golf shirt. Will that do?".

"Near enough", said David. George was unusually unsure of himself. Reassurance given, Chris went back to his room and reacquainted himself with a sprawling Bonnie.

The two young lovers left the hotel hand in hand a couple of hours later and headed straight for the pier to take in the bracing sea air. The Palace Pier, in Edwardian times, had been a resplendent and civilised place for prim and proper ladies to promenade under the protection of frail, lacy parasols and dapper, moustachioed beaux. These elegant gentlefolk would invariably enjoy the thrill of parading themselves as they sauntered along the quarter mile iron folly that jutted out into the English Channel. In the summer evenings in that long-lost period, the theatre at its end saw packed Brighton audiences convulsing in laughter at the stage appearances of such greats as Charlie Chaplin and Stan Laurel. At Christmas, it was the pantomime. Sadly, since that dignified era, all that courtly charm had been lost, although the Pier still retained its ability to attract huge crowds. Every year, millions of fun-loving, casually dressed tourists were still taking a leisurely stroll to its end, not, however, to enjoy the theatrical entertainment or the demure tearoom, but to unload coins into the noisy slot machines and to take manic rides on the dodgems.

Chris and Bonnie dawdled down the pier as if they belonged to that former age, arm in arm, at a refined snail's pace. The sight of a seafood stall proved too tempting for Chris, who immediately tried to persuade Bonnie to indulge in a plate of succulent whelks, something she declined with an unladylike spewing gesture. He treated himself to a carton of cockles, which came with a wooden cocktail stick to be used as a spear, and they continued their amble. They had barely gone ten strides when they saw a group of six Japanese girls giggling as one of their party took photos of the others. Chris put his cockles down onto a large wooden lifebelt box next to the railings and offered to take a picture that they could all be in. No sooner had the tittering lasses started to pose than a huge herring gull divebombed them and promptly flew off with Chris' cockle carton, scattering the orange molluscs into the sea. Bonnie thought this was quite the best thing that had happened all day and laughed hysterically. The Japanese girls just looked shocked. Chris, after swearing at the huge bird in words the Japanese had not yet learned, somehow managed to recover his composure and returned, unabashed, to get a replacement boxful.

Next stop was the fortune-teller. A small booth invited them to come inside to have their future told and their past exposed. In spite of Chris saying that he thought it was a load of old nonsense, Bonnie pushed him forward, telling to have a go and saying that it was all just for a laugh. She pulled back the curtain to reveal an elderly lady in a bejewelled Romany veil and a black silk tasselled gown, leaning over a small baize-covered table. The wizened old crone beckoned them in.

"My friend would like his fortune told", Bonnie explained. The crumpled clairvoyant directed him to the chair opposite him and told him to lay his hands on the table. She took them in her fingers and turned the palms upwards. She then proceeded to present her well-worn patter in a hoarse whisper and a strong mid-European accent. The oracle spoke.

"My name is Roma Taragosa. I have learned the mystical secrets of Kings and uncovered the damnatory deceits of Queens. I can see into the inner spirit. The soul. Now what is your name?". He told her. "Chris. You have had many interesting moments in your life. You were much loved throughout your youth. But something always troubled you. I see you playing on your own. Are you an only child?". That got his attention. He nodded and found himself suddenly listening more intently. "I see you were often lonely and yearned for a brother or a sister". He turned to Bonnie open-mouthed as if a discovery had been made. "You have had many jobs, Chris. People close to you say you should be less adventurous. Some say that you are crazy. Ha, you may be crazy, but you are as crazy as a fox". Chris sniggered. By now, he was very impressed. Ms Taragosa continued. Chris concentrated. "They want you to listen. They want you to heed the words of the wise man. They want you to be like them. They want you to fit in. But you are an adventurer. A free spirit. You prefer to take a chance rather than play safe. I see betting, gambling. A casino or racing perhaps?".

"Greyhound racing", chipped in Chris. "I worked at a dog track here in Brighton and loved it. That's incredible". Sceptical Bonnie thought that probably the old girl had seen him on the track with his microphone when she was gambling her week's takings on a Saturday night.

"And I see a book. No, a magazine. No, a newspaper. Yes, a newspaper". Chris nearly fell off his seat at that point. The seer went on with some other prophecies about travel and sunshine, a trip to the west, the Caribbean perhaps. That meant nothing to Chris, who felt that she had struck lucky with her early predictions and had now completely lost the plot, until, that was, she mentioned his love life. "I am seeing a parting. I see sadness". Bonnie put her hand over her mouth, immediately thinking that she was forecasting their impending doom. "I see an old love lost. But, wait, there's new one found. Yes, the pain of the past is behind you. You have a new beginning. A new enlightenment. I see it glowing like a furnace, a furnace that cannot be put out. I see a blazing cauldron of love. Could it be this young lady here today? Is it you, m'dear?". Chris grinned with pride in affirmation. Bonnie twinkled. The veiled soothsayer went on. "Finally, Chris. I have some advice. Do not listen to the wise men. Wise men sit cross-legged while the world passes them by. Life is too short and the world is too large. Go find it. It will not find you. Chase it down. Stay curious. Listen to your heart. Release your spirit. Follow your dream. Love and faith in yourself will always find a way. I wish you every happiness. That will be £5".

Apart from the mercenary ending, Chris and Bonnie left sharing an incredulity and an unexpected belief. It was as if their lives together had just received a Romany blessing.

Next, they set off for the rides and amusements at the end of the pier, a mix of traditional fairground favourites and some modern thrill seekers' delights. Joining the carnage on the dodgems was a must and Chris drove Bonnie around like a demented demon, careering into everyone and everything around them. The more sedate carousel, with its gilded horses, was chosen next, in preference to the Turbo Coaster which gyrated you round until your head spun and your stomach churned. A trip on the Ghost Train was irresistible. Halfway round, Chris tried unsuccessfully to steal a kiss, only to have a tatty dangling fish net, which was meant to be a spider's web, envelope his face.

They decided that that was enough of the pier for one day and headed off to the Lanes, which Bonnie had always adored. Over two hundred years before, Brighton had been a small fishing hamlet called Brighthelmstone. It had comprised of a tangled warren of narrow, twisting alleyways, which still survived and had become known as 'The Lanes', although the shops no longer sold local fish and market produce as they had all those years ago. The maze of twitters, as Sussex folk call these passages, was now home to countless cramped boutiques, cosy pubs and, above all else, tiny antique jewellery shops. One particular shop window-display transfixed Bonnie. Behind the glass was a treasure trove of Victorian brooches, necklaces and Art Deco rings. Rubies, amethysts, pearls and sparkling diamonds glistened in their gold and silver mountings. Her particular penchant was for the early 1900's style and she pointed out several enticing pieces that caught her attention. She was like a joyful child peering into an old-fashioned sweet store and pointing out her favourites.

"Look at these, Chris. They are just fabulous. Can you see that emerald, oh, and look at that topaz. I just adore Art Deco jewellery. Wow, I cannot believe that one with that large Asscher cut diamond and sapphires. That is simply fabulous, so exquisite and perfectly of its time."

They walked on, Bonnie never tiring of looking at more gems in the other shops, until they found themselves out of the labyrinth of lanes and into bustling Duke Street. Seeing one of his old haunts, Chris then suggested a bite of lunch and they crossed the road to Browns, a place they both knew well. On entering, they were lucky enough to be guided to a table in the window, allowing them to watch Brighton life meander by as they enjoyed the sanctuary of their stylish surroundings.

"Oh, I'm sure you'll go for the cockle cocktail or would you prefer gull's eggs?", Bonnie joked as she perused the menu, only to receive a sarcastic 'ha ha' from Chris. They decided to share the pan-fried wild Atlantic scallops for a starter and she then ordered the fish pie, 'with extra cockles, please', while he went for the haddock and chips. The doting couple looked into each other's eyes and immersed themselves in their past experiences during their former times in their old hometown, sharing stories of their days of late drunken nights in various pubs, hikes in the Sussex sunshine across the sprawling Downs and debauched parties, all the time sipping their unhurried Provençale Rosé. Although there had been so many things that they had discussed doing in Brighton, just sitting at the table in the window of Browns, chatting harmoniously about times gone by, could not be bettered and the quick snack lunch they envisaged unwound into a two-hour feature, all washed down with more glasses of the delicious French wine. "This", said Chris, "right here, right now, is what memories are made of".

At one point, George and David passed by the window, presumably on their way back from the Royal Pavilion to English's for a late lunch. Chris automatically raised himself up and was about to rap on the window. Bonnie seized his arm.

"No, Chris. Let this be just us", she said with an affectionate smile. Chris, without any word of disagreement, resumed his seat, his haddock and his magical afternoon with Bonnie.

By the time they had paid the bill, it was after three o'clock. Chris put forward an idea with that glint in his eye that she was beginning to recognise.

"Why don't we go back to the hotel and have an afternoon nap, or a lie down anyway? Late night tonight, remember."

Bonnie saw right through this poorly designed seduction routine but was a willing accomplice and they left, arms around one another.

At 5.15pm, the phone shrilled, rudely jerking Chris and Bonnie out of their catnap. It was David, telling them to start getting ready and repeating the instruction to meet in the bar at six. They assembled as instructed in their gig-gear, with George appearing in his Polo shirt looking as if he would be more at home at the nineteenth hole at Wentworth Golf Club. Bonnie was every inch the rock chick in her skin-tight black jeans, studded cowboy boots and black, fringed suede jacket.

It was decided that they would grab something Italian at Donatello's in the Lanes and get to the club just before 8pm.

They were in a boisterous mood as they made their way through Brighton on the first stage of their night on the town. Everyone had had a glorious day, playing at being stupid bloody tourists, or 'grockles' as they were referred to in these parts, and now they were thrilled at the prospect of seeing Ricky on stage with his band. They felt the highlight of the weekend was yet to come.

After their swift pizza dinner, they set off again, feeling a mounting sense of excitement welling up inside them. They were almost fit to burst by the time they walked past the pier entrance and into Madeira Drive, which ran along the coast with the stony beach on one side and the aquamarine cast-iron arches of the Madeira Terrace on the other. This historic terrace is a half-mile long covered walkway, designed in the same ornamental, marine-inspired style as the Palace Pier. Built in the 1890's, it had provided the Victorian gentry with protection against the English summer sun and the inevitable showers, while still allowing them to enjoy an uninterrupted view out across the English Channel. With its completion over a hundred years before, the aristocratic ladies and their gentlemen were no longer restricted to taking a blustery promenade on the Palace Pier or along the esplanade, but they could also give their well-covered legs a stretch along the seafront in the shade of the sheltering canopy. The Victorians were very keen on their seaside saunters, not so keen on suntans. Most had arrived on the packed steam trains, each puffing heavily under the burden of several hundred passengers. They pulled into the station in the heart of town regularly throughout the day, disgorging their cargo of tourists, all of whom were seeking a fleeting escape from London's chimney smoke and choking pollution. Brighton had always met the challenge of entertaining them royally as they took their leisurely walks along the front and through the Lanes, breathing in the restorative salty air.

Hidden within Madeira Terrace, there had once been a refined tearoom that had served the day-trippers and holidaymakers with a well-earned pot of Earl Grey to accompany some perfectly baked scones with strawberry jam and Devon cream. Now, this genteel saloon, where the loudest sound had been that of a silver teaspoon clinking against the inside of a china cup as it stirred a sugar cube into the hot milky tea, had been transformed into Concorde, one of the most loved rock venues on the south coast. This totally incongruous reincarnation, from bone china to heavy metal, added to its charisma and fans flocked into the decorative venue to see the rebellious rantings of their favourite bands. Tonight, it was Ricky's turn to rock the place and the four Street Fire groupies, George, David, Chris and Bonnie, strode valiantly up to the front entrance, George albeit slightly less comfortable than the others.

The assertive David thought that he was important enough, and senior enough, not to have to join the queue of young people that lined up outside and headed straight up to the front of the line to collect their tickets. Fortunately, not all teenagers and twenty-somethings were unkind to older folk and, with his polite 'excuse me', the couple at the front of the column let him in. The diminutive young lady behind the desk gawped back at him, and uttered the briefest welcome.

"Yes?", she snapped.

"Ricky Wilde of Street Fire left us four tickets", he announced proudly, loud enough for the people around him to hear. She handed over the tickets without looking at him and he went back to the others. They then headed straight for the long bar in the front hall and David shoehorned himself into the massed herd of jeans and T-shirts. He had mastered over the years the art of attracting the barman's attention with a single authoritative glance and, in no time, he was reversing out of the melee and back to his pals with four overflowing plastic beer cups. Chris and Bonnie could not wait to see the stage and they all moved quickly into the auditorium. There is always something exciting and anticipatory about a stage set up for a concert, devoid of performers, the cluster of drums surrounding an empty seat, the small lights glowing on the amplifiers and the lead singer's unattended microphone gripped by its tall stand. What gave them a tingling thrill was the huge Street Fire logo dominating the back wall. On seeing it, Chris felt a crescendo of excitement and gave Bonnie a squeeze. They then raised their beers to a good evening. "I think you are going to enjoy this", Chris whispered into her ear, suspiciously knowingly.

It was only after they had taken in the drama of the stage that they took time to look around the hall itself. The original pillars, lined up down the right-hand side, acted as a permanent reminder of those stylish bygone years, as did the row of stained-glass windows. There were, of course, lights strapped everywhere, all controlled from the sound and light desk at the rear. What it lacked in class, it made up for in fun and vitality. You could feel the friendly energy from the two or three hundred eager fans already claiming their square foot of standing room at the front of the stage. Meanwhile, the debate began about where the gang should base themselves.

"Let's get as near to the front as possible", demanded a buoyant Chris, with the smiling approval of Bonnie.

"Not bloody likely", retorted a more conservative George. "There's a little alcove over there, on the left. Let's put ourselves there. This isn't a big place. The stage is well raised so we should be able to see perfectly well from there".

As ever, George's ruling decided things. They moved away from the front row mayhem and into a huddle on the side of the hall to await Ricky's big entrance.

"Hey, this is great", said Chris, now converted to the sanctuary of the alcove. "And we have our own little bar at the back. More drinks, anyone?". In one move, the other three sank their pints and thrust their cups at Chris.

Young fans started to teem in. Ricky had told them it should be a sell-out night, adding that Brighton was a fantastic audience. The pressure of anticipation grew until it positively exploded when the lights went down and the band, less Ricky, came out and set themselves up. The mass of fans roared and hollered, bringing the hall alive. The drummer and the two guitarists started a soft, background riff and the screaming got still louder. Mitch, flicking his drumsticks like a juggler and thumping his bass drum, then announced over the deafening speakers, "Ladies and Gentlemen. We are Street Fire. And this is Ricky Wilde". The crowd went berserk, joined from the alcove by the uncontrollable Bonnie and Chris, who flailed their arms in the air and shouted thunderously. David and George kept their composure and stood motionless like UN peace observers.

Ricky swaggered onto the stage with the arrogant strut of a star, raising his hand in salute to the fan's cheers. He carried his Fender Stratocaster around his neck and plugged it in to power it up. In his studded biker's jacket, black T-shirt, grungy jeans and blue canvas shoes, he then posed momentarily behind his microphone, soaking up the adoration of the crowd. In one smooth move, he turned to his band, threw his guitar back over his head, Jimi Hendrix-style, and, with an ear-shattering strike, attacked it with the opening chords of the Stone's 'Start Me Up'. They went mad. That moment set the intensity and tone for the evening, with each number shaking the old building to its foundations. If it had been a hundred years earlier, he would have shattered every teacup in the room with the opening chord.

Even George started to move a bit when they broke into their version of 'Shake Your Money Maker'. He felt a glow of pride and privilege that Ricky had actually consulted him about what he thought he should sing live in Brighton and it was he who had suggested the old 12-bar classic. George now felt a part of the whole experience. He started to roll his shoulders and tap his heels in support. When Ricky broke into "Feel Like Making Love", another song they had discussed, he positively rocked. David loved every minute of it, by now bopping away with Chris and Bonnie, who were completely taken over in the euphoric hysteria.

Ricky then brought the temperature and the lights down as he announced he would like to play his new song. Fans tend to go quieter with 'new songs', preferring the tribal familiarity of the older stuff. As the stage lights dimmed further, except for the blinding spotlight that picked out the lone figure of the lead singer, he spoke softly to the crowd "Let me introduce to you the first ever performance of a very special song to me. It's dedicated to a very special friend of mine. It's called 'Lying In Love'". The audience hushed respectfully for the slower number.

At that point, Chris said apologetically to Bonnie that he had to go the loo and would get some drinks on the way back, so he might be some time. Bonnie was slightly annoyed that he could not wait but let him go and clung on to David's arm as Ricky sang powerfully and emotionally. At the end, the stage lights went up and the crowd raised the roof once again. He gracefully accepted their praise before bursting into one of his own ear-splitting rock anthems.

After he had played two more thunderous songs, he put his hands up and spoke to the crowd.

"You have been an amazing audience and now we have a surprise guest for you. I want to bring on now someone who has just come from Brixton, the prison, not the Academy. He has travelled the world, appearing in far off places like Crawley and Croydon, but by the wonders of modern travel and medical science he is here with us tonight. His latest release was from jail. Ladies and Gentlemen. The King is not dead. He is here, although barely alive. Long Live the King. Let's give a rapturous Brighton welcome to the greatest of all time. Elvis is in the room!". With that, the fans went ecstatic as an Elvis Presley stepped on stage, garbed in dark glasses, a wig with the trademark greasy quiff, a sensational gold suit and blue suede shoes. He brought with him an old-fashioned microphone on its stand and positioned it next to Ricky, who went straight into it, with his 'one, two, one, two, three, four". They smashed into "Jailhouse Rock". At first, you could feel a hesitancy in the hall, as Elvis' vocals were shaking more than his wobbly pelvis, a lot more. But Ricky saved the day by dominating the song in his own inimitable way.

David shouted to Bonnie. "What the hell is that? What is happening? It doesn't sound good at all".

Bonnie leaned into David's ear, equally bemused. "I have absolutely no idea what's going on. I wish Chris was here to see it, though. Where the hell is he?". Just then Elvis sang the line 'You're the cutest jailbird I ever did see' and pointed directly at her. There was no mistaking it. She had been picked out by The King. "Oh, no", she thought "Oh, God, no, it can't be. It bloody well is. It's Chris", and she turned her thoughts into words, yelling at David and George, "That's bloody Chris out there!". They would have been shocked less if the real Elvis had just tapped them on the shoulder.

Ricky and the band bravely carried Chris through his moment of fame with their supportive backing. Ricky sang with him, guiding him back into tune when he drifted off-key. In fact, after

a couple of verses, it was Ricky who was Elvis's voice. The sound desk had wisely turned his vocals up and Chris's down. But everyone loved it, especially Bonnie, who was in hysterics when he attempted some ridiculous hip-swivelling. By the end of it, Ricky had taken over and he got the whole audience to sing the last chorus with him.
'Let's rock, everybody, let's rock
Everybody in the whole cell block
Was dancing to the Jailhouse Rock'.

Chris' Elvis had by now become more of a prop. Ricky was in complete control. The whole show, though, had brought the house down and Elvis left the stage with an outstretched wave to the audience and a tweak of his lip, turning directly to Bonnie to give a thumbs up and a theatrical exaggerated wink.

Meanwhile, Ricky spoke to the crowd. "He's off back to Brixton prison now. Back inside for his bad behaviour. Hope you enjoyed that. That was my dear friend, Chris Adams. We did it for a bet. Chris won. He is indeed crap! Thanks, Chris, see you later. Now let's get on with the show".

Ricky opened up again with another of his rock numbers. In the dark of the alcove, George and David hugged Bonnie, asking, in a shout over the music, whether she knew that was going to happen.

"No. No. Not a bloody clue. I knew I couldn't trust the little bugger". Luckily, this time, she was joking and the expression on her face was a mixture of pride and surprise. He may not have a future as an Elvis impersonator, but tonight he was, in her eyes, the King of Brighton.

After what was a deceptively short time, Chris returned, with four beers, creeping up behind Bonnie, dressed in his normal gear. "Have I missed anything?", he said nonchalantly. She swung round and was about to hurl herself at him when she spotted the drinks in his hand. She just managed to balance herself, taking two precariously clutched cups off him and passing them to David. She then took the other two that Chris was holding and gave them to George. In one quick movement, she jumped up onto Chris, clenching him around his neck, legs locked around those Elvis hips and speaking right into his face.

"I bloody love you, Chris Adams. Don't you ever leave me", and she gave him the most fervid kiss, which had his eyes popping.

Now it was Chris who was almost in tears. The couple looked lovingly at one another, retrieved their beers and returned their attention to what was happening on stage, Chris, as Elvis, with his arm wrapped possessively around her shoulder.

Ricky's last number was a hard rock version of 'All Right Now', which threw the crowd into a frenzy as they shouted every word back at the enigmatic lead singer. They left the stage to the raucous clamour of 'More! More! More!'. The band gave them five minutes to press their demands for an encore, before coming back and breaking into 'Satisfaction'.

It had been an extraordinary night. Street Life left the stage to tumultuous cheers and the house lights came up.

"Christopher, you were amazing. Don't give up your day job yet though, dear boy", George told him in his avuncular way.

David also heaped praise on his friend. "That was incredible. Ricky was just brilliant. How long have you two been planning that little coup? Did you get to rehearse it?".

Chris explained that they had thought of it one night, when they were alone and Ricky was trying out his new songs. He told them that it was Ricky's idea, how he had initially been reluctant, but that the Brighton gig then came up. He had repeatedly told Ricky that he was not actually any good, but Ricky kept insisting, saying 'Do it for Bonnie. I bet you'll be terrific'.

"But enough of this", Chris announced. "We rockers like to go backstage with our groupies after the show. Let's finish our drinks and go see Ricky. Come on, Bonnie. Let's do it".

By the time they got to the door on the left of the stage, the hall was virtually empty. They thumped on it heavily and it was opened from the other side by a bouncer. They told him who they were. "The room at the end", said the colossal doorman, letting them through.

As they walked into the dressing room, Ricky was telling Mitch, Rupert and Jake, to their complete amazement, how excellent they had been and how that was one of the best gigs he had ever played. They took this rare compliment with a piece of a salt. They knew for sure that the irascible, testy Ricky that they had come to know so well would doubtlessly return the next time they played to lambast them as usual. On seeing Chris, Ricky mockingly aimed his praise at Elvis.

"But it was all down to this guy. Well done, Chris, mate. How did you like that?"

Chris gave him a hefty hug. "It was just incredible. Thank you so much, Ricky. And you lot were fantastic. I really appreciate how you backed me up, all of you. I was never a solo artist", he joked.

"Only in bed", chipped in Mitch, with smutty innuendo and a joint between his fingers.

They grabbed cans of beer and talked about how fantastic the set had been and how great the audience was, while the band packed up. Meanwhile, Stardust, the roadie, had enlisted some extra help and was busy bundling up cables and shunting amplifiers out of the hall and into their hired truck.

"Let's get back to the hotel and grab a decent drink", commanded Ricky. "Let's go. I need a blast of that famous Brighton sea air, especially with Mitch puffing away on that bloody thing. We can't stay long though as we have to get back to London. Stardust will pick us up at the hotel".

The flatmates fell in behind Ricky and the boys as they set off under the arches towards the Grand Hotel, chatting and laughing about the great night they had just had. When they got to the hotel, some fans who had been at the show mobbed Ricky, who patiently signed every autograph and spoke with each one of them. The others headed for the bar and grabbed a table near the large bay window. Although it was late, the curtains were pulled back, revealing the effulgent illuminations on the pier and the colourful seafront lights strung along the esplanade, lighting up their view out to sea.

At David's instruction, two bottles of Moët arrived almost immediately, along with a tray of glasses. The white-coated waiter poured the champagne and they all raised them together in celebration.

"To Street Fire. The greatest band in the universe", David proclaimed as Ricky joined them. "To Street Fire", they all obediently voiced back.

An hour passed quickly, helped by more champagne and more raucous laughter that repeatedly rose from their circle. Predictably, George was the first to leave, getting up with his customary "Got to go". It was well after midnight and long past his bedtime. David was not far behind, courteously thanking the boys in the band for a 'splendid evening' and signalling to the barman for two more bottles to keep the boys' excessive thirst satiated in his absence.

Chris and Bonnie stayed a while longer, Chris feeling a new ease with the group. He was a fellow performer after all. Bonnie enjoyed the steady flow of flirtations from Mitch, Jake and Rupert, all of whom were unable to take their eyes off her. At one point, Chris did brazenly ask whether his Elvis routine should become a regular feature but got his short shrift in the form of a spontaneous burst of side-splitting howling from his unappreciative fellow musicians. Street Fire, in spite of their earlier plans for just a quick drink, continued chortling their litany of weird 'on the road' stories into the night. It must have been 2am when the two exhausted sweethearts left. They staggered back to their room and crashed into the enormity of the bed, completely drained by the exhilaration of the day.

Bonnie lay her head on Chris' shoulder. "You aren't that bad an Elvis, you know", she said, before adding a light-hearted barb "That was Elvis you were impersonating, wasn't it?'.

Chris kissed her and simply said "I love you" as he closed his eyes.

"I love you too, you hound dog", she laughed, prodding him with her finger. "Thanks for a fabulous weekend, Chris. We love Brighton, don't we".

She got no answer. The heavy breathing from Chris told her he had already fallen into a helpless sleep. She nestled her body deeper into his and joined him.

SUNDAY, SEPTEMBER 22

The next morning, heads pounding, the four packed their bags with hardly a word spoken and checked out of the Grand. With the help of the front doorman, who David tipped handsomely, they piled into a large taxi to the station. They then slept for almost the whole journey back to Victoria Station.

Once home, it was straight to bed. David was the only one who hung around, making a cup of tea before collapsing into a chair. As he stared vacantly out towards St Paul's, his mind was agitating over his date with Alex in the park on Tuesday. 'How the hell did I get into this?", he mulled. "Oh yes, I started it".

MONDAY, SEPTEMBER 23

Ricky emerged from his room, a bedraggled zombie in search of food. David sprung up like an alert butler to make him a bacon sandwich and a cup of tea.

The singer was nursing a hangover that he had thoroughly earned after treating the band to steak and chips in the pub the night before. What had been amazing to the boys in the band was that he had still been unusually pleasant all evening, suspiciously so, heaping praise on each of his backing musicians in turn, while buying round after round of beers. A new, anger-free, affable Ricky was emerging from his old, irascible, angst-ridden chrysalis.

"That was a brilliant weekend Ricky. You were amazing". David said appreciatively. "How are you feeling?" Stupid questions demand short answers. "Shit", came the scholarly reply.

David took an immediate break from any attempt at a reasonable conversation even though he was desperate to talk to Ricky about Alex. However, it did not seem the right time to discuss it, with his long-haired pal in such a monosyllabic mood. He handed the sandwich and the tea over to Ricky, extracting a terse 'ta' from him. In spite of his reservations, David pressed home his question.

"Not now, but sometime today, could we talk about Alex?".

Ricky was unexpectedly responsive. "Sure. Let's do it now. Number one, is he the best guy I have ever met? Yes. And two, it's your job is to get us back together. Next?'.

"I understand that, Ricky, and I promise I'll do everything I can. You know that. It will help me though if I can have as much insight as possible, even though you gave me a lot at dinner the other night. For example, you two, did you used to have any rows in the marriage, was it honestly all about just this one lapse? I find it hard to imagine that there wasn't a bit more to it than that".

"You're not wrong, mate. Generally, we got on really, really well. There was this thing with my temper though. Alex is the most laid-back and unargumentative person on the planet. Not like me. I admit I do have my flare-ups, well did, and I got mad at him sometimes over little things, like his irritating tidiness. He is so bloody tidy. With Alex, everything has to be in the right place, everything in the kitchen has to go into the right drawer, clothes have to be hung facing the same direction, the furniture couldn't be moved an inch. It did drove me mad sometimes. It would anybody".

"You'll be able to accept all that now?", David pushed.

"Too bloody right. My stroppy moods have to go. I can see my mistakes and I believe I'm genuinely getting better. Someone once said it was down to insecurities, but I am far too talented and beautiful to have those. I haven't ever shouted at any of you lot, have I? No, my time here has proved to me that I can calm down. I am even starting to be nice to my band, it's that bad. I don't know why though, the wankers".

"There you go, Ricky. I honestly think this has to stop and you will have to convince Alex that you have changed, that you are a new man. I can't help you out with that though, because, remember, I don't know you".

"You're right. All I want you to do is lay down the ground so that he'll take my calls. I'll do the rest. You know, I must be getting old. The 'angry young man' thing is definitely mellowing and I know Alex and me will be fine if we can start speaking again. There is so much I want to say. Get him to call me and I can do the rest. Or at least get him to pick up the bloody phone when I ring".

"OK. Now tell me. What does he like apart from dancing?", David enquired further.

"Italian food, and margaritas, and small dogs, and old black and white movies, and interior design, and seedless grapes, and he hates Marmite…".

David stopped him at mention of the yeast extract spread. "I think I have enough. That's plenty to start on. So, I am meeting him tomorrow in the park and do you think we should go to lunch or just for a stroll?".

"Both. He's a really gentle guy. I'd have a bite of something in the park and then go for a long walk, get him to talk. He'd like that. He'll have a tuna mayonnaise sandwich, if they do it. Have a nice long chat with him. He is very easy to talk to. Ask him all about his dancing. You'll like him. He may have to work so he'll probably want to be away by 3.30 latest. Don't worry about it. It'll be fine".

"What should I wear?".

"David, wear what you like. Don't think we all go around in high heels and suspenders. You've been watching too much bloody Cabaret. Just wear whatever you feel good in. Leave the Quentin Crisp fedora at home though".

At that, the conversation ended. David took himself back to his chair to resume reading his paper, all the time, his rendezvous in the park spinning in his head.

"We can talk some more tonight, if you want. You might get more sense out of me then", Ricky stated helpfully.

"Can't tonight", David said from behind his Telegraph. "Got to go out to dinner".

"Oh, yes. How is your legal eagle, apart from being the hungriest lawyer in the land. Must be the size of a bus by now", said Ricky mockingly. David just smiled.

Chris hated Mondays back at work at the best of times. This one was particularly rough. He had had a fantastic weekend and now faced the back-to-work realities at the Post. He hoped and prayed that the Editor had more important people to see that day and that he could remain in his shell at his desk undisturbed. Suddenly, the spectre of Moira loomed large. This was one task that could not be averted. He headed for the lifts, with his phone in his hand. She answered almost instantly.

"Hi, Moira. It's Brian. Good to hear you. Did you have a nice weekend with the children? Excellent. Me? Not much really. Caught up on some sleep. Yes, we are still on for October 14th. Looking forward to it. Have you sorted the children out with your ex yet? So, you'll talk to him today? Great. This is exciting. The annoying thing is that I have to go up to our office in Glasgow from tomorrow for the rest of the week. It's a bloody nuisance. We are having a big sales push up there. And I have promised to go to see Chelsea with my mates on Saturday, it's a big game, so I might not see you till next week, which is a real bummer. You can come up early next week? That'd be brilliant. You sure you don't mind coming up here? We could go for dinner somewhere and take it from there. I shall call you later in the week. Got to get back to work, the Editor is in a foul mood. Venice here we come! You, too. Bye".

He went back to his desk, only to be told Jill wanted to see him. He took a deep breath and knocked on her door.

"Come in and close the door, Chris. Sit down". This sounded a bit serious, thought Chris. Jill had her stern face on. "I've just had a call from a certain elderly lady. She said that a man in this office was very rude to her this morning".

"Ah. Her. Yes, I did speak with some old loony".

"What happened?", probed his boss.

"Well, you remember the Free Art Print for Every Reader promotion we did last month? We had thousands of prints of ten different masterpieces run off and we sent them out at random to readers who sent in five tokens. What could possibly go wrong? Well, I had just got in and this potty woman came on the phone complaining about the picture we'd sent her. It could have been any one of them. We had Constable's Haywain, the Birth of Venus by Botticelli, Van Gogh's self-portrait, stuff like that. Well, she got The Vitruvian Man by Leonardo da Vinci. You know, the one with this bloke in a circle stretching out four arms and four legs. She was incandescent, saying it was pornographic because he was naked and that she had never seen anything like it in her life. A nude man sticking his you-know-what right in her face, she complained. She went on and on about it. She didn't mind his eight limbs, just his old todger".

"Don't be crude, Chris. What did you say?"

"I just said, politely, that artists have always loved painting naked ladies and that hers happened to be of a naked man and that it was a Leonardo da Vinci. She shouted back that she didn't care what his name was and that he should put some proper clothes on. She said it was pure filth and we shouldn't go round shocking people with pornography. I tried to calm her down and I just told her to hang it carefully on the wall and people could say what a well-hung Leonardo it was."

"Not funny, Chris. That potty old lady only happens to be Mrs Arbuthnot, the wife of one of our main board directors".

"Oh, bugger", said Chris. "How was I to know?".

"Do be careful, Chris. Not all our readers are lunatics". Her face broke into a smile. "Only half of them. Now off you go".

Chris found it all very amusing and, if Jill had meant him to take the reprimand seriously, she had failed dismally. He sat down and told the whole story to the girls, who listened amidst some hushed, girlish chuckles. He needed that light-hearted relief after his chat with Moira.

Next thing, his phone rang. He assumed it was Moira back again. Pulling it out of his pocket, he answered quickly.

"Wow, that was quick. Have you told David about, you know, you and me?", he said in a hushed voice.

"But, dearest, this is so sudden. I thought 'you and me' was our little secret", said a sultry male voice. It as George.

"For Pete's sake, George. What do you want?".

"Now, Christopher, when is your lunch hour tomorrow and are you free?".

"George. Sorry about that. Yes,1 till 2. And yes, I'm free", he replied. "Why?".

"Fancy a stroll in St James's Park? You never know who you might bump into. David is having his date with Alex and I thought we could, you know, share the park in a covert observation operation. Should be quite amusing".

"You cunning old rogue. I forgot. It's tomorrow, isn't it? Where exactly are they meeting?"

"The café at 1pm. It'll be hilarious".

"Wouldn't miss it for the world. It'll be a walk in the park. I'll wear my watching briefs", said Chris. "Let's talk about it tonight. And we should also talk to Ricky about where he is going on Thursday with Kate. That sounds a good one as well". Chris never missed out on impish devilry. He was just amazed that George, Mr Straight, was getting into it so enthusiastically.

"Oh, I know all about his plans. I'll tell you when I see you. David is out but both Ricky and I are in. See you later". George rang off. Chris could not wait to hear what lay in store for Ricky's night out with the sultry sex-kitten, Kate.

When Chris arrived home, the welcome smell of curry hit him.

"I got you a chicken madras, pilau rice and a Peshwari nan. Is that OK?", asked George, who knew the answer full well. Chris gave him a brotherly hug of approval and got himself a beer, before helping his friend put the food onto the dining table. They called Ricky out of his room and the three sat around their Indian feast. It did not take long before Chris brought up Ricky's assignation with the hot-blooded Señora.

"Where are you taking Kate on Thursday?", Chris asked. George's ears pricked up with a sharply honed interest.

"Long story", answered Ricky. "She told me she really wanted to go dancing so I am taking her to the best dance place in London. Eden 86. If she wants dancing, I'll give her bloody dancing".

"That's the big gay club, isn't it?', Chris enquired.

"You know it then. Funny, I have never seen you in there".

"Not yet", said Chris puckishly. "Soon maybe".

The penny dropped with Ricky immediately. "I get it. You're coming along too on Thursday, is that right? You bastard. Not you too, George?".

George had only just heard that the venue was Eden 86. He thought quickly and then, to the surprise of the other two, spoke excitedly.

"Wouldn't miss it for the world, Richard dear boy. You and my ex-wife having your first date in a damn gay club, this is just wonderful". George then set the record straight, very straight. "Christopher and I are going along as chums though, aren't we, Christopher. I am absolutely not dancing with you. Oh, and David says he is up for it too. We're all coming.".

They listened in fascination as Ricky gave the enlightening details about Thursday nights at Eden 86, what people got up to, how they dressed and much more. George gave a sudden start.

"What if Kate sees me? That would be really awkward, not to mention embarrassing".

The other two pondered this dilemma for a minute and then Ricky said casually, "There's only one thing to do. You'll have to go in disguise. It is a gay club after all. Anything goes. You can't go in your usual 'Captain Sensible' style anyway, George. They'd laugh at you". Chris bucked in his chair with laughter. Ricky had got the solution. It was all back on track again.

"Let's go out tomorrow and get some gear. Where is a good shop to go to for, you know, 'gay stuff', Ricky?", Chris queried.

"Best place is that shop near Leicester Square. It is a ridiculously gay clothes boutique, although it gets used a lot by straight people for fancy dress. They also have loads of wigs, bondage gear and sex toys, all that kind of stuff. You'll love it, George. It's definitely your sort of place. You did go to public school after all, didn't you? I think it's called 'This Way, That Way' or something like that".

"I'll stick to the wigs, thank you", George insisted.

George and Chris agreed to meet at the shop at 6pm the next night, following on from their lunchtime 'walk in the park', and then go to the Wellington afterwards for a drink. George thought that they would definitely need a pint after all that intrigue with David and some flamboyant gay shopping later on. For almost an hour, they discussed the intricate conspiracies they had plotted, while devouring their curries and sinking their Kingfisher beers.

David came home around 10.30 pm, jauntily throwing his jacket over the back of a chair. Without a word, he went into the kitchen and poured himself a glass of wine.

"Bingo, boys. Bingo", he cried out as he sat down in the lounge. "Chris, you are a genius. It worked a dream".

"What worked like a dream?", asked Ricky.

"I know", Chris butted in, "Moira rang you, right?".

"Yes, she did", said David. "And she told me she had thought about it and generously agreed that I could take the Jess and Robbie to Disneyland, that she had decided it was the best thing to do 'for the children'. She was actually dangerously near being pleasant to me. All fake, of course. You were brilliant, Chris, correction, Brian. Bloody brilliant. Well done, mate". The others let out a victorious cheer.

"Project EX is on a successful trajectory. Alert the media", Chris rejoiced.

"Not yet, Chris", interjected David. "We still have to keep the lid on it until I leave for Paris. Oh, and Ricky, I don't suppose I could cancel my date now? It doesn't seem necessary any longer".

Ricky jumped straight back at him. "No way, bro. You've got your job to do. I've got mine. Everything stays the same. Remember our chat this morning? And I am actually looking forward to my night out with Kate. All for one and all that. Isn't that what we agreed?". Chris and George were in total agreement. David just laughed.

CHAPTER TEN
ONE DATE ON TOP OF ANOTHER

TUESDAY, SEPTEMBER 24

David thought about wearing a cravat with his open necked shirt for his date with Alex. He tried on the green paisley one and came to conclusion that he looked far too much like a very British film star in a very British 1940's film, about to climb into his drophead MG. He chose instead his trendy chinos, a dark blue shirt and long cashmere coat, which he decided that he would let hang casually open. As it was his first gay date, he needed to look right. He wanted to make a good impression, after all. Preened to perfection, he set off for St James's Park at 12.30, grabbing a taxi.

"Going anywhere nice?", asked the cabby.

"Don't ask, or I might tell you". London black cab drivers get the message in an instant and the rest of the drive was in silence. He got out in the Mall and ambled leisurely towards the café in the park. It was a chilly, but beautiful autumnal day, with a clear blue sky and the first fall of crispy, brown leaves lying around the trees. The outdoor patio was almost empty and there were plenty of tables to select from. Choosing one next to the five-foot hedge for a bit more privacy, he decided to be a gentleman and save the seat looking out over the park for his guest. He ordered a coffee while he waited anxiously, but after no more than a few minutes, he heard his name in a soft, velvet voice over his shoulder. "David?"

David stood up and greeted his date. "Alex. It's lovely to meet you. Thank you for seeing me today".

Alex was a pleasant surprise to David. He was slender, without being skinny, with an athletic build, without being muscle bound. His eyes showed a kindness within and his shining white smile gave him an instant attraction. David then had a sensation which shocked him. 'I can see why Ricky likes him so much', he thought. Alex was, after all, a faultless physical being.

They chatted freely from the word go, initially about how Alex had been named by his mother after Alexander Cooper, one of the most famous Jamaican artists. He talked with genuine warmth, in a rich West Indian accent, about the great man's paintings, most of which reflected daily life and traditions on the Caribbean island. Ricky had been right. He was a most engaging lunch companion. While nattering away, they ordered some food, together with a glass of crisp South African Chenin Blanc. To Alex's pleasure, they did a tuna and cucumber sandwich, so, to be sociable, David ordered the same. The conversation got round to Alex's dancing and he told him about how he was currently in a show in a small theatre and loving it.

"Are you dancing tonight?", David enquired.

"Yes, every night except Sunday. I don't ever normally drink at lunchtime but, to be honest, I was a shade nervous about meeting you", said Alex, "I haven't ever done this sort of thing before. Have you?".

"No, never. I'm new to the whole thing". David replied. He meant the computer dating. Alex took that as meaning new to his sexuality.

"When did you come out then, David?".

"Oh, about an hour ago. I left home soon after 12.30. Got a taxi straight here", David replied.

Alex looked confused. "No, I meant come out, as in 'come out'", he explained.

"Oh, that". David took a second and then continued with uncertainty. "Well, sort of a few years ago really".

"How did you realise you were gay?", Alex asked sympathetically.

David was now getting fidgety. This was one area he had not covered in his mental rehearsals. He had thought that the conversation would stick to things like where they lived, what they did and where they went on holiday. This was a challenge he had not prepared himself for. Before he could answer, a head popped up over the hedge like a large glove puppet. It was George gazing straight at him. Then up popped up another head. Chris was not going to miss out. David was utterly bamboozled and tried to pick up the dialogue, but not before flashing his two pals a disapproving glare. His reply come out before his brain could take control.

"Oh, that. Well, it was all down to a Wham video. Club Tropicana it was, and I watched George Michael and, wham, I felt a twitch and a tingle, if you know what I mean". David was desperate to change the subject. "I suppose you have danced in a lot of places, Alex. All over the country? Tell me, I am really interested".

"All over the world actually. I had a job on the cruise ships for a couple of years. That was great. The highlights, I suppose, were dancing at charity gigs at the Palladium and the Albert Hall. You mentioned in your profile that you danced, David. Have you danced in many interesting places?".

"Dance? Me? Oh, yes, of course. Not many really. A lot in London, a few times in Brighton, and I remember there was Bristol. Oh, and one unforgettable night in Bournemouth. There must have been a few other places as well but it was all quite a while ago".

"Where did you dance?", asked Alex, expecting a professional answer.

"Parties, mostly. I have been known to dance at parties. And weddings. Only after one too many, of course". Alex just stared back in bemusement.

George and Chris placed themselves at the table two away from the suitors, alongside Alex but in David's full view, and, with hardly anyone there, they could hear every word. George was highly noticeable. He had taken his spying challenge seriously and had a pair of large binoculars hanging around his neck.

Alex got back to main issue. "Have you got a boyfriend?". Chris just managed to stop himself collapsing into hysterics, getting a sharp kick under the table and a 'shush' from George.

"No, not at the moment", David responded. "How about you?".

"No. I was married. That went wrong and we got divorced. It was very sad. I haven't been out with anyone since".

This was David's opening he had been waiting for. "Tell me about your husband, sorry, ex-husband".

"His name was Ricky. I adored him. He's a rock singer, a very good one. We had so much in common. It was a shame that he was such an idiot".

"What happened?", David probed.

"The usual. He went off with someone and I found out. I just couldn't forgive him. I trusted him and he cheated on me. And then he lied. It was horrible. And he was so messy. It drove me mad. And grumpy too. So, basically, I kicked him out. It sounds terrible. In truth, I regret it. He wasn't really that bad. I guess I am just too picky. I have come to realise that. I am not sure where he is now, although I hear he still plays a good many gigs in London".

"Don't you speak with him?".

"No, I just can't bring myself to. He rings now and again, but I just can't take his calls. I can't pretend it didn't happen, David. To be fair, he has apologised a thousand times. I am not very forgiving, I guess. My life has been tough. Can you imagine what it was like growing up in a Caribbean family knowing you're gay. They are all so homophobic. And my Dad was originally from Jamaica. You just can't fit into society. It's impossible. You can't talk to anyone about it, and that included my parents. I told my sister one day. She seemed to understand, although she couldn't do anything to help me. When it eventually came out into the open, I was 18. I was basically kicked out of the family. It was awful. I left with no money, with just a suitcase full of clothes and somehow managed to get a job on a cruise ship. That's where I met Ricky. He was the first person who was really kind to me, who understood me and I fell in love with him, and the rest is history. I feel so differently now. I want to hear his voice so badly and I need to say sorry too, but I can't bring myself to do it. It was a huge overreaction on my part, I admit now, and I miss him dreadfully, but I just can't". Alex then woke up to where he was and who he was with. "Oh, sorry, David. Forgive me. I don't know why I am telling you all this. We are meant to be on a date. I'm so sorry". Alex's eyes welled up.

Chris was listening from his table and emotion overcame him as well. He too had a tear in his eye. George tapped his arm in consolation. "Don't blub, old chap", he softly comforted his friend, taking out his pristine white handkerchief and handing it to him. Chris accepted it graciously, wiped his eyes, blew his nose and handed it back.

"I do believe though that time heals all things and that, perhaps, you are a conversation short with him", David encouraged. "It seems, from what you say, that he is a thoroughly nice chap at heart and maybe he has changed his ways. Perhaps he is calmer now. Who knows? It could be that he has learned his lesson. He might even be a bit tidier. Don't ever give up, Alex. Never say never".

"You're right. We should speak. But the lying is hard to get over. Yes, you are absolutely right. After all, I reckon there's no harm in talking, is there?".

They sat chatting for a while longer, paid the bill and Alex suggested they go for a walk. Things were easier for David now that he had, in his opinion, completed the main part of his mission and he seemed to have achieved its goal. Alex did still love Ricky, that was clear, and it sounded like he was going to take Ricky's phone call. They ambled leisurely down the path, talking more about Alex's married life. Meanwhile, George and Chris tagged after them stealthily, trying to hide in plain sight. This presented a thorny problem for the two sleuths. In keeping a discreet distance behind the other two, they could not hear a word they were saying. They then saw Alex invite David to sit on a bench up ahead, on the right of the path. The intrepid spies needed a new tactic or they would have no alternative other than to walk straight past them and away out of the park. George spotted another bench on the left, which was situated in front of a shrubbery with an uninterrupted view of the seat opposite where their targets were sitting. They settled down and George lifted his binoculars to his eyes.

"Have they kissed yet?", quizzed Chris, tight-mouthed.

"Don't be silly. Hold on. Wait. It looks like Alex is touching David", George whispered back.

Chris needed more. "What? Where, how, what are they doing? Are they having a grope?".

"No", said George, "he just has his hand on David's thigh".

"What do you mean? Like sexily? Like how? Give me the binoculars", asked the prurient Chris.

"Like this", and George spread his palm gently over Chris' right thigh, refusing to part with the glasses. At that exact moment, a deep voice bellowed from behind them.

"Hello. Hello. What do we have here?". It was an elderly park warden, with a wrinkled face and a well-ironed uniform, looming large behind them. "Don't tell me you're birdwatching. Men-watching more like. Let me make it clear. I have nothing against the LBCBBC community. We accept all types these days. It is none of my business, apparently. If you want to touch each other, that's your affair, but we draw a line at spying on your like-minded types. You couple of weirdos are bang out of order and I must ask you to leave the Royal Park forthwith".

The embarrassed pair pleaded their innocence in vain. David looked over in amazement to see his flatmates being marched unceremoniously off the premises by the Park guard.

"That was great", Chris said sarcastically. "Another park I can't go back to. Thanks, George". Chris continued his embarrassed moan as they got into a taxi and headed down the Mall to Trafalgar Square. He jumped out at his office with George staying on board to get home.

"Don't forget. 6pm at the This Way, That Way or Whatever Way shop in Leicester Square", reminded George.

"Shit, I'd forgotten about that. So, I am now going to a gay sex shop with you, George. Where else can we be thrown out of? See you at 6".

Meanwhile, back in the park, David and Alex were saying their farewells. It had been less of a date, more of a counselling session. But a huge success for David. He had been bursting to come clean, to tell his affable date the truth about his stupid scam, but had decided against it, especially in the light of Alex's sensitive nature. He had done his duty and thought it better that Ricky use his questionable skills to reveal the truth in due course. They shook hands at the gate, David wishing him well before suggesting again that he and Ricky really should be talking.

"You never know, that might be just what he is waiting for too. Why don't you phone him?", David urged.

"No. It is for him to phone me", Alex huffed, then appeared stubbornly angry. With more than hint of bitchiness, he added,

"I'm not the one who went off shagging strangers". David suddenly saw the possibility of his plan unravelling if they went on and he left abruptly to catch a cab. No mention of another date was made by either man.

George and Chris met up again outside the Leicester Square store as they had planned. David had been invited to join the shopping spree but told them that he had been to gay clubs before and that he already had all the gear he needed. The two men dwelt for a minute outside the window.

"Us two again", said Chris. "What a gay day we are having. Thrown out of the park and now going shopping in this place. Do you mind if we don't go in together? We don't want to look like an item. I think I'd prefer it that way. Anyway, you're not my type".

"Come on", said an emboldened George. "They've seen all this before. Just act naturally, whatever that is".

"I don't know what the hell has happened to you, George", Chris exclaimed.

On entering, they were confronted with an array of clothing hanging on circular rails and against the side walls. George noticed that there was a great deal of leather and lace. As they courageously ventured further in, they found themselves approaching the back wall, which was covered with a menacing menagerie of whips, chains and bizarre torture devices. A very effeminate assistant mugged them in an instant.

"Can I help you boys? Looking for something a bit naughty, are we?", he chirped, airily. George put on his most macho voice.

"Thank you. No, we are fine. Our girlfriends are taking us to this posh fancy-dress party tomorrow. We want to go as something like those Village People, but much straighter. Sorry. When I mean straighter, I didn't mean any offence. I mean not completely...".

The effete man spared bumbling George's blushes and offered to help find them some interesting outfits. They perused rail after rail, trying on studded leather jackets, glittery waistcoats, cowboys' chaps, sailors' uniforms, not to mention the American Indian headdresses. In the end, they played it safe. George went for the lumberjack look, topped off with a Mexican straight-hair wig and a wide-brimmed cowboy hat for extra disguise, while Chris chose a white wife-beater vest, some black patent-leather trousers, finished off with a black shiny peaked cap. They paid and were ready to scurry out, laden down with bags, when Chris, for some reason, headed once more to the back of the store, to the dozens of the sadistic devices that would have been more at home in the Chamber of Horrors, all in full display on the wall. Chris studied them all intensely, wondering, in his naivety, what they did and, more importantly, where some of them went, while thinking at the same time that some people out there seemed to be having so much more fun than he was. On the counter, there was a selection of large vibrators standing on end like shiny soldiers, pink ones, bent ones, rabbity ones, knobbly ones, one like a yellow sweetcorn, all sorts. As the assistant was elsewhere, he picked up the biggest and waved it at an unsettled George, mouthing 'Want one?'. All he got back was a frown and he started to place it back on its end on the glass countertop, only clumsily to let it fall over and it started whirring. Loudly. It took on a life of its own, rattling against the glass and making a deafening thrumming that resounded throughout the whole store. Chris did not dare touch it again and fled, like a startled coward, out of the door, with George hot on his heels.

"That was horrible. Bloody thing had a life of its own. Let's get a pint", Chris cried out. They headed for the pub.

The first thing they saw when they went into the Wellington was Bonnie, lighting up the bar with her radiance. Chris was more delighted than usual to see her. He leaned over and kissed her intensely.

"What's all this?", she said, seeing the boys carrying their shopping bags. "What have you been up to? Been shopping, have we? Did you get me anything nice?".

She then saw the bags with the name of the store on the side.

"Uh oh". She looked at Chris disapprovingly. "You are joking, aren't you? What have you bought?".

Chris hurriedly explained. "I think that if I had got you something from where we have just been, you'd probably be buzzing with excitement".

"Well, why didn't you?", she said coquettishly. "Embarrassed, were we?".

Chris began to go over the events of their day, from the park incident to the sex toys, omitting any mention of the vibrator incident. George quietly assumed his favourite barstool, happy to be back on his beloved seat, in safe surroundings, with a beer in his hand. He let Chris do the talking. He had had an interesting but, at times, uncomfortable day, especially in the park. People like George do not often get kicked out of public parks for being dirty old men. He had never been ejected from anywhere, let alone from one of the Queen's finest gardens. However, he still managed a scampish smile as he said 'cheers' to Chris and Bonnie.

"Your turn tomorrow", said Chris, jogging George's memory. The latter's expression changed at a stroke to one of disquiet.

"Where are you off to tomorrow, George?", enquired Bonnie.

"He is out flirting with my ex-wife", interjected Chris. "He's in for a thrilling day with Angela, going to some art gallery or other. I'm definitely not going to be a fly on the wall for that one. Too much excitement, more than I could possibly take".

At that moment, David came in and was greeted like a conquering hero. They all exchanged their day's experiences and David announced his delight at the way things had gone, in spite of his friends' antics. He felt he had set Ricky up for a big reunion and had escaped being asked out for a second date. That, he considered, was the perfect outcome and he beamed with self-congratulation at his magnificent performance.

Chris heralded another success for his Project EX. David had got the children for half term, Ricky only had to pick up the phone. If George and Angela can walk into the sunset, he thought, and Ricky and Kate can trip the gay fantastic on Thursday, then they had all heroically accomplished everything they had set out to achieve. It was all going well. But tomorrow was another day.

WEDNESDAY, SEPTEMBER 25

George had arranged to meet Angela in the entrance of the National Gallery. He looked like the quintessential British diplomat as he climbed the steps, under the watchful surviving eye of Lord Nelson at the top of his lofty column. In his casual, light-tanned suit, open-necked obligatory blue shirt, with well-polished brown leather shoes, his appearance was distinctly ambassadorial, a suaveness he comported elegantly.

Angela was fluttery when she drew closer to the columned façade of the Gallery, which so regally dominated the Trafalgar Square backdrop. This was the first date since her divorce, having apprehensively put her name on a dating website on the advice of her good friend Beth, who had assured her that online dating did not have to be all about sex and tawdry liaisons, but that she might actually meet some truly interesting people. She also advised her not to be afraid of going out with someone a bit older. Angela herself was an old soul. She had found George's profile and thought it had mirrored her own artistic and literary interests and decided that she would 'give it a go', with much encouragement from Beth.

Today, the world saw a revitalised, embellished, graceful and prettified Angela. Her hair had had some expert attention, designed into the soft bob that she loved, now finished off with dazzling highlights. She wore a smart floral, pleated midi-dress in autumn colours with a cashmere jacket and knee-length, beige suede boots. A pale blue pashmina adorned her neck. She oozed pizzazz.

She had left the house with a determined stride, having caught an encouraging glimpse of herself, with all her fresh sassiness, in the hall mirror. However, as she advanced up the steps, her poise became less assured. She felt a sudden diffidence about the whole idea. For a moment, she hesitated, considering whether listening to her friend Beth had been a good idea or not. Nonetheless, a subconscious momentum drove her on. Fortunately, she did not have long to wait. George had seen her coming up the steps and gone out to greet her.

He was pure charm itself. "Angela. I am so pleased to meet you. Thank you so much for finding the time to join me today. I have been looking forward to this enormously".

She relaxed immediately, warmed by his urbane greeting. He certainly showed the refined and courteous manner of a true gentleman, something that she appreciated after all those years with Chris. Her ex-husband was never discourteous, but he certainly lacked style and culture. Dapper George was the epitome of both these.

He loved what he saw. This gracile, fetching young lady was not what he had expected. His first thought was that she was very different from the Angela that Chris had described, far more sophisticated than he had been led to believe, and lovelier, much lovelier. If Kate had been a thorny rose, Angela was a lissom, soft petalled camelia.

Introductions over, they decided to go directly to the Vermeer Exhibition, eager to find the 'Girl with the Pearl Earring'. When they stood before it, Angela was spellbound. She spoke without taking her eyes off the portrait.

"I have always wanted to see this painting. He worked so slowly, you know, meticulously. Each and every brushstroke mattered, and it shows. His mastery of light is genius. To think he actually stepped back to study this work over three hundred years ago, just as we are doing now. She is meant to be Turkish, allegedly. It's a 'tronie', that's what they called the Dutch style of painting faces in the 17th century. They were not meant as portraits but were studies in expression and character".

As she spoke, she did not take her eyes off the painting, while George could not take his eyes off her.

"You know so much. I am most impressed, Angela".

"I read a great deal, George, and the Dutch Golden Age fascinates me". They continued on their tour, only on Angela's condition that they could come back to the masterpiece after they had seen the other paintings. They absorbed and discussed the fineness of the 'View of Delft', the concentration captured on the face of 'The Lacemaker', the inquisitiveness of 'The Astronomer' and 'The Geographer'. Referring to the last two, Angela continued her tutorial. "There are only about 50

Vermeers that remain, and these are the only two with a single male subject. Do you notice it's the same man in both? Isn't that interesting? The artists of this era loved painting scientists. Not like today".

For once, George was lost for words. He was entranced by her and what she was saying. He stood motionless by her side, gripped by every engaging word, in total awe of her knowledge. Eventually, after being beguiled by the mastery of other Dutch painters from this period, they returned to the classic 'Girl with a Pearl Earring'.

"It used to be called, 'Girl with a Turban'. 'Girl with a Pearl Earring' sounds so much better, don't you think, although some experts say it's not a pearl, but a piece of tin. 'Girl with a Piece of Tin on her Ear' doesn't sound so great, does it?", she chuckled.

They spent the whole afternoon drifting from one masterwork to another around the vast galleries in full veneration of what was before them. Together, they shared their appraisal of each work of art in a refreshing merging of intellects that they both enjoyed. Time passed rapidly and soon it was nearly 5pm.

"David, it's been absolutely lovely, but I think I should be thinking of going", said an enthralled and somewhat reluctant Angela.

"Let's try to put that thought right out of your mind and go for a drink. How about a glass of champagne or something at London's oldest and finest cocktail bar, the American Bar at the Savoy?".

She readily agreed and they set off jauntily on their ten-minute walk down the Strand, Angela putting her arm through his in a companionship way. After they swung through the revolving door of the unique Savoy Hotel, they found themselves turning left into the famous bar once frequented by such luminaries as Winston Churchill and Ernest Hemingway. A correct, white-jacketed waiter directed them to their table and, in no time, brought them his Manhattan (Scotch, not Bourbon) and her Kir Royale. They both relaxed, perfectly at home in the luxurious setting. Luxury suited them. She had come from a good middle-class family and was accustomed to the occasional fizz in fine places. While she might have appeared to the wide world as dowdy and dull, in truth she was anything but that. Sipping her champagne cocktail, she realised that, looking back over the past ten years, she had been entrapped in mundanity for so long that she had become unremarkable. Today, however, in sharing an afternoon of art and aesthetics, following on with an evening of flair and elegance, she found herself totally fulfilled as a person. With George, she had discovered an immediate assimilation and attachment and she was thoroughly loving every moment of it. When he suggested that they grab a bite to eat next door at Simpson's, she did not flinch to accept the invitation.

What had started out as an anxious walk up the steps to meet a stranger had become a memorable day of inspiration, conviviality and erudition. In George, she had found a mature intellect that matched her own. While Chris had been the comic beer buddy for so many years, in George she had found a complementary soul with whom she could effortlessly relate.

Simpsons-in-the-Strand remained a resilient bastion of classic English cooking, a glorious throwback to the country's imperial greatness. With its dependable staple menu of traditional roasts, it was the perfect place for a true Englishman like George to take lunch or dinner, especially after savouring a cocktail or two at the Savoy. 'Proper food', he called it. The interior of the restaurant retained a similar stateliness to the legendary neighbouring hotel. It had started out as the country's premier chess club in 1828, the Wimbledon of the chequered board, and it still encapsulated all the imposing Victorian, wood-panelled distinction of a Pall Mall gentleman's club. Here, under the glittering crystal chandeliers, you could expect only traditional fare, with master-carvers bringing roast meats right to your table on the original trolleys. George always felt entirely at home in the sumptuous, conservative comfort of Simpsons. Mr Granby was such an old-fashioned Englishman at heart.

It seemed an apt place for the couple to continue their lavish evening and Angela found it equally befitting. Their free-flowing banter rolled on, seamlessly bringing new subjects into the conversation. George was fascinated by Angela's intellect. As much as he had loved Kate, and still did, she was no match for his current scholarly companion. They talked about opera, the

Queen, the Mona Lisa, private education, holidays and, of course, their failed marriages. She was attracted to his sophistication and his worldly wisdom, both of which Chris had lacked. Now she was loving their sharing of stories. Together, they harmonised on so many levels.

Angela had lost all track of time and it was George who suggested that she should think about catching her train before it got too late. She checked her watch.

"Goodness", she exclaimed softly. "Is that the time? I suppose all good things must come to an end. George, I cannot thank you enough. I have honestly loved every second of today. You have been a real gentleman".

There was some significance in that last statement, for what Angela had been missing in her life was the fellowship of a 'real gentleman', a mature, polished cavalier. She knew in an instant that she had found that in George.

"The pleasure has been all mine, Angela. To meet you has been an absolute delight."

He, like David had earlier, then had a quandary. He felt a burning need to be honest with Angela about how this date had come about. He was uncomfortable with playing this silly, callow game with something so priceless, although he knew that if he did decide to own up to the truth, he had to get his story right. One false move, one clumsy word, and the whole day could end very badly. He gathered his thoughts for a second, while the wine waiter topped up their glasses.

"Angela, I have a confession", he said, gutsily. A worried look seized her face. "I want you to know that I have always lived by honesty and, meeting you, I cannot tell you how elated I feel. Let me explain". He sipped his wine before settling in to divulge the real version of how they had got to meet. He convinced himself that telling her the truth, or something near the truth, at this early stage would be better than peddling a lie throughout any further dates. He was fully aware that it came with risks and that he did not want to do anything that would jeopardise their new-found friendship, but he felt this was the time. Where untruths and deceit might have been justifiable for one date, this relationship was already starting to mean so much more to him.

"I want to come clean, Angela. Now please don't go mad. Hear me out. Please". He took a deep intake of breath. "I do actually know Chris. I know him very well actually. Let me put it this way, he is my best friend and is also my flatmate". Silence fell like a dark blanket.

Angela looked shaken to the core. He flinched at her desperate facial expression, one of shock and, above all, of overwhelming disappointment. He had nothing to add and could only watch, speechless, as she bowed her head and processed what she had heard. Eventually she looked up.

"Oh, George. I get it. You are George, Chris' drinking buddy. What an idiot I have been. So, this is all a childish joke, or a bet or something, is it?". She started to rise from her seat, her anger obvious.

"No, Angela, no. Please. Please sit down. Hear me out. It isn't anything like that. I need to explain. I just want to be totally honest with you. I have known Chris for a couple of years now and he has always talked well of you, even though he has made play of the fact that you two were so different. He, as we both know, can be a bit two-dimensional. He may just be one of the nicest guys in the world and that's why this is all so difficult. I have listened to him going on about things at home for ages. We both know Chris. The tales he would tell I would listen to for hours in the pub and, the more I heard, the more I felt a sympathy for your side. This is not a conspiracy. And I don't want to be disloyal to Chris. The truth is that I wanted the chance to meet you, you fascinated me, and then Chris mentioned you were on this online thing and I saw my chance. Thank heavens I did, Angela. I want to be totally upfront with you. How could I have asked my best pal's wife to meet me when you and he were still living together in the same house? I couldn't, even though I could see that the marriage was over in reality. Then you got divorced. I had thought about ringing you up, but it seemed wrong, what with me living with Chris and him being my best friend. Last week, the perfect opportunity arose. Chris mentioned that you were on this dating site. Yes, he found you on it. It isn't the sort of thing I do. But then I saw a way that I could put myself in front of you to see if you would like to meet up with me. It might not have happened if not for that. It was just two people reaching out to each other. I was fully expecting you to say 'no'. Fortunately for me, you didn't, because meeting you today has been incredible. Please, Angela, I meant no harm. Please, I beg you, don't let this ruin everything. It doesn't, does it?".

She ignored the question. "Does Chris know? About the date?", she asked stiffly. George had to think quickly, considering whether lying further by saying 'no' could create even further repercussions or whether being truthful by saying 'yes' would make it sound like a puerile conspiracy, which in fact it had been. He knew that his answer could be pivotal to what happened next. He decided on a bit of both routes. He preferred to think of it as not lying but that, in self-justification, he was really just being slightly economical with the truth.

"Honestly, and I am being nothing but honest, I told him last night. He was OK with it, laughed, as you'd expect from Chris, then he wished me luck and said he thought that, actually, we might get along really well. That's the truth. He did add that we were all grown-ups and that he would love to see you happy. No hard feelings and all that.".

"Does it put you in a bad place with Chris? He is your friend after all. I can't see how this will work, with you living with my ex-husband".

He took a positive out of this as he read into her words that she too had been having thoughts that their chance meeting could possibly grow into a more meaningful future relationship and he was heartened by that. He knew that he had to be very careful. He had to try to steer the conversation away from the duplicity in which he had become embroiled.

"It isn't a problem, Angela. A bit unusual, maybe. But I am sure it would be fine. Chris is a thoroughly good egg underneath. He knows that you and he were not particularly well-matched, if you know what I mean. He has admitted as much to me and he bears absolutely no resentment towards you and tells me you have none towards him. By the way, the manner in which you two handled your divorce was exemplary and I give you personally huge credit for that. You two can still be friends and our, er, 'friendship' shouldn't affect that. It sounds to me, if you don't mind my saying, that you two had a typical 'married too soon' situation with short-term, not long-term attraction. I hope you don't mind my being personal about your marriage?".

"Chris and I, you're right, we fell out of love with each other years ago, if we are honest. I certainly did. It was not his fault. It was nobody's fault. We were just not right for each other. Wow. This is a bombshell. I am going to have to think about this whole thing. So, you are THE George? Unbelievable".

"I am sorry about any misunderstanding. I have tried to be honest with you and I hope you can forgive me. Let me tell you, Angela. I really, really like you. This has been a simply wonderful day for me". Angela gave him an indecipherable glare, taking her time before responding.

"I think I should go home. I can get a cab. It has been fabulous, now this has come as a shock. I need to think about where we go from here".

George decided to take a chance and be authoritative.

"Angela. Please listen. I am not going to let you just walk away like that. Meeting you has been the most extraordinary thing that has happened to me in years. Please don't think I am playing games. I am not. I have never met anyone like you. And this is after only a couple of hours of Vermeer and a few slices of rare roast beef. Please, don't think bad of me. Now, this is what's going to happen. I will get the bill, we shall share a taxi and I will see you safely to the station. OK?". Angela gathered herself.

"How could a girl say no, George? Let me be equally honest. I have had the most amazing day too and I feel much the same way. I did not expect this last bit though. Well, I guess I didn't expect any of it. You get the bill and let's get me back to my train".

There was now a weighty atmosphere between the two. The conversation that had been smooth and effortless throughout the evening had now stalled. Although George was craving to get things back as they were, he knew that she needed some uninterrupted, quiet time for reflection.

They sat in the back of the taxi without a word being exchanged. George thought it best not to break her silence. They walked across the station concourse, awkwardly not holding hands or linking arms, and stopped at the platform barrier, as neither knew what to do next.

"Thank you for today, George. I've had a lovely day. Everything was wonderful". She went to kiss him politely on the cheek. As her face drew closer to his, she then did the totally unexpected. She spontaneously put her arms around his neck in slow motion and kissed him firmly on the lips. He embraced her tightly in return. With that kiss they felt completely comfortable, without any embarrassment or self-consciousness. After some time, enfolded together, wordless, George looked her into her eyes and spoke softly to her.

"Angela, this has all been simply incredible. I just can't believe what has happened today. You are just an unbelievable woman. I think we could have something special. Let's keep this between us for now. Let's not let anything get in our way. Today was meant to be, it has surprised us both and it's not like me to express my emotions".

She kissed him again. "You're right. We should keep Chris out of this. It has nothing to do with him. Actually, I don't know what I was so worried about. I was thinking in the cab that I am, after all, a single woman now and Chris is a single man. What matters is that you and I met. It is not about Chris. That was then and this is now. I am so pleased to have met you, George. It is weird though, isn't it? You being that George. Oh, I haven't even given you my mobile number".

They exchanged details and George remained assertive. "Theatre on Saturday night? I insist. What would you like to see?".

She threw her head backwards and laughed. "Not exactly Mr Reticent, are we? No, I'd love that. Can I tell you what I would really like to see? I don't suppose we could try and get tickets for Madame Butterfly at the Albert Hall, could we? I have heard it is excellent. There may be none left, but that would be fantastic".

"There's always a way, Angela, there's always a way. Why don't you come up at lunchtime, then we can make a day of it?", George proposed. The mood had completely lightened.

"Sounds like a plan. I'll let you know what train I shall be on. If you can't get tickets for Madame Butterfly, anything will be wonderful. This is lovely". The conductor blew the whistle to get the last remaining passengers on board. "Thank you, George. I can't believe all this. You have been simply lovely. I'll see you on Saturday then".

"Bye, Angela. And thank you. Our secret, for now. See you Saturday". With that, she kissed him yet again and scurried through the barrier. George stood glued to the spot until she boarded the train, giving him one last wave, which he returned.

He travelled home replaying the whole wondrous day in his head. He had not expected any of this, not in the slightest. Angela was just extraordinary. It had started out as Chris' bit of fun, but he would never have guessed it would turn out anything like this. He never had been a good liar and, somehow, he had also managed to banish the lies into the bin. By being honest, well, mostly honest, he felt cleansed of all the duplicity of this stupid game. Now he had to think of tomorrow and what he would say to his friend, her ex-husband. 'Of all the women in the bloody world, I have to fall for this one. I can never do things the easy way, can I?', he thought, with a huge smile on his face. He felt young and vital again. Then he remembered another date he had coming up. Ironically, with Chris in a gay club the next night. He could not stop a snigger at the absurdity of Project EX.

CHAPTER ELEVEN
Dancing Queen

THURSDAY, SEPTEMBER 26

By 6pm, Ricky had been primping himself for at least an hour, attending every tiny detail of his appearance in readiness for his hot date with Kate, his dancing queen. He had been captivated by the exotic apparition he had seen in the photos, with the tumbling raven mane and the pouting red lips. What was more, he was enthralled by her sexy, sultry voice and that steamy Spanish accent on the phone. A good half-hour had been spent immersed under the foam bubbles in the bath, washing his lanky dark hair under the shower and then grooming his long locks to perfection, before putting on a smart white shirt, black leather trousers and, of course, his favourite dancing shoes. He was ready to party.

At the same time, in the privacy of his own room, George was concentrating on his metamorphosis into a living gay icon. In fact, he was quietly enjoying the attention that he was showing himself. When George did something, he liked to do it properly. He had zero preconceptions of what to expect at the club, being too scared to google 'What to wear to a gay dance' in case it got stuck on his computer's memory and popped up at the wrong moment sometime in the future. But he went at it with gusto. First, he had to squeeze his lower torso into his only jeans, a beaten-up pair that he had bought at least ten years and which, by now, he had well outgrown. To get them anywhere near on he had to breathe in to collapse his middle-aged paunch and then jump up and down. When that proved only half successful, he ended up lying on the floor, pulling them up hard with both hands. Once the zipper had locked him in, he stood up painfully and put on his red and black checked lumberjack shirt but not before he had wrestled himself into a matching elastic chest harness. While he had not wanted to buy this ludicrous, functionless piece of 'queer gear', as the assistant called it, he had been told that it was essential kit if he wanted to have that authentic butch look. Eager not to get into a long debate about chest harnesses, he had humbly acquiesced. Next was his Mexican wig, with the last touch being his droopy moustache, which he affixed carefully to his upper lip. The disguise was then complete, or 'completo' as they say South of the Border.

While all this pampering was going on, Chris came in from work to find the lounge empty. He headed for his room, grabbing a beer on the way. After a quick shower, a heavy splashing of deodorant and a drag of a comb through his greased-back hair, he slipped into his patent leather trousers, donned his new sexy vest and put on his shiny black cap. As he admired his reflection in the mirror, he did not hesitate in complimenting himself out loud. "I didn't know you could look so damn hunky. You're gorgeous", he boasted.

Ricky had by now moved in the lounge. He called out to the others. "I'm off now guys. Hope I don't see you later".

Chris was dying to see him and also to be seen. He sprung out of his room, only to be confronted by what looked like his own mirror image.

"What the hell…? I see you're getting into the mood. At least my strides are real leather, not like the bin-liners you're wearing", mocked Ricky.

Chris felt both embarrassed that his dress scheme was virtually identical to that of his gay friend's garb and, at the same time, relieved that he seemed to have chosen the acceptable garb for the occasion. Now all he wanted to see was George in his garb.

"George, come out here", he cried out.

George then made his entrance, walking in as if onto the set of a spaghetti western, hiding his face under large black, sombrero-style cowboy hat. He raised the rim to reveal the bandit moustache perched precariously on his upper lip.

The other two creased up in stitches. "You're not bloody serious. Hey, gringo, cómo éstas?", Ricky mocked. "Well, if it isn't El Bandido, the Mexican Lumberjack Outlaw Advertising

Man. Well done, Georgie. That'll do nicely. A gay bandit who chops down trees".

"You're looking very nacho, George. No, sorry, that's should be 'macho'. Seriously, you look fantastic, irresistible. The boys will love you", Chris said with as much sincerity as he could muster, lending his support. "Don't listen to Ricky. What does he know? I'll be proud to have the first dance with you".

"You bloody well won't. I am not doing any the damn dancing. I just want to see Richard here tackling Kate. Above all else, I don't want Kate to recognise me. That's why I added the moustache. Do you think she might know it's me?".

"Oh, I don't think so. No way. Not you, George. Not until I tell her, that is", Chris added impishly.

Just then, Ricky's phone rang and he flustered, moving purposefully into the far corner of the room. Chris took the opportunity to challenge George. Although this was not the best time, he could not stop himself asking about his date.

"So, how did it go with Angela?", he whispered in George's ear, with an expectant expression on his face. "She's not that bad is she. No beauty perhaps but she cleans up nicely and there is no doubt she is very bright".

George jerked upright, involuntarily wanting to jump to her defence.

"She is actually extremely attractive. She's not like you make out at all. In fact, you are being very unkind. We had an excellent day at the Vermeer Exhibition and then we went for a superb dinner at Simpson's. All very civilised. Yes, it was lovely and she is actually wonderful company".

Anyone other than Chris would have picked up a clear nuance in these words and asked whether there was, perhaps, a little spark between them? However, Chris did not do nuances and sparks. If it did not hit him like a steam train, he just would not get it.

"I am glad you had a nice time. When she makes the effort, she can look quite good in a certain light, or no light at all", Chris came back cruelly.

George glared at him, his face flushing bright red around his droopy moustache as he suppressed his anger, but, in true style, he managed to hold himself back. Fortuitously, just at that moment, Ricky joined them again. He said only three words and any tension was immediately diffused.

"That was Alex", he grinned, unable to hide his joy. The other two whooped and hugged their friend, who simply simmered and glowed. "It seems that we are all good. Just like that. We are going to have a long chat tomorrow. We have a way to go but it's brilliant. We're talking again. And it's all thanks to David. He's a bloody miracle worker".

"That's fantastic, Ricky", said Chris. "I am so happy for you, mate. It all seems to be coming together nicely. Talking about successful dates, where is David, your horny love rival? He's going to be late".

At that exact moment, David walked in and his jaw dropped. "What the hell is this? Are you serious? Sorry, wrong place. I seem to have checked into the YMCA. Are you really going like that, you two? George, all you need is your horse. Must be tied up outside. I guess the lift wasn't big enough for El Trigger", he sniggered.

"I'm a lumberjack, not some bloody Mexican bandit, you idiots. Isn't it obvious?".

"The hat has to go. Yes, definitely, get rid of the hat. A lumberjack in a sombrero just doesn't work", commanded David.

"Then Kate will recognise me in a second, stupid. Perhaps I should have worn a Lone Ranger eye mask, only I don't have one. The hat has to stay. I have no other choice". George insisted.

Ricky chipped in, drawing the attention away from George. "Listen, David mate. Alex just phoned. He actually phoned me. We are talking again. I can't say how much I owe you. I won't go into it now. It was only a quick call but a mega step forward. But, David, you did brilliantly. Let's talk later. I have to go. Now listen up, guys, tonight is Thursday night, so there will be loads of people there. As the line outside will be massive, I have arranged three tickets for you. Just go round the corner and pick them up at the stage door. They're in my name. Have fun, boys. Just keep well away from me. Don't do anyone I wouldn't do", he said smuttily. With that, he turned and dashed out of the door with a triumphant grin on his face.

The others took a while glancing up and down at one another's attire in amused silence, before David broke the pause.

"OK. Whoever thought that this was in any way a good idea? Look at you, George. What bloody idiot came up with this nonsense?".

"You did" the other two barked together, loudly.

"Good point", said David. "I keep forgetting. I suppose I did get the ball rolling. But I never thought it would roll into this, a bloody gay ball".

"Are you going to slip into your Cinderella frock then, David?", teased Chris. "Don't forget your glass slippers, Cinders love. You have to be home by midnight, remember".

"Just go and get us some beers, while I get changed", said David. "There's no way I am going to do this sober".

Ricky had arranged that he and Kate should meet up in a trendy bar just around the corner from Eden 86. The place was packed young men, all heavily engaged in exuberant, animated chitter-chatter. An excited buzz hung over the room. Ricky shuffled his way sideways through the tightly-bunched horde of vests and bare flesh in search of Kate, acknowledging with a smile the several friendly shouts of 'Hi, Ricky' directed at him. There was no sign of Kate. Unsuccessful in his search, he emerged back through the lively throng just as the double front doors were pulled open in a synchronised swing by two sexily clad young bucks. A ravishing diva swept through. It was a Hollywood entrance by any standard as this dazzling creature, her long, satiny hair flowing obediently behind her, swished in, clad in a flowing, full-length, low-cut black lace dress adorned with red flowers and two colourful peacocks. Waist-down, it had a flamboyant, Spanish abundancy, with the floral-embroidered hem rising up to her thighs at the front to reveal her long, shapely, tanned legs and her shiny black high heels. Her lithe, smooth arms, slightly bent out at the elbows, finished off that composed catwalk poise. She strode straight up to an aghast Ricky and hurled her arms around his neck.

"Ricky, darling. This is fabulous. Thank you for asking me. I am so pleased to meet you, darling".

Kate had this ability to stun men into silence. It was not only the way she dressed but also the way she comported herself, that ridiculously steamy accent and that racy smile. She drove men crazy and Ricky, whose preferences lay elsewhere, was her latest conquest. Although he was perfectly accustomed to fans throwing themselves at him, when challenged by Kate, he was rendered frozen and he just about managed a nervous, monosyllabic stutter in reply.

"Hi Kate. You look terrific. Thanks for coming. Great to meet you. Did I say you looked terrific? Yes, I did. Sorry. What are you drinking?"

Such was her instant allure that dozens of the pretty young boys in the bar turned their heads, with more than a few whistles ringing out. She loved it. With flick of her tresses and a flash of that smile, she bewitched her admirers. With Ricky in tow, the waves of drinkers parted in a Moses-like miracle, opening up a path to the bar as her gaping disciples stepped back to allow her gliding passage through the multitude. It was showbiz in biblical proportions. She was definitely the Queen of the night.

After a few beers for courage, the three absurd amigos left the apartment and stood together on the curb trying to flag a taxi. Each time they saw the orange light of a cab coming out of the distance, George, beneath his huge hat, put out his arm to hail it, only to see the light go off and the accelerating cab zoom past. Four times this happened, as the abuse from the boys grew louder with each rejection. Eventually David told the other two to go and hide somewhere and he took over. Immediately a taxi stopped. He beckoned his gaily dressed friends from out of the shadows and they all piled in.

"Don't tell me. Let me guess. It's either Eden 86 or some fancy-dress party", the cabby said in his cheeky Cockney accent.

"How clever of you", complimented George. "Well, it is indeed a fancy-dress party. Funnily enough though, it just happens to be near Eden 86, so please drop us anywhere nearby. Our girlfriends are meeting us there, you see".

"Don't listen to him. He is just a confused old queen", Chris ridiculed.

"Thank you, Christopher. I didn't need that", said George, sarcastically.

When they drove slowly past the club, they saw the long line of clubbers stretched along the pavement. The driver asked where they would like to be dropped.

"Oh, not here. It's a bit further yet. It isn't actually Eden 86. Just near it. Keep going", said George with a pant, with his two friends glaring at him disapprovingly. "This will do. I think it is in this building", he added, handing over a ten-pound note and rushing out of the vehicle, holding on tightly to his expansive sombrero.

"Brilliant", rebuked David. "Now we have to walk all the way back. Thank you, George. Great plan".

To get to the stage door, they would have had to have walked back past the line of vividly attired clubbers, meaning they had to run the gauntlet of all the boys, and some girls, in the queue. A quick discussion took place on whether they should cross to the other side of the road. They decided, on a split vote (George was against), that they should 'man up', be proud to be what they were and march boldly straight past. As they went by, they held their heads high, ignoring the spatter of ridiculing catcalls and the curious ogling that escorted them.

To their great relief, a nice old security man on the stage door gave them their tickets and let them go straight through, meaning they did not have to go all the way back to the entrance, facing their belittlers once more. Unfortunately, however, they misunderstood the doorman's directions, took the wrong door and suddenly made an unexpected entrance onto the small floodlit stage, right next to the DJ. The lighting guy at the back of the hall spotted the intruders at once and mischievously floodlit the stage. The arrival into the spotlight of a lumberjack and two shiny new romantics caused the throng of stoked-up clubbers to give them a rapturous, taunting welcome. Caught in the headlights, the shamed trio scuttled sheepishly off the stage, down a small set of steps, to immerse themselves in the mocking mass on the floor. Fortunately, it was all very good natured and they were generously applauded as they made their ignominious way towards the bar.

The dance floor was not as big as they had been led to believe. But was already seething with an eclectic mix of the LBGTQIA community at play. And, boy, they knew how to party. It was not yet 10pm and already the techno music was pulsating. Flashing lights swung over the dancing crowd in a choreographed swirl. The frenzied atmosphere was driven by the deafening drum and bass Ibiza sounds that boomed out, so loud that the place positively throbbed. Our courageous three headed stoically towards the bar, cutting through a clamour of affectionate derision and jibes, George's moustache getting special attention. Unlike with Ricky and Kate, who had been welcomed deferentially as celebrities, they had to shuffle unceremoniously through the swarm of numerous bare-chested fellow hombres and scantily clad carousers. All the people they brushed against got an apologetic 'excuse me' from David, as they gawked back in astonishment on seeing the full close-up splendour of these ridiculous clowns that had made such a public entrance. In no time, they had become the centre of attention and a circle of admirers gathered around them.

Ricky and Kate, meanwhile, had headed directly to the front of the line outside, enjoying the attention. As the bouncers saw them coming, the brass hook of the red rope was unhitched, allowing them to shimmy through without breaking their stride. Once inside, Ricky was greeted like a hero and, with the heavenly accoutrement of Kate on his arm, their VIP status was guaranteed all night. It seemed everyone wanted to fete the rock star and his beauteous partner. In no time, not only was a private table found for them but also a bottle of champagne in an ice bucket was placed at its centre. They chatted together spiritedly, before taking to the floor for an exuberant jive that caught the attention of all around them.

Across the hall, the boys had eventually escaped their stalkers and they battled through the crush with their beers to find and spy on Ricky and Kate, who were by now back sitting cosily at their small table. The voyeurs stood and stared, shoulder to shoulder, rather too obviously. The two daters, now with iconic status, were knocking back their expensive champagne, rock style. While David and Chris, gripping their beers, watched on in envy, George felt his world fall around his ankles. Kate had never looked more beautiful. Immediately, his thoughts flashed back to that afternoon in Miami when, for a mad couple of hours, he had cavorted with Kama Sutra Kate in her hotel room. A crushing sense of failure and regret came over him. His light-heartedness suddenly evaporated and a sense of sadness engulfed him. Here he was, dressed like a buffoon, looking on while his gorgeous ex-wife quaffed Bollinger with a rock star. David could read the expression on his friend's face and rushed to support him.

"Come on old chap. Let's leave them to it. What's done is done. Remember, the best is yet to come."

"George looks like he's seen a ghost. Is he feeling OK or just a little queer", Chris asked David, who failed to find the predictable jibe even remotely amusing.

They returned to the bar, David with his arm around George, nothing unusual in Eden 86. George removed the consoling arm, took off his hat and left it on the bar. In no time, a group of genial young men had clustered around the compadres. From the moment they had stepped onto that stage, they were an instant hit with the boys, who loved their outfits. A fellow lumberjack, in an identical black and red check shirt, was monopolising George, who naïvely failed to recognise his twittering as a chat up and just thought he was being jolly friendly. Both shared a laugh at their similar outfits and swilled their beers together like a couple of old tree-felling chums. Chris and David meanwhile were encircled by a gang of jovial lads who were firing all manner of questions at them. In no time, all their intuitions got lost in the music and they were dancing on the spot with their new best friends.

Thursday nights was known as 'Dance Night' for good reason. The loud music forced you on to the floor. The main feature was one full hour of the greatest anthems, shown on a large video screen with a deafening sound system, belting out every classic from "I Will Survive" to "YMCA". It started off with a quick dance contest, where three couples were picked out of the crowd to perform to a hit of their choice. The MC was a lissom young boychick called Pretty Boy Garrett. He was squeezed into the tightest shorts known to man, naked from the waist up and invariably took to the stage to a raucous welcome. Behind him, at the back of the stage was the giant screen.

"Gentlemen, ladies, laddies, girls", proclaimed the host to a roar. "This is the Power Hour. Sixty minutes of what made this country great. The best music, the best dancing, the best-looking presenter in London". The cheers turned to sarcastic jeers. "But first, the world-famous Eden 86 Dance Off. The prize for the plucky winner tonight? – an Eden 86 'I Can't Even Think Straight' coffee mug, an undersized, fully developed framed photo of Boy George and £100 in cash. Remember, it is you out there who decides who wins. The loudest shout picks the winner. So, make some noise, guys".

It had become a tradition at the club that, at this point, Garrett took on the old London music hall trait of using the longest, most obscure adjectives he could think of to introduce the rival dancers. It was also customary that the audience cheered or jeered at every elephantine word he used.

"Let's the dance-off begin. Please welcome our first contestants, the splendiferous (cheers), thaumaturgic (jeers) – it means magical, love - the sagacious (cheers) Julian and Todd from Brixton". Two pliable black men, their muscular bodies glistening with oil under the spotlights, skipped on, while behind them the video of the Pet Shop Boys performing 'Go West' filled the screen. Their bodies twisted and turned around one another. It went well until Todd attempted to lift the slippery Julian but failed miserably as a lubricious Julian slid right through Todd's strong hands like a wet bar of soap. Nonetheless, they finished to a worthily loud ovation. The MC stepped forward again.

"Next up is a Sapphic showstopper, two pulchritudinous (cheers), perspicacious (jeers), pullulating (cheers), pusillanimous princesses (jeers). They won't want the Eden 86 mug. They prefer to drink from the furry cup. Let's give them a massive, throbbing welcome, all the way from Wimbledon, new balls please, the tribadic, the eupeptic Kelly and Dani". Two girls ran on to the strains of 'Believe' by Cher, who loomed large on the big screen. The girl with long blonde hair looked snazzy in her tight top and miniskirt, while her friend, who sported a mannish mousey crop and wore raffish baggy trousers, took the terrifying lead. They swayed, twirled and twisted uncontrollably and inelegantly. This time the audience's appreciation seemed less enthusiastic, although it was still boisterous and supportive.

"Now we come to our final pair. Can there ever be too much excitement at Eden 86?", announced Garrett. "We welcome onto the stage one of our heroes. The deific (cheers), terpsichorean (cheers) - it means dancing, dears – the Promethean (jeers), our very own, the one and only, Ricky Wilde of Street Fire, and his ambrosian (cheers), paradisiacal (jeers), drop dead gorgeous partner, Kate, from somewhere just round the corner".

George, David and Chris were so busy having a good time that they nearly missed what was going on. Luckily, they all caught Ricky's name and immediately joined the thunderous clamour for their friend and George's glamorous ex-wife. The already frenzied crowd went completely berserk when the two new darlings of Eden 86, both with identical lustrous locks, strolled on demurely, hand in hand, as if about to embark on a Viennese waltz. After settling into their pose, they exploded into Ricky Martin's 'Livin' La Vida Loca'. The hall was thrown into a dancing delirium. Kate was a sensation as she swirled, whirled and jived, throwing in an occasional flick of her heel, Argentine Tango-style. How Ricky kept up with the Hispanic showgirl was a mystery, but somehow, he managed to match her masterfully, step for step.

The uproar at the end nearly took the roof off. Pretty Boy Garrett rushed back on stage while they were still taking their bows for the inexhaustible applause.

"The results are in. It is that quick. The hi-tech, state-of-the-art clapometer (my ears) declares that, in third place, it's Kelly and Dani. In second place, it's Julian and Todd. That means one thing. Tonight's winners: let's hear a cornucopian Eden 86 cheer for Ricky and Kate. Now, on with the Power Hour". 'YMCA' blasted out of the speakers.

Deep within the capacity crowd, David and Chris howled with delight at their friend's victory. George was pensively quiet. The three were huddled in a cluster, encircled by a curious collection of butch admirers, who pulsated energetically around them, drawn to the novelty of the gaily dressed lumberjack and his motley crew of buddies. The moment the first, predictable song started with 'Young Man...', they all found themselves jumping up and down and shouting out every word of the infectious chorus. Arms flailed and clashed as they tried to spell out Y-M-C-A above their heads. George tried hard, concentration on his face, but got into a hell of a mess with his pathetic attempt at semaphore, his wobbly efforts reading more like F-U-C-U.

When the Village People stopped, the three 'Apartment People' started back to the bar.

"Shall we make this the last one?". David hollered over the shattering music. "Time to leave before George gets pulled by a randy logger".

"He looks a nice enough feller. Get it? Feller?", joked Chris.

As George left in the company of his two friends, he cast his eye back to see Ricky gazing deeply into Kate's absorbing brown eyes. He afforded himself a smile as he put jealousy out of his mind. Ricky, after all, would never fall for a woman. 'Or would he?', he thought, his confidence buckling.

Ricky and Kate had returned to their table to pick up their conversation. He knew that this flourishing friendship would remain at best just that, a friendship. Kate, however, had other ideas. Even if her suitor was not the usual suave, erudite, sartorial Englishman that tickled her fancy, her poorly controlled sensuality found something irresistibly animalistic in this untamed savage. They were drawn even closer together by their epic success on stage and were massaging one another's egos with effusive praise for their amazing performance. Somehow, though, he managed to resist any temptation to tell her of his sexual proclivity. It was, he thought, their first and only date so there was no need to complicate it. As they stared into one another's eyes, stories of their colourful lives were exchanged, without a single mention of George or Alex. It was Kate who suggested that they leave. She had had all the dancing she wanted, her evening with her lucky-dip partner had fulfilled her every desire to revisit the disco scene of her youth and the pangs of hunger were becoming more compelling to her.

"Ricky darling, let us go to grab something to eat. We have just won a £100. That's a lot of sushi. It is too noisy here and I noticed there's a great Japanese restaurant around the corner".

Unlike their entrance, no-one noticed their low-key exit. They snuck out inconspicuously into the chilly London air. She grabbed his arm and snuggled her head into his shoulder as they left the pandemonium and headed for the calm revolutions of the sushi-go-round. They disappeared into the anonymity London night, huddled together in close harmony, looking like a pair of young lovers.

SATURDAY, SEPTEMBER 28

By two o'clock in the afternoon, David had returned to the apartment with Jess and Robbie. On the drive back from Kent, the only conversation was about their half-term trip to Disneyland. It was just two weeks away. Robbie had already been to the Park and was desperate to describe every ride to his sister, especially Big Thunder Mountain and 'Indiana Jones et le Temple du Péril', which Robbie pronounced perfectly in his best schoolboy French. David felt some justification for paying years of expensive school fees on hearing his son's word-perfect gallic accent. The children were squealing with excitement about the upcoming trip and, unusually, were not calling for the radio to be turned up. Moira had, for once, been almost normal for the handover, amenable even, and he felt a momentary pang of guilt about the trick that was being played on her by 'Brian'. But then, he reconciled, she had treated him so badly throughout the divorce that this was his only way to make it happen. Seeing the children in such a buoyant, carefree mood fully vindicated his deception. Thanks to Chris' artful dodging, they could all thoroughly look forward to the moment when they could get on the train through the Channel Tunnel to France. But this weekend there was still a lot in store, more than the children realised.

"Is Ricky at the flat?", Jess enquired. David told them that he was, although he would be out that night as he had a date. What he failed to explain, understandably, was that Ricky was going on a date with someone called Alex, who was his former spouse and who their Dad had once dated, but who was actually a man. He wisely thought that there was just too much detail to get into and chose instead to talk about Disney hotels and the Eurostar train.

To the children's delight, Ricky was strumming his guitar as they entered the apartment. They dropped their rucksacks as they crossed the threshold and ran over to him, hurling their arms around his neck. He was in the best mood, putting down his guitar to give them both a huge, favourite uncle kind of hug.

"How is the music going, Ricky? Have you played any good gigs?", asked Robbie. David smiled when he heard his young son using such groovy vernacular.

"We did a great show at Brighton last weekend. Your Dad came. And Chris did too, and so did George. It was a blast."

"Daddy told us. He said you were great. Did you play 'Lying In Love'?", pressed Jess. They had adopted that song as their own.

"Yeah, it went down a storm. All down to you guys helping me write it. I recorded it with Street Fire last week. I'll get you a copy when its ready". The two youngsters chortled with pride. "Well, what are you doing with Daddy this weekend? Anything nice?", queried Ricky.

"Daddy said we are going to the OXO Tower for dinner tonight, so we are getting all dressed up. What are you up to?", Jess asked.

"Well, it's a bit complicated really". Ricky stalled, stuck in the same quandary that David had found himself in when trying to explain his date. He thought it best to simplify his answer. "Just going to dinner with an old friend", he replied, skirting a more accurate explanation. But he did add, "Looks like we are all going out to dinner with people we love".

"Can we all go together then?", enquired Robbie in his innocence.

Ricky dwelt on his answer before saying that perhaps next time would be better. Unknown to him, there was something prescient in those words. He then took up his guitar once more and a sing-along started.

Across town in Kensington, Chris had woken up late in Bonnie's bed, having met up with her after work the night before. She had only a few more weeks before rehearsals began and was getting both nervous and excited about her hitting the big stage in her first major West End show. The music from West Side Story still filled her flat at every opportunity and, as they rose from their slumbers, she put it on quietly yet again. Their weekend in Brighton had been an unqualified success and it had somehow moved their relationship onto a new plane. It seemed that suddenly everything was more peaceful, more idyllic. That initial flush of energetic love had mellowed into a calm, close and seamless union. No longer did they feel the need to party every time they got together, preferring now to snuggle down on the settee in front of a good film or just share a home-cooked dinner for two. It was as if they were nesting. The exhilaration of getting to know one another had ripened and matured into a merging of spirits, while that unbridled passion of first attraction had evolved into a more clement fusion of love.

Back at Thames Tower, George was in his room. He had spent all the previous day not only recovering from that Thursday crazy night but also suppressing his anxieties of what might have happened after he had left the club. Interestingly, he had not asked Ricky a single question about his date with Kate, about what she had said of him and, especially, how it had all ended up. He had decided he had to look forward. After all, as someone used to say, 'the best is yet to come'.

He had by now brushed that evening aside, not wanting to look like some jealous ex-husband pining over a lost love. Rather than dwelling on the past in his failed marriage, he was by now in a state of eager anticipation. Unlike his former dispassionate self, he was all 'atingle' about the night that lay ahead. He had managed, at a cost, to get good seats in the Albert Hall, row 7, centre aisle, and the thought of watching one of his favourite operas in the company of the delectable Angela filled him with an adolescent excitement. Furthermore, the intense prospect of a blossoming romance was heightened still further by the clandestine nature of the affair. George had agreed with his new squeeze that Chris, her former husband and, ironically, with whom he lived, should not be made aware of this burgeoning 'courtship'. As George came out of his room, Ricky acknowledged him, looking up from his guitar, with his superfans on either side.

"You look chuffed with yourself today, Georgie Boy", he commented.

"Do I, Richard? Do I, indeed", George replied, trying to not make it look too obvious. "Just happy to be alive, old boy. Hi, children. Lovely to see you. What are you up to today?".

"Daddy is taking us to the OXO Tower and Ricky is seeing someone special, but he won't tell us who", Jess said.

"I am seeing someone special too, actually. And we are going to see Madam Butterfly. It's an opera by Puccini and has some terrific tunes in it".

Jess came back snippily. "I know what Madam Butterfly is. We watched a bit of it in music lessons at school". George, in spite of the curt reply, was impressed and reassured that the old qualities of a decent private education still lived on in some finer British schools.

David, having taken the children's bags to their room, came out and headed for the kitchen.

"Anyone fancy a late lunchtime snack? I have hot dogs from the deli and some oven chips, if anyone's interested. We've got a big dinner tonight, so I didn't get much".

"Yes, please", shouted the gleeful Jess and Robbie.

"If you force me", said Ricky, who immediately hit his guitar strings and broke into Elvis' classic. "You ain't nothing but a hot dog, fryin' all the time," much to the amusement of the children.

By six o'clock, there had been flurry of bathing, dressing and grooming in the household. Jess in particular had been energetically making herself look elegant for her dinner with her Daddy at a very posh restaurant. Robbie, being a male of the species, required far less time in the bathroom than his sister, just enough for a fleeting splash of water over his face, the flash of a comb through his hair and a quick change of clothes. In all of ten minutes, he was dressed, ready and lying on his bed watching cartoons. Jess, by contrast, took her time, attentive to every small detail. The only thing that had worried her was that her mother had picked out her clothes and she opened her bag uneasily. However, for once, Jess did not totally disagree with the choice. Usually, she hated the frumpy, 'uncool' outfits she was made to wear, but tonight she felt like a million-dollar girl about to join London's jet set in her miniskirt and tights. Her shiny patent shoes even had slight heels that made her feel so much more grown up. That moment that she looked at herself in the mirror, makeover completed, was perhaps her first 'selfie' experience, a preoccupation with vanity that would become an obsession with her for the next ten or more years of her young life, as it does with every teenager. She stood tall and proud as she left her room to join her father as he watched the news in the lounge. He felt a wash of pride as he saw her, realising that his little girl was rapidly growing into a very beautiful young woman. Nevertheless, when she sat demurely next to him, she was his child again and he gave her that close cuddle they had always enjoyed, although he could not help thinking that there may not be many more moments like this to come as she grew into her future.

When it comes to self-preening, however, no-one could out-compete Ricky. He too was prone to stare at the mirror in self-admiration. However, at one point, he broke off from his preparations to sit on the bed for a minute for some deep reflection, something that was not customary in the musician's carefree life. He realised that, just occasionally, some things matter. He was over the moon that his relationship with Alex was hopefully about to be restored, while he was still anxious that it was something over which he had no control. He considered his stupidity that had caused the failure of what he took for granted as a lifelong partnership, a union that he thought could never be broken. He had thought that their marriage was rock-solid. How wrong he had been. After David's report of their date, Ricky had seen that perhaps he could have a second chance and he had sent Alex a bouquet of birds of paradise, his favourite flowers, with a card that read simply, 'Alex. I am sorry. I have been an idiot. But I shall always be your idiot. Forgive me. Love you, R'. It had therefore been no surprise that he had been a bag of nerves when Alex had rung.

Ricky had been terrified of what Alex might say. In the event, he seemed very receptive to meeting, albeit talking in a dispassionate, courteous and passive manner. Dinner was agreed. Ricky recognised that there was still much mending to be done and that he would have to tread carefully. He put on his suede jacket and left the apartment in thoughtful silence, nervous about how the night would go.

They had agreed to meet at 7.30pm at Babylon, also known as the Kensington Roof Gardens Restaurant. This exceptional eatery sits on the summit of a seven-storey building that had formerly been a well-known department store, Derry & Toms, but which had subsequently been converted into an office block. That is all apart from the roof, which had been retained as an extraordinarily magical and unique venue, 100ft above Derry Street, a secret garden. It had recently been restored to its former glory by its creative owner Sir Richard Branson and it also just happened to be Alex's special place. He loved to enjoy the uninterrupted views over the city while wandering through the exotic rooftop oasis in central London. The restaurant sat in the middle of this aerial park, surrounded by three spectacular gardens. One had a Moorish-Spanish theme, with walkways, fountains, palms and vines, another was Tudor in style, with archetypal English plants such as roses, lilies and wisteria, and then there was the water garden with over 30 species of trees and a stream running through it into a pond, where once four famous flamingos, Bill, Ben, Splosh and Pecks, had stood, usually on one leg. This botanical wonderland was often the scene of colourful showbiz bashes, society parties and countless weddings, but tonight it was the perfect place for a quiet reunion.

As he travelled across town in his cab, Ricky had started to think about how he should handle the conversation, especially about his regretted infidelity. Alex was hardly the most forgiving man in the world, as he had shown. Ricky knew that he had to take the utmost care with every word. The best tactic, he thought, was not to rush in and pour out apology after apology. He had tried that before and it got him nowhere. That approach would also mean that the whole evening would start negatively with a regurgitation of the break-up. No, he decided to be positive, to look to the future, to be honest about his commitment to change. Suddenly, that word 'honest' resounded in his head. How could he be honest, he thought, when he has just duped him into a date with his flatmate? If Alex found that out, he would probably lose all trust in him again and he would then lose forever the one person he loved. He needed a plan. As he thought it through, the complexity became greater. If Alex and he did get back together again, he was bound to meet David at some point. How could he possibly lead a normal life without Alex coming to the apartment and bumping into his former date? He was in a cold sweat as he weighed up options, aware that one wrong word could ruin everything. The more he thought it over, the more he woke up to the fact that there was, in fact, no choice. The truth must out.

He was shaking with trepidation as he stepped out of his taxi and into the unassuming foyer of the building. The small lift was in no hurry to get him to the top floor and moved far more slowly than his own mind that was rushing with feverish anxiety. As ever, the greeting by the manager was warm and friendly. He had been here many times before and loved the staff, a happy crew who managed to create a wonderfully friendly and relaxed environment. The front tables were laid out against the plate glass window, which stretched from one end to the other, overlooking the city skyline. The one that he had asked for was right at the far end, on the front row, and, as ever, his request was dealt with as a command. He sat with his back to the wall, facing out towards the entrance. If it had been summer, he would have chosen to sit on the terrace outside, a place that Alex once called 'his London heaven'. When the waiter came over to ask what he was drinking, he could only mumble that he was waiting for his guest and would like just a glass of water, which his quivering hands could hardly steer to his dry mouth.

Then he saw Alex. He looked more handsome than ever, tall, vigorous and ebony beautiful. As he advanced, Ricky felt the same pangs that he had felt when they had first met all those years ago on the cruise ship. He stood up on his uncertain legs to greet his guest.

"Alex. It is so good to see you. Thanks for coming tonight. I hope this is OK, choosing Babylon. I know you love it here".

As always in these situations, Ricky could hear himself speak and he knew that what had come out was diffident, bland and thoroughly inadequate. His whole demeanour was stiff and totally unrelaxed, whereas the collected and lissom Alex was as cool as a cucumber.

"Good to see you too, Ricky. How have you been?".

"Not bad. Still playing some good gigs, and still playing some not so good ones. But the band are getting better. In fact, I think we have the best thing going that we have ever had".

"Well, coming from you, that really is a compliment, Ricky. You never had anything good to say about them before. Where are you living now?".

"I am sharing a lovely apartment with three other guys, all straight mind you, on the South Bank, not far from Blackfriars Bridge". Ricky immediately thought of David and felt a shiver of apprehension. He kept going. "How is the flat, Alex? Still got the noisy toilet and even noisier neighbours?".

"That hasn't changed but I have decorated the bedroom. It is really splendid now".

Ricky felt a sort of left-out jealousy. He was about to say that he would love to see it but thought better of it. Too soon, he thought, stay calm.

"That's great. Is Jeff upstairs still bashing out Led Zep every night?".

"No, his tastes seem to have changed. He seems to be getting into the Eagles and Foreigner, which is much more acceptable. We all mellow as we get older, I guess. Shall we have a drink?", said Alex, taking the lead.

"Oh yes, of course, sorry", Ricky replied meekly as he beckoned the waiter over. "What will you have? A dark 'n' stormy? Or champagne for a change". Ricky knew most things that Alex liked.

"What do you think?".

Ricky turned to the waiter. "Two dark 'n' stormies please. Goslings if you have it".

They spoke correctly to one another, talking about their individual lives since the split, not yet touching on their previous time together or on the break-up. As they drank their rum and ginger beers, the mood softened and they started to act not as if they were carrying a bagful of bitterness but as two people who had a closer, deeper connection, a harmony, a true affinity. Ricky began to unwind, leaning forward towards Alex as the tension drained from his body. He had come into the meeting with this feeling of being completely on the back foot and Alex's serenity had put him at ease. Ricky now felt his equal once again and the conversation started to flow naturally as it gradually ventured back to their time together.

By the time they were enjoying their food, with the added delight of a bottle of Viognier, there was a congeniality between them that only comes out of genuine affection. They began to reminisce on happier times, exchanging their favourite memories. Nostalgia started to create the foundation for a rekindling of the flame that had been smothered by events, but never extinguished. That flame grew brighter and hotter by the minute. In no time, it was hot enough to melt their Eton Mess, Ricky's favourite, which they shared as they laughed together, just like in the old days. Their heads drew closer across the table. It was then that Ricky felt it was the right time to present his badly overprepared speech.

"Alex. I want to get something off my chest. I have been waiting for the chance to say this for too long. Alex, right from the beginning, you were, and still, are the one, the only one. You are, and always will be, the most amazing, the most special person I have ever met. Being with you has brought so much light and so much love into my life. Without you, I am not whole, life is meaningless. I know that now. It was my stupidity that made me realise this and I paid a high price. I have changed, Alex. Genuinely changed. I look back at my tantrums and all that and see someone different. As you said, I even get on with the boys in the band now. In fact, now I can see that they are actually quite good. You were angry with me for all the right reasons and I am so, so sorry. I am not that angry young man anymore. I must be getting older, I guess. I want you to try and find it in you to move on, to park history, to be assured that I shall never, ever, be anything but yours. For my part, I just want you back, I want us to be together, I want our lives together. Without that, it all means nothing. I want to say this. I will never stop loving you. You are my happy-ever-after". He paused, sighed a sigh of relief, took a gulp of his wine and then added, "There, I've said it".

There was silence. Alex's expression did not change. Ricky tried to find some hope in the softening of an eye or an encouraging turn of the mouth. He found none and, as he stared back at the love of his life, he felt his dreams slipping away. Eventually, Alex's face relaxed and the hint of a smile broke out.

"Ricky. You know my story. You know the hurt I have been through. How my family, my own parents for Christ's sake, the people I trusted and relied on, rejected me after eighteen years because of what I am, something I couldn't help. Only my sister, Tianna, had any understanding words for me. She was the only one to shed a tear when I left Antigua. Well, my mother perhaps, but I never saw it. When I joined the cruise ship, I had to fight to find a life there. I was too young to be alone, dragging behind me my anger, resentment and confusion. It was you, Ricky, who rescued me. You gave me the support I needed. It was you who revived my life. All because I knew you loved me. In no time, I gave you the trust in people that I had lost, or that had been snatched from me more like. I shall never forget that. We had something special. When I left home, I felt I could never trust anyone again. The greatest gift I gave you was my trust. I gave you the ability to hurt me. It was my gift to you. I had nothing else to give. And then you hurt me. You betrayed that trust, Ricky. You took that gift and tore it up. How could you have done that? I never ever want that to happen again".

Ricky could feel it all slipping away. His heart was pounding. Alex went on.

"Let me tell you something. I have had just one date since we broke up, well, it wasn't what you'd call a date really. I met this guy, a nice man, called David and we just went for a walk in the park and chatted. He is the one that got me thinking about it all and about trying to start again. He was incredibly astute. He was actually quite attractive, I admit, but I could never think of being with anyone other than you. You are the only man I have ever loved, the only man I will ever love but the sad thing is that I don't know if I can trust you".

Ricky was downhearted at how this was all going. He realised trust was the issue and that you cannot have trust without honesty. He knew he had no choice. He had to put his cards on the table. Fearfully, he played his hand.

"Alex. I want this more than anything. I want to regain your trust. I will do anything to achieve that. But I do have to tell you something". Alex sat back. Ricky continued. "Please, I have something I have to own up to. Hear me out." He took a deep breath. "I do actually know David, your date. It was me who wanted David to meet you. When you refused to talk to me, I was at my wit's end. I missed you so much that I would have done anything. David is my flatmate". Alex's eyes widened. Ricky continued. "You're right, he is a really nice guy. I asked him to meet you, under the guise of this website shit, so that he could find out how you felt about me. It was David that got us together. I had already decided that, if you had lost all feelings for me, I would have to move on with my life. Mind you, I'm not sure I meant it. But I needed to know. David liked you too by the way, but he is as straight as they come. He came back convinced that there were still feelings there. I have been a bloody fool. I am only too aware that it was my damn stupidity that broke us up. I won't lie to you, Alex. I am now fighting for you in every way I know and David meeting up with you was the only way I could see to beat this communications breakdown. Now you know. If you are upset, I am sorry. If you are not, please smile and tell me you forgive me. I was thinking when I came out tonight that I would say that, after tonight, we shall either walk out of here back together or go our separate ways. But I can't say that, because I don't think I will ever stop fighting for you, whatever it takes".

Alex dwelt on Ricky's words, before his whole face broke into the kindliest of smiles. Both men reached out a hand and briefly clinched the other's. They sat focussing on one another in silence, as their happy and relieved expressions spoke more than words could ever express.

Little did they to know that, just a few hundred yards away, another unpredicted love story was being played out.

For, at the same time as Ricky and Alex were reuniting, by pure coincidence, George and Angela were huddled together in their own discreet corner in the top floor bar of the Royal Garden Hotel. Here, they were locked into each other's company, sipping slowly on their champagne, still glowing from the sheer exhilaration of Puccini's heart-rendering Madam Butterfly. Even though they had been seated in the very heart of the packed stalls of the glorious Royal Albert Hall, encircled by elegant boxes which encased the hierarchy of bejewelled opera lovers, the two had remained oblivious to everything and everyone around them throughout the evening, apart from the powerful allegorical story being performed so beautifully on the vast stage and, of course, one another. The comfort they felt together was exclusive and to share such an evening felt miraculously natural to them both. After the deafening applause had eventually died down, they had left the auditorium hand in hand and had walked slowly through the chilly, clear night along a busy Knightsbridge towards High Street Kensington. As they passed the shimmering gilded statue of Queen Victoria's adored consort, Prince Albert, standing proudly opposite his classic colosseum, observing his masterpiece, they paused and threw him a respectful glance and playfully thanked him for creating his own, very English Taj Mahal, a hallowed place that had become the spiritual home to the finest music for generations.

The conversation flowed freely between the two like-minded spirits as they discussed in earnest not just the production but also how times had changed, how honour and duty had become things of the past. This was a subject that defined the old-fashioned George to a tee. The sheer beauty and drama of the tragic tale of teenage self-sacrifice, staged in such a magnificent setting, had not been lost on either of them and they exchanged views on this abiding tale of love, misunderstanding and, ultimately, tragic suicide. The two theatre and opera devotees hardly drew breath as they talked constantly. As they conversed, looking out over Kensington Palace, George took her hands in his and kissed them delicately. What they did not talk about, but what they both knew in their hearts, was that tonight was not just a date, but a special evening, a connection of souls, that was about to reshape their lives.

Across town, Chris and Bonnie had also locked out the world. In Bonnie's little flat, they had nested themselves away, wallowing in doing absolutely nothing. They had been set for an all-night slouch in front of the TV. However, this was not to be. Bonnie suddenly, unexpectedly, leaped up off the settee, turned to Chris and made a forceful announcement.

"I have made an executive decision. Get dressed. It's Saturday and we are not yet ready for a night in on a Saturday. We are going out. Come on. There's somewhere I want to take you. My treat. Let's go, big boy. I'm taking you out".

"Where the hell did that come from? Hang on. Did you say 'my treat'?" said Chris. That was all he needed to hear to get into gear. "I like the sound of that. Well, now that's an offer I can't refuse. Can I choose where we go?".

"No. Absolutely not. I have decided and it's a surprise. This is something I need to do. Now go and get ready", Bonnie commanded.

Half an hour later they were back in Covent Garden and she guided him straight to the restaurant they had gone to on their first special date. They hovered outside for a second.

"I needed to purge any ghosts and bring you here." Bonnie said as she squeezed his arm possessively. "It scares me how near I came to finishing with you. I have always hated jealousy and, in spite of what I said, I fell for it. I was so bloody daft. I want to say sorry and make it up to you. Would you care to have dinner with me, Mr Adams?".

"My honour, Miss Carter. But if the former Mrs Adams is in there, it ain't nothing' to do with me". She smiled at him and they walked in, arm in arm.

By 10 o'clock, David and the children were back at home. He had put them straight to bed and was reading a good night story, perched at Robbie's feet. He had chosen Peter Pan deliberately. "I think we should all go on Peter Pan's Flight when we get to Disneyland".

On the word 'Disneyland', the children, who he had just settled down quietly, jumped up from beneath the sheets and bounced up and down hysterically, chanting "We're going to Disney! We're going to Disney!".

"That's brilliant", proclaimed their father sarcastically. "I just get you quietened down and now I've got to do it all again. Now back into bed". They laughed, obeyed the instruction and he tucked them in once again. "Now no more mention of Disney", he repeated. At that, up they jumped again, crying out their 'We're going to Disney!' mantra.

"You mentioned it, Daddy", Robbie laughed.

They settled down yet again and David said "Robbie, do you want to tell Jess about the Peter Pan ride at 'you know where' or shall I?".

"You do it, Daddy. You remember things better than me".

"I am not sure of that but here goes". He kissed them both on their foreheads, turned down the light still further and sat down on the end of Robbie's bed, talking very slowly and softly. "When you go in, it's all dark and you get into a little ship with a mast and it starts off by going through the bedroom of an old Victorian house with children and a dog, then you fly right over London, over Big Ben and the River Thames, all lit up in the dark, and then over a magical island with buccaneer ships where there are pirates fighting with swords and Captain Hook holding the alligator's mouth open with his feet and...". He tailed off slowly and saw that the children had already fallen fast asleep. He kissed them gently on their foreheads. Creeping out, he glowed with happiness, although he questioned whether their dropping off so quickly meant that he was a very good children's storyteller or a very bad one. He then took himself off to his bed, lay there for a minute thinking about his plans for the next day and then, like his children, fell smoothly into a deep slumber.

SUNDAY, SEPTEMBER 29

As usual, the children were early to rise. It was the sound of their TV that woke David up. He sprung out of bed, excited about the prospect of the day, and went into their room. They were both lying on their beds.

"Morning you two. Sleep well? I've been thinking. Why don't we get up, have breakfast and go the zoo?". Immediately, the children shot up and bounced on their beds again, shouting out "The Zoo! The Zoo!".

David shushed them and said, "Great. You get yourselves ready and I'll get breakfast. Is that OK? If we go early, we can have a good three hours there before I drive you back to Mummy's". They loved Daddy's cooked breakfast almost as much as the idea of the zoo and let out a loud cheer. David admonished them gently. "Hey, calm down, you two. Don't wake the others. They'll still be asleep".

Closing their door quietly behind him, he went to put on the kettle. The last time the children were there, he cooked their special Sunday breakfast in an overcrowded kitchen as Chris, George and Ricky came in and out, one after the other, grabbing cups of coffee and popping slices of bread into the toaster. This weekend, he had decided to do all the cooking himself, buying enough for a big breakfast for everyone. Bacon and sausages galore started to sizzle in one large pan, baked beans bubbled in another, while ten eggs, vigorously beaten, sat in a bowl ready for scrambling.

It was almost 9.00am and he thought it was time to alert his flatmates that breakfast was ready. First, he knocked on Chris' door. There was no answer, so he knocked again and opened it noiselessly, whispering "Chris?". There was zero sign of life. He assumed he must be having another night at Bonnie's.

Quietly, he moved to Ricky's door. He tapped gently and whispered his name. No response came back. He tried again. Nothing. Turning the knob silently, he eased open the door and peered in. The bed had not been slept in.

"Bloody hell", David mumbled to himself. "The plan worked. He must've got back with Alex. Brilliant. Well done, David", he muttered in praise of himself.

Finally, he knocked on dependable George's door. He knew he would be awake by now. He rapped loudly. "Wake up, George, breakfast". He burst in without ceremony and, to his complete surprise, his bed had not been slept in either. "Bloody hell", he said to himself, "now the world has gone mad. Even George is at it, the dirty old devil. What is the world coming to? I wonder where the hell he is?".

On returning to the kitchen, poor David now faced enough food for a small army. While Jess and Robbie loved their Daddy's full English breakfast as it was something they never got at home, this was just too much. Although they certainly did considerable damage to the huge plate of bacon, leaving only five rashers, the sausages were too great a challenge with only four of them taken.

"You've cooked rather a lot, Daddy", commented Jess looking at a vat of scrambled eggs.

"Yes, you see, er, I thought you might be hungry".

"What, after that huge dinner last night? Anyway, the others can have some when they get up, can't they", she deduced.

"Yes. That's a good thought. But I think Chris and Ricky might have already driven off to see a friend in Birmingham", David invented quickly.

"Funny. Ricky never mentioned that. And George?", said an intrigued Jess.

"George, yes George. He may have got up to play golf or tennis or something. Not really sure. More orange juice?".

"But it is hardly light, Daddy. So why did you cook all this food if you thought they might not be here?", the ever-questioning Jess logically pointed out. David evaded answering.

"Come on. You guys get ready while I clear up".

An hour later, they were in a taxi, on their way to London Zoo, chatting all the way there about the animals that they would like to see. As they approached Regent's Park, David matter-of-factly dropped something into the conversation.

"Oh, children, I meant to tell you, we are meeting up with a friend. She rang me yesterday and I happened to mention that we were going to the zoo and she asked nicely if she could come. I said of course she could. The more the merrier I say."

Both children gave him a dubious look and went quiet before the astute Jess enquired. "She, Daddy. Is she a new girlfriend?". Although he had prepared himself for this inquisition, he stumbled on his words.

"Er. No. Just a good friend. She is very nice though. I think you'll like her".

"So, would you like her to be your girlfriend?", Robbie probed innocently.

"Robbie, Jess, please", pleaded David, buckling under the relentless probing. "Let's just enjoy the day. She is a good friend. That's all".

The two children looked at one another with suspicion in their eyes and fell silent.

London Zoo is a spectacular place to take the family. It is the oldest scientific zoo in the world and has city folk flocking there in their droves throughout the year to peer at the myriad of weird and wonderful wildlife from around the globe. With almost 20,000 animals, there was going to be plenty for them to see in their limited time and they started talking about what they should seek out first. As the taxi pulled up at the entrance, a stylish figure dressed in a loose-fitting camel-hair coat stood by the rank. She waved demurely at the approaching cab. The children did not return the wave, although they did manage a polite and hesitant smile back.

"Is that her, Daddy? She is very pretty". Jess observed.

"Is she?" replied Daddy, as if he had not noticed. "Yes, that's Sophie. Now be nice to her, won't you".

They climbed out of the vehicle and Sophie came to greet them, first shaking David's hand in a cordial manner before crouching down and shaking the little hands of the children.

"Hello. I am Sophie. It is so lovely to meet you both. It's Jess, isn't it? And you must be Robbie? Thank you for letting me join you with Daddy today. I have never been to the zoo. I am so excited. Now what is it that you want to see most, the lions, the tigers, the elephants or what about the rhinoceroses? Where shall we go first?"

The children competed be the quickest to shout out their favourite. "The gorillas", yelled Jess. "The snakes", barked Robbie.

"Oh no. Not snakes. I hate snakes", Sophie feigned fear. "Will you look after me? They frighten me". In a typical boyish way, Robbie seized his chance to terrify the timid Sophie.

"Hissssss!", he taunted, right up to her face, before they all broke into giggles.

"I'm with Jess. I think I'd rather see the gorillas", Sophie said. That brought a huge smile of satisfaction from the young girl.

David could not have been more pleased. This whole scenario had, of course, been set up in advance. Over their most recent dinner together, he had told Sophie that it was time, that they had played this game long enough. She had reassured him that, if necessary, she would wait for as long as it took for him to be absolutely comfortable about the children meeting her, also adding the advice that, in her professional experience as a family lawyer, the first meeting should be conducted in a gentle, welcoming way in an outdoor environment that they enjoyed. That way, she had said, it would be less intense for them.

"I've given it a great deal of thought, Sophie", David had said, "and if you were 'only a girlfriend' I don't think I would do it, but you have become so much more, someone very special in my life, so I really do think that this is the right time".

She had returned his words of commitment and affection and together they had hatched this 'Sunday at the Zoo" ploy as the perfect way to introduce her to the children. It had been her idea, explaining it by saying it would be a much better way to break the ice than just sitting having lunch, which, she said, would 'make them feel forced'. As ever, she was right. They could now all share the distraction of the animals while getting to know one another.

It started off with the four of them walking rather formally side-by-side. Soon, though, after lots of laughs with Sophie about what monkeys eat and where hippos live, the little hands of Jess, to her left, and Robbie, to her right, crept into hers and they all skipped along joyfully to the next enclosure, a very happy David in close attendance. They went to the gorillas first. There were four of them, two adults and two young ones, living on an island. Jess was fascinated and Sophie promised they could watch a documentary about gorilla families in Africa when they next got together. David and Sophie, guessing that Robbie would choose snakes or spiders or something scary, had already decided that they should do that last to keep him in anticipation. If they pretended to be frightened, she suggested, it would give him a chance to be in charge for a few minutes.

They must have spent almost three hours touring around, visiting as many animals as they could. Having seen every kind of creature, from aardvarks to zebras, and finally the snakes, they wandered back to the taxi rank, Jess holding Sophie's hand and Robbie his father's. David could not be more delighted. Although it pained him to have to contain any emotion towards Sophie, he could not feel more pleased that the day had gone so well nor prouder of her as the children fell for her charms. Even the perceptive Jess had not noticed any of the discreet loving glances that their Dad and Sophie had surreptitiously exchanged. It was what Sophie later described as 'a very tantric day'.

When it came to the time for farewells, the children hugged Sophie in turn, politely saying their goodbyes and thanking her for a lovely day before clambering into a taxi. David gave Sophie a formal hug and whispered in her ear.

"You were brilliant. See you later". He gave her a warm, appreciative smile and climbed into the cab.

"Have a good journey back to Kent", Sophie said through the open window of the vehicle before standing back and waving her goodbyes. The children returned the gesture with exaggerated waves and an enthusiastic farewell shout out of the window.

"Daddy", Jess spoke, as they drove away. "Sophie is lovely. You should go out with her". David grinned. His little daughter really was growing up. He looked back out of the rear window and gave Sophie one last wave. Jess just grinned at her father knowingly.

MONDAY, SEPTEMBER 30

Chris found himself back at Boisdale. That had not been his plan when he had woken up that morning. However, as he had been peacefully sitting at his office desk, minding his own business, his phone had vibrated violently in his pocket. He had put the ringer on silent. He had then dashed to the lifts, rightly guessing it was Moira.

"Hi, Brian. How's things? How was Scotland? How was the football? I see Chelsea won", Moira had asked cheerily.

"Where? Oh Scotland. Oh, yes. It was fine. Listen Moira, I don't want to be rude. I can't really talk because I am just about to go into an important meeting, with the Editor".

"He is quite demanding, isn't he, your Editor. No problem. Are you free tonight?".

Chris hadn't had time to come up with an excuse. "Tonight?".

"Look, I am coming up to London tonight. Can I take you for dinner? I don't mind the same place if it's convenient for you. Is that OK? Yes? Good. I'll see you there at 7".

She had rung off abruptly, leaving Chris stunned into a paralysis of powerlessness. He had nothing arranged for that evening and it now seemed that he had no choice other than to endure another night with Moira. His sense of duty to David and the children was being tested to the limit but had somehow prevailed.

At the station later that evening, Moira strode up to him on the platform, put her arms around him and went to kiss him, in a way that was usually reserved for those old films when the uniformed war hero was welcomed home from the Front by his beloved. His very un-movielike reaction was entirely involuntary as he turned his head to one side to fend off the advance. She looked momentarily offended, although her smile quickly returned as she put her arm through his and dragged him off to the restaurant.

Moira talked incessantly all evening. It was clear that she had moved on to the next stage in her own mind. He hardly got a word in. She seemed to have convinced herself that she was embedded in a full-on, proper relationship. Chris had done his job too well. He still tried to play the interested date, but, somehow, he was becoming less convincing. He found himself back again in his cartoon, this time in the last frame, the one with the man yawning. After the third occasion when pushy Moira had to say, 'are you listening?', she paused and changed her tone.

"Look, Brian. If this isn't working for you, I do understand, you know. I am not stupid. We can just leave it at that and call it a day, if you'd rather. It isn't a big deal for me. I really like you, but it has to be a two-way street. If you don't feel anything for me, that's OK. We can just stay friends and go our own ways".

Chris was about to say 'fine' when he woke up to his predicament. He had to keep this going for a bit longer, long enough to keep her on the hook until at least half-term, so that David could get away with the children.

"No, no. It's not like that at all. What about Venice? Don't you want to come?", he asked.

"Of course I do. But don't worry about it. If you don't want me to come, I will get over it", Moira conceded.

"No. No. No. I do want you to come", Chris insisted, desperate to protect the final, crucial stage of his precious Project EX.

"Well, I have said already that we can go as friends", said Moira, accommodatingly. "We don't have to jump into bed together. We can just enjoy the time as tourists. And you will have a lot of work to do too with your demanding Editor. That is if you still want me to come".

"Yes, yes. That is what I want". He said, possibly too enthusiastically, then realising he had to bring down his mood. He suddenly felt that he could keep up the pretence no longer and continued in a more subdued tone, almost serious by Chris' standards. "No, that's not what I mean. What I mean is... Oh, I don't know. I guess I am not getting all the feelings I should and I don't want to lie to you". He bit his lip and he saw the irony in those last words, coming as they were out of 'Brian's' mouth. "Honestly, Moira, I really like you and you are a great person, but I don't think I'm falling in love with you... yet. It's as simple as that. But, look, I'd still love you to come to Venice. Would that work with you?".

Moira was not unknown to rejection and saw this lack of unbridled enthusiasm as just that. Over the years, she had learned how to handle herself with dignity and coolness in such situations.

"That would be great. I totally understand. Let's have a nice few days in Italy and then, if we never see one another again, so be it. But let's leave as friends".

He felt that a reprieve had been granted. In his mind, he had managed the situation to perfection. All the stress went out of his body. He had got what he wanted. After all, he could and would never betray Bonnie, who he knew was coming to the end of her tether with this charade, and yet he had kept the masterplan in place for David's sake.

"Let's have another drink. I am glad we have got that sorted", he said as he lifted his wine glass to her. "Cheers. To friends".

"To friends. And to Venice. Saluti", returned Moira, albeit with a lightly sarcastic sneer.

SATURDAY, OCTOBER 12

The next two weeks had passed quickly and uneventfully. After the hectic week of dating games, the respite was welcome. Little had been seen of Ricky. He had brought Alex back to the apartment on just two occasions, preferring to settle back into their old home life. David felt particularly pleased with the part he had played when he saw them so happy to be back together again, clearly having buried their past differences. Ricky, according to Alex, was indeed a changed man, putting every pot into its assigned kitchen cupboard and hanging all his clothes the right way round. The meeting between David and Alex was one hurdle that they had all been worried about. In the event, Alex went directly up to him and warmly hugged his one-time date and the two of them let out an affectionate hoot of laughter at the whole situation. Ricky joined in the group hug as they celebrated. Above all else, the fact that Ricky had, through their cynical liaison, recovered his true love and, with it, his mojo made David very proud of the playacting he had put himself through. Each man kept his lips well and truly sealed about the duplicitous Project EX. The underhand four had agreed that the real truth, the whole truth must never out.

David and Sophie had been together more frequently of late. The passion of their relationship had increased over the past few weeks, both in its intensity and the time shared together. However, David had recently revealed the existence of his new love to his flatmates, which came as absolutely no shock to Ricky, who just reacted with a 'Now there's a surprise', followed by some smutty line about lawyer's briefs.

Chris and Bonnie had become inseparable. Since Brighton, their commitment to each other had become set in stone. The more time they spent together, the more they looked like a match made in heaven. They were now spending most of their nights at her flat, where they found a cosier refuge and far greater privacy.

Back at the apartment, there was more often than not, a feeling of vacancy about the place. With Ricky gone and Chris so often absent, it had been left to George and David to keep the place going, even though they too enjoyed their nocturnal absences on a regular basis. However, their time alone had seen their male bonding grow stronger and they had plenty of opportunity to share confidences. They would sit out on the balcony, wrapped up against the chilly weather, with a glass of red wine in hand, presenting to one another reflective confessionals about what life had brought them, their loves and their regrets, the good times and the bad. During their candid heart-to-hearts there had been major divulgences between the two men. George spilled out all his fiery marriage tales, even owning up to his ambivalent emotions towards Karma Sutra Kate since the divorce. He revealed the full, grim story of his ignominious departure from Forsyte Manners, which still riled him, before finding himself comfortable enough to unleash the depth of feeling that he had developed for Angela, something he described with uncustomary candour. David could not hide his surprise about the unlikely romance. He had always believed Angela to be a dowdy frump, having only ever heard Chris' jaundiced account of his former wife. Familiarity must have bred both contempt and myopia, he fathomed. Also, the whole relationship was disturbingly close to home. However, when a besotted George opened up about the depth of love he was experiencing, David saw the sincerity of his pal's heartfelt feelings. George had looked genuinely pained when he spelled out his anxiety over the awkwardness of the situation, causing David to rush headlong to give support to his lovestruck friend. Over a late-night glass of Laphroaig whisky, David, while agreeing that it was definitely right not to tell Chris too much too soon, bolstered his flatmate's self-assurance by stressing that there was no reason whatsoever why he and Angela should not be together. Loosened by the drink, George even revealed that they had already slept together many times and that it was just 'perfect'. At that point, David made it clear that it was not necessary to disclose every gory detail and abruptly switched the subject to unveil some home truths about his own new love, including the truth about the night he said he was visiting friends in Guildford, when he was in fact staying with Sophie for the first time. He went on to explain at length how difficult it had been with the children, before confessing about the ploy when he had introduced Sophie into their lives at the zoo, adding that everything was now going 'brilliantly'. He did make it clear though that he would be taking the children to Paris alone to find some long-overdue 'family time'. They both concluded that the scams they had played along with had, in the end, produced some very unforeseen but excellent results. Project EX had indeed achieved all its objectives, and more. George called it 'a triumph of mischievousness'.

Today was twelfth day of October, the day when the final act was to be staged, the day when all this pretence and skulduggery came to fruition. It was the date that had been etched in David's mind for many weeks, the long-awaited, eagerly anticipated glorious twelfth, the special day that he had been waiting for. Up at the crack of dawn, he had packed and was ready to go down to pick up the children for their half-term trip to Paris. As he drove down the country road towards his old house, the sun was shining, his windows were down, the road was clear, Chris Isaak's 'Wicked Game' was on the radio. Life could not get better than this, he thought. 'Let the final drama begin', he said to himself out loud as he drew the car up outside the house.

His finger was not quite on the bell when the door flew inwards. Jess and Robbie bundled themselves out, coats over their shoulders while heaving overpacked suitcases with both hands, barely managing to lift them off the ground. They dragged them out to the Range Rover with a huff and a puff. David clicked the boot open and helped each load them in. The children jumped into the car and David was left for a moment alone with Moira. Predictably, while he was hoping that, by now, she would have curbed her vitriol and controlled her anger towards him, her natural bossiness could not resist the opportunity to spill out as she dished out instructions about what to do and what not to do with the children, as well as ramming home that they had to be back by next Sunday at 4pm sharp. As she handed over the passports, he looked at her and felt a strange sincere sadness, although he knew that anything he said would only serve as a trigger for her next outburst against him. His one-time anger for the way she had, deliberately and unnecessarily, dragged him and the children through the most torturous divorce, inflicting as much damage as possible as she went along, had given way to a sense of pity, a pity that she was wasting her life by being so eaten up with hate. He looked at her for a second with genuine sadness for her plight. He truly wanted for her to be happy, for if she was happy, they would all be happy. He wished that he did not have to have such a major identity in her life, that she would move on, let go and not keep playing the victim, his victim. A guilty qualm almost came over him about the impending cancellation of the Venice trip, but then the coldness in her expression on the doorstep against the warmth of the smiles on the children's faces through the car window made it easy for him to find justification for all his sly shenanigans. Unscrupulous tactics, such as they were, had been the only way to achieve what he considered as his perfectly reasonable objective. And this was the moment. As the door was closed behind him and he turned to see Jess and Robbie in the car, he was overcome with a sense of victory. He turned the key, the engine revved, the radio was on and children were singing. He was on his way.

"Thank you, Daddy. We love you", said Robbie. "It's lovely having Jess with us this time". The sister and brother hugged each other. David sighed with pleasure. Mission accomplished, he thought.

That evening, Chris and Bonnie had the apartment to themselves. George was away for the night 'seeing friends' and they had the place to themselves. Chris was working himself into a right old lather over how to break the news to Moira. Bonnie listened patiently as he voiced his anxieties.

"You have to tell her tonight", she strongly advised. "David will be well on his way by now. You don't need to delay a moment longer. You must do the decent thing. One, she will already be busy picking out clothes to pack into her case. Two, her excitement will only heighten as the trip gets nearer. You have to let her down as soon as possible, Chris. It's only fair, if anything is fair about any of this. One thing though, if it was David doing it, he would have got his revenge by leaving her stranded at the airport. That would have been awful. At least you are doing it nicely. Tell her that the conference is cancelled because the Editor found out about the jolly and went ballistic. Yes, that's it, blame the Editor. Or, no, better just say you have come down with the flu. That's easier. Plain and simple. But you'll have to sound dreadful. Can you do that?".

"Oi tink so", said a nasal Chris, starting to get into character. "OK, but can I do it in the morning, like I woke up with this horrible bug?".

"No, Chris. Don't be a wimp. Do it now. Say it's been getting worse throughout the day. You had hoped it would get better, but it's got steadily worse. Go on. It has to be done".

He realised he could not resist and hesitantly picked up his phone, mumbling through his nose to himself to get the right sounds.

Now there is an art to telling lies. Firstly, you have to have a very good memory and secondly you must speak confidently and, most importantly of all, you must never waffle. Chris failed on every point.

"Hoi, Moira. I 'ave some werry bad noos".

"Hi, Brian, what's up?".

Chris chuntered through his adenoids, all the time blundering from one lie to another in his unpersuasive attempt to convince his date that he was on death's door. For some reason, he seemed to think that the more lies he told and the more he repeated them, the more believable his excuses became. He could not have been more wrong. She went deafeningly quiet. This made him chunter on even more, stupidly filling her silences with additional, irrelevant blather, making the flimsiest excuses less and less credible. He then stupidly started muttering something incomprehensible about the Editor and that he had it too. Bonnie began to wave her hands frantically, signalling for him to end the call before he completely gave the game away with his floundering gibberish. But it was too late.

"Brian, you are a bloody liar. And a bloody awful one. You haven't even got the guts to tell me the truth. You are such a coward. I told you we were going as just friends. You could have had the guts to call it off when we had dinner. I hate weak men. You're a bloody chicken. That's what you are, a bloody chicken. Anyway, I couldn't give a shit. You're not worth it. You are not the only one you know. I am seeing someone else and he is twice the man you are. You are pathetic. I hope your fantasy flu bloody kills you. You're a damn liar". With that, she slammed down the phone. He had witnessed for himself Moira's barbed tongue. He looked tentatively at Bonnie.

"That went well", she said. "You should've stopped sooner, Chris. She rumbled you in the first five seconds. Did anyone tell you that you are a useless liar? But, hell, who cares. David is on his way to Paris and your stupid games are over, thank heaven. Now, it's gin and tonic time. Come here, give me a hug and get me a bloody drink. We're free again".

Shell-shocked Chris complied obediently with her demands, although he was still reeling from the attack. He could never cope with people being cross with him. They sat side by side out on the balcony, holding hands, swathed in thick woollen blankets to keep out the autumn shivers as they gazed out over the London skyline. Bonnie's words slowly sank into his head. It was finally all over. The curtain had come down on this mad, underhand pantomime of farcical subterfuge. Ironically, neither of them was aware of the full extent of the success of the cunning scheme. They knew that David was on his way to Disneyland with his children. They knew too that Ricky was blissfully reunited with his ex-husband. That alone was enough for Chris to hail the unqualified success of the unprincipled scheme. What he was not aware of, as they enjoyed their drink and the view over the Thames to St Paul's, was that his ex-wife and George had found true love and were at that very moment snuggled up in one another's arms on the sofa at his former home and David too was all loved up.

"You know what they say, Bonnie", he said as he put his arm lovingly around her. "The best is yet to come". As the sunset turned the river into a candescent orange, she smiled back at him, lay her head on his shoulder and thought of his words. She had her man, her huge theatrical success and her wonderful life in London. What more could a girl ask for? Life was, as David would say, simply 'brilliant'.

CHAPTER TWELVE
EMERGENCY

SATURDAY, NOVEMBER 9

"Exactly where are you taking me, Sophie?", enquired a curious David.

"Ah. That's for me to know and you to find out", answered Sophie with a playful smile.

She was sitting at the wheel of David's Range Rover, driving through the green Sussex countryside. He knew they were heading south but had absolutely no idea where this magical mystery tour would end up.

"It is your birthday today after all and this is my surprise", Sophie continued. "Now sit back and enjoy it. We need to make up for Golden Oak just having his first defeat. Good job that I have chosen somewhere special. Don't worry. I know you'll love it".

They had just left Lingfield Park racecourse in Surrey. His valiant racehorse had just run his first ever two-mile race over hurdles. This time, unlike with his races on the Flat, he had been slightly less than heroic. The flashy chestnut had had a short rest since his win at Sandown, had been turned out into the paddocks to enjoy the late summer grass for a few weeks in preparation for the 'jump' season ahead. After being brought back to fitness with daily gallops, all under the eagle eye of his trainer Charlie Walsh, he had then been schooled over practice hurdles that Charlie had installed in his compact, circular training arena. Surrounded by a six-foot fence, Golden Oak had been cantered around and around, repeatedly tackling the hurdle on each side of the circuit, improving his skills with leap. He quickly showed a natural aptitude to the jumping game. Charlie wanted him spot on for his first hurdles race. It was Sophie who had mentioned David's birthday to him, when they were up at the stables visiting the yard a couple of weeks earlier. 'Now I know, I'll see if I can find a race on that day. It's a Saturday, so we should find something. Hopefully, I'll give him a birthday winner', Charlie had said, with his characteristic optimism.

As it happened, the horse had run well, albeit a tad too keenly. David put that down to his exuberance of youth. So happy was the handsome horse to be back on the racecourse that, from the moment the race started, he nearly pulled the jockey's arms out of their sockets as he strode out in front. This was probably his undoing. He led all the way from the start but, jumping the last, he rapped the top of the hurdle and, showing signs of tiredness after his lay-off, he got caught by another horse, who took advantage of his mistake and swept past him. Sophie thought David would be disappointed, when he was anything but. He had been in the game long enough to know that second in his first race over jumps was a good result. The connections had shared a bottle of champagne afterwards and, as is the wont with racing folk, looked forward to the next race and to what might be in the future.

The conversation in the car had moved on from racing. After David had spent a few minutes unsuccessfully guessing where she was taking him, they talked at length about the children and how pleased they were that Sophie had met them at the zoo that day. It brought them such happiness that both Jess and Robbie had instantly taken to her and, although she had spent only a few hours with them since, Sophie had fallen for them equally. Jess in particular was becoming inseparable from her, encouraged by their spending 'girl time' together, while Robbie sat with his Daddy, playing video games and watching TV. David then joyously repeated some of the tales of his Disneyland trip with the children. The whole adventure had been an immense success from the moment they stepped into their first-class compartment on Eurostar, to their three nights in the luxurious Disneyland Paris Hotel and, of course, to spending those magical, exhausting days in the Park, riding all the attractions, each one at least once. But for David, the best times were when they all sat down to dinner in the evening, especially in Captain Jack's, hidden in the wonderland of the Pirates of the

Caribbean. They loved it so much they went back there on their last night. Every night closed with a walk down Main Street to marvel at the awe-inspiring firework display, a crescendo of rockets and pyrotechnics that lit up Sleeping Beauty's fairytale castle. His time in Paris with his precious children, so much longer than the short weekends every fortnight, had regenerated the closeness and the devotion they all had for one another. Above all, it had been a time of calm and had helped wash away so many unhappy memories of the bad old days.

It was starting to drizzle. The windscreen wipers began their intermittent sweeps. The weather, against Sophie's wishes, had turned cloudy and grey. David recognised where he was as they joined the A21 road to the coast and started to have his suspicions about what she was up to.

"Ah, is it...?", he started to guess.

"Be quiet", Sophie snapped jokingly. "This is meant to be a surprise. Don't spoil it. All will be revealed".

Half an hour later, they approached the beautiful old town of Rye, famous for its cobbled lanes and Tudor houses. David had already worked out the destination with certainty. He had guessed that there was only one place in this part of the country that stylish Sophie would have chosen for them to stay. Sure enough, they pulled into the car park of The Mermaid, one of the best-known pubs in the south of England. The original tavern had been established in the 1156 but was rebuilt in its current form as recently as 1420. It had been the haunt of smugglers for generations and was riddled with underground passages and cellars. Today though, it had ditched the rum-running and eye-patches for fine wine and silver service in its award-winning restaurant. It also had spectacular beamed bedrooms, some of which were reportedly still stalked by ghosts. A lady in white appeared occasionally in Room 1, while a man in old-fashioned dress had been seen to enjoy an aimless wander around Room 19. Other apparitions had appeared in several of the other rooms, to the delight or horror of the occupants.

"Darling, this is brilliant", enthused David. "You are fantastic. I couldn't think of a better place to be. This is going to be a wonderful weekend. Thank you".

They checked in and were given room 17, the Elizabethan Room. As she handed over the key, the receptionist nonchalantly added the tale about the alleged duel that had taken place in the room back in the 16th century, with one of the smugglers ending up being killed by his merciless adversary. Since then, many poltergeist incidents had been reported and they were warned by the kindly lady not to be alarmed if bottles or china ornaments inexplicably fell off shelves and crash to the floor for no accountable reason. And that's not all. The troubled soul of another smuggler's girlfriend, who had been brutally murdered by the dead man's gang because she knew too much, had also been observed haunting that very same room in ghostly form in the middle of the night.

Unfazed and unpacked, they settled into the room before wrapping themselves up warmly against the chilly weather to set off for a stroll through the nooks and crannies of the historic town. Walking hand in hand, they meandered down the cobbled streets, past the venerable churches and old timbered houses. Dating back to Roman times, Rye is steeped in romantic history. It had once been a teeming and important seaside community, one of the five busy and strategically important Cinque Ports, but the harbour had silted up after violent storms seven hundred years ago and the town was now completely cut off from the sea. A good Gallic sacking and burning by the French in 1377 had not helped either.

As they strolled around, absorbed in their theatrical setting, the sun broke through, lighting up the whole historic scene. David pulled Sophie close as they looked into each other's eyes.

"You know what I love about you, Sophie Cavendish? Everything".

They eventually arrived back at the hotel for a gin and tonic, enlivened by the obligatory dash of Angostura bitters, nestling by the fire which flickered in the inglenook fireplace.

After Sophie had enjoyed the luxury of a long, leisurely bath, surrounded by candles, they went down for dinner in the panelled dining room. It was the perfect romantic setting as they leaned forward towards each other, both thoroughly revelling in David's birthday celebration.

Suddenly, David's phone rang in his pocket.

"Blast. Sorry about this. I'll have to take it outside. I won't be a second".

He got up and left the dining room, leaving Sophie alone at her table, in the company of her glass of white Burgundy.

David had been gone less than two minutes when he rushed back in, his demeanour completely changed. He was visibly shaking as he came close to Sophie.

"We have to go. There's been an accident. We have to go," he repeated, turning on his heels and heading towards the door. Without question, she hastily followed him back to their room, carefully trying not to disrupt their fellow guests.

"David. What's happening? You're frightening me. Tell me", begged Sophie.

"There's been a car crash. Jess and Sophie have been hurt. We have to get to the County Hospital. I don't know anything else".

"Oh my God. Is it bad? Are they OK?", asked a troubled Sophie.

"I don't know. That was Roy on the phone, my old neighbour. Their car went off the road into a ditch. He found out about it and rushed to the hospital. He doesn't know much more. I said I'd ring him once we were on the road".

They got up and dashed back to their room. After throwing everything back into their cases, they hurried to the car.

"What about the bill?", Sophie asked.

"We'll sort that out later. Let's just throw our things back in the cases. We have to get there now".

"I'll drive. You just tell me where to go", Sophie insisted.

As the headlights did their best to cut through the dark, drizzly night, the winding country roads made driving difficult. Once on their way, David phoned Roy again. Sophie tried desperately to make sense of it all from hearing one side of the conversation. When he finished the call, he sat back quietly for a second before passing on the information to Sophie.

"Apparently, they were in Moira's car. It happened as they were coming back towards the village late this afternoon. Roy doesn't know exactly what caused it, but he was told the car skidded and ended up in a ditch. Moira is in pretty bad shape he thinks. Luckily the children were in the back. He says Jess has a bad arm. It might be broken. Robbie is fine, shaken up naturally, but Roy says he isn't injured".

"Oh, David. This is awful. I hope they are OK. At least they are in hospital and being looked after. I am so sorry, darling".

They drove on in silence, both engulfed in the horror of the unknown. Sophie wanted to say something supportive. However, when she saw David's paralysed face in the dashboard light, she said nothing and concentrated on driving.

Once at the hospital, they ran in and straight up to the front desk.

"Jess and Robbie Nugent. Can you tell me where they are? Please hurry", David implored.

"One minute, sir", the girl said dispassionately as she fingered her keyboard, with no hint of urgency. "Jessie Nugent is in Casualty, sir. I believe her brother is in the waiting room there with some friends".

As they scurried into the Casualty Department, Roy got up from his chair and dashed over to greet them.

"David. It's OK. Jess is going to be fine. The doctor told Margaret that there are no bones broken, just bad bruising. She will be sore for a while, but she'll be OK in a few days. Margaret is in there with her now while they patch her up".

"Thank God for that", David said, with an audible sigh of relief. At that moment, he saw Robbie, sitting alone next to where Roy had been seated, reading a page of cartoons in a children's magazine. He went straight over, carefully trying not to show his real emotions. Robbie's expressionless face stared directly into the cartoons.

The anxious father crouched down and hugged his son. "Robbie. Are you alright, mate? That was pretty horrible, wasn't it? But you are OK now. And so is your sister. It is all going to be fine".

"Mummy got hurt, Daddy. I think she bumped her head badly. There was blood everywhere," the little boy said, his head bowed.

"Oh, I am sure she will be fine, darling. These doctors are brilliant. They can fix anything." He looked across the room and there was Jess, her arm in a sling, walking slowly towards him between a supporting nurse and Margaret. She looked stunned. David went immediately to her and kissed her.

"Jess, darling, are you OK?".

"I am alright, Daddy. It hurts a bit. The doctor says nothing is broken. Mummy isn't good though, Daddy. We came here by ambulance and she was on a stretcher. I hope she'll be alright." She started to cry.

"Darling, the doctors will make her better". David could not help but be moved by the love and concern Jess had for her mother.

The nurse brought some calm authority into the conversation. "I take it you are Jess' father. She has been very brave, Mr Nugent. You should be very proud of her. We took some X-rays and fortunately nothing is broken. She was very lucky. It was a nasty crash. With lots of rest and tender loving care, she'll be as right as rain. You can take her home whenever you like".

"She'll get lots of both, for sure. Thanks for looking after her. We are all really grateful", David replied.

Sophie came over, knelt down and gave Sophie a gentle hug. She then looked up at David.

"What can I do to help? Should we take the children to a hotel?"

"No. No way. Don't even think about it", interjected Roy. "You can all stay at our house. Since the kids left home, we have plenty of room".

"Thanks, Roy. That's a great idea", said David. "Sophie, will you kindly take the children back with Roy and Margaret, if that's OK, Roy. I think I should just check on Moira. The children are very worried about her and I need to know what's going on".

"Of course, David. Are you sure you're OK to drive?", enquired a caring Sophie.

"Perfectly. I just want to see how she is. I won't be far behind you".

He kissed Sophie and escorted them all out to Roy's car before hurrying back to the front desk.

"Moira Nugent, please".

"One moment, sir", said the spiritless girl, returning to her computer. "She is just out of surgery, but you can speak to the doctor to find out more. She's in the Nightingale Ward on Floor 2. The doctor should be up there now".

"Thank you", he said, already rushing to the lifts.

The lift seemed to take forever to struggle to the second floor where he caught the attention of a nurse in the corridor. After explaining about Moira, he then asked if he could have a word with the doctor. He was shown into a small room, which had a dozen or so functional chairs parked unimaginatively against the jaded walls, a table in the centre strewn with well-fingered magazines and one other occupant, a man in his early forties, reading a National Geographic, sitting in the far corner. Two bright fluorescent strip lights emitted a cold and unwelcoming aura over the austere scene. David took a seat. Before long, a doctor in a white coat came in.

"Mr Nugent?". David stood up. "Your wife has had a nasty bump on the head". David resisted correcting him on their marital status. "I had to put some stitches in a wound and I took some X-rays as she appears to have suffered some whiplash, which is understandable. It doesn't look too serious, but I shall have another look tomorrow. Thankfully nothing appears broken although she may be suffering from mild concussion. I think she should be left to sleep tonight. I have given her a mild sedative. But don't worry too much. I couldn't find anything too be overly concerned about but we shall know more in the morning".

"Do you know what happened?", David asked.

"Well, she is very bleary, understandably, but she said she thought a deer or something ran out, they swerved and skidded off the road to the left. Unfortunately, your wife was in the front passenger seat and got the worst of it".

David looked completely shocked.

"The passenger seat? Who was driving then?".

"It was a complete accident, Mr Nugent. But I believe the driver was her friend over there", the doctor said, looking at the other man in the room. David went rigid but kept his composure.

"Thank you, doctor. You have been brilliant. What a horrible night".

"Just another night for me, I am afraid", retorted the doctor, who then turned and left, inevitably moving on to his next medical emergency.

David was left alone with the other man. He turned to him.

"Who the hell are you? What the hell is going on?".

"David, isn't it?", said the man politely. "My name is Gary Michaels. I am Moira's friend. I am so sorry about this. It was all an accident. We were coming back from Cawston Holt with the kids in the back and this bloody little deer ran out across the road. It was getting dark and I just automatically went to avoid it. It was awful".

David lost it. "You could have killed my children, you damned idiot."

"Calm down. Please. This is no time for this".

David's anger swelled up further. "Don't tell me to bloody calm down. Who the hell do you think you are driving my children around, anyway?".

Gary's politeness disappeared in a flash. He jumped up and snapped back defensively. "Don't lecture me on how to behave, you of all people. If anyone should have bloody well been there, it was you. You're the one that ran off and left them all. Don't you bloody dare lecture me".

The nurse burst in on hearing the ruckus.

"Gentlemen, please. We have some very sick patients here. Please keep your fighting for outside the hospital". Both men look chastened and embarrassed. David muttered humble apologies to the nurse, while Gary took his seat once more.

"Now, Moira is still awake. I have just been talking to her and she is asking for you", said the nurse. Gary got up and started to walk towards the door.

"No, not you, Mr Michaels. She has asked to see Mr Nugent". Gary looked surprised and glared at David, before resuming his seat.

The nurse then accompanied David into the Nightingale Ward. Moira was attached to a electrocardiograph machine, with the rolling green graph following her heartbeat. Bandages were wrapped around her head and she wore a rigid neck collar. On seeing her, he immediately regained his composure and pulled up a chair beside the bed.

"Hi, Moira. I am so sorry. This is horrible. But I have just spoken to the doctor and you are going to be fine. Just a few headaches for the next few days, he says. It sounds like you were lucky".

"So, this is what you call lucky, is it, David? Very funny. I think it will be more than a few days. The nurse told be more like a few weeks. I feel like I have been hit by a bus. Now listen to me, David. I am really tired, but I need to say something to you. I know you. The fact is that my boyfriend, Gary, was driving but it was not his fault. Not at all. In fact, he may have saved our lives. No-one could have stopped this happening. This deer jumped out of nowhere. There were cars coming the other way. For Christ's sake, we could have had a head-on crash and all be dead. He did the only thing he could do. He swerved to the left and we landed in a ditch. If you bump into him, please don't get mad", she implored.

"Well, actually he and I have already had words outside", David said, with his feathers still ruffled from his spat with Gary.

"That's exactly what I didn't want to happen. Don't go there. He's a nice guy and I like him a lot, OK? I don't interfere with you and your precious Sophie. It was just an accident. We had all been to an Autumn Fair. The children had had a great day. And he was the one that put their seatbelts on in the back. So just leave it. Now, David, I am exhausted. I'm not going into a long discussion with you about my boyfriend. Can you make sure, please, that you look after Jess and Robbie. I gather Roy and Maureen Harrison are taking care of them at the moment. The doctor tells me they are both shaken up and that Jess has a badly bruised arm. They can do without any of your histrionics. There have been enough arguments between us. I don't want any more so please take care of them and don't start on at Gary. I have to trust you. Just look after them, won't you", she pleaded.

David looked at her in her sorry state and felt subdued.

"Obviously I will, Moira, as if you have to ask. Don't worry. Whatever has gone on, you are right. This is when they need a lot of love. They love you very much too by the way. Jess is so worried about you".

"Tell her not to worry. I'll be fine. Go now, David. And if Gary is still outside, don't start off at him and would you ask him to come in, please. I'd like to see him".

"He is in the little room next door and I will, of course".

"Now off you go. Tell the children I love them and let's keep in touch by phone. I would like to see them tomorrow if that's possible. And look after them, David".

"Of course," replied David before giving her a reassuring smile before leaving.

He paused in contemplation outside the waiting room door for a good thirty seconds, in a moment self-pacification. He thought of everything Moira had said and then walked into the little room.

Gary was still alone and stood up warily when David entered.

David spoke with a measured voice. "Gary, I owe you an apology. I'm sorry for that outburst just now. I am sorry I flared up. I said things I shouldn't have. But it was the shock of it all, but then I should not have flown at you. I'm very sorry. In fact, I owe you my thanks".

Gary's face relaxed in relief and he stretched out his hand. David grabbed it and pulled him into his shoulder.

"Thank you," David continued. You may have just saved my children's lives. Moira explained what happened. You did a good job. Now, Moira is asking for you. You must go and see her". He then turned towards the door, walked down the long sterile corridor to the lift and out to his car.

When he got to Roy's house, his friend opened the door and David stepped inside, only to be almost bowled over by the wildly over-excited Billy, who Roy had collected from his neighbour's house and who was squirming with uncontrolled excitement at seeing his old master. The dog had been waiting a long time for this moment. Master and servant greeted one another like the long-lost friends that they were. When the reunion had quietened down, Roy took David upstairs to the children. Jess was cuddled up in a double bed, with Sophie lying on top of the covers, reading a fairy story by the dim light of a bedside lamp. He crept in trying not to disturb them. Sophie gave him a subtle 'everything is good' look and he went over to Jess, sat on the edge of the bed and spoke softly to his daughter.

"Mummy is doing fine, darling. I have just seen her. She sends all her love. You needn't worry. Although she has a nasty bump on her head, the doctor said she will be right as rain in no time. So, you get some sleep and we shall go and see Mummy in the morning".

"I love you, Daddy. I am pleased Mummy is going to be alright. Sophie, can you stay with me tonight? Is that alright, Daddy? Please? Please". Sophie naturally agreed and David blew them both a kiss, before he crept back out of the door. In the next room, Robbie was fast asleep in one of the twin beds, while Margaret sat on the other.

"I'll stay here until you come to bed, David. Why not have a drink with Roy downstairs? You have hardly had a great birthday", whispered Margaret.

David and Roy went quietly downstairs and spent the next couple of hours talking, a large whisky by their sides. The shock of the evening had hit both of them hard and a medicinal shot of Scotch was just what the doctor ordered.

The next day, David took Jess and Robbie to see their mother. The parents decided that it would be best to take the children out of school for a few days and that they should stay in Thames Tower, at least until Moira was back to full strength. The doctor had already said she should stay in hospital for at least a week. Billie, meanwhile, continued his holiday with Roy and Margaret.

As it happened, Jess and Robbie bounced back in no time, helped by Ricky coming round with his guitar for a couple of sessions with his 'superfans'. The regular phone calls with their mother helped to reassure them that she was on the mend and that life would soon be back to normal. Everyone was moving on from that frightful, rainy Saturday night.

THURSDAY, NOVEMBER 14

Sophie had taken the week off work to help David look after the children and was, by now, becoming acquainted with the ritzy apartment as well as getting to know the not-so-ritzy flatmates, who came and went erratically. At David's invitation, they had all gathered en masse at the apartment on Tuesday night to meet Sophie. The children had laid the table with the canapés that David had bought, together with all the plates and the other accoutrements. Ricky arrived first, with Alex, both irritatingly happy at being back together. Chris also came along on his own as Bonnie was on duty behind the bar at the Wellington, Bonnie had popped in to meet Sophie earlier that morning and the two hit it off from the word 'wine', as David thought they would. George too was flying solo as he continued to squirrel Angela away out of the limelight, terrified that Chris would find out about their burgeoning relationship. It was not as if he did not want to tell Chris. It was just that they had such a special relationship that he did not want to take the risk of losing such a great friend. As they all sat around the table, with the children predictably monopolising Ricky, the conversation was remarkably proper and polite, even though Chris was champing at the bit to get to all the juicy bits. But he managed to contain himself. The aura of the cultivated Sophie, and the presence of the children, had put them all on their very best behaviour. By 9.30 the unusually gentlemanly evening came to an early end, with Chris, Ricky and Alex bidding uncharacteristic, middle-class farewells as if they were leaving a suburban sherry evening. As the closed the door, David and Sophie gave each other a relieved look and a hug, knowing that, at last, they no longer had to duck and weave between country hotels and a host of restaurants to keep their relationship secret.

"I'll clear up. David, why don't you put the children to bed and I'll come in in a minute and we can read them a story", proposed Sophie. "George, you can lend me a hand, can't you? It won't take long".

"Of course," said George, "but I will have to leave in ten minutes. I hope you don't mind".

David gave his friend a knowing glance.

"No problem. You go, George. We can manage. There's not much to do that the machine can't do. I know you have more interesting things to do than clearing up plates. Now off you go. And give Angela our love".

"Thanks, David. I hope it won't be long before we can have our own version of a night like tonight. I hate all this masquerade, but it is such a difficult situation. Thanks for being my pal through it all. See you soon". With that, after kissing Sophie on the cheek, he grabbed his coat and fled through the door.

It was now 10.30. She and David had put Jess and Robbie to bed with a story and grabbed the chance of some grown-up time alone on the balcony. Armed with a bottle of wine, they pulled up two chairs and rested their feet on the shiny steel ropes that stretched between the posts. There was a nip in the air as they looked out across the London skyline, which was silhouetted under the stars in the clear winter sky, and Sophie pulled a blanket over her legs. They sat quietly, unwinding from all that had happened over the past few days. Sophie, who was never one for inane chatter at the best of times, was unusually quiet and pensive. That was until she shuffled her chair closer to his. She then spoke to him softly.

"David. There has been something I have wanted to tell you for a while". He looked sideways at her with some apprehension but said nothing. "I want you to know how much my life has changed since you came into it. You have brought me something I thought I would never find. I can't say I have been exactly searching for you all my life, but I have been waiting for you to arrive. You are everything that I ever dreamed of, even as a young girl. You are truly my handsome prince and I have come to love you so much. I have never told you this but I was in one other serious relationship before. I haven't mentioned it until now because there was no need to. It's all in the past. We moved in together for a while and even talked about marriage. But there was always something missing. Something that made a commitment impossible. He loved me, I know that, too much in many ways, but I knew I couldn't give him all that he wanted – and was entitled to. You see, David, I can't have children. I have to tell you that. I have a medical issue and it seems I wasn't given the blessing of being able to have a baby. It took me a long time to come to terms with that. It is hard to explain. In the end, I learned to live with it. It's a lonely sort of feeling. I can't describe it, a sort of unfulfilled emptiness. You question life itself, knowing that you will have no family, no legacy, no heritage. For a while, there seemed no purpose, no value in life.

But something's happened to me. Something you brought into my life. Suddenly, I don't worry about what I don't have and am just so thrilled at what I do have. With Jess and Robbie, I have found everything I could ask for from a family. Especially with Jess, I have to admit. She is such a gem. I love them both so much. They are providing me with everything I need to feel that fulfilment, that wholeness, that reason to exist that I thought I'd lost. Suddenly I have everything I ever wanted".

She breathed deeply, looked deep into his eyes and continued.

"David, you are so important to me. At work, I can always be that forthright, bossy, confrontational lawyer, but that is not me. This is me, sat here now, with the man I love. I love you, Mr Nugent. Like no other love there has ever been". She paused, took a sip of her drink and took his hand, appearing to lighten up. "So, what I am trying to say, Mr Nugent, is simply this. If you were to ask me to marry you one day, I would".

David was completely taken aback. He said nothing but gawped at her in aghast adoration.

"Are you asking me to marry you, Sophie?", he said, almost glibly.

"No, of course not. I told you, I am not that pushy. But perhaps I am asking you to ask me?".

Without a moment's hesitation, David got up and pulled his chair away before going down gallantly on one knee. Sophie remained seated, unable to restrain a reflexive nervous laugh. Taking a deep breath, he looked her directly in her eyes and spoke.

"I don't need to be asked twice", said David eagerly. "I hope you are really ready for this. OK, here goes... Sophie, you are the most amazing person on this planet. I never knew I could feel such love for someone. I know I am not worthy of you but... Sophie Cavendish, will you marry me?". He stopped for a second and then corrected himself. "No, let me do that again". Sophie laughed, partly out of nerves. David set off again. "Sophie Cavendish... will you do me the enormous honour of agreeing to become my wife and join me, Jess and Robbie to make our family complete?".

With a tear in her eye, she fell onto her knees with him. "Yes, yes, I will marry you". They then both rose to their feet and wrapped themselves into a lovers' knot before David dashed to the kitchen and came back with a bottle of champagne and two tall glasses. Drinks poured, they burst into full tilt, making plans, excitedly talking about how to tell the children the news, what guests they should invite, what colour Jess' bridesmaid's dress might be, how Robbie would feel about a pageboy suit and, importantly, where the venue might be. When it came to the date, they both said simultaneously, 'soon'. They were ecstatic, overflowing with joy as they continued their excited planning late into the night. They kept coming back to where on earth they should have the wedding. There were so many possibilities, grand places, historic places, quirky places, romantic places.

Suddenly, David had a brainwave. "How about this for a thought? What about running away together to that tropical beach I talked about? You did promise to take me there one day, remember? Now's your chance. How about it?"

"That's a wonderful idea. Just you and me and the children. Oh my, that would be sensational. But hang on, David. What about the boys? I guess they'll want to come. We can hardly leave them out after everything you guys have been through together".

"No, we couldn't not have the boys there. George wouldn't miss it for the world, I'm certain of that", reassured David. "I wouldn't want him to. He's been such a mate. Trouble is, I'm not sure Chris could afford it. Same with Ricky. This isn't going to be a cheap 'gig', as he'd say. Mind you, I think he may have the money as he's really done well recently, but then he wouldn't come without Alex and that could all be too expensive for them right now".

"David, it's my turn for an idea. Why don't we treat them? We have the money and they have been such amazing friends to you".

"That's a brilliant thought, Sophie. This whole thing here has been exceptional and they have all been such great mates. They certainly got me over the Moira stuff and those dreadful times. Let's do it. Are you sure don't mind? And then we have to talk about who you want there".

Sophie paused thoughtfully.

"You know David. I just want to be with you and the children. We are not a close family these days and the only one I'd really want there is my Mum, but she isn't well enough for a long flight".

"Well, we have plenty of time to talk that through. I just want you to be happy. In the meantime, here's another brilliant Nugent idea. What about this. How about Christmas - in Antigua? I love that place and so does George. And you will too".

"Christmas? Wow, you're a fast worker ,Mr Nugent. I'm all for it. The sooner the better, in my opinion. Antigua. Interesting. Isn't that where Alex comes from? I seem to remember hearing that somewhere". A lawyer's brain retains everything.

"Blimey. I think you're right", responded David. "Yes, I believe it is. That's a massive coincidence. Well, that decides it. And it gives me yet another idea". He went back down onto one knee.

"Sophie, let me rephrase my proposal. I think I can be a bit more precise. Ready? Sophie Cavendish, will you marry me on the beach at English Harbour, Antigua at 3pm on Christmas Day? How's that for detail?".

"David, I will", she replied. "Of course, I will. I love you so much. I am a very lucky girl".

They both drew themselves together and kissed.

"Bloody hell. What have I just said?", David added. Sophie looked surprised. "I've just realised that I'll be making the ultimate sacrifice. I shall be missing the Queen's Speech for the first time ever. See what you have done to me? You've turned me into a Republican", David chuckled.

"That's nothing", Sophie gasped. "I have a million things to be getting on with. If you are serious about Christmas, we have so little time. I'd better start working on it right now". She then paused and a seriousness gripped her face.

"Goodness. There is so much to be done. Most importantly though, how shall we tell Jess and Robbie? How shall we do that?"

"I think that is one job that I have to do on my own", David replied. "I am sure they will be alright with it because they really do love you, but we know that their mother will go ballistic. I don't understand why, but she will. If Moira is anything, she is consistently unreasonable. This needs to be handled carefully. But you never know, with a bit of luck, she will be well into her new relationship with Gary and be pleased I am out of the way. Well, we can dream, can't we? What do you think? Should I tell them on my own?".

"Absolutely. This is such a personal, close family thing. You are the only one who can do this. If I may suggest, why not tell them tomorrow before it leaks out. We won't be able to keep it quiet and Jess picks up everything. And anyway, we will have to call all the boys back again as soon as possible. We'll have to tell them quickly if we are going to invite them to the wedding. Oh my god, that word. I am talking about our wedding. I just cannot believe I am talking about my own wedding. I am so happy, David".

"This is all incredible. Now, I think you should find some shopping to do tomorrow morning, while I tell Jess and Robbie about our news. That shouldn't be too difficult, should it?", David joked.

"I think I could manage that", she said with a playful smirk. "But I think I should go back to work on Tuesday. I'm going to have to take some time off at Christmas if I have a honeymoon to consider".

CHAPTER THIRTEEN
WEDDING PLANS

As is almost always the case, following hot on the heels of the euphoria of the proposal and the exultation of its acceptance is the daunting reality of all the wedding planning that has to be done. The countdown for David and Sophie began at the moment she said 'yes'. There was the venue to be booked, the catering and entertainment to be agreed, the photographer, the vicar, the cars, and of course, the guest list and invitations. The 'to do' list was as long as the bridal train. But for David, there was only one starting point.

"Now, Jess. Robbie. I need you to sit here at the table with me. I have some news", commanded David gently. Sophie had left on her shopping spree and the children were alone in the apartment with their father. Their faces were etched in curiosity, but they obediently got slowly to their feet and wandered over to where their father was seated.

David, a man who could address a packed hall of high-flying business people without a scintilla of apprehension, felt a heart-fluttering diffidence about making his pronouncement to his two offspring. Their eyes focussed on him intently, as if they knew something significant was coming. David had turned over any number of opening gambits in his head over past couple of hours. In the event, he drew a deep breath, smiled affectionately and launched himself.

"You two are amazing. You have put up with so much and been so strong. I know we've had some really hard times, but we've got through them together, haven't we". He wavered for a second before going on. "Now, you have got to know Sophie really well over the past weeks. She is such a lovely person and...".

"Are you going to marry her, Daddy?", crashed in Jess, as sharp as ever. Robbie sat bolt upright in his big chair.

"Are you, Daddy?", Robbie compounded.

"Well...", he said falteringly, after a short pause. "Sophie and I have been talking and, yes, we have decided that it would be nice if we got married. Nice for us and, I hope, nice for you".

Their expressionless reaction was frozen in stillness. A second felt like a minute as David tried to evaluate what they were thinking. Both children took on an almost empty mien, clearly processing the news. He was about to break the silence when Jess spoke.

"Won't Mummy be cross?", she said quietly and rather pathetically. Robbie looked at his father for an answer.

"Oh darling. I don't think so", David said reassuringly, before losing his confidence and garbling edgily. "I am taking you back home on Sunday and I shall tell her all about it before then, don't worry. Mummy and I may have had our ups and downs, but we have put all that behind us. We both love you more than anything. It was just that we couldn't be together forever. But we will both always be there for you. You know that you are the two most important things in our world and now Sophie wants to join that world and I would love her to be part of it. Can she join us?".

"Oh, Daddy", Jess replied. "Oh, yes, of course she can. We love Sophie, don't we Robbie. But we are just worried Mummy might be unhappy. She gets so sad sometimes and very cross when things upset her. It's just that we don't know what she'll do when she finds out".

"I understand that. But let me talk to her first and I am sure we can sort it out. Let's try not to worry too much. I think she will be OK with it all. But how do you feel about it? Are you OK with me marrying Sophie?".

To David's utter relief, Robbie spoke up.

"I think Sophie's great. She is really kind and is always treating us to things".

"Yes, Daddy", Jess added, reclaiming her role as spokeswoman for the pair. "We really really like Sophie and I think we knew you would marry her, even on that day at the zoo. She's lovely. So, is there going to be a big wedding?"

"No, quite a small one. And here's a nice surprise". David saw his chance to change the mood completely. "It's going to be in the Caribbean and you are going to be there to help us with it all. How does that sound?".

That brought an immediate, involuntary yelp of excitement.

"When, Daddy? When is the wedding?".

"How does Christmas sound? The idea is that we are all going to Antigua in the Caribbean for Christmas and we'll get married on Christmas Day. But we are going to need your help".

"Are we coming too?". Jess lit up. "Wow, that's amazing! This is going to be great, Daddy. Are there lovely beaches?"

"Absolutely, the best", David told them.

"Where is the Carra Been?", asked Robbie in his innocence.

"It's the Caribbean, silly. Just like in Pirates of the Caribbean", his sister explained. "It's hot and sunny with palm trees. And the sea is amazing. Thanks, Daddy. It's a great idea. Where's Sophie? I want to give her a hug".

"She'll be back soon then we can all celebrate. So, we are all OK with everything?". The children smiled keenly and nodded. "Thanks, guys. This is going to be brilliant. And you are going to have the time of your life. I promise".

His next task was to tell Moira. He primed himself for her response when he rang her from his bedroom. And, within the first minute, the hysterics began.

"Now, shut up and listen", barked the fiery Moira. By now, David was able predict every well-worn, vitriolic line almost word perfectly, or imperfectly to be more accurate. However, after years of matching her anger, often blow for blow, toe to toe, he had finally realised the futility of trying to get the last line in against her, electing to let her run uninterrupted until she simply ran out of steam. When he had picked up his phone to ring her, he had momentarily held out an inkling of hope in his head that the accident might have somehow mellowed her, that she might miraculously have become a changed woman, someone reasoned, someone more gentle. But no chance. She had hurled herself headlong into her old, hostile self the moment she had heard his voice. She could not help herself. It was an automatic, almost Pavlovian reaction. Not that he had not fully prepared himself for the latest hissy fit as he had hit her name on his phone. He was ready for it and she did not disappoint.

However, to his amazement, the call did not go totally as expected. He had started calmly, talking about the children and how they had missed her. Then he threw the pebble into the pond.

"Moira, I want you to be the first to know. Sophie and I are getting married", he had announced in a brief, almost casual, throw-away manner. He had lit the fuse and waited for the explosion. There was a weighty pause at the other end of the line before she burst into her usual mantra.

"Now, shut up and listen. I want the children back here by 4pm. I hope you haven't filled their heads with lies and nonsense. I know you. They are going back to school on Monday, so I don't want them too tired and make sure you bring all their clothes back".

David broke in. "Moira, please listen for a second. We need to talk. Are you alright? Have you recovered OK? We have all been worried about you".

Moira surprised David by immediately regaining her composure. "I am fine. How nice of you to ask," she said with a slash of sarcasm. "It is good to be home. I hated that hospital. I suppose I should thank you for coming to see me and for looking after Jess and Robbie. I have really missed them. I can't wait to see them".

"They are very excited about seeing you too. I am so pleased you are home, Moira. That was a horrible experience".

All of a sudden, they were sharing a rare moment. They were actually having a relatively normal conversation.

"Yes. It was pretty ghastly. But I think I am fine now. I feel fine, anyway. Just a few headaches. David, congratulations on you and Sophie. I know we have had our differences, but Gary has convinced me over the past few weeks that we all need to move on. He always says that we have to be happy with what we've got. I am happy that you are happy".

"And I am happy that you are happy, Moira," said David, resisting the temptation of adding 'because if you are happy, we're all happy'.

David could not believe his ears. They were having 'happy talk', like ordinary people, and continued to do so for a good few minutes before the call ended on an amenable note, apart from a barb that Moira could not resist.

"I am delighted for you, David", she said before adding, "I just hope you make a better job of marriage that you did with me. But I guess it takes two to tango. I'll see you on Sunday. Please don't be late".

David decided to seize this moment of truce.

"One thing, Moira. Would it be OK if the children came to the wedding? You know that it would be lovely if they could be there", he asked politely.

"I am sure they would like that", Moira responded curtly, without a flinch.

"That's a 'yes' then?".

"David, I am not an unreasonable person".

With that, the conversation ended and, as that was as good as it gets with Moira, David allowed himself a smug smile of satisfaction.

And it did not stop there. When he took Jess and Robbie back home two days later, he was staggered that, after throwing open the door to hug the children, she greeted him like an old friend. As he drove away, his smile turned into the broadest beam, even though he had somehow conveniently 'forgotten' to mention Antigua.

"One hurdle at a time", he said to himself in racing terminology with a wry chuckle. "That Gary is doing a bloody brilliant job. Maybe I was the wrong person for her all that time after all. Perhaps, maybe, it's just possible, it did have something to do with me".

Telling his flatmates was a much more pleasant task. Following his clarion call to the clan, the boys rallied back to the apartment to hear David's happy news. After handing each man a glass of champagne, they gathered around expectantly as he made his proclamation.

"So, this is it. One of us had to go first. One of us had to surrender his new-found freedom to the manacles of marriage. Well, gentlemen, it fell on me to be the one. I am pleased to tell you that we are about to welcome another Mrs Nugent into the world, poor girl. Sophie has, bizarrely, agreed to marry me".

George clenched his fist in celebration and was the first to offer his congratulations. "Bloody good show, David, old chap. This is wonderful news. Sophie is absolutely gorgeous and you two will be amazing together".

Ricky and Alex then both grabbed him for a hug and embraced him with love and good wishes. Chris' reaction was typically Chris.

"This is great, mate, so where's the stag night?", he bellowed, without so much as a 'well done', his priority firmly fixed.

David dismissed the question like a batsman skilfully glancing the ball through the slips. A stag night was the very last thing on his mind.

"Don't worry, David", Chris persisted. "I'll organise it. You have nothing to worry about. You have enough to do. Leave it all to me".

"God help us", exclaimed Ricky. "Chris has taken over the helm. Man the bloody lifeboats. The party's starting".

Chris was already in organising mode. "George, Ricky, Alex. Tomorrow night, 6.30. We need a board meeting in the Wellington". The sighs were audible, but they agreed.

David took the floor once more. "Getting back to the wedding, one small detail...we have decided that the wedding is taking place... wait for it... on Christmas Day... on the beach... in Antigua... and you are all going to be there... as my guests. I shall not take no for an answer".

"Are you serious?", cried Chris.

David looked at each man in turn to gauge their reaction. While Chris was unable to contain his boyish excitement, George looked stunned, clearly compromised by the secrecy of his covert relationship with Angela. Alex appeared concerned at the word 'Antigua' as Ricky's jaw dropped to the floor.

"This is the dog's bollocks. Can Bonnie come?", roared Chris.

"I hate that expression, Chris", George reprimanded.

"OK. Sorry, George. David, my dear friend, do I get the honour and privilege of bringing Miss Bonnie along with me?".

"Absolutely. Partners included, of course".

George sunk into a still deeper cogitation. David suddenly realised he had not taken George and Angela's situation into account and he saw that he had challenges ahead that he had not considered properly. 'Weddings are notoriously problematic,' he thought to himself, before turning to optimism for support. 'But there's always a way'. He gave both George and Alex a sensitive and reassuring glance.

Time was of the essence. The clock was ticking away and, as if the wedding alone was not enough, it was all happening thousands of miles away, on the other side of the Atlantic. David and Sophie burned the midnight oil finding the right hotel, reserving rooms, booking flights and having numerous excited chats on the phone with the engaging young wedding planner called Gabrielle. She was based at the hotel and quickly brought order and control into their plans. The only major downside was that George remained emphatic that he did not wish to produce Angela from out of the shadows. He was adamant that he did not want to risk telling Chris. Their relationship was both long-standing and trusted, but his concerns about his reaction to his dating his friend's ex-wife were, to him, insurmountable. David tried repeatedly to get him to move forward, even offering to act as a good broker, but there was no way George could face bringing the clandestine affair out into the open. In the end, due to time pressures, David reluctantly had to accept that his great pal would be coming on his own, or even not at all. This cast a shadow over his joy, but David pragmatically accepted that he had tried his best and could do no more about it.

"If you change your mind about Angela, George, you only have to let me know. I want you there whatever happens. It won't be that same without you". These were David's last words on the matter.

Chris, meanwhile, had his own party to organise. His first port of call was the Wellington, where he enlisted the enthusiastic support of Gerry, the barman. The two of them in tandem made an unstoppable force. Gerry flew into action. He said that a Monday would be ideal for him because it is usually a quiet night in the pub and he picked December 9. He offered to supply the food, to be served in the private room. He would arrange a small stage for some music near the main bar and he would also supply a bevy of colourful young things to liven up the party and boost the numbers. Chris fell in with it all, bouncing up and down with excitement at the whole prospect.

At the 'board meeting' at the Wellington, Chris and Gerry presented their proposal to Ricky, a pensive Alex and a sombre George. Bonnie was there too, listening quietly as the plans for the evening evolved.

"Hey. Have you got a band yet? I'll play", declared Ricky. "I'll get the boys together and we'll bash a few old numbers out. How would that be? I always said I would never be a wedding singer, but this is for old Dave".

"That'd be fantastic", enthused Chris.

"I've got my pal Sebastian to do a disco too", added Gerry.

They played around with an invitation list, adding names of friends and workmates, and they all agreed to chip in some money to cover the food.

"What about strippers?", asked Chris. The disapproving frown from George did enough to see Chris shrink back. "Only joking", he relented, even though he had not been.

Sophie found the whole idea of a hen night both utterly unappealing and completely infra dig. Nevertheless, she told David that she would like a dinner with her few good friends who would not be able to come to the wedding and suggested that she took a room at Mosimann's Club, arguably London's finest and most exclusive Michelin restaurant, in the heart of Belgravia. As it was a former church, it seemed the perfect venue, she said, and suggested that she should pick the same night as the stag night at the Wellington, Monday, December 9.

When it came to choosing the dress, she started right at the top and headed for London's most iconic bridal store, where she was made to feel at ease as she was shown fairy-tale gowns from the lavish collections from some of the world's top designers. They explained that the choice was limited because of the time but showed her all they had in stock at that moment. Sophie had made up her mind that her wedding was not going to be just about the day, but also about all the wonderful experiences along the way. Choosing her dress was her highlight. She made an appointment for a Saturday so that Jess could accompany her to this hall of high fashion, an experience that the young girl was never to forget. They were shown all they had, but when the Vera Wang dress was reverently produced it was love at first sight.

"Oh, Sophie. That's the one. You'll look like a princess", gasped Jess.

"I'll feel like one", said Sophie, before arranging to come back the following week for alterations. "Now, let's go shopping for my special Maid of Honour".

The unforgettable girls' day ended with them picking out Jess' bridesmaid dress and having their nails done. By now, Sophie and Jess were bonded like giggling sisters. It was as if Jess, in one afternoon, had taken that giant step into adolescence.

MONDAY, DECEMBER 9

When Chris arrived at the Wellington, the hallowed pub was empty apart from a couple of unfamiliar bar staff and Gerry, who was putting the final touches to the decor. In the front corner, near the window, there was now a small stage. The unattended drums and equipment were already in place and gave the room a feeling of expectancy. The side room, red curtains pulled back, had been laid out for the buffet and awaited the delivery of the trays of food. A tall, Victorian candelabra dominated the centre.

Chris carefully positioned George's barstool in its proper place before producing a sticker out of his pocket and putting it carefully across the seat. He stood back an admired his work and read the inscription - 'Reserved for King George'.

By seven o'clock, the first guests had started to pour in, mostly made up of Gerry's countless young things who had been attracted by his offer of free food and drink all night. There must have been at least sixty of them. Gerry had given himself and Bonnie the night off from behind the bar, bringing in guest staff to look after the evening. His friend, Sebastian, the deejay for the night, was fiddling expertly with his deck as some chilled Ibiza sounds softly filled the room. In no time the place seemed packed and at 8 o'clock, on cue, George escorted David through the door to the choreographed cheers of the assembled mass. Gerry had done his preparatory work perfectly. With them came Bonnie, looking as fabulous as ever. Chris rushed over to greet them.

"This is it, David. Welcome to your send-off. George, your throne awaits".

As they approached the bar, Gerry shouted out their order and, as George positioned himself on his seat, two pints of their usual were promptly set down before them.

"Thank you, guys", said David. "This is amazing. Thank you for doing all this work. I am not sure who all these people are but it looks like it's going to be a hell of a party. Hey, are we having a band as well? This is brilliant. You have gone to so much work".

"Come and look at the grub", Chris said to David over the music before leading him into the private room. The lights were dimmed and the tempting food gleamed under the flicker of the candles in a true gothic scene.

"This is incredible. I wish Sophie was here to see it", lamented David.

"Where is she tonight?", enquired Chris.

"Oh, she's taken some girlfriends to Mosimann's for a slap-up dinner, although I know she'd rather be here".

"Well, there are loads of hot chicks out there, so you'd better make the most of your time as a single man", jested Chris. David just laughed. At that point, Chris spotted the girls from his office in the main bar, together with his boss, Jill, and he rushed over to talk to them. That left David alone to admire the spread and feel the pleasure of knowing that all this was for him. His moment of solitude was rudely interrupted when Ricky saw his moment to catch to David for a private word. He put his arm around the party boy and gave him a shameless, lingering peck on the cheek.

"Wow, Ricky. That is some greeting".

"You, mate, are the best", said Ricky. "You changed my life, you cunning devil. Not just the way you got Alex and me back together but how you got me back into life again when I came into the apartment. I was at such a low point then. I will always love my pal David. And now I am so happy for you, mate. Congratulations. You and Sophie are top drawer".

As the two men returned to the bar, they spotted Gerry at far end, all over Samantha like a rash, in the boisterous company of Bonnie and Adya, who had her new adoring boyfriend close by her side. David and Ricky huddled themselves around George, who sat imperially on his stool. It was like the good old times were back.

"It was a cracking idea coming back here to the Wellington, don't you think, George? It is such a special place. This is fabulous", said David, before raising his glass in turn to his friends. "And I can't thank Chris and Gerry enough. Just look at them. They really are in their element, surrounded by a coterie of gorgeous creatures. Have you seen Gerry and Samantha at the end of the bar? They really should get a room. And look at Chris out there. He looks like he is having his own Christmas office party. This is incredible. What a great start to my wedding. Brilliant. Here's cheers to you, George. You have been at the centre of all the unbelievable things that have happened in the past six months. You are such a good sport and I'll never be able to thank you enough".

George grinned warmly, but David was able to spot a hint of loneliness behind his smile.

"Never forget, the best is yet to come, George. Keep your spirits up, dear friend. And here's to you too, Ricky. And Alex, of course. Where is he, by the way?"

"He'll be along later", replied Ricky. "He got the night off his show just so he could have his second date with you. I'm watching you, you crafty old Lothario".

"As much as I like Alex, I hereby officially give up the fight. Ricky, he's all yours. I could never compete with you anyway".

The music had now stepped up a beat and all the youngsters, especially Gerry's gang and Chris' office crowd, were dancing away feverishly. Suddenly, the doors flew open and in stepped two stunning figures, a striking, swarthy, extremely handsome

Latin man in an immaculate suit, with a ravishing goddess, adorned like a diva, on his arm. They strode radiantly up to the bar. George's face was thunderstruck.

"Georgie, darling. How lovely to see you". It was Kate. "Ricky asked me along. I hope you don't mind. You didn't know I knew him, did you. I had a date with him once. It's a long story. Darling, you look wonderful. This is Antonio. He is from Argentina. Antonio, darling, meet George, one of the most special people on this planet".

Antonio reached out and firmly shook George's quivering hand. The Englishman was so taken aback that he could hardly utter a sound.

"Nice to meet you, Antonio. Kate, this is such a surprise. How lovely to see you". George stood up off his stool. "Let me get you all a drink".

"That's George for you. Always the gentleman", commented Ricky. "Mine's a pint".

Once George had regained his composure, his conversation with Kate flowed effortlessly. He realised as he relaxed that his own confidence had been boosted by the presence of Angela in his life and he suddenly wished she was there by his side. At the same time, Chris started chatting to Antonio, asking all about Argentina and what he did for a living. On hearing the word 'polo' through the music, he wrongly assumed that the Argentinian was referring to the men's shirts.

"So, you're in the rag trade. That's great. I really like their shirts. I get them in the sale. They're really good. I've still got a couple but they're a bit ropey nowadays", said Chris, only to have it explained to him by the sophisticated Antonio, the son of a Buenos Aires' multi-millionaire, that he actually rode horses and did not work in a men's clothing store. David then joined in, saving Chris from further faux pas, and, as the room throbbed, the laughter rose from around George's seat, just like it had in the old days.

No-one had noticed that Ricky and Bonnie had quietly disappeared, that was until a loud voice bellowed over the sound system.

"Good evening, you lot. Welcome to the Wellington. I am Ricky and we are Street Fire. We are here to give our old mate

David the biggest send-off so let's get the party started. Let's go". With that, he burst straight into Johnny Be Goode. Everyone started dancing in a frenzy, with the exception, predictably, of David and George, who remained in a fixed state of dignity. A couple of girls, clearly following Gerry's instructions, then dragged David off by both arms and forced him into some bone-twisting rock 'n' roll contortions. He was still there three numbers later. At the same time, while Antonio danced stylishly with a starry-eyed young girl, Kate returned to George.

"Are you OK, darling? You look well. Muy contento. Is life being good to you, darling?'.

"Oh, Kate. You are exceptional. Yes, life is being very good to me. I cannot tell you about it but something special has happened and I am very happy. And it is good to see you happy too. Antonio looks very nice".

"He is so precioso, darling. I adore him. But you know I shall always have mucho amor for you, Georgie. But perhaps you have found a little amor yourself, George, you naughty boy?", Kate said with a mischievous chuckle.

"Kate. You are so funny. You will always be so special to me. Now go dance with your knight in shining armour before he rides off into the sunset with some young floozy".

"I shall never let him do that. He is too 'especial'. Take care, George. Tony and I are not staying long. Ricky suggested we pop in and how could I say no. I wanted to see you and wish you well. Adios, Georgie. Thanks for the good times. Stay happy".

With that, she eased herself into the dancing mass, took her man's hand and slipped out as gracefully as she had entered. George thought for a minute, grinned and signalled out to David to join him once more.

"I think it's called closure, David. That's it. Kate has just walked out of my life and become a treasured part of my past. My new life starts for real right here, right now".

David looked at his friend. "Does this mean you can tell everyone about you and Angela? Come on, Geroge, it's time. Let's get this out of the way".

George stepped up off his stool and took David's arm.

"No, not just yet David. I can't do that yet. But saying goodbye to Kate has cleared my head. I am on my way but I have to move forward in my own time. I'd love to come along to the wedding with Angela but the situation with Chris is so complicated. I don't want anything to ruin your big day. Please, I have to do this my own way".

"I understand, George. I really do", said David, comforting his friend.

At that precise moment, Ricky started another announcement.

"Ladies and gentlemen, as a special treat, will you welcome onstage two incredible singers, our very own Two Degrees".

With that, the band started and two dazzling divas in dark wigs and shimmering full-length gowns stepped up and broke straight into the Crystals' hit, 'Going to the chapel and we're gonna to get married'.

Chris sidled up to David and George.

"Look at these two crackers", he said loudly. "Which one do you fancy, Dave?".

As David looked at the two illuminated singers, the penny dropped. It was Bonnie and, amazingly, his Sophie.

"Bloody hell. What the... B-b-but she's at Mosimann's".

"Ha.! Ha! Got you back properly this time, David, my old chum", gloated Chris.

The three flatmates stood in stunned adoration. Sophie and Bonnie had practised so hard and were word and move perfect in their routine. After the cheers had died down, they went into 'My Guy', pointing straight at the bar to identify their men, which made David and Chris swell up with pride as heads turned to look at them. At the end of the song, the girls stayed rooted to the stage as they soaked up the shouts of 'More! More!'.

"Hey", announced Ricky, "shouldn't there be three degrees. Hang on. We are missing a degree. Worry not, here he comes. Ladies and gentlemen, please give a big hand for The THREE degrees".

With that, Alex appeared, looking majestically Motown in a silver lame suit and shiny black patent shoes. He stood tall between the two girls as they sang Lionel Richie's 'All Night Long' to the roar of the audience, all the time with Alex gyrating his lithe body to the acclamation of the crowd. The performance brought the whole night to a climax and, after Ricky eventually handed back over to the deejay, everyone headed for the bar.

David was stupefied by the whole event. He shook his head in disbelief before setting about mercilessly chastising Chris, who was positively vainglorious is his successful masterstroke of surprise and deception. It had been his idea to get Bonnie and Sophie to sing. Alex had put himself forward as the Third Degree just a few days before, after being pushed by Ricky to join in the fun.

As the stag night drank and danced it way into the early hours, David and Sophie decided to make a discreet exit, quietly saying goodbye to their friends one by one, leaving them totally absorbed in the haze of the revelry. As they walked out into the winter air, David prepared his arm to hail a cab. Sophie grabbed it and pulled him to her side.

"No, David. Let's walk".

As they crossed Blackfriars Bridge, the glowing moon glistened on the still water of the River Thames.

"Have I told you I love you, tonight?", said David.

"No", replied Sophie.

"I love you tonight".

They stopped halfway across the bridge, pulled one another together and kissed. They then continued to walk slowly along the empty pavement, arm in arm, with the moon for light and their silence for company.

On arriving back at the apartment, David turned to his bride-to-be as he put the key in the door.

"Now, young lady, that's the hard work done. You and I have another job to do. Let's go get married".

CHAPTER FOURTEEN
THE AZURE PALACE

THURSDAY, DECEMBER 19

"Welcome to the Azure Palace, Mr Nugent and Ms Cavendish. And a special congratulations on your upcoming wedding. Congratulations to you both. And you two must be Miss Jess and Master Robbie. I am very happy that you will be staying with us. Your rooms are ready for you and we hope you will all enjoy your stay with us in English Harbour". The children grinned with self-importance.

Joseph, the smart, imposing reception manager with a golden West Indian accent, had stepped out from behind his long counter in the stylish, open lobby as he greeted his latest guests. David and Sophie smiled a tired smile back, drained from their long transatlantic journey, yet enlivened by the prospect of ten days of sheer indulgence in the luxury of this lavish hotel.

Arriving in Antigua, they had miraculously stepped into a sunnier clime, a far cry from the dull and damp London weather that they had left behind in the vapour-trail of their plane. Their dour journey from the apartment to Heathrow in the back of a black cab had only served to heighten the anticipation of being magically transported to this summery paradise. By complete contrast, once they had all arrived at V.C. Bird International Airport, a limousine had whisked them smoothly away for the 40-minute drive to their fabulous beach hotel. David had planned it all with precision. This was going to be special. It was time for a splurge. Everything was good in David's world. Here, he was in paradise with the woman he adored and with his much-loved children at his side.

The greeting from the warm, Caribbean sun had instantly embraced them like a warm blanket. They had chosen well. From the moment you walked in, the Azure Palace had that stamp of relaxed class about it, a refreshing change from the soulless foyers of many big European hotels that they had often been to on business over the years. They had stepped into a world of palm trees, blue skies and white sand. The children were fascinated by the centrepiece of flowers in the lobby, an extravagance of exotic blooms, a cornucopia of colour, from shiny red anthuriums to the beak-like heads of the regal birds of paradise that protruded out of the centre. They had never seen anything like it. Within seconds, a tropically dressed young lady presented them with a tray bearing mimosas in tall champagne glasses and fruit cocktails for the children, while another offered lukewarm face towels to wipe away the fatigue from their weary brows. Two uniformed porters discreetly took their bags away on a brass trolley. Above their heads, fans turned silently at an unhurried pace, while the mannerly receptionist efficiently produced their key cards from under his desk. At that point, yet another elegant girl sidled up to them, to be directed by Joseph to show the guests to their rooms. With a gracile extension of her arm, she guided the joyous new arrivals through the hotel, around the expansive pool and along a wide path that ran parallel to the edge of a pristine beach. The children's heads were spinning as they took in the exotic scene around them, while, all the time, David squeezed Sophie's hand as all the cares and worries of the past few weeks instantly vapourised into the warm Caribbean breeze.

Their accommodation for the next ten days, comprising two interconnecting rooms, was set in a discreet row of ground floor suites, which sat on a beautifully manicured greensward, a stone's throw away from the warm cerulean water. Each suite was treated to its own private patio, with bright red bougainvillea adorning the white walls. Sophie mentioned that it felt more like they were on a Greek island. They immediately saw themselves drinking their leisurely cocktails outside their room, while looking out over the benign blue sea which stretched to the horizon where it seamlessly joined the cloudless sky. Ten long days and nights of doing nothing lay ahead of them and they could not be more elated. There was one thing that needed their attention, however. They had to deal with the small matter of organising a wedding.

It had been only a matter of weeks since David had proposed to Sophie on their Thames Tower balcony. They had then come up with all manner of tantalising ideas on where to get married, such as the Kensington Roof Garden, the Royal Pavilion in Brighton and that picture-book little church in Rye. But here they were in Antigua, waiting for their friends to arrive for what was going to be a spectacular party in the sun. Their guests from London were equally excited as they prepared to leave the London drizzle for the delights of the Caribbean.

Bonnie had been busy buying new clothes for the trip. Luckily, there was a break in rehearsals over Christmas and Chris had somehow managed to persuade Jill to agree to him bunking off work over the Yuletide. He was only released, however, with a stern reminder that the newspaper business does not stop for things as trivial as the festive season and weddings and that next year he would not be so lucky.

Ricky and Alex could not turn down David's his generous offer, although Ricky had to be back for a big gig at the Blue Bell on New Year's Eve. Alex managed to hide his anxieties about returning to his homeland.

The less adventurous George was still prevaricating over coming. David just could not get him to commit. He knew that he was keen, but he had said that he would not come without Angela and that he was not at all sure that she would want to come. They still had not told Chris about the relationship and both were worried about what his reaction would be.

David had done all the planning for his flatmates' trip with detailed planning, booking the flights and the Azure Palace for them and their guests, except for George who was still humming and hawing, in spite of David's repeated insistence.

But that was not what was in the happy couples' minds as they were shown into their suite. The children burst past them and they went straight through to their very own room and, predictably, immediately bounced onto their beds as on a trampoline. David and Sophie collapsed onto their bed for a minute, hand in hand, exhausted, before Sophie bounced up and started the unenviable task of unpacking everyone's clothes and putting them into the appropriate cupboards.

Suddenly, the children burst in, jumping uncontrollably up and down around the comatose father.

"Can we go into the sea, Daddy?", cried Jess.

"Please, Daddy. Please. Can we?", added Robbie.

Sophie looked at David. "Well, Daddy. You can hardly say no, can you?".

David sighed and flashed Sophie a tired look before getting up and giving the children a big hug. It was their special holiday too, he reminded himself.

"Come on then. Let's do it. Sophie, could you kindly get the swimming costumes out. We have a date with the Caribbean".

Sophie, who had packed meticulously, immediately went to the swimwear in the case and passed the costumes round. She had bought new ones for everyone.

"Here. Put these on. I bought them specially for you. This is your new bikini, Jess, and these are your trunks, Robbie. Now go into your room and pop them on".

"Thank you, Sophie. I love it", squealed Jess.

"Now, you guys go and enjoy yourselves and I shall finish the unpacking. I'll be along in a minute and then Daddy can get me a cocktail. Isn't that right, Daddy?"

"Absolutely. You are an angel. Come on guys, let's get ready". The children went back into their room and slipped into their costumes. "Thanks, Sophie".

"What for, David?", asked Sophie

"Just for being you. I cannot believe we are here. And, in a few days, we shall be married. What did I do in an earlier life to deserve you? I could not be happier", and he took her in his arms and kissed her. It was not long before their lingering embrace was interrupted by two eager children grabbing his legs.

"Come on, Daddy. Get changed. Let's go to the sea", said Jess in her stylish new bikini.

He put on his swimming trunks in the bathroom, took the children's hands and set off for the gentle waves.

While they were gone, Sophie did all the unpacking, starting with the grown-ups' cases. She had been keen to be left alone as she had to pull out the neatly wrapped Christmas presents to hide them, the larger ones in their wardrobe and the smaller ones at the back of drawers. Then she went into the children's room and saw to their cases.

After a playful hour in the water, a drink by the pool and an early dinner on in the veranda restaurant, they all crashed heavily into their beds and sank into a deep, travel-weary sleep.

FRIDAY, DECEMBER 20

After emerging from their room at around 10am, David and Sophie headed straight for a leisurely buffet breakfast with Jess and Robbie. There, waiting for them, was the best possible start to any day. The serving table, overladen with bacon, sausages, fried bread and the other English essential elements, was a spread of pure heaven to David and the children and to attack their piled-high plates in the Caribbean sunshine was an exceptional joy indeed. Sophie selected a far more modest and responsible diet of cereals and fruit.

The hotel boasted a wonderful Children's Club and he had booked them in for the course of the stay, fully prepared to change plans if they did not enjoy it. At the end of breakfast, a lovely young Antiguan girl came over and introduced herself to Jess and Robbie as Mia, the Club 'Captain'. She and the children immediately hit it off and they went off together with barely a goodbye.

The bridal pair had a lot to do that day and wanted to be refreshed before the meeting with the wedding planner. They had spoken to her on the phone but knew there was still much to organise once at the hotel. They arranged to meet in the foyer, where she came over and shook their hands courteously, with a broad smile. Sophie immediately took to her. Her name was Gabrielle, 'like the angel', she had joked on the phone. That was entirely appropriate as David had put to her that he wanted Christmas Day for the ceremony, something unheard of in Antigua, or anywhere else for that matter. But David knew that, until a hundred years ago, Christmas Day weddings were very much the thing and Sophie loved the idea of being different and having one superlative day of celebration. When she raised the date with the hotel management, the staff could not believe it. 'Only the British', someone had said. However, although they warned that would cost a bit more, they said it could be done and David did not care about any extra expense. Above all else, he liked the theatre of it all, added to the fact that he could never forget the date of his anniversary thereafter.

The couple walked down to the beach with Gabrielle to inspect the white trellised wedding venue, already bedecked in flowers for another wedding later that day. In spite of their ambitious request that it be draped in traditional holly and ivy proving impossible, it looked idyllic as it was and they could instantly envisage their perfect wedding on the white sand, against the backdrop of the lapping waters of the azure sea.

Next, they went to the outside dining room to talk about the catering. It had been agreed that they would host a pre-wedding dinner for their guests the night before. They selected the large table with the best view over the ocean. David had already booked a traditional English menu with roast turkey and all the trimmings for the wedding breakfast ceremony at the same table, including the obligatory crackers and Christmas pudding. It was uncomplicated as there would be only a few guests, after all. They had wanted to keep it small. Chris and Bonnie were definitely coming, as were Ricky and Alex. There was still a slim chance that George and Angela would miraculously appear, but that was still uncertain. Sophie's parents were sadly unable to make it. Her mother had been ill and was now very frail. She and David had therefore had a celebratory dinner with her before they left, where the kindly lady had shown a generous and genuine delight at the union and given them her blessing.

After agreeing on the food and drinks menu, Gabrielle took them downtown to sort out the legalities for the licence and sign the necessary marital papers. She then left them, saying that she had to get back to the hotel, so David and Sophie took the opportunity to grab an early lunchtime snack at a local bar.

Suddenly, David looked up at Sophie.

"Darling, there's one thing I have to do. I would like you to come with me. Trust me. I know it sounds mysterious, but all will be revealed. Is that OK?". She looked suitably perplexed but complied without question.

When they returned to the hotel a couple of hours later, they were able to find time for themselves before the children returned from Children's Club and took a glass of wine back to their patio.

"Well, how do you feel?", David asked as they looked out over the beach. "Are you sure you are doing the right thing? No second thoughts?".

"Second thoughts? Mm, let me think." She paused for thought. "Well, actually, yes, I think I do in a way", David's spirits sank. "Let me put it this way", Sophie continued. "My first thoughts are that I am the luckiest, happiest girl in the world and being here is paradise. And my second thoughts are that I just could not love you more than I do today and all I want to do is make you happy for the rest of your life. How's that for second thoughts?".

David was left speechless and simply went over and kissed her.

"Shall we go inside and have a little siesta?", he suggested.

"Those were my third thoughts, exactly", said Sophie.

An hour passed before there was a knock on the door. It was Mia and the children, who were clutching colourful paintings. Jess and Robbie were beside themselves with excitement.

"Daddy", Jess squealed, "we had such a great time. We've made lots of friends and tomorrow we are going to play on the beach and there's a lady coming to show us how to make animals out of leaves".

"And Daddy", Robbie continued, handing him their pictures "we've painted these for you and Sophie".

"And Daddy". Jess took over again. "Do you mind if we don't have dinner with you and Sophie. Mia says we can have dinner with our friends and watch the... what are they called, Mia?".

"The steel band, Jess. Remember what I told you? Tell your Daddy".

"Oh, yes", stuttered Jess. "There's a steel band and, Daddy, they play on old oil drums. And afterwards there's a Disney film. Can we? Is that OK, Daddy?".

"Of course, darling. This is your holiday". David then looked at Mia. "Thank you, Mia. You're doing a wonderful job. Brilliant. Thank you very much".

"My pleasure, Mr Nugent. Your children are adorable. We are going to have a lot of fun. And Robbie has made friends with a boy from Paris and Jess gets on well with a lovely girl from Italy. I think they are going to love it here". She turned to the children. "Now I suggest you two have a little nap. We want you to be wide awake for tonight, don't we". With that she patted the children on the head and left. "See you later, Jess, and you too Robbie. Six o'clock remember. In the Clubhouse".

As the children ran into their room and lay on their beds, Sophie looked lovingly at David. "Isn't it nice to see them so happy. They seem to have completely forgotten about the accident. Well, it looks like dinner for two tonight. Fancy a date night, Mr Nugent?".

"That sounds wonderful, Miss Cavendish. It's funny but this could be the last time I shall have a date alone with Miss Cavendish. In a couple of days, my dates will be with a certain Mrs Nugent".

"They might just get better, Mr Nugent. You will be dating a married woman after all. Now, I must settle the children down for a short nap or they won't get through the evening."

"I'll do that, Sophie".

"No, do you mind if I do? It is so special for me".

"Carry on, Miss Cavendish. I am at your command". David then fell back onto the bed and resumed his siesta.

SUNDAY, DECEMBER 22

The next couple of days had been spent sunbathing on the beach, swimming in the sea and spending as much time as possible eating, drinking and sleeping. They had established a later afternoon routine, swimming up to the pool bar for a cocktail at 5pm, climbing astride their stool seats which lay just below the water level and ordering their Tequila Sunrises. Today was no exception.

Jess and Robbie could not be kept away from the Children's Club. They loved every minute and sprung out of bed early each morning, dressed themselves in a rush and were ready to go in no time.

David and Sophie dined 'al fresco' each night in the casual Italian restaurant, under a spider's web of patio lights with a classical Spanish guitarist plucking away merrily in the background. They had talked a great deal about the wedding, discussing who, if anyone, would make speeches, before deciding that oratory seemed unnecessary with so few guests. They could just talk among themselves. But, mostly, they took a long look back over the dramatic events of the past year, especially the accident, recognising how precious their new life together was and how important the children were to both of them.

As they talked, half submerged, at the pool bar, a couple came up and sat alongside them, unnoticed. David and Sophie were absorbed in their chat, sipping their drinks through ornate straws, giving each other undivided attention. David, with his back to the other couple, suddenly heard a man's loud voice.

"And then there was bloke, some posh City drop-out, who ran off to the Caribbean with his bloody gorgeous divorce lawyer. We never saw them again".

That immediately got David's attention. He swung round, only to see Ricky and Alex grinning on the adjacent stools, looking right at him. "Good afternoon, Mr and Mrs Nugent, Well, almost", Ricky joked.

David fell over backwards into the water, in mock surprise, taking what was left of his cocktail with him.

"You bastards", he yelled in his public school accent as he came up to the surface, followed by an apologetic "excuse the language, Sophie." As he emerged with his mouth, and his glass, full of pool water, he spat out, "I'll get you back for that, Ricky." He then gave each of them a soaking wet hug before clambering back onto his stool and ordering a round of drinks. Sophie retained her composed dignity throughout the whole proceedings.

Ricky spoke. "Hi, Sophie. You look so, well, svelte and gorgeous. I'll be honest, after all those lunches and dinners with David, I had expected to see with, well, a fat lass". The gauche Ricky was trying to be funny but missed the target. Alex gave him a disapproving glare. Sophie returned a confused look.

"I'm sorry, Ricky? I don't understand?", the refined Sophie replied, remaining unfazed. "I would have fattened myself up just to meet you if I'd known". David put a protective arm around her.

"Ricky's only having a laugh. It's a bit of an in-joke", he whispered in her ear.

"No offence meant, Sophie. It's bloody good to see you and you look gorgeous", Ricky said awkwardly, holding out his hand. She took it and he kissed her on the cheek graciously.

"So, having fun are we, you two lovebirds?", said Ricky, "How's your drink? I see you prefer your tequila with water these days, David? Thanks for arranging all this, mate. It's fabulous here. This is an amazing hotel. It's horrible back in London. Rain and cold".

"We couldn't wait to leave London. The weather's been awful", added the ebony skinned Alex.

"No, it's not bad here, is it. Shame you had to come with this idiot though, Alex", David jested.

All of sudden two other wet creatures emerged from the depths.

"Oh, no, looks who's just turned up. It's bloody love unlimited", Ricky announced.

Chris and Bonnie then swished out of the water to claim the other two seats by the bar.

"Hi, guys", beamed Chris. "Fancy seeing you. Who do you have to sleep with to get a drink round here?".

"Here's trouble", replied David. "Hey, welcome you guys. Terrific to see you. I'll get those drinks. How was the flight?".

"It was good actually. I hate flying normally", piped up Chris. "But the pilot came on the PA and he had a posh voice and said his name was Nigel so I knew we were OK".

"It was lovely, thank you, David", said Bonnie. "The boys almost behaved well, except for Ricky getting the whole plane to sing 'Desmond Has A Barrow In The Marketplace'".

"... Molly Is A Singer In The Band", added Ricky in full voice.

They laughed and chatted away, catching up on the latest news, such as it was. Ricky bought a round, then Chris bought another and, in no time, they were all completely chilled. Alex then asked who else would be at the wedding. Sophie explained that it was going to be a small affair and that basically the whole congregation was sitting the bar.

"Is George coming?", Ricky asked casually.

"Not sure. I think he might. He seemed a bit reluctant when we left", Chris replied.

"My guess is that he's probably worried about bringing Angela," the rock star blurted out. "How are you with that, Chris?". There was a deathly silence. The air went heavy. Chris looked puzzled. Ricky repeated the question.

"Are you OK with him bringing Angela, mate? It must feel a bit funny?". Ricky then saw the surprise on Chris' face, at the same time as he felt Alex's sharp kick on his ankle. Bonnie sat bemused. This was news for her too. Chris turned to Ricky.

"Are you serious? What the hell... Oh, my God". The penny dropped and Chris started gabbling. "Are you seriously saying that George and Angela...an item? Bloody hell. Really? I can't believe it. Yes. Now it all makes sense. Ever since that date he has been behaving really weirdly, even for George. That's, er, that's amazing, very weird, but amazing. That George, eh. There's no stopping him. So that's where he has been going, the cunning devil. He never said a word. One trip to the National Gallery and whoosh. Artful little bugger, our George. Wow, I need a minute to take this in". He slurped on his drink.

Ricky looked apologetic. "Sorry, mate. I thought you knew. I only found out because I overheard George on the phone. He has been seeing her for ages, I reckon. All that stuff about seeing friends and it was Angela all the time, ever since that first date. I think he has really fallen for her".

Alex stepped in. "Ricky, you are so clumsy. You never could keep a secret. You have such a big mouth". Ricky looked suitable chastised.

Chris reassured his friends. "No, no, it's fine. Shit, I hope George hasn't decided not to come because of me. That would be awful. I hope not. No, I am delighted for both of them, for him and for Angela. It's fantastic when you think about it. George and Angela. I used to joke to him that they'd make a good couple. Now they can bore each other to death talking endlessly about the books, opera and the bloody Mona Lisa".

"Well, it looks as if they won't be here for the wedding anyway. It's a shame but there you go", said David disappointedly. "Can't be helped".

A hushed awkwardness descended over the six. Bonnie took hold of Chris' hand to settle him down, softly comforting him as he came to terms with the latest surprise development in his crazy Project EX. But Chris was never down for long and, in no time, it was back to the boozy, nonsensical banter, with Chris taking every opportunity to have a friendly joke at George's and Angela's expense. Bonnie, ever the emotional logician of the pair, whispered something lengthy into Chris' ear. Having taken in what she had said, he staggered up without a word, waded through the water, wobbled across the deck and disappeared.

"Where's he gone now?', enquired Ricky. "I haven't upset him again, have I? He's a sensitive little flower that Chris.".

"No, not at all. There's just something I've told him he has to do", Bonnie reassured him.

Twenty minutes later, Chris bounced back noisily to make a loud proclamation to David and Sophie in the guise of a tipsy town crier. He pretended to ring a handbell.

"Ding! Ding! Hear ye! Hear ye! Listen up, bride and groom. I am pleased to announce that The Honourable, Sir George Granby and Her Right Royal Excellency, The Princess Angela, are coming to Antigua for a wedding. Not theirs, I don't think. Yours". Ricky and Alex let out a cheer. Chris went on with his speech. "I have just spoken to George, told him I know all about his disgusting, filthy goings-on with my ex-wife and have given the happy couple my gracious blessing. He seemed bloody relieved to be honest. So, he is now busy talking to Angela, checking flight schedules for tomorrow and I bet he is online as we speak, trying to book flights for them both. Actually, I think it is really, really great, and I told him so. A few times. I love old Gorgeous George and Angela is basically a very nice person. Anyway, she'd be better off with an older, more boring man. Don't you think so, Bonnie?".

"That's not very nice, Chris, but, yes, I do think it's great. Honestly, I do. And thanks for ringing him. Now, come and sit down before you fall down". Bonnie, whilst worried about Chris' inebriated state, was naturally pleased to see Angela out of the frame and more than happy to encourage the relationship.

"Yes. Bloody good show, mate", said Ricky to Chris. "You took this really well. Sorry I opened my big mouth".

"Well done, Chris. It takes the bigger man", Alex added.

"Hey, David", interrupted Ricky rudely, changing the subject. "What have you done with my superfans? I hope you haven't bloody sold them. I need all the fans I can get".

"They're having a brilliant time, Ricky", explained David. "They love the Children's Club here. We can't keep them out of it".

"That's superb. I'll have to get my guitar out and sing for the kids one day".

"That", said Sophie, "would be wonderful of you, Ricky. They'd love that".

Chris, by now, was well over the surprise, feeling proud of himself for coming to grips with the situation and he celebrated by shouting 'more drinks' to the barman. The rest of the late afternoon slid away into a haze, with all of them crashing out back in their rooms, unconscious to most things, most notably to the fact that George had already booked his flights and was scheduled to arrive in Antigua for Christmas Eve.

TUESDAY, DECEMBER 24

Monday had understandably been a recovery day after their Sunday night antics. The hungover adults collapsed on their sunbeds, taking everything very, very slowly, recharging their batteries before what looked like being an electrifying Christmas Day. The children were well and happily immersed in their Club, making tie-dye T-shirts and learning calypsos as Mia strummed her guitar. The hotel had well and truly swung into the festive mood. They had made every effort to make their guests feel the seasonal comfort and joy. A huge artificial tree, bedecked in hundreds of lights and decorations, set the theme in the lobby and there were garlands of colourful bunting and streamers throughout the restaurants and bars. David and Sophie had successfully spent the day away from the bar, saving their energy for the pre-wedding dinner with their guests later that night.

After a day lazing around in the sun on the beach, Ricky and Alex were busy preparing for the festivities to start. By four o'clock, they were back on their patio, sipping a relaxed cup of tea and nibbling on digestive biscuits. Suddenly, Alex looked up, only to spot David, Sophie and a lissom West Indian girl heading towards him down the path. As they got closer, he recognised, to his complete surprise, that it was Tianna, his sister. He sprung up and strode out towards her, his arms outstretched in a familial greeting. Her pace quickened as she rushed into his brotherly arms. To see this affection between the two siblings was to witness the reunion of two people who clearly had a deep love for one another but who had been forced apart for too long. Tianna held on to him tightly as they walked back to the patio. They had not seen one another for so many years, yet the bond instantly returned to the same unbreakable strength that it had had when they were growing up as children.

"We'll leave you guys to it. Tianna will explain everything", David said as he led Sophie off to their own patio.

"Oh my God. This is amazing. Tianna, you're actually here. Hey, this is Ricky. Ricky, meet Tianna, my lovely, special sister". She took a second to take in Ricky's rock appearance, his long hair, his confident manner and his infectious grin.

"Lovely to meet you at last, Ricky. Thanks for helping David track me down. It got me here to see my brother again", she said, reaching out for him to shake her hand.

"Oh. Come here, sis". He replied, pulling her into a friendly bear hug.

The first thing that everyone noticed about Tianna was her wonderfully clear shimmer of youth. Her enticing smile drew you in and captivated you. Her eyes glistened with a soft kindness and honesty, while her fresh, faultless skin gave her a glow of good health. She had straightened her dark hair and looked for every inch a catwalk model, complemented with an approachable, girl-next-door warmth. In a silk floral top with a matching full-length skirt, she eased her spry figure down next to her handsome brother. No-one could mistake the fact that they were brother and sister.

First, she explained how this had all come about.

"I got a call completely out of the blue from David, who I had never heard of. He said that you, Ricky, had somehow got my number and set the whole thing up. Then David and Sophie, who are lovely by the way, came to see me on Friday and we had a long chat. And, well, here I am". Alex leaned back in amazement at this web of intrigue.

She then brought her brother up to date with all the family news and it was not long before their parents became the topic of conversation. Alex expressed his concern about his mother and asked how she was. He still had a heartfelt love for her, but he had always been frustrated by her preference to stay in the background as the dutiful wife, never saying boo to a goose. Her lack of strength had caused great hurt to Alex, who had tried again and again throughout his teens to reach out to her about the complexity of his sexuality. His appeals for understanding had fallen on deaf ears. His Mama seemed completely unable to summon the courage to challenge her strong husband's views on anything. Alex could never forget that day he broke down and sobbed like a baby in front of her, remembering clearly her distant coldness as she held his head, saying nothing. That moment was indelibly etched onto his memory. She would never get involved, hating rows of any kind, and, throughout the forty years of her loyal marriage, she had avoided arguments with her husband by completely surrendering her own identity and capitulating to his prejudices, without necessarily agreeing with them. She might have appeared on the outside the exemplary wife, loyal, unquestioning and hard-working, but she had not been, in Alex's eyes, the kind of mother she should have been. Yes, she had done her job. She had fed, bathed and clothed them as children, but that special, soft maternal love had never broken the surface. Yet, he could find no anger for her. That he reserved for his father, whom he blamed exclusively. As he and Tianna began to explore the deep resentments that had arisen out of their intolerant upbringing, Tianna managed to reach into Alex's heart as only a close sister could and he was heeding every word she spoke with concentration and respect.

"Alex, Daddy is getting old. I know that he regrets losing you. He misses having a son around. I know that. He is still so stubborn though. He is such a proud man. He just cannot make himself drop his guard. I have begged him to contact you, countless times over the years. He just won't budge. Or can't more like. You hear of families getting stuck in these situations, and that is exactly what has happened. He is as stubborn as an old mule".

"I just wasn't the son he wanted, I know that", Alex said sadly.

"Like father, like son", Ricky chipped in. Alex looked up at him.

"What? What do you mean by that?", Alex snapped at Ricky.

"You know exactly what I mean", he said. "Tianna, your brother seems to have some of same traits as his Dad, I reckon, just the same. He showed a similar stubborn streak when we broke up and he would never have rung me afterwards, that was until I came up with my little ruse. Alex, you two really need your heads knocking together. If you have learned anything from the past few months, it must be that life is too short for all this. You and your Dad are fighting your own stubbornness as much as each other. You two sound like peas in a pod".

Alex did not take kindly to the reprimand. Nevertheless, he still pondered on what both of them had said, especially the words of his sister, who had always been on his side, albeit powerless, throughout those bad teenage days when he was so alone.

"I don't know if I can ever forgive him. I'm sorry, Tianna. I know you want me to try. It is just that he made my life hell. I should have been happy, gone to college and made my way in life with my family around me. He ruined all that. He just cast me aside. It is too much to forgive. I just can't".

"Well, I tried", Tianna sighed. "Just as I have been trying all my life. And I will continue to try. Hey, listen, darling brother. You could always do it for me. Think about it".

That struck home and Alex went quiet. Ricky broke the awkwardness with a question to Tianna about her favourite music, leaving Alex to have a moment of contemplation. The hirsute rocker and Caribbean beauty, an incongruous pair, chatted away affably until Alex suggested that they should start to get ready for their night out.

"You wait here, Tianna, we won't be long. Can I get you a beer, or would you prefer a glass of wine?", Ricky asked.

"A beer would be great. A Wadadli if you have it. Thanks, Ricky. I am so pleased Alex has you to look after him. I guess we have all let him down. I love my brother and it has been so unfair on him. He has had it tough".

"We'll sort this out. Have faith".

"Ricky, faith is something I lost years ago", Tianna lamented. "With a father like mine, you don't have faith, you have obedience. He is quietening down with age though. I guess we should never say never".

"My words exactly", said Ricky. "Now, I'll just go and tell David we have one more for dinner tonight. You will stay for dinner, won't you?", Ricky said, touching her hand. Tianna smiled in affirmation.

Chris and Bonnie were busy getting dressed for the evening. They were also talking about their next stop, Universal Studios in Florida. He had changed their flight home to grab two days on the amusements, especially the Harry Potter ride and The Incredible Hulk Roller Coaster, before flying home from there. Bonnie would rather have spent the time on the beach with the others, but she could not keep Chris from his rides after coming all this way.

He then reminded Bonnie that their two-centre holiday meant that they would have to leave the morning after Christmas, with a midday flight from Antigua to Orlando. He reminded her too that they would have to pack their bags the night before and leave them outside their door last thing on Christmas night for overnight collection. The airline had efficiently arranged a separate transfer for the luggage to the airport.

As they left the room, they were aware that, unusually, they were ready ahead of schedule and they decide to go for a cocktail. As they approached, Chris saw a recognisable rear-view figure. It was the unmistakably shape of his good friend

George, seated at the bar, a shape he had so often seen in the Wellington. He was just about to shout out. Instead, he grabbed Bonnie's arm.

"It's George. He's with Angela", he said in a hushed voice. "Bloody hell. I don't know what to say. This is really awkward. Help me".

"Don't be silly, Chris. Just act naturally. No, better than that, just follow me".

She went straight up to them. "Hi Angela. Hi, George. How was your flight? Welcome to paradise".

Chris followed. He looked at Angela. She looked back at him. George looked at Chris. Chris looked back at George. Chris then broke the silence.

"Bloody hell", said Chris in his unsubtle way. "This is so bloody weird. But, hey, let's have a drink. My round. Georgie, come here, I love you". He threw his arms around his friend. "Hello, Angela, I am very happy for you. I am happy for you both. There, now that's over. Margaritas all round. Great to see you guys".

Bonnie was not best pleased by Chris' graceless reaction and his insincere greeting, quickly stepping in to smooth it all over with her engaging charm. One cocktail later, thanks to the natural balm in her gentle manner, it was as if life had always been like this. George felt free to pull Angela close to him and she was comfortable putting her arm on his shoulder.

After a few minutes, George got up to visit the men's room. Chris followed and, as they stood side by side, facing the wall, George was the first to speak.

"Thanks for being understanding, Chris. You and I have been mates a long time and you know I feel very uncomfortable about this. This sounds pathetic but I want you to know that I really do love Angela. As crazy as it sounds, it just happened. It came as a complete surprise to me. I am sorry it didn't work out between you two, but we just hit it off from that first date. I agree it is totally weird, but I really hope you are OK with it, or will be in time".

"George, of course I am. It was just a bit of a shock, that's all. You know Angela was not happy with me for years and I can see in her face now how different she is. She looks great. And that makes me happy. And you are happy. Angela's happy. We are all bloody happy. I tell you what, when we go back to the bar, why don't I give Angela a happy hug and you give Bonnie a happy hug. How does that sound? Happy hugs all round. Agreed?"

"That'd be great, Chris. It will break the ice and it will help Angela relax no end if you show that you are fine with it all. She has been dreading this".

"Bollocks", said Chris, in his ungallant way. "She has no reason to feel worried or anything. It's all good. Or, as David would say, it's all brilliant".

As they got back to the bar, the plan was executed to their theatrical best, and, even if the girls did realise it was totally contrived, it was appreciated. George came behind Bonnie and puckered a gawky kiss on her cheek, while Chris gave Angela an insincere embrace.

In spite of the lack of sincerity in his gesture, Chris was unusually genuine in his words. "You are very special Angela", he whispered into her ear. "To see you happy again means everything. George is a great guy and you two look made for each other. I can see it a mile away". Angela felt small tears of relief moistening her fluttering eyes, but was determined not to show emotion.

David then appeared, looking every inch the Englishman abroad in his blue blazer, cream slacks and pink shirt, together with Sophie. They both welcomed George and Angela and put them totally at their ease.

Ricky arrived with Alex and Tianna, who proved an enormous hit, with George and Chris almost salivating over her exotic beauty, so much so that Bonnie had to reproach her distracted boyfriend with a 'down boy'. As they gathered back together, the party started in earnest. The reunited friends took over the bar. Suddenly, all their attention was distracted by two shrill voices, shouting in their direction.

"Ricky, Ricky", yelled the high-pitched voices in full bellow. He turned round to see the over-excited Jess and Robbie, having just left the Children's Club, sprinting towards the bar, ignoring everyone else, and hurling themselves at their long-haired friend. David then reminded them of their manners. The children toned down their excitement. "Sorry. Hi, everyone. Oh, hello George. Have you just got here?".

George told her all about his flight and introduced Angela. Introductions over, Jess and Robbie rushed over to Ricky, almost bowling him over.

David made an announcement. "Hey, everyone. Listen up. I just want to say how pleased Sophie and I are that George and Angela could make it and how unbelievably brilliant it is that you are all here. Big day tomorrow and it is just fantastic for us that we have our dearest friends around us. Jess, we are proud of you too, and you have a big job to do. I know you'll be the prettiest bridesmaid ever while also doubling up as Sophie's special maid-of-honour. And this handsome young man will be our page boy. How about that?". Jess beamed. Robbie looked completely embarrassed and gave Ricky's arm another tweak.

As they went back to their drinking, George sidled up to David.

"This is amazing, David. You haven't told me. How on earth did manage to get the children for Christmas?",

"Get me a drink and I'll tell you". George ordered another two margaritas and two non-alcoholic Planter's Punches for the children, while Sophie talked to Angela. David proceeded to tell his pal the story. "Well, it was incredible. A bloody miracle more like. Moira has mellowed so much since the accident and she phoned me and asked if I would like the children over Christmas, just like that. It was at the time Sophie and I were in deep discussion over the wedding, so it all fell into place. I couldn't believe my luck". He then lowered his voice so that the children couldn't hear. "She has a new boyfriend, a proper one this time, which explains everything. A bloke called Gary. He is OK actually, poor blighter. As I have always said, if Moira is happy, we are all happy. So, here we all are". More drinks were handed round. The two then joined their partners and David put his arm around Sophie and raised his glass. "Cheers, everyone. Thanks for coming. Better together, I say. Normal service is resumed". They then proceeded to party like rock stars, all the time with the children clinging onto Ricky, gazing at him is adoration, like the superfans they were. He loved it.

As dusk approached, Tianna, who had been in deep conversation with her brother, stealthily stole him away without anyone noticing. She led him by the hand through the lobby to the softly-lit coffee area. The leather seats were empty apart from one elderly couple. Alex froze. Sitting there on their own were his Mum and Dad. Tianna tugged his arm and then held it tightly to her. His father stood up, tall, formidable, dark and strong. He stretched out his hand. Alex remained rooted to the spot, staring at him directly, expressionless. Tianna gave his arm another squeeze and directed him gently. "Go on, Alex. Do this for me". He looked at her and broke into a slow forward movement. He approached the imposing man tentatively and took his hand. His father promptly pulled Alex into his strong embrace, enveloping him in his arms. Alex complied, rigidly. His father spoke directly to him.

"Son, I have let you down. I have come to apologise. I should have known better. I am so sorry I wasn't a better Dad to you". This was as good an effort as the dispassionate man could muster, and, in spite of its lack of warmth, there was a genuine sense of atonement about his words. "Now, give your Mum a hug. She has missed you. We have all missed you". His elderly mother stood up and she and Alex wrapped themselves around one another, sobbing uncontrollably, the tears washing away so many years of heartache and suffering. Tianna joined Alex and their mother in a family clinch.

His father watched the flow of emotion placidly. "I am proud of you, Alex", he went on. "So proud of you. You went out into the world, alone, and conquered it. You are the real man. What more could a father ask for? We have missed you. Every day. Every single day. Welcome home".

The tears and self-recrimination continued until the hairy rock 'n' roll figure of Ricky came round the corner. Alex was immediately overcome with anxiety about how this would go. He nervously introduced him, watching every move in his father's face, knowing that his sincerity in his search for redemption was about to be seriously tested. To his complete surprise and relief, the older man reached out his hand, without a flinch.

"Good to meet you, Ricky. I am Tarone, Alex's father. I want to thank you for looking after my son for all these years. Tianna has told me all about you. We have a lot to thank you for. Come and meet Alvita, Alex's Mum".

Without further ado, Alex then led his parents into the bar to meet the others. While the flatmates may not have known his family, they were certainly aware of his painful estrangement from his kith and kin. As they witnessed the family coming back together, they wanted to show their delight at the breakthrough and they greeted them all warmly. Bonnie went over to Alvita and started chatting while David and George both shook Tarone by his huge hand and offered him a drink, something he readily accepted. He had, after all, just been made to go through an epiphany on the road to the Azure Palace. In one fell swoop, he had put all his lifelong bigotry behind him. As Tianna had said, he may never really approve, but his acceptance of Alex and Ricky had brought his family back together once more and of that he was pleased and proud.

After a bustle of restaurant staff had busied themselves putting tables together to accommodate the increased number of guests, they all sat down for dinner. The red candles and napkins, together with a red and white floral centrepiece, gave it a colourful, festive appearance. It was Christmas Eve after all. At David's insistence, Alex was positioned at the end, with his father and Ricky on his left, his mother and Tianna on the right. The levity of the early evening had by now understandably settled down to a slightly less boisterous mood. The bride and groom positioned themselves at the centre, with the children opposite and Chris, Bonnie, George and Angela to their right.

The dinner went with a bang, everyone buzzing with the excitement of spending Christmas away from chilly London amongst friends in such a magical, summerlike setting. However, it was not long before tiredness had caught up with the George and Angela, although there was enough time to ask the children what they thought Santa would be bringing them and whether they had told him where they were so that he could bring their presents. Robbie's fears that Santa would drop them off at Mummy's house were allayed by their adept father.

"He will probably leave some there and get Rudolf and his friends to drive him here", he convinced his son. A sceptical Jess said nothing but gave her Dad a meaningful grin.

By 9.30pm, there was general agreement that an early night in readiness for the big day was in order. To face the Christmas celebrations and a wedding rolled into one demanded fresh energy. David and Sophie were the first to leave, taking the exhausted children off to their beds, but only after insisting to Alex's family that they must cancel all their Christmas plans and join them at the wedding. Tarone looked at Alex and said they would be honoured to attend. George and Angela followed soon after. Ricky, Alex, Tarone, Alvita and Tianna remained at the table, locked in deep conversation, as Bonnie nudged Chris to find their privacy and they headed to the barstools for a sambuca, complete with its floating coffee bean and dancing blue flame.

"It will take some time for me to stop thinking of my friend George tucked up in bed with Angela. Do you think they sit up all night reading books?", Chris asked.

"Somehow, dear Chris, I think they may have something more novel to do to amuse themselves", Bonnie joked. Chris just groaned.

"Suddenly, I don't want to think about it a moment longer", he responded with a smirk.

CHRISTMAS DAY IN THE CARIBBEAN

It was entirely foreseeable that Jess and Ricky would be the first to wake up. The door between the two rooms had been left slightly ajar and, as dawn broke, Jess peered through, only to see her father and Sophie lying fast asleep. She softly and silently pushed the door closed, without so much as a click. As she crept back into bed, she spotted two large red stockings laying neatly on the floor at the foot of each bed. With a muffled squeal, she picked them up, checked the labels and handed one to her brother, telling him that Father Christmas had been. Robbie was beside himself. Jess put her finger to her mouth and 'shushed' him, telling him that they must not wake Daddy and Sophie. After excitedly pulling out all manner of small toys and treats, they opened a pack of jelly babies, settled down again, clutching their most prized gift, and turned on the cartoons. However, they were simply unable to contain their bursting excitement and it took less than one episode of Sesame Street before they decided that the grown-ups had slept quite long enough and that it was now the perfect time for them to be woken up. It was Christmas Day after all. So they tiptoed in and, with one synchronised leap, gave them the rudest of rude awakenings by hurling themselves on the sleeping pair.

Sophie, woken on her wedding day with a such a start, somehow managed to maintain her defining kindly countenance. Without fuss, she gave them a hug and went to retrieve the children's presents from their hiding places, but not before she had made two cups of tea and poured two orange juices from the fridge for Santa's overactive elves. David tried to ignore it all but, as the archetypal Englishman, eventually stirred when the cup of tea appeared by his bed and sat up as Sophie lay the gifts on the bed.

The first presents were handed out by Jess and Robbie, huddled on the big bed, next to their bleary-eyed father and to Sophie. David was first to go and unwrapped their gift. It turned out to be a pristine, first-edition copy of his precious The Observer's Book of Birds, bought thoughtfully online by Sophie on behalf of the children. It was accompanied by a prompted comment from Robbie about how his old one was falling apart. Sophie then opened her present, a beautiful turquoise pashmina that Jess and David had bought at the airport in a quiet moment of deceptive shopping. Everyone was delighted. By now, the children were agitating for their presents. David handed Jess her small package and she took the paper off daintily, as Sophie had done, trying not to make a tear in the Christmas wrapping. Inside, she discovered a small, sky-blue box, which she opened like a princess, to reveal a shining Tiffany silver heart tag bracelet, which she excitedly rolled onto her right wrist before throwing her arms around her father's neck in gratitude. Next, it was Robbie's turn. This time, Sophie did the honours. Robbie was over the moon to see that he was getting a much bigger package, deducing that, thankfully, he was not going to get jewellery. He tore the paper off maniacally with both hands to find that he was now the proud owner of a stunning, hi-tech drone. With hardly a thank-you, he immediately asked if could take his new helicopter outside and Sophie got out of bed to open the curtains and to slide open the glass door. They watched with joy as the young boy placed himself on the grass and prepared his aircraft for its maiden flight.

On her way back to bed, Sophie pulled a present from out of her drawer. She had that smile of anticipation on her face, having found what she thought was the perfect present for David. She was then thrilled to see his face light up as he opened the small case, which held a pair of gold and enamel cufflinks bearing his own yellow and blue racing colours.

David then produced Sophie's gift, which she opened unhurriedly after giving him a grateful kiss. It was also another Tiffany treasure, this time an 18-carat white gold and sapphire bracelet, which she immediately slipped on to her wrist, stretching it out and admiring it effusively, all the time watched intently by Jess.

"Now we both have posh bracelets", she said to Sophie, in a moment of bonding.

"I thought you could both wear them to the wedding. They're not quite something old, something new, something borrowed, something blue. But we are half-way there. They are definitely new - and they did come in a blue box".

Further down the row of suites, Chris had woken up and was, predictably, as energised as any little boy at Christmas. Rustling in the cupboard, he brought out two presents that he had wrapped himself, badly. Going over to Bonnie's side of the bed, he sneakily lay them on the floor beside her, before slithering back under the sheets. He kissed her gently, pretending to try not to wake her but, in reality, with the hope that his attentions might bring her back to consciousness. An abrupt tug of the sheets over her head made it clear that she was in no way ready to be wakened. She eventually reappeared from under the covers, eased open one eye, mumbling something about getting ten minutes more sleep, and then turned over. Chris lay back in bed, disappointed at the lack of response, and stared blankly at the spinning fan while emitting the occasional audible sigh of frustration. Bonnie gave in.

"Alright. Happy Christmas, Chris. You are such a child sometimes".

"It's Christmas Day", Chris bubbled enthusiastically, in justification of his pent-up enthusiasm. "Father Christmas has been. Look on the floor by your side". Chris could never keep a surprise for long. Bonnie gave up all hope of having a longer lie-in and sat up. Chris ran round, half-opened the window blinds and handed her the presents, before getting straight back into bed. She tore off the Christmas paper on the first and found a framed, 8" by 10" West Side Story print, actually autographed by Rita Morena and Natalie Wood. He had found it online and paid what he thought was a fortune for it. Bonnie sprung awake, was beyond ecstatic and could not take her eyes off it.

"Do you like it? Do you really like it? It's the West Side Story stars", cried out the frenzied Chris.

"I think I know that, Chris. And I absolutely adore it. Thank you so much. It's fabulous", said Bonnie, before giving him a thank-you kiss.

Bonnie then handed over her beautifully wrapped present for Chris. He kissed her excitedly and wasted no time in tearing the parcel open to reveal his favourite John Varvatos aftershave, plus a smart leather man's bracelet, all wrapped up in a colourful pair of Polo boxer shorts. He slipped the bracelet over his wrist and sprayed himself from the bottle before hurriedly whipping on his smart underpants.

"Wow, now I am completely irresistible to women. Thanks Bonnie. They're great. Happy Christmas, darling. I love you so much", he gushed before kissing her.

As always with Chris, he did not dwell on any one moment. In no time, he impatiently thrusted another gift at her, with an impatient grin.

"Here's another. Open it!". This one, a large Chelsea shirt, received a more muted response, but she feigned elation and kissed him again, before returning to gazing in awe at the signed print. Chris took the Chelsea shirt in his hands.

"Go on, put it on", Chris implored Bonnie, who was fixated on the photo.

"What? Now? Are you serious Chris?", she implored.

"I'd love to see you in it. I know it's a bit big and baggy, but that's how I like them".

Bonnie knew she had little choice other than to indulge him and disappeared into the bathroom to slip the oversized blue shirt over her head. She then ran a brush through her hair and emerged into the fractured sunlight that fought to break through the blinds. Chris sat upright.

"Bloody hell. You look absolutely gorgeous Bonnie. Now, give us a twirl".

She spun round, displaying the big number 9 on the back, above it her name, Carter. "I see it now. You didn't buy it for me at all. You bought it for yourself. You've got weird fantasies, Chris", she said.

He pulled back the bed covers, tapping the bottom sheet to invite back her in. As she nestled into his arms, he whispered in her ear.

"You're right. I have always had this fantasy about scoring in a Chelsea shirt".

Bonnie matched him, line for line. "That is very forward of you, Mr Adams. Stop your dribbling and come here".

George and Angela were early risers by habit and today were sitting peacefully on their veranda in a very English scene, still in their hotel dressing gowns, with a pot of tea, some toast and a jug of orange juice. George had recently reverted to having Darjeeling tea with his breakfast. Their gift-giving had been a much politer affair. George had taken time to babble, typically apologetically, about how it had been hard to pack anything large and that he had meant to buy something else but that he had had no chance to go shopping as they had left in such a hurry. He humbly handed over a beautiful old-fashioned Christmas card with a touching message of everlasting love. Inside, he had included two tickets, front row balcony, for the Royal Ballet's The Sleeping Beauty with Carlos Acosta and Tamara Rojo. That was perfect bliss for Angela. He could not have given her anything better. In return, she presented him an orange box containing a yellow Hermes tie that she said would go nicely with his countless blue shirts. Then, coincidentally like Sophie, she presented him with a small box containing a handsome pair of cufflinks, thoughtfully carrying his initials, something he would come to treasure.

Ricky and Alex decided that this holiday was their gift to one another, no presents, just five unforgettable days in the Caribbean. They had ordered a full English breakfast on their patio under the clear blue sky. As they struggled through their poached eggs, streaky bacon and local sausages, they were enjoying some quiet time alone before the start of the big day ahead. As the wedding was not until 3pm, they had decided to have an easy morning, perhaps going for a walk along the beach before taking a light lunch by the pool. David's plan was that everyone should have their own Christmas morning before getting together at around 2pm in the Tiki Bar for a quick drink, after which they would all progress down to the beach for the ceremony. It was going to be a long day and a long night, so they were very happy to start slowly.

Chris and Bonnie had fallen back to sleep after their exciting and energetic exchange of presents. It was around 11am when they showered, put on some casual beach clothes and colourful flip-flops and set off for a stroll along the beach.
As they walked barefoot on the warm white sand, accompanied only by the sound of the small tumbling waves, Chris saw the wedding arch, already overdressed in white flowers and dark green ivy, and they went over. In front of it, there were just two rows of seats placed correctly on the sand, four on each side of a matted aisle.
Chris led Bonnie, his arm around her shoulder, to the start of the aisle. "I'm dying to have a go at this. Do me a favour, Bonnie. Bear with me. Would you walk down the aisle with me?".
"You are such an idiot. Don't be so silly".
Chris insisted. "No, I want to see how David will feel this afternoon. Come on. Let's do it. Just like Maria and Tony in that dress shop in West Side Story. Please".
She reluctantly consented to his ridiculous piece of childish theatre. Chris took her hand in his and they marched solemnly down the walkway, side by side, to the 'altar', with Chris

humming 'Here Comes The Bride'. He then turned, interlocked their hands and they looked at each other.

The 'bridegroom' cleared his throat and spoke softly to his 'bride'. "Bonnie. I have wanted to walk down the aisle with you for a long time". She thought he was joking and let out a chuckle.

"For God's sake, Chris. We don't have to act out the whole thing, do we?"

He responded by suddenly dropping to one knee and producing a small box out of his pocket. Her eyes widened and she put her hand over her mouth, knowing what was coming next.

"Oh, shit. You're being serious, aren't you".

"Bonnie Carter. You know how much I love you. You know I'll love you forever. Thank you for loving me, for trusting me and for being my best friend". He paused for a second. "Miss Carter, would you do me the honour of walking down the aisle properly, with me by your side, and becoming my wife? To have and to hold and all that?".

He opened the box and she gasped at what she saw. It was the diamond and sapphire art deco ring.

"Oh, Chris. It's the one we saw in Brighton", and she started to cry. "It's just fabulous. You are so clever", she added through the tears.

"But you haven't said 'yes' yet. You don't get the rock until you say 'yes'. It's only yours when I hear that word".

"Yes, yes, yes", she replied determinedly. "Yes, of course I'll marry you. That's all I ever wanted". She pulled him to his feet, threw herself at him and kissed him. He then slipped the ring onto her finger. "I love you, Chris Adams, you crazy man - and I think Bonnie Adams sounds quite nice, don't you? Chris and Bonnie Adams. I love it".

She walked back down the aisle, holding his hand, while all the time extending her left hand out in front of her as she admired the sparkling gems.

There was something different about George these days. The old, serious George had been totally replaced by this new, relaxed man about town. He was carefree and seemed twenty years younger than the morose, brooding company executive who had spent hours holding court on his stool at the Wellington. Clearly, the miraculous transformation had everything to do with Angela. They sauntered along the path towards the hotel closely together to find Chris and Bonnie back on their balcony, with a bottle of champagne on the table. George was carrying a special gift for his friend.

"Morning Bonnie. Morning Chris. Merry Christmas, you two lovebirds". They joined the happy couple, Chris fetching two more glasses from the bathroom and pouring them a nice sip of yuletide champagne. George had a surprise gift for Chris, but it had to wait. His thunder was stolen. Bonnie was pointing her ring finger towards them.

"Look", exclaimed an elated Bonnie, her eyes fixed on the brilliant stones, "Chris has just proposed". She paused as a cold chill ran through her. She looked at Angela, realising that she was in the process of announcing her engagement to his ex-wife. Angela flashed a gracious, approving smile both to Bonnie and then to her former husband, making them all feel instantly at ease. She then raised her glass.

"Chris, Bonnie, I couldn't be happier for the two of you. Congratulations. This is wonderful news. I hope, no, I absolutely know, that you will be very happy together."

George added his congratulations to the elated couple before changing the subject back to the reason for his mission.

"That's all bloody marvellous. Well done, you guys. But before we get carried away, I have bought you a little present, Chris. It seems a bit superfluous now, but I want you to have it anyway", George announced, eager to get the gift into Chris' hands.

"You shouldn't have", Chris said bashfully. "I haven't got you anything".

"That doesn't matter, mate. It was just that I was out shopping the other day at my favourite shop and found something I know you really wanted. So, we got it for you. Actually, it isn't so much a present as a trophy". He handed over the gaily wrapped box. Chris was mystified.

"Well, thank you guys. That is really nice and very unexpected. I am a bit embarrassed".

"Oh, you will be", said George menacingly. "You will be".

Chris tore off the paper and rolled back in hysterics when he saw what it was. There, in a long box, was a gargantuan, pink vibrator. He immediately recognised it as the one that he had waved at George in that sex shop, the one that had exploded into life on the counter.

"That is excellent", laughed Chris. "Just what I need on my wedding night. Not", he joked.

"Angela thought you could put it on a shelf. Like a trophy. It is a sort of permanent reminder of your stupid Project EX. As far as I am concerned, you can put it where the hell you like". More smutty laughter followed and, with the celebratory champagne now flowing, they knew it was going to be a great day.

At 2pm, they all came out of their rooms, dressed for the occasion, following the theme of light tropical clothing. George was wearing the same suit that he had worn when he first met Angela, a blue shirt, with his new cufflinks, and his dazzling new tie. Chris, in a lightweight suit, had allowed Bonnie to brush his normally unkempt hair and, for reasons best known to herself, she had given him a side parting, making him look more like a naughty schoolboy than ever. Bonnie sparkled like her new ring in a pale-yellow minidress. Ricky and Alex wore identical white suits, ignoring the tradition of not competing with the bride.

The other guests in the hotel, already in their own good Christmas spirits, delighted at the sight of the well turned out gathering. It was a very British occasion, smart and dignified in a colonial way and the onlookers seemed suitably impressed. George had been asked by David to organise the group, insisting that he use his powers of persuasion and his shepherding skills to get everyone seated on the beach by 2.45pm, 'and not too pissed', David had instructed. David had a seating plan in his head. George and Angela would nab the front seats on the left, with Chris and Bonnie. Ricky and Alex would sit on the right with two spare seats for the children if they need to sit down. Alex's mother, father and sister would sit behind.

As David gave the green light, they moved slowly to the ceremony, Bonnie gripping Chris' hand with the nerves of a bride, as if it was her own dress rehearsal. Once seated, the music started. By now, many other inquisitive hotel guests had gathered around at the back. After five minutes, Etta James and 'At Last' blasted out of the speakers on the beach. The minister, a rotund Pickwickian man with a jovial face, shuffled down the aisle and took his place centre stage, laying his bible reverently on the round small table that served as an altar.

"Ladies and Gentlemen. My name is Joshua and I have the privilege of performing this wonderful Christmas Day wedding ceremony. The Good Lord is working overtime today. As am I". Polite laughter came from the congregation. "Thank you for being here. Now, may I ask you to please stand and welcome the happy couple. David and Sophie".

They all rose and turned their heads. David, in an immaculate light fawn suit, came first with little Robbie the pageboy, and best man, by his side. They walked slowly up to the trellis and positioned themselves by Reverend Joshua's side. There was then a pause in the music before Richard Wagner's 1850's Bridal March from his Lohengrin opera, better known as 'Here Comes The Bride", filled the air and Sophie, accompanied by Jess, took to the aisle. She looked radiant bearing her bouquet, in her fabulous Vera Wang off-the-shoulder, buttoned-back crepe wedding dress, accompanied by Jess, looking sensational in a suitably floral minidress and eye-catching red patent shoes. As she floated towards her future husband, Sophie paused to give a broad smile to her new friends. What the scene may have lacked in numbers, it made up in unconfined emotion. Bonnie took out the handkerchief that she had put in Chris pocket and dabbed her eyes.

As Sophie and Jess reached David, they all moved behind the table with Joshua in the middle.

"We are gathered here today to celebrate the marriage between with David and Sophie, to seal the love they have discovered in each other and to share their joy. By being here, you are giving your support to their decision to commit themselves to one another for the rest of their lives. This afternoon we are here to celebrate their love and to bear witness to their joining together in marriage. God has brought

David and Sophie together for a reason, to make the world a better, happier, more loving place".

The bride and groom turned to face each other, holding hands.

He turned to Sophie. "Sophie Annabel Cavendish, do you take David as your lawful wedded husband, to have and to hold from this day forward, for better, for worse, for richer, for poorer, in sickness and in health, to love and respect always, to be truthful, to stand by him, in joy and sorrow, and forsaking all others?"

"I do", said Sophie.

The pronouncement was then made again to David Dominic Nugent, who also proudly proclaimed, "I do".

"The rings, please". David had already placed them on the table and the reverend set them on his open bible. "Repeat after me, please. With this ring, I thee wed. And with it I bestow upon thee my love, my trust and my faith. Please wear this ring as a symbol of eternal love". David and Sophie recited the words before each slid their ring over their partner's finger. The jolly minister went on. "Being deeply loved by someone gives you strength, while loving someone deeply gives you courage. May God go with you and bless this union. It is now my honour to be the first to introduce David and Sophie as a married couple. Partners in life... for life. Ladies and Gentlemen, please greet Mrs and Mrs Nugent".

A clamorous, impassioned cheer filled the air. The guests were on their feet, clapping and hooting in a heartfelt outburst of approval, joined by the assembled onlookers. The newlyweds held hands and they gave each other a small, meaningful kiss before turning to the joyous congregation. Beyoncé's 'Single Ladies (Put a Ring on It)' burst out. By now, quite a crowd had gathered, including beachgoers in their scanty swimwear, and everyone started clapping and dancing. Before taking the walk back down the aisle as a married couple, they shook the hand of the cheery vicar, then that of each and every attendee, starting with Jess and Robbie, who had done such a sterling job and who got a bonus hug. Alex turned and embraced his mother. Mr and Mrs Nugent then escorted everyone back towards the hotel. The table, which had been palatially festooned with festive flowers. Before long, they had taken up their same seats as the night before. Spirits were high, with smiles and laughter on every face. Towards the end of the meal, the merriment was paused as several clinks on a glass beckoned silence. David stood up.

"I am going to be brief. Oh, before I begin, Happy Christmas, everyone". They all cheered. "I was always told that the best way to make a speech is to stand up, speak up and shut up. So, this will be mercifully short. It isn't really a speech at all. I just want to say a big thank-you to each and every one of you for sharing this special moment with Sophie and me and to say that I am the proudest and most privileged man in the world right now to be able to say that this beautiful woman is my wife. I have married a truly remarkable lady and I am exceptionally lucky. I am sorry guys that I married a lawyer. You may see it as sleeping with the enemy. But, I assure you, when she is on your side, she is the best friend you could ever have. We have been through a scary time recently but, thank God, lovely Jess and handsome Robbie are here with us today. You guys were the best maid-of-honour and pageboy ever. I am also delighted that Tarone, Alvita and Tianna are with us. It is truly lovely to meet you all. I hope we didn't upset your Christmas plans too much. But then, you can just have another Christmas Day tomorrow. I hope we can get to show you London one day. Make sure you get them over there soon, Alex. Now what can I say about George and Chris. You guys have been my true friends from that daft Sweeney Todd introduction in the Wellington. Every day since that moment has been step after unbelievable step on an epic journey together, most of which is best kept between us boys. No-one here would believe half the stories even if I told them, which I won't. If I did, we might not live long enough to enjoy the rest of our holiday. Anyway, I guess it seems to be coming to an end. My guess is that you, Ricky, will be the first to break ranks. We are so pleased to see you and Alex back together. Getting back together was just a walk in the park, wasn't it. George, you are such a dark horse. You are a new man nowadays and I know that that has everything to do with Angela. I think George and I are similar in so many ways and it is an honour to call you my friend. And Angela, it is so lovely to get to know you and I know that you and George will be perfect together. One tip though. Just make sure you never steal his barstool. That was always, and still is, and will always be an unforgivable sin".

"Chris and Bonnie. What can I say about you two? One is sexy, funny, provocative, elegant and intelligent, while Bonnie... Only joking, Bonnie. You are both fabulous. We can't wait to see you taking the official lead in West Side Story. It is all amazing and we are so proud of you as you should be of yourself. We all love you. You're the best former barmaid turned international superstar we know. As for Chris, where do I start. You're a one-off, mate. The world needs you. You bring sunshine and laughter into all our lives. None of this would have been fun without you... and your Sunday breakfasts. Now, today, you got engaged. That made our day even more special. Well done, you two. And good luck, Bonnie. It's going to be one hell of a ride with him by your side. But you two are brilliant together and I can see it is curtain up on a long and happy showtime". He took a sip of champagne and glanced lovingly down at his bride. "Finally, I want to come back to my lovely wife. Quite what you saw in me I shall never understand. But you overruled your better judgment and married me. I am a bloody lucky man. Thank you, Sophie, and thank you all. This is just brilliant. Enjoy Christmas dinner and pull another cracker, in addition to the one by your side. We love you all. Thanks again".

With that and some heavy clapping, George stood up and asked everyone to raise their glass. "To David and Sophie", they all cried.

There was no holding Chris back and he stood up to take the stage, receiving a sarcastic groan. He began with a serious look on his face, holding up a hand to get everyone's attention. "Hang on, I haven't started yet." A supportive chuckle went around the table in anticipation of what was to come next. He started unimaginatively. "Congratulations to the bride and groom and a massive thank you for letting us be here to share the amazing day. David, the whole apartment thing has been the best time ever and you, our pal, are just an amazing friend who made it happen. Boy, have we had some fun. Sadly, I can't tell you all just how much fun we have had but, believe me, these past few months have been unreal. Now, I want to wish you and Sophie all the happiness in the world. We all need a good lawyer, don't we David. I needed one last year, Sophie, when I sued an airline company after they mislaid my luggage. I lost my case." A groan went around the table. "Anyway, I hope, Sophie, now the 'courting' days are over, that David will never lose his appeal and that you both celebrate tonight with a jolly good.... I can't finish that line. It's what they call a suspended sentence. And remember, nothing comes easy in life. Take this morning. Even Santa came with a clause. Cheers everyone". He raised his glass. "Here's to David and Sophie".

Everyone drank a toast to the bride and groom before giving Chris a generous burst of applause. He soaked it up and gave Bonnie a big hug as she clapped more loudly than anyone. Ricky then stood up.

"Hi. I'm Ricky. I sing and play a bit of guitar. I'll keep this very short. Firstly, Alex and I want to congratulate David and Sophie. And then I want to give commiserations to Bonnie. Bonnie, darling, have you any idea what you are doing? After Brighton, we can confirm that he is the worst Elvis impersonator ever. He ran an Elvis phone-in contest in his paper recently. You had to let them know what prize you want, $500 or tickets to see Chris singing with Street Fire". Ricky then burst into song. "You had to press '1 For the Money, 2 for the Show...'. I gather only two people entered - both chose the money. We played in a steak house a few weeks ago when Chris came on stage and started singing, 'Love Meat Tender, Love Meat Rare...'. Do you really have any idea what you are doing, girl? Seriously, though, we couldn't be happier for you. Now, getting back to the bride and groom. On behalf of me and Alex, we want to give our heartiest congratulations. You two look fab together. We want you all to know how lucky we are to have such incredible friends, even you Chris. It is amazing that we have so many gorgeous girls here too, Sophie, of course, the blushing bride, Angela, Bonnie, and Alvita, it's lovely fir us to meet you on such a happy occasion. Now, let me give a special mention to the fabulous Tianna. Not only are you drop dead gorgeous, Tianna, but you have played such a big part in bringing everyone back together again. You're amazing. I can't thank you enough. And big thanks to you too, Tarone. I am so proud to have been so welcomed into your lovely family. And didn't my superfans do well today? Jess and Robbie, you guys looked terrific and made the day extra-special. What can I say? Hey, I have some more good news, too. You know I dedicated our latest single to you two? What do you think? I got a call from my manager this morning to wish us a happy Christmas and do you know what? 'Lying In Love' is number 23 in Japan and climbing. Alex, baby, you'd better brush up your Japanese, I can see a tour coming on. What we don't need is any more Elvis impersonators singing in Japanese though. Sorry, Chris mate. Now moving on to tonight, David says there's a karaoke in the disco and that we are all cordially invited. Bonnie, we want our own West End star up there. Chris, we want Elvis in the room one more time. We'll be 'All Shook Up...' if you don't get up there. I don't know what you two, David and George, can do. The Pet Shop Boys perhaps? No, I think George would prefer the Village People. He's had more practice at that. Anyway, cheers to you two, David and Sophie. Well done. Keep on rocking. Now I am going to get off the stage. And there is no encore so don't start screaming."

After the applause died down, David stood up again.

"Ricky beat me to it. Yes, there is karaoke tonight, at 9pm. I suggest we all wear the gaudiest tropical beach gear you can find. Let's have a great Christmas dinner and then I suggest that we all take a little break or have a drink or do whatever it is that couples who have just got engaged do and then get ready to party. Oh, and before I forget, can we all meet for breakfast at 9am tomorrow morning? Sorry it is so early, but Chris and Bonnie are off to Orlando, so we need a group photo before they go. If it is OK with you, we'll meet down here in the outside restaurant. Back to tonight. Let's gather together here at the bar around eight. Remember to leave your reputations at home. They're mostly ruined anyway so it's time to behave badly. On behalf of my wife and me, thanks again for coming all this way, everyone. You have made our day very special".

He sat down to rapturous bawling and cheering.

There was no way that David and Sophie could take a nap as the children, who had been so adult all day, desperately wanted to get back to being children, playing in the pool. After the turkey dinner and Christmas pudding, the newlyweds somewhat reluctantly changed into their bathing suits and took the two youngsters off for a swim, David allowing himself to be pushed in as Sophie lay back on her lounger and soaked up the glorious sun. George and Angela joined them on the sunbeds, sipping slowly on their Pina Coladas. Meanwhile, the newly engaged couple chose to retire to their room.

    At 8pm, they began to gather at the bar. David had arranged for Mia to babysit. She and Jess had really hit it off. Robbie was happy to watch cartoons, while lovingly cradling his prized drone. Sophie and David put on their most colourful gear. He radiated in a bright Hawaiian shirt and she simmered in a stunning summer dress. Happy that the children were in Mia's good hands, they set off to join the others. A couple of drinks later, they all, including Alex's brave parents, moved off to the disco, where about fifty other hotel guests were already in full swing. The party mood could not have been better. In no time, Ricky was on stage, boosted by a copious intake of the local Cavalier rum. He had a word with the DJ and broke sharply into a deafening version of Bad Company's 'Can't Get Enough of your Love', which brought the house down. Chris, in a flowery shirt and blinding red shorts, could not be held back and threw himself headlong into 'Jailhouse Rock". To everyone's amazement, Tarone then stepped up. His throaty version of Bob Marley's 'Buffalo Soldier' may not have been the best reggae they had ever heard, but it was certainly unforgettable. As the evening went on, things were getting more and more delirious. By now, the whole wedding party was in a mad euphoria and the chant of "Bonnie, Bonnie, Bonnie" rose up. To the unbridled delight of the crowd, she modestly made her way to the stage, looking every inch the West End star, in a tight top, a loose sixties miniskirt and white shoes. With a single raise of her hand, a respectful hush came over the room as she stood authoritatively with her microphone in hand. She had not chosen a rock song or a festival anthem, but instead a ballad with which she had become all too familiar. She broke the silence gently by easing into the most idyllic rendition of 'Tonight' from West Side Story. Chris could not help himself and started crying all over again, with tears of happiness and pride filling his eyes. As George put his arm around him, Chris leaned into his ear and said, "However did I get someone so bloody perfect?". George just said back, "I have been asking myself that same question for months. I have absolutely no bloody idea, dear boy. It's not your money or good looks, that's for sure. Perhaps it's some kind of charity work". With the help of the DJ, who had cued up the next song, she then got the party going again as she broke into her own raucous version of 'America', complete with the skirt-swishing and foot-stomping that she and Sam had excelled in at the audition.

After a few hours of increasing mayhem, the night started to come to its close, the DJ announced that there would be just one more song and he invited the crowd to tell him who they wanted. There was a unanimous shout for Ricky, who took no persuading to get back up on stage. He had a word with the host and then spoke to the audience.

"This has been the most amazing day. Thank you, David and Sophie. You are both bloody incredible. Thank you from the bottom of my old rock 'n' roll heart. But this next song is for you, Alex. And for you, Mum, Dad and Tianna. And for all our cool friends. I'm going to miss you. Now, let's take the roof off this place. Play it maestro". The anthem strains of 'You'll Never Walk Alone' engulfed the room. Everyone huddled in lines, arms over their neighbours' shoulders, singing at full volume. And so the day ended in the greatest way. Together. They all drifted out and returned slowly to their rooms. It had been an unforgettable but exhausting day and they could at last settle into a well-deserved night's sleep.

Chris and Bonnie wobbled back to their room with Chris fumbling for his key card. After four failed attempts to put it in the slot, he then fell right through the door, crashing onto the floor. Bonnie helped him up and let him fall onto the bed. She too was completely sloshed and staggered across into the bathroom, throwing off her clothes as she went and struggling to put on her Chelsea shirt as nightwear. She collapsed on to the bed next to her unconscious fiancé and turned off the light.

Ten seconds later, she shot up again and put the light back on. "Shit. The bags", she yelled out loud to herself. She had suddenly remembered what Chris had told her. They had to put the suitcases outside for collection overnight. They had both completely forgotten. She panicked, put on all the lights, pulled out the cases and stuffed them with the contents of the wardrobe together with the hastily gathered stray clothes that were scattered around the floor. She even cleared out the bathroom, leaving just two toothbrushes and a tube of toothpaste. She then put the labels on the bags, dragged them outside and crawled back to bed, happy that the job had been done, even without Chris' help. Before she put out the bedside light, she looked across at the crumpled body of her snoring man, still in his flowery shirt, totally comatose. 'What have I done?', she asked herself with a smile. She arranged the covers over him, kissed him on the head, turned out the light and fell straight asleep.

THURSDAY, DECEMBER 26 – BOXING DAY

The alarm buzzed them awake at 8.30am the next morning. Bonnie's head was pounding. She climbed out of bed and went to the bathroom. It was all a blur. It was completely bare except for two toothbrushes and a tube of toothpaste. No make-up, no wash bags, nothing. Even the hotel towels had gone. She came out and slid the wardrobe door open. The cupboard was bare. "What the ...?", she said to herself. She looked around the room. Nothing. No clothes. No shoes. Nothing. A faint, blurry memory came back. "Shit. I packed bloody everything. Everything, except this stupid Chelsea shirt".

It took three increasingly rough shakes to wake Chris up. By now she was in a state of hysteria and garbled to him what had happened. Her task was made more difficult because of his inability to understand a single word of English.

"Chris. This is serious. I packed last night before I came to bed, with no help from you, I may add".

He looked at her blearily. "Well done, Bonnie. Thanks for that. I completely forgot".

"You were completed pissed more like. But listen. You don't get it. I didn't just pack stuff. I packed everything".

"Everything? Do you mean…?".

"Yes. Everything. Every single thing. Our clothes, our presents, everything", Bonnie replied.

"That's great, Bonnie. Thanks". He muttered.

"No, Chris. You don't understand. I packed EVERYTHING! We have NOTHING!".

Chris remained unruffled.

"You're exaggerating, Bonnie. Not everything. You still have that fantastic Chelsea shirt. Good job I got it for you. Now, don't panic. We can go to the gift shop. They have loads of things there. Why don't you put on the hotel dressing gown?".

"Uh huh. That got packed too. Everything. And the gift shop doesn't open till 10. We have got to have this stupid group picture in half an hour. You're alright. You're still wearing last night's clothes. All I've got is this ridiculous shirt".

"Ridiculous? How dare you? That's Chelsea. You can't call Chelsea ridiculous. You look champion in it. At least, our passports and money and things are in the safe. Or did you pack that too? Now come back to bed and let's have 45 minutes each way".

"Shut up, Chris", screamed Bonnie, starting to get angry. "Come up. Get up. We can't let David and Sophie down".

By 9am, over at the outside breakfast area, the others were busy reaching for the orange juice jugs, trying to swill away their hangovers as best they could. David was standing with the hotel photographer and began to martial people into some sort of order for the farewell photo.

"Get together, guys. Sophie, you and I should be in the middle with the children and everyone else can just gather around and look happy. Try not to look like you've been out all night. George, are you actually alive? You look bloody awful, mate". George managed a sarcastic grin back.

The guests complied with David's directions and were soon in place, when he suddenly realised two of their cast were missing. "Where are Chris and Bonnie?".

"One guess", said Ricky, adding something about rabbits.

At that moment, the two late arrivals appeared. Chris lumbered over in the same floral shirt and bright red shorts that he had worn the night before and Bonnie straggled behind in nothing but her blue football shirt, pulling down the hem to maintain her decency. A jeer went up and they drifted into the line-up.

"I didn't know it was fancy dress", commented Ricky. "Hands up, who scored last night?'. Bonnie just smirked back at him, sarcastically.

The photographer called for everyone to smile and the camera flashed.

"You're not the only one that's flashing, Bonnie", Ricky called out. Bonnie blushed in embarrassment.

In spite of how tired and emotional they all felt, it was not lost on the flatmates that, deep down, that this was a highly poignant moment. They knew that they were coming to the end of their insane journey, not the trip to Antigua, but the whole long episode of four disparate, divorced, depressed men meeting in a London pub and then rebuilding their lives together in a short-lived, crazy world of cross-dating, luxurious living and rock 'n' roll. Photos over, Chris, to everyone's surprise, stepped forward and stood next the photographer.

"Wait, everyone. Stay right there. Can we do a couple more, please, Mr Photographer?". He stood right next to the camera, directing the assembly. "This time let's have the Thames Tower boys in the middle. This one's for the four amigos". As instructed, George, David and Ricky took the centre stage. Chris had one more thought. "Hang on. It's not right. There is something missing". He disappeared into the hotel and came back with a stool from the bar, placing it in the middle. "George", Chris directed. "Please take your throne". George hitched himself up onto the seat and Chris continued to manage the group. "David, you stand on George's left with Sophie, Jess and Robbie. Ricky, you go on George's right, with Alex. I'll stand behind George, with you, Bonnie and Angela".

The scene was now complete, with George sitting in his usual pose, while Chris, David and Ricky put their hands on his shoulders, raising their heads proudly, like in a Victorian family portrait.

"Right, Mr Photographer. Do your damnedest. Now smile everybody. Say cheese. This one is for King George, the Grand Old Duke of Wellington and the Magnificent Four".

With that, the Thames Tower era came to an end, in a flash. The boys now had their own individual destinies laid out before them and it was time for them to go their different ways, to find new lives, back in a new normality. Their rehabilitation was complete. Ironically, it had been divorce, which is so often defined by bitterness, division, anger and pain, that had ultimately brought the happy band together. The Gang of Four had emerged out of their darkness and into the uplifting light of their next horizons. What they had thought at that desperate time had been the end had, in fact, turned out to be just the beginning. George and David, who had once taken for granted all the status and prestige that went with those big City jobs, the nice homes, good standing and enviable wealth, had come to realise the vacuity of power and riches. They had discovered that real opulence lay not in the corporate offices of London or in how many houses you own, but in the shared company of friends. As for Chris, he will remain for always a Peter Pan, or, as the fortune-teller in Brighton had told him, as 'crazy as a fox'. He had never listened to the 'cross-legged wise men' and never would, choosing always to live in the moment and to chase down his latest dream. Ricky had also found what is important in his life, turning regret and adversity into optimism and opportunity. Like the words in his new song, he had listened, used the time and used his head.

Looking back, all the men had suffered moments of divorce despair. But now, through their shared ingenuity and strength, each man had finally found his renaissance, having broken through the walls of confrontation and intolerance. David in particular had had a bruising time but, seeing his contented smile as he held his new wife's hand, it was clear to all that he had now put the whole episode behind him. If truth be told, he still felt an anger that, in those dark days, the children had suffered unnecessarily from the divisive, brutal tactics of the legal process and also pangs of guilt that, while the parents had fought in the spotlight, they were forced to hide in the shadows. However, the light had finally appeared on the horizon, under the Caribbean sun. It may have taken cynical deceit and cunning, but through the boys' guile they had each found a fresh start in life.

For this is a story with a happy ending and proves that freedom and happiness are always worth fighting for. The things that define us can never be measured by acquisition and prestige.

All we need to discover is true love, good friends and a sense of adventure. Sounds easy, I know. But our four lads proved once and for all that all you need is love, a free spirit, good health, a great pub, a bit of money... oh, and the right date.

VALETE
By David Nugent

I was delighted when I was asked to write a short post-script to our little story as you may be wondering what happened to us all next. Let me try to bring you up to date.

The six months since we got back from the wedding have gone really quickly, but a lot has happened. Ricky, as predicted, moved out of the apartment completely and back in with Alex and their noisy neighbours. Ricky's song reached number 5 in the Japan charts and Street Life are going off to Tokyo for a short tour later this year, hopefully playing to sell-out crowds. I gather Alex is going too. I guess that he does not want to let Ricky out of his sight. Sophie and I had dinner with them recently and Alex was incredibly excited to tell us that he has been booked for the Christmas pantomime at the Palladium. He is also looking forward to his Mum, Dad and Tianna coming over in early September. Sophie and I thought we would take them to the races, hopefully when Golden Oak is running. Ricky still pops over to the apartment to see his superfans whenever he can. They still adore him. Oh, and he has had a haircut. It makes him look almost debonair. He told me that Alex prefers it that way.

Bonnie, Samantha and the cast of West Side Story are playing to full houses every night. The show is a massive success. Bonnie takes the lead at least twice a week, mostly matinées, always to thunderous applause. She is brilliant in it and has one eye on a permanent lead role in the not-too-distant future.

Chris' newspaper career is still going pretty well, but you know Chris. If you listen to his version of events, he is a rising star, the Editor's protégé, although he did confess to having a minor hiccup with his Lucky Car Numbers scratch card game when, instead of having the expected outright single winner, no less than ninety-seven people claimed the prize of a smart new Jaguar. The printers had messed up apparently. That got the Editor's attention and had Jaguar futures going through the roof. He got out of it somehow, as only Chris can. He and Bonnie continue to dote on each other and are now living in a flat in Wandsworth. They are a lovely couple. I cannot wait to go to their Autumn wedding in October. Her friend Samantha is another one with wedding bells on her mind. She is going very steady with Gerry, I gather. 'Watch this space', she told me the last time I saw her in the Wellington. Could be a double wedding?

George and I still live in Thames Tower, but we are not alone. After the wedding, we persuaded new two recruits to join us in the apartment, my wife Sophie, of course, and just recently Angela moved in. The girls have struck up quite a friendship, which is brilliant. Angela has found a good job at a major book publishing company in London and rented out her house to her friend Beth, who had recently split up with her boyfriend and needed somewhere to live. Sophie has just been promoted to a top job at her London law firm and is doing exceptionally well. She tells me she should become a partner soon. I am so proud of her. The apartment is a much quieter place these days, but everyone gets on tremendously well. The lease expires soon, although we are seriously thinking of renewing it as we all like being together so much.

My little Jess is doing really well at school and this term she got a lead part in Annie, with some expert audition help from Bonnie. She now thinks she wants to make a career on the stage, although I am not so sure. Wee Robbie is a star in the cricket team. His spin bowling is a sensation. He got seven wickets in his latest match. I can't wait for him to play for England. All that money spent on their education and they just want to sing and play cricket. That's life, I guess. They still stay with me every other weekend, but now with another member of the Nugent family. Remember Billy, my devoted dog? He is now allowed to pile into my car, drying his feet first of course, for weekends with us in London. It is just lovely to be back with him.

In August, we are having a family holiday with him on the Norfolk Broads.

There is news on the work front too. Greg Chapman, Sophie's friend, and I have formed the Chapman Nugent Partnership, which is going very well, touch wood. And George tells me that he is about to start a bit of freelancing with a new, up-and-coming agency, but nothing too serious. He also told me a few days ago that Kate is still crazy about her Argentinian polo player and gets to rub shoulders with the Royal, rich and famous. George generously says he is very happy for her, but I am not so sure that he doesn't still hold a bit of a candle for her though. If you pop into the Wellington around 6pm on any night, you might still find him sitting on his stool. Angela often meets up with him after she finishes work. Chris joins them at least twice a week, filling time after work when Bonnie has to be at the theatre.

Well, I think that is about it. Thanks for reading our story. I hope you enjoyed it. Oh, I completely forgot someone. What about my dear Moira? I am pleased to report that she has completely recovered from her injuries and we are still having the odd decent conversation. She has definitely calmed down and mellowed. Perhaps it is as a result of the blow on the head or possibly the success of her relationship with Gary, which seems to be flourishing. Or it could be just with age. But I like to think it has more than something to do with her bruising flirtation with that cad Brian. Whatever it is, it is good news for all of us. You know what I always say, 'If Moira's happy, we are all happy'. I guess her boyfriend doesn't like dogs much, which is good as it means I get time with Billy. She amazed me when she was so relaxed about my taking Jess and Robbie to Antigua. Maybe the lesson she learned with Brian has put me in a better light and that she thinks I was not so bad after all. Thanks, Chris.

However, I do see one possible dark cloud on the horizon. Last week, Jess told me that her Mum had asked, for reasons best known to her, to see the Christmas photos on her phone again and she unfortunately stumbled across that last group picture for the first time. You know, the one on Boxing Day, with George on his stool and the delectable Bonnie in a Chelsea shirt (and little else). To be honest, I had asked Jess to delete it, but she obviously forgot. Apparently, Moira was OK with all the pictures, saying she thought the children looked lovely. But then, Jess said, she came across this one at the end and she started to study it more carefully. Jess says that 'Mummy went white and looked at her in a really bad way', as she put it. What Moira said next sent a chill down my spine.

Jess said she breathed deeply, her face went bright red and looked like she was going to explode.

"Wait. Hang on a minute", she hollered, looking Jess straight in the eyes. "What the hell was Brian doing there?".

Printed in Poland
by Amazon Fulfillment
Poland Sp. z o.o., Wrocław